THE
ELEPHANT GOD

GORDON CASSERLY

1ˢᵗ WORLD
LIBRARY
Literary Society

The Elephant God

Gordon Casserly

© 1st World Library – Literary Society, 2005
PO Box 2211
Fairfield, IA 52556
www.1stworldlibrary.org
First Edition

LCCN: 2006905700

Softcover ISBN: 1-4218-2129-X
Hardcover ISBN: 1-4218-2029-3
eBook ISBN: 1-4218-2229-6

Purchase *"The Elephant God"*
as a traditional bound book at:
www.1stWorldLibrary.org/purchase.asp?ISBN=1-4218-2129-X

1st World Library Literary Society is a nonprofit
organization dedicated to promoting literacy by:

- Creating a free internet library accessible from any
  computer worldwide.
- Hosting writing competitions and offering book
  publishing scholarships.

**Readers interested in supporting literacy
through sponsorship, donations or
membership please contact:
literacy@1stworldlibrary.org
Check us out at: www.1stworldlibrary.ORG
and start downloading free ebooks today.**

The Elephant God
contributed by Tim, Ed & Rodney
in support of
1st World Library Literary Society

TO A CERTAIN ROGUE ELEPHANT RESIDENT IN
THE TERAI FOREST

THE SLAYER OF DIVERS MEN AND WOMEN

THIS BOOK IS DEDICATED BY THE AUTHOR IN
GRATEFUL ACKNOWLEDGMENT OF MUCH
INSTRUCTION AND IN THE HOPE THAT SOME DAY
IN THE HAPPY HUNTING GROUNDS
THEY MAY MEET AGAIN AND DECIDE THE ISSUE

FOREWORD TO AMERICAN EDITION

Twenty years ago I dedicated my first book, *The Land of the Boxers; or China Under the Allies*, to the American officers and soldiers of the expeditionary forces then fighting in the Celestial Empire - as well as to their British comrades. And when, some years afterwards, I was visiting their country, right glad I was that I had thus offered my slight tribute to the valour of the United States Army. For from the Pacific to the Atlantic I met with a hospitality and a kindness that no other land could excel and few could equal. And ever since then, I have felt deep in debt to all Americans and have tried in many parts of our Empire to repay to those who serve under the Star Spangled Banner a little of what I owe to their fellow-countrymen.

Only those who have experienced that sympathetic American kindness can realise what it is. It is all that gives me courage to face the reading public as a writer of fiction and attempt to depict to it the fascinating world of an Indian jungle, the weird beasts that people it, and the stranger humans that battle with them in it. The magic pen of a Kipling alone could do justice to that wonderful realm of mountain and forest that is called the Terai - that fantastic region of woodland that stretches for hundreds of miles along the foot of the Himalayas, that harbours in its dim recesses the monsters of the animal kingdom, quaint survivals of a vanished race - the rhinoceros, the elephant, the bison, and the hamadryad, that great and terrible snake which can, and does, pursue and overtake a mounted man, and which with a touch of its poisoned fang can slay the most powerful brute. The huge Himalayan bear roams under the giant trees, feeding on fruit and honey, yet ready to shatter unprovoked the skull of a poor woodcutter. Those savage striped and spotted cats, the tiger and the panther, steal through it on velvet paw and take toll of its harmless denizens.

But, if I cannot describe it as I would, at least I have lived the life of the wild in the spacious realm of the Terai. I would that I had the power to make others feel what I have felt, the thrill that comes when facing the onrush of the bloodthirstiest of all fierce brutes, a rogue elephant, or the joy of seeing a charging tiger check and crumple up at the arresting blow of a heavy bullet.

I have followed day after day from dawn to dark and fought again and again a fierce outlaw tusker elephant that from sheer lust of slaughter had killed men, women, and children and carried on for years a career of crime unbelievable.

No one that knows the jungle well will refuse to credit the strangest story of what wild animals will do. Of all the swarming herds of wild elephants in the Terai, the Mysore, or the Ceylon jungles no man, white or black, has ever seen one that had died a natural death. Yet many have watched them climbing up the great mountain rampart of the Himalayas towards regions where human foot never followed. The Death Place of the Elephants is a legend in which all jungle races firmly believe, but no man has ever found it. The mammoths live a century and a half--but the time comes when each of them must die. Yet no human eye watches its death agony.

Those who know elephants best will most readily credit the strangest tales of their doings. And there are men--white men--whose power over wild beasts and wilder fellow men outstrips the novelist's imagination, the true tale of whose doings no resident in a civilised land would believe.

GORDON CASSERLY.

CONTENTS

CHAPTER I

THE SECRET MISSION

"The letters, sahib," said the post orderly, blocking up the doorway of the bungalow.

Kevin Dermot put down his book as the speaker, a Punjaubi Mohammedan in white undress, slipped off his loose native shoes and entered the room barefoot, as is the custom in India.

"For this one a receipt is needed," continued the sepoy, holding out a long official envelope registered and insured and addressed, like all the others, to "The Officer Commanding, Ranga Duar, Eastern Bengal."

Major Dermot signed the receipt and handed it to the man. As he did so the scream of an elephant in pain came to his ears.

"What is that?" he asked the post orderly.

"It is the *mahout*, Chand Khan, beating his *hathi* (elephant), sahib," replied the sepoy looking out.

Dermot threw the unopened letters on the table, and, going out on the verandah of his bungalow, gazed down on the parade ground which lay a hundred feet below. Beyond it at the foot of the small hill on which stood the Fort was a group of trees, to two of which a transport elephant was shackled by a fore and a hind leg in such a way as to render it powerless. Its *mahout,* or driver, keeping out of reach of its trunk, was beating it savagely on the head with a bamboo. Mad with rage, the man, a grey-bearded old Mohammedan, swung the long stick with both hands and brought it down again and again with all his force. From the gateway of the Fort above the *havildar,* or native sergeant, of the guard shouted to the *mahout* to desist. But the angry man ignored him and continued to belabour his unfortunate animal, which, at the risk of dislocating its leg, struggled wildly to free itself and screamed shrilly each time that the bamboo fell. This surprised Dermont, for an elephant's skull is so thick that a blow even from the *ankus* or iron goad used to drive it, is scarcely felt.

The puzzled officer re-entered the bungalow and brought out a pair of field-glasses, which revealed the reason of the poor tethered brute's screams. For they showed that in the end of the bamboo were stuck long, sharp nails which pierced and tore the flesh of its head.

Major Dermot was not only a keen sportsman and a lover of animals, but he had an especial liking for elephants, of which he had had much experience. So with a muttered oath he put down the binoculars and, seizing his helmet, ran down the steep slope from his bungalow to the parade ground. As he went he shouted to the *mahout* to stop. But the man was too engrossed in his brutality to hear him or the *havildar,* who repeated the Major's order. It was not until Dermot actually seized his arm and dragged him back that he perceived his commanding officer. Dropping the bamboo he strove to justify his ill-treatment of the elephant by alleging some petty act of disobedience on its part.

His excuses were cut short.

"*Choop raho!* (Be silent!) You are not fit to have charge of an animal," cried the indignant officer, picking up and examining the cruel weapon. The sharp points of the nails were stained with blood, and morsels of skin and flesh adhered to them. Dermot felt a strong inclination to thrash the brutal *mahout* with the unarmed end of the bamboo, but, restraining himself, he turned to the elephant. With the instinct of its kind it was scraping a little pile of dust together with its toes, snuffing it up in its trunk and blowing it on the bleeding cuts on its lacerated head.

"You poor beast! You mustn't do that. We'll find something better for you," said the Major compassionately.

He called across the parade ground to his white-clad Mussulman butler, who was looking down at him from the bungalow.

"Bring that fruit off my table," he said in Hindustani. "Also the little medicine chest and a bowl of water."

When the servant had brought them Dermot approached the elephant.

"*Khubbadar* - (take care) - sahib!" cried a coolie, the *mahout's* assistant. "He is suffering and angry. He may do you harm."

But, while the rebuked *mahout* glared malevolently and inwardly hoped that the animal might kill him, Dermot walked calmly toward it, holding out his hand with the fruit. The elephant, regarding him nervously and suspiciously out of its little eyes, shifted uneasily from foot to foot, and at first shrank from him. But, as the officer stood quietly in front of it, it stretched out its trunk and smelled the extended hand. Then it touched the arm and felt it up to the shoulder, on which it let the tip of the trunk rest for a few seconds. At last it seemed satisfied that the white man was a friend and did not intend to hurt it.

During the ordeal Dermot had never moved; although there was every reason to fear that the animal, either from sheer nervousness or from resentment at the ill-treatment that it had just received, might attack him and trample him to death. Indeed, many tame elephants, being unused to Europeans, will not allow white men to approach them. So the Hindu coolie stood trembling with fright, while the *havildar* and the butler were alarmed at their sahib's peril.

But Dermot coolly peeled a banana and placed it in the elephant's mouth. The gift was tried and approved by the huge beast, which graciously accepted the rest of the fruit. Then the Major said to it in the *mahouts'* tongue:

"*Buth!* (Lie down!)"

The elephant slowly sank down to the ground and allowed the Major to examine its head, which was badly lacerated by the spikes. Dermot cleansed the wounds thoroughly and applied an antiseptic to them. The animal bore it patiently and seemed to recognise that it had found a friend; for, when it rose to its feet again, it laid its trunk almost caressingly on Dermot's shoulder.

The officer stroked it and then turned to the *mahout*, who was standing in the background.

"Chand Khan, you are not to come near this elephant again," he said. "I suspend you from charge of it and shall report you for dismissal. *Jao!* (Go!)"

The man slunk away scowling. Dermot beckoned to the Hindu, who approached salaaming.

"Are you this animal's coolie?"

(The Government of India very properly recognises the lordliness of the elephant and provides him in captivity with no less than two body-servants, a *mahout* and a coolie, whose mission in life is to wait on him.)

The Hindu salaamed again.

"Yes, *Huzoor* (The Presence)," he replied.

"How long have you been with it?"

"Five years, *Huzoor*."

"What is its name?"

"*Badshah* (The King). And indeed he is a *badshah* among elephants. No one but a Mussulman would treat him with disrespect. Your Honour sees that he is a *Gunesh* and worthy of reverence."

The animal, which was a large and well-shaped male, possessed only one tusk, the right. The other had never grown. Dermot knew that an elephant thus marked by Nature would be regarded by Hindus as sacred to *Gunesh*, their God of Wisdom, who is represented as having the head of an elephant with a single tusk, the right. Many natives would consider the animal to be a manifestation of the god himself and worship it as a deity. So the Major made no comment on the coolie's remark, but said:

"What is your name?"

"Ramnath, *Huzoor*."

"Very well, Ramnath. You are to have sole charge of Badshah until I can get someone to help you. You will be his *mahout*. Take this medicine that I have been using and put it on as you have seen me do. Don't let the animal blow dust on the cuts. Keep them clean, and bring him up tomorrow for me to see."

He handed the man the antiseptic and swabs. Then he turned to the elephant and patted it.

"Good-bye, Badshah, old boy," he said. "I don't think that Ramnath will ill-treat you."

The huge beast seemed to understand him and again touched him with the tip of its trunk.

"Badshah knows Your Honour," said the Hindu. "He will regard you always now as his *ma-bap* (mother and father)."

Dermot smiled at this very usual vernacular expression. He was accustomed to being called it by his sepoys; but he was amused at being regarded as the combined parents of so large an offspring.

"Badshah has never let a white man approach him before today, *Huzoor*," continued Ramnath. "He has always been afraid of the sahibs. But he sees you are his friend. *Salaam kuro*, Badshah!"

And the elephant raised his trunk vertically in the air and trumpeted the *Salaamut* or royal salute that he had been taught to make. Then, at Ramnath's signal, he lowered his trunk and crooked it. The man put his barefoot on it, at the same time seizing one of the great ears. Then Badshah lifted him up with the trunk until he could get on to the head into position astride the neck. Then the new *mahout*, salaaming again to the officer, started his huge charge off, and the elephant lumbered away with swaying stride to its *peelkhana*, or stable, two thousand feet below in the forest at the foot of the hills on which stood the Fort of Ranga Duar. For this outpost, which was garrisoned by Dermot's Double Company of a Military Police Battalion, guarded one of the *duars*, or passes, through the Himalayas into India from the wild and little-known country of Bhutan.

Its Commanding Officer watched the elephant disappear down the hill before returning to his little stone bungalow, which stood in a small garden shaded by giant mango and jack-fruit trees and gay with the flaming lines of bougainvillias and poinsettias.

Dismissing the post orderly, who was still waiting, Dermot threw himself into a long chair and took up the letters that he had flung down when Badshah's screams attracted his attention. They were all routine official correspondence contained in the usual long envelopes marked "On His Majesty's Service." The registered one, however, held a smaller envelope heavily sealed, marked "Secret" and addressed to him by name. In this was a letter in cipher.

Dermot got up from his chair and, going into his bedroom, opened a trunk and lifted out of it a steel despatch box, which he unlocked. From this he extracted a sealed envelope, which he carried back to the sitting-room. First examining the seals to make sure that they were intact, he opened the envelope and took from it two papers. One was a cipher code and on the other was the keyword to the official cipher used by the military authorities throughout India. This word is changed once a year. On the receipt of the new one every officer entitled to be in possession of it must burn the paper on which is written the old word and send a signed declaration to that effect to Army Headquarters.

Taking a pencil and a blank sheet of paper Dermot proceeded to decipher the letter that he had just received. It was dated from the Adjutant General's Office at Simla, and headed "Secret." It ran:

"Sir:

"In continuation of the instructions already given you orally, I have the honour to convey to you the further orders of His Excellency the Commander-in-Chief in India.

"Begins: 'Information received from the Secretary to the Foreign Department, Government of India, confirms the intelligence that Chinese emissaries have for some time past been endeavouring to re-establish the former predominance of their nation over Tibet and Bhutan. In the former country they appear to have met with little success; but in Bhutan, taking advantage of the hereditary jealousies of the *Penlops*, the great feudal chieftains, they appear to have gained many adherents. They aim at instigating the Bhutanese to attempt an invasion of India through the *duars* leading into Eastern

Bengal, their object being to provoke a war. The danger to this country from an invading force of Bhutanese, even if armed, equipped, and led by Chinese, is not great. But its political importance must not be minimised.

"'For the most serious feature of the movement is that information received by the Political Department gives rise to the grave suspicion that, not only many extremists in Bengal, but even some of the lesser rajahs and nawabs, are in treasonable communication with these outside enemies.

"'Major Dermot, at present commanding the detachment of the Military Battalion stationed at Ranga Duar, has been specially selected, on account of his acquaintance with the districts and dialects of the *duars* and that part of the Terai Forest bordering on Bhutan, to carry out a particular mission. You are to direct him to inspect and report on the suitability, for the purposes of defence against an invasion from the north, of:

(*a*) The line of the mountain passes at an altitude of from 3000 to 6000 feet.

(*b*) A line established in the Terai Forest itself.

"'In addition, if this officer in the course of his investigations discovers any evidence of communication between the disloyal elements inside our territory and possible enemies across the border, he will at once inform you direct.' Ends.

"Please note His Excellency's orders and proceed to carry them out forthwith. You can pursue your investigations under the pretence of big game shooting in the hills and jungle. The British officer next in seniority to you will command the detachment in your absences You may communicate to him as much of the contents of this letter as you deem advisable, impressing upon him the necessity for the strictest secrecy.

"You will in all matters communicate directly and

confidentially with this office.

"I have the honour to be, Sir,

"Your most obedient servant."

Here followed the signature of one of the highest military authorities in India.

Dermot stared at the letter.

"So that's it!" he thought. "It's a bigger thing than I imagined."

He had known when he consented to being transferred from a staff appointment in Simla to the command of a small detachment of a Military Police Battalion garrisoning an unimportant frontier fort on the face of the Himalayas that he was being sent there for a special purpose. He had consented gladly; for to him the great attraction of his new post was that he would find himself once more in the great Terai Jungle. To him it was Paradise. Before going to Simla he had been stationed with a Double Company of the Indian Infantry Regiment to which he belonged in a similar outpost in the mountains not many miles away. This outpost had now been abolished. But while in it he used to spend all his spare time in the marvellous jungle that extended to his very door.

The great Terai Forest stretches for hundreds of miles along the foot of the Himalayas, from Assam through Bengal to Garwhal and up into Nepal. It is a sportsman's heaven; for it shelters in its recesses wild elephants, rhinoceros, bison, bears, tigers, panthers, and many of the deer tribes. Dermot loved it. He was a mighty hunter, but a discriminating one. He did not kill for sheer lust of slaughter, and preferred to study the ways of the harmless animals rather than shoot them. Only against dangerous beasts did he wage relentless war.

Dermot knew that he could very well leave the routine work of the little post to his Second in Command. The fort was practically a block of fortified stone barracks, easily defensible against attacks of badly armed hillmen and accommodating a couple of hundred sepoys. It was to hold the *duar* or pass of Ranga through the Himalayas against raiders from Bhutan that the little post had been built.

For centuries past the wild dwellers beyond the mountains were used to swooping down from the hills on the less warlike plainsmen in search of loot, women, and slaves. But the war with Bhutan in 1864-5 brought the borderland under the English flag, and the Pax Britannica settled on it. Yet even now temptation was sometimes too strong for lawless men. Occasionally swift-footed parties of fierce swordsmen swept down through the unguarded passes and raided the tea-gardens that are springing up in the foothills and the forests below them. For hundreds of coolies work on these big estates, and large consignments of silver coin come to the gardens for their payment.

But there was bigger game afoot than these badly-armed raiders. The task set Dermot showed it; and his soldier's heart warmed at the thought of helping to stage a fierce little frontier war in which he might come early on the scene.

Carefully sealing up again and locking away the cipher code and keyword, he went out on the back verandah and shouted for his orderly. The dwellings of Europeans upcountry in India are not luxurious - far from it. Away from the big cities like Bombay, Calcutta, or Karachi, the amenities of civilisation are sadly lacking. The bungalows are lit only by oil-lamps, their floors are generally of pounded earth covered with poor matting harbouring fleas and other insect pests, their roofs are of thatch or tiles, and such luxuries as bells, electric or otherwise, are unknown. So the servants, who reside outside the bungalows in the compounds, or enclosures, are summoned by the simple expedient of shouting "Boy".

Presently the orderly appeared.

"Shaikh Ismail," said the Major, "go to the Mess, give my salaams to Parker Sahib, and ask him to come here."

The sepoy, a smart young Punjabi Mussulman, clad in the white undress of the Indian Army, saluted and strode off up the hill to the pretty mess-bungalow of the British officers of the detachment. In it the subaltern occupied one room.

When he received Dermot's message, this officer, a tall, good-looking man of about twenty-eight years of age, accompanied the orderly to his senior's quarters.

"Come in and have a smoke, Parker," said the Major cheerily.

The subaltern entered and helped himself to a cigarette from an open box on the table before looking for a chair in the scantily-furnished room.

As he struck a match he said,

"Ismail Khan tells me you've just had trouble with that surly beast, Chand Khan".

Dermot told him what had occurred.

"What a *soor!* (swine!)" exclaimed Parker indignantly. "I always knew he was a cruel devil; but I didn't think he was quite such a brute. And to poor old Badshah too. It's a damned shame".

"He's a good elephant, isn't he?" asked the senior.

"A ripper. Splendid to shoot from and absolutely staunch to tiger," said the subaltern enthusiastically. "Major Smith - our Commandant before you, sir - was charged by a tiger he had wounded in a beat near Alipur Duar. He missed the beast with his second barrel. The tiger sprang at the howdah, but Badshah caught him cleverly on his one tusk and knocked him silly.

The Major reloaded and killed the beast before it could recover."

"Good for Badshah. He seemed to me to be a fine animal," said Dermot.

"One of the best. We all like him; though he'll never let any white man handle him. By the way, Ismail Khan says he permitted you to do it."

"I doctored up his cuts. Besides, I'm used to elephants."

"All the same you're the first sahib I've heard Of that Badshah has allowed to touch him. Do you know, the Hindus worship him. He's a *Gunesh* - I supposed you noticed that. I've seen some of them simply go down on their faces in the dust before him and pray to him. There's a curious thing about Badshah, too. Have you heard?"

"No. What is it?" asked the Major.

"Well, it's a rummy thing. He's usually awfully quiet and obedient. But sometimes he gets very restless, breaks loose, and goes off on his own into the jungle. After a week or two he comes back by himself, as quiet as a lamb. But when the fit's on him nothing will hold him. He bursts the stoutest ropes, breaks iron chains; and I believe he'd pull down the *peelkhana* if he couldn't get away."

"Oh, that often happens with domesticated male elephants," said Dermot. "They have periodic fits of sexual excitement - get *must*, you know - and go mad while these last."

"Oh, no. It's not that," replied the subaltern confidently. "Badshah doesn't go *must*. It's something quite different. The jungle men around here have a quaint belief about it. You see, Badshah was captured by the Kheddah Department here years ago - twenty, I think. He's about forty now. He was taken away to other parts of India, Mhow for one -"

"Yes, they used to have an elephant battery there," broke in the Major.

"But somehow or other he got here eventually. Rather curious that he should have been sent back to his birthplace. Anyhow, the natives believe that when he breaks away he goes off to family reunions or to meet old pals."

"I shouldn't be surprised," remarked Dermot, meditatively. "They're strange beasts, elephants. No one really knows much about them. I expect the jungle calls to them, as it does to me."

He lit a cigarette and went on,

"But I've sent for you to talk over something important. Read that."

He handed Parker his transcription of the cipher letter. As the subaltern read it his eyes opened wider and wider. When he had finished he exclaimed joyfully,

"By Jove, Major, that's great. Do you think there's anything in it? How ripping it'll be if they try to come in by this pass! Won't we just knock them! Couldn't we get some machine guns?"

"I'm afraid we couldn't hold the Fort of Ranga Duar against a whole invading army, Parker. You know it isn't really defensible against a serious attack."

"Oh, I say! Do you mean, sir, that we'd give it up to a lot of Chinks and bare-legged Bhuttias without firing a shot?"

The Major smiled at his junior's indignation.

"You must remember, Parker, that if an invasion comes off it will be on a scale that two hundred men won't stop. The Bhutanese are badly armed; but they are fanatically brave. They showed that in their war with us in '64 and '65. They had only swords, bows, and arrows; but they licked one of our columns hollow and drove our men in headlong flight. But cheer up, Parker, if there is a show it won't be my fault if you and I don't have a good look in."

"Thank you, Major," said the subaltern gratefully.

He smoked in silence for a while and then said:

"D'you know, sir, I had an idea there was something up when Major Smith was suddenly ordered away and you, who didn't belong to us, were sent here from Simla. I'd heard of you before, not only as a great *shikari* - the natives everywhere in these jungles talk a lot about you - but also as a keen soldier. A fellow doesn't usually come straight from a staff job at Army Headquarters to a small outpost like this for nothing."

Dermot laughed.

"Unless he has got into trouble and is sent off as a punishment," he said. "But that didn't happen to be my case. However, I was delighted to leave Simla. Better the jungle a thousand times."

"Yes; Simla's rather a rotten place, I believe," remarked the subaltern meditatively. "Too many brass hats and women. They're the curse of India, each of them. And I'm sure the women do the most harm."

"Well, steer clear of the latter, and don't become one of the former," said Dermot with a laugh, rising from his chair, "then you'll have a peaceful life - but you won't get on in your profession."

CHAPTER II

A ROGUE ELEPHANT

The four transport elephants attached to the garrison of Ranga Duar for the purpose of bringing supplies for the men from the far distant railway were stabled in a *peelkhana* at the foot of the hills and a couple of thousand feet below the Fort. This building, a high-walled shed with thatched roof and brick standings for the animals, was erected beside the narrow road that zig-zagged down from the mountains into the forest and eventually joined a broader one leading to the narrow-gauge railway that pierced the jungle many miles away.

One morning, about three weeks after Dermot's first introduction to Badshah, the Major tramped down the rough track to the *peelkhana*, carrying a rifle and cartridge belt and a haversack containing his food for the day. Nearing the stables he blew a whistle, and a shrill trumpeting answered him from the building, as Badshah recognised his signal. Ramnath, hurriedly entering the impatient elephant's stall, loosed him from the iron shackles that held his legs. Then the huge beast walked with stately tread out of the building and went straight to where Dermot awaited him. For during these weeks the intimacy between man and animal had progressed rapidly. Elephants, though of an affectionate disposition, are not demonstrative as a rule. But Badshah always showed unmistakable signs of fondness for the white man, whom he seemed to regard as his friend and protector.

Dermot was in the habit of taking him out into the jungle every day, where he went ostensibly to shoot. After the first few occasions he displaced Ramnath from the guiding seat on Badshah's neck and acted as *mahout* himself. But, instead of using the *ankus* - the heavy iron implement shaped like a boat-hook head which natives use to emphasise their orders to their charges - the Major simply touched the huge head with his open hand. And his method proved equally, if not more, effective. He was soon able to dispense altogether with Ramnath on his expeditions, which was his object. For he did not want any witness to his secret explorations of the forest and the hills.

An elephant, when used as a beast of burden or for shooting from in thick jungle, carries on its back only a "pad" - a heavy, straw-stuffed mattress reaching from neck to tail and fastened on by a rope surcingle passing round the body. On this pad, if passengers are to be carried, a wooden seat with footboards hanging by cords from it and called a *charjama* is placed. Only for sport in open country or high grass jungle is the cage-like howdah employed.

Dermot replaced Badshah's heavy pad by a small, light one, especially made, or else took him out absolutely bare. No shackles were needed to secure the elephant when his white rider dismounted from his neck, for he followed Dermot like a dog, came to his whistle, or stood without moving from the spot where he had been ordered to remain. The most perfect understanding existed between the two; and the superstitious Hindus regarded with awe the extraordinary subjection of their sacred and revered *Gunesh* to the white man.

Now, after a greeting and a palatable gift to Badshah, Dermot seized the huge ears, placed his foot on the trunk which was curled to receive it and was swung up on to the neck by the well-trained animal. Then, answering the *salaams* of the *mahouts* and coolies, who invariably gathered to witness and wonder at his daily meeting with Badshah, he touched the elephant under the ears with his toe and was borne away into the jungle.

His object this day was not to explore but to shoot a deer to replenish the mess larder. Fresh meat was otherwise unprocurable in Ranga Duar; and an unvaried diet of tinned food was apt to become wearisome, especially as it was not helped out by bread and fresh vegetables. These were luxuries unknown to the British officers in this, as in many other, outposts.

The sea of vegetation closed around Badshah and submerged him, as he turned off a footpath and plunged into the dense undergrowth. The trees were mostly straight-stemmed giants of teak, branchless for some distance from the ground. Each strove to thrust its head above the others through the leafy canopy overhead, fighting for its share of the life-giving sunlight. In the green gloom below tangled masses of bushes, covered with large, bell-shaped flowers and tall grasses in which lurked countless thorny plants obstructed the view between the tree-trunks. Above and below was a bewildering confusion of creepers forming an intricate network, swinging from the upper branches and twisting around the boles, biting deep into the bark, strangling the life out of the stoutest trees or holding up the withered, lifeless trunks of others long dead. They filled the space between the tree-tops and the undergrowth, entangled, crisscrossed, festooned, like a petrified mass of writhing snakes.

Through this maddening obstacle Badshah forced his way; while Dermot hacked at the impeding *lianas* with a sharp *kukri*, the heavy-bladed Gurkha knife. The elephant moved on at an easy pace, shouldering aside the surging waves of vegetation and bursting the clinging hold of the creepers. As he went he swept huge bunches of grass up in his trunk, tore down leafy trails or broke off small branches, and crammed them all impartially into his mouth. At a touch of Dermot's foot or the guiding pressure of his hand he swerved aside to avoid a tree or a particularly thorny bush.

There was little life to be seen. But occasionally, with a

whirring sound of rushing wings, a bright-plumaged jungle cock with his attendant bevy of sober-clad hens swept up with startled squawks from under the huge feet and flew to perch high up on neighbouring trees, chattering and clucking indignantly in their fright. The pretty black and white Giant Squirrel ran along the upper branches; or a troop of little brown monkeys leapt away among the tree tops.

It was fascinating to be borne along without effort through the enchanted wood in the luminous green gloom that filled it, lulled by the swaying motion of the elephant's stride. The soothing silence of the woodland was broken only by the crowing of a jungle cock. The thick, leafy screen overhead excluded the glare of the tropic sunlight; and the heat was tempered to a welcome coolness by the dense shade.

But, despite the soporific motion of his huge charger, Dermot's vigilant eye searched the apparently lifeless jungle as he was borne along. Presently it was caught by a warm patch of colour, the bright chestnut hide of a deer; and he detected among the trees the graceful form of a *sambhur* hind. Accustomed to seeing wild elephants the animal gazed without apprehension at Badshah and failed to mark the man on his neck. But females of the deer tribe are sacred to the sportsman; and the hunter passed on. Half a mile farther on, in the deepest shadow of the undergrowth, he saw something darker still. It was the dull black hide of a *sambhur* stag, a fine beast fourteen hands high, with sharp brow antlers and thick horns branching into double points. Knowing the value of motionlessness as a concealment the animal never moved; and only an eye trained to the jungle would have detected it. Dermot noted it, but let it remain unscathed; for he knew well the exceeding toughness of its flesh. What he sought was a *kakur*, or barking deer, a much smaller but infinitely more palatable beast.

Hours passed; and he and Badshah had wandered for miles without finding what he wanted. He looked at his watch; for the sun was invisible. It was nearly noon. In a space free from undergrowth he halted the elephant and, patting the skull with his open hand, said:

"*Buth!*"

Badshah at the word sank slowly down until he rested on his breast and belly with fore and hind legs stuck out stiffly along the ground. Dermot slipped off his neck and stretched his cramped limbs; for sitting long upright on an elephant without any support to the back is tiring. Then he reclined under a tree with his loaded rifle beside him - for the peaceful-seeming forest has its dangers. He made a frugal lunch off a packet of sandwiches from his haversack.

Eating made him thirsty. He had forgotten to bring his water-bottle with him; and he knew that there was no stream to be met with in the jungle for many miles. But he was aware that the forest could supply his wants. Rising, he drew his *kukri* and looked around him. Among the tangle of creepers festooned between the trees he detected the writhing coils of one with withered, cork-like bark, four-sided and about two inches in diameter. He walked over to it and, grasping it in his left hand, cut it through with a blow of his heavy knife. Its interior consisted of a white, moist pulp. With another blow he severed a piece a couple of feet long. Taking a metal cup from his haversack he cut the length of creeper into small pieces and held all their ends together over the little vessel. From them water began to drip, the drops came faster and finally little streams from the pulpy interior filled the cup to the brim with a cool, clear, and palatable liquid. The *liana* was the wonderful *pani-bel,* or water-creeper.

Dermot drank until his thirst was quenched, then sat down with his back against a tree and lit his pipe. He smoked contentedly and watched Badshah grazing. The elephant plucked the long grass with a scythe-like sweep of his trunk, tore down succulent creepers and broke off small branches from the trees, chewing the wood and leaves with equal enjoyment. From time to time he looked towards his master, but, receiving no signal to prepare to move on, continued his meal.

At last the Major knocked out the ashes of his pipe, grinding them into the earth with his heel lest a chance spark might start a forest fire, and whistled to Badshah. The elephant came at once to him. From his haversack Dermot took out a couple of bananas and held them up. The snake-like trunk shot out and grasped them, then curving back placed them in the huge mouth. Dermot stood up and, slinging his rifle over his shoulder, seized Badshah's ears and was lifted again to his place astride the neck.

Once more the jungle closed about them, as the elephant moved off. The rider, unslinging his rifle and laying it across his thighs, glanced from side to side as they proceeded. The forest grew more open. The undergrowth thinned; and occasionally they came to open glades carpeted with tall bracken and looking almost like an English wood. But the great boughs of the giant trees were matted thick with the glossy green leaves of orchid plants, from which drooped long trails of delicate mauve and white flowers.

Just as they were emerging from dense undergrowth on to such a glade, Dermot's eye was caught by something moving ahead of them. He checked Badshah; and they remained concealed in in the thick vegetation. Then through the trees came a trim little *kakur* buck, stepping daintily in advance of his doe which followed a few yards behind. As they moved their long ears twitched incessantly, pointing now in this, now in that, direction for any sound that might warn them of danger. But they did not detect the hidden peril. Dermot noiselessly raised his rifle, aimed hurriedly at the leader's shoulder and fired. The loud report sounded like thunder through the silent forest. The stricken buck sprang convulsively into the air, then fell in a heap; while his startled mate leaped over his body and disappeared in bounding flight.

At the touch of his rider's foot the elephant moved forward

into the open; and without waiting for him to sink down Dermot slid to the ground. Old hunter that he was, the Major could never repress a feeling of pity when he looked on any harmless animal that he had shot; and he had long ago given up killing such except for food. He propped his rifle against a tree and, taking off his coat and rolling up his sleeves, drew his *kukri* and proceeded to disembowel and clean the *kakur*. While he was thus employed Badshah strayed away into the jungle to graze, for elephants feed incessantly.

When Dermot had finished his unpleasant task, it still remained to bind the buck's legs together and tie him on to Badshah's back. For this he would need cords; but he relied on the inexhaustible jungle to supply him with these.

While searching for the udal tree whose inner bark would furnish him with long, tough strips, he heard a crashing in the undergrowth not far away, but, concluding that it was caused by Badshah, he did not trouble to look round. Having got the cordage that he needed, he turned to go back to the spot where he had left the *kakur*. As he fought his way impatiently through the thorny tangled vegetation, he again heard the breaking of twigs and the trampling down of the undergrowth. He glanced in the direction of the sound, expecting to see Badshah appear.

To his dismay his eyes fell on a strange elephant, a large double-tusker. It had caught sight of him and, contrary to the usual habit of its kind, was advancing towards him instead of retreating. This showed that it was the most terrible of all wild animals, a man-killing "rogue" elephant, than which there is no more vicious or deadly brute on the earth.

Dermot instantly recognised his danger. It was very great. His rifle was some distance away, and before he could reach it the tusker would probably overtake him. He stopped and stood still, hoping that the rogue had not caught sight of him. But he saw at once that there was no doubt of this. The brute had its murderous little eyes fixed on him and was quickening its pace. The undergrowth that almost held the man a prisoner was no obstacle to this powerful beast.

Dermot realised that it meant to attack him. His heart nearly stopped, for he knew the terrible death that awaited him. He had seen the crushed bodies, battered to pulp and with the limbs torn away, of men killed by rogue elephants. The only hope of escape, a faint one, lay in flight.

Madly he strove to tear himself free from the clutching thorns and the grip of the entangling creepers that held him. He flung all his weight into his efforts to fight his way out clear of the malignant vegetation, that seemed a cruel, living thing striving to drag him to his death. The elephant saw his desperate struggles. It trumpeted shrilly and, with head held high, trunk curled up, and the lust of murder in its heart, it charged.

The tangled network of interlaced undergrowth parted like gossamer before it. Small trees went down and the tallest bushes were trampled flat; the stoutest creepers broke like pack-thread before its weight.

Dermot tore himself free from the clutch of the last clinging, curving thorns that rent his garments and cut deep into his flesh. Gaining comparatively open ground he ran for his life. But he had lost all sense of direction and could not remember where his rifle stood. Escape seemed hopeless. He knew only too well that in the jungle a pursuing elephant will always overtake a fleeing man. The trees offered no refuge, for the lowest branches were high above his reach and the trunks too thick and straight to climb. He fled, knowing that each moment might be his last. A false step, a trip over a root or a creeper and he was lost. He would be gored, battered to death, stamped out of existence, torn limb from limb by the vicious brute.

The rogue was almost upon him. He swerved suddenly and with failing breath and fiercely beating heart ran madly on. But the respite was momentary. His head was dizzy, his legs heavy as lead, his strength almost gone. He could hear the terrible pursuer only a few yards behind him.

Already the great beast's uncurled trunk was stretched out to seize its prey. Dermot's last moment had come when, with a fierce, shrill scream, a huge body burst out of the jungle and hurled itself at his assailant. Badshah had come to the rescue of his man.

Before the rogue could swing round to meet him the gallant animal had charged furiously into it, driving his single tusk with all his immense weight behind it into the strange elephant's side. The shock staggered the murderous brute and almost knocked it to the ground. Only the fact of its having turned slightly at Badshah's cry, so that his tusk inflicted a somewhat slanting blow, had saved it from a mortal wound. Before it could recover its footing Badshah gored it again.

Dermot, plucked at the last moment from the most terrible of deaths, staggered panting to a tree and tried to stand, supporting himself against the trunk. But the strain had been too great. He turned faint and sank exhausted to the earth, almost unconscious. But the remembrance of Badshah's peril from a better-armed antagonist - for the possession of two tusks gave the rogue a great advantage - nerved him. Holding on to the tree he dragged himself up and looked around for his rifle. He could not see it, and he dared not cross the arena in which the two huge combatants were fighting.

As Badshah drew back to gain impetus for another charge, the rogue regained its feet and prepared to hurl itself on the unexpected assailant. Dermot was in despair at being unable to aid his saviour, who he feared must succumb to the superior weapons of his opponent. He gazed fascinated at the titanic combat.

The rogue trumpeted a shrill challenge. Then it curled its trunk between its tusks out of harm's way and with ears cocked forward and tail erect rushed to the assault. But suddenly it propped on stiffened forelegs and stopped dead. It stared at Badshah, who was about to charge again, and backed slowly, seemingly panic-stricken. Then as the tame elephant moved forward to the attack the rogue screamed with terror, swung about, and with ears and tail dropped, bolted into the undergrowth.

With a trumpet of triumph Badshah pursued. Dermot, left alone, could hardly credit the passing of the danger. The whole episode seemed a hideous nightmare from which he had just awaked. He could scarcely believe that it had actually taken place, although the trampled vegetation and the crashing sounds of the great animals' progress through the undergrowth were evidence of its reality. The need for action had not passed. The rogue might return, for a fight between wild bull-elephants often lasts a whole day and consists of short and desperate encounters, retreats, pursuits, and fresh battles. So he hurriedly searched for his rifle, which he eventually found some distance away. He opened the breach and replaced the soft-nosed bullets with solid ones, more suitable for such big game. Then, once more feeling a strong man armed, he waited expectantly. The sounds of the chase had died away. But after a while he heard a heavy body forcing a passage through the undergrowth and held his rifle ready. Then through the tangle of bushes and creepers Badshah's head appeared. The elephant came straight to him and touched him all over with outstretched trunk, just as mother-elephants do their calves, as if to assure himself of his man's safety.

Dermot could have kissed the soft, snake-like proboscis, and he patted the animal affectionately and murmured his thanks to him. Badshah seemed to understand him and wrapped his trunk around his friend's shoulders. Then, apparently satisfied, he moved away and began to graze calmly, as if nothing out of the common had taken place.

Dermot pulled himself together. Near the foot of the tree at which he had sunk down he found the cord-like strips of bark which he had cut. Picking them up he went to the carcase of the buck and tied its legs together. A whistle brought the elephant to him, and, hoisting the deer on to the pad, he fastened it to the surcingle. Then, grasping the elephant's ears, he was lifted to his place on the neck.

Turning Badshah's head towards home he started off; but, as he went, he looked back at the trampled glade and thanked Heaven that his body was not lying there, crushed and lifeless.

CHAPTER III

A GIRL OF THE TERAI

"How beautiful! How wonderful!" murmured the girl on the verandah, her eyes turned to the long line of the Himalayas filling the horizon to the north.

Clear against the blue sky the shining, ice-clad peaks of Kinchinjunga, a hundred miles away, towered high in air. Mystic, lovely, they seemed to float above the earth, as unsubstantial as the clouds from which they rose. They belonged to another world, a fairy world altogether apart from the rugged, tumbled masses, the awe-inspiring precipices and tremendous cliffs, of the nearer mountains. These were majestic, overpowering, but plainly of this earth, unlike the pure, white summits that seemed unreal, impossible in their beauty.

"Do come and look, Fred," said the girl aloud. "I've never seen the Snows so clearly."

She spoke to the solitary occupant of the dining-room of the bungalow. The young man at the breakfast table answered laughingly:

"I don't want to look at those confounded hills, Sis. I've seen them, nothing but them, all through these long months, until I begin to hate the sight of them."

"Oh, but do come, dear!" she pleaded. "Kinchinjunga has

Gordon Casserly

never seemed so beautiful as it does this morning. And it looks so near. Who could believe that it was all those miles away?"

With an air of pretended boredom and martyr-like resignation, her brother put down his coffee-cup and came out on the verandah.

"Isn't it like Fairyland?" said the girl in an awed voice.

He put his arm affectionately round her, as he replied:

"Then it's where you belong, kiddie, for you look like a fairy this morning."

The hackneyed compliment, unusual from the lips of a brother, was not far-fetched. If a dainty little figure, an exquisitely pretty dimpled face, a shell-pink complexion, violet eyes with long, thick lashes, and naturally wavy golden hair be the hallmarks of the fairies, then Noreen Daleham might claim to be one. Her face in repose had a somewhat sad expression, due to the pathetic droop of the corners of her little mouth and a wistful look in her eyes that made most men instinctively desire to caress and console her. But the sadness and the wistfulness were unconscious and untrue, for the girl was of a sunny and happy disposition. And the men that desired to pet her were kept at a distance by her natural self-respect, which made them respect her, too.

She was, perhaps, somewhat unusual in her generation in that she did not indulge in flirtations and would have strongly objected to being the object of promiscuous caresses and light lovemaking. Her innate purity and innocence kept such things at a distance from her. It never occurred to her that a girl might indulge in a hundred flirtations without reproach. Without being sentimental she had her own inward, unexpressed feelings of romance and vague dreams of Love and a Lover - but not of loves and lovers in the plural.

No one so far had shattered her belief in the chivalrous feeling of respect of the other sex for her own. Men as a rule, especially British men - though they are no more virtuous than those of alien nations - treat a woman as she inwardly wants them to treat her. And, although this girl was over twenty, she had never yet had reason to suspect that men could behave to her with anything but respect.

Her small and shapely figure looked to advantage in the well-cut riding costume of khaki drill that she wore this morning. A cloth habit would have been too warm for even these early days of an Eastern Bengal hot weather. She was ready to accompany her brother in his early ride through the tea-garden (of which he was assistant manager) in the Duars, as this district of the Terai below the mountains is called. From the verandah on which they stood they could look over acres of trim and tidy bushes planted in orderly rows, a strong contrast to the wild disorder of the big trees and masses of foliage of the forest that lay beyond them and stretched to and along the foothills of the Himalayas only a few miles away.

Daleham's father, a retired colonel, has died just as the boy was preparing to go up for the entrance examination for the Royal Military College at Sandhurst. To his great grief he was obliged to give up all hope of becoming a soldier, and, when he left school, entered an office in the city. Passionately desirous of an open-air and active life he had afterwards eagerly snatched at an offer of employment by one of the great tea companies that are dotting the Terai with their plantations and sweeping away glorious spaces of wild, primeval forest to replace the trees by orderly rows of tea-bushes and unsightly iron-roofed factories.

Left with a small income inherited from her mother, Noreen Daleham, who was two years her brother's junior, had gladly given up the dulness of a home with an aunt in a small country town to accompany her brother and keep house for him.

To most girls life on an Indian tea-garden would not seem alluring; for they would find themselves far from social gaieties and the society of their kind. Existence is lonely and lacking in the comforts, as well as the luxuries, of civilisation. Dances, theatres, concerts, even shops, are far, very far away. A woman must have mental resources to enable her to face contentedly life in a scantily-furnished, comfortless bungalow, dumped down in a monotonous stretch of unlovely tea-bushes. With little to occupy her she must rely for days at a time on the sole companionship of her man. To a young bride very much in love that may seem no hardship. But when the glamour has vanished she may change her mind.

To Noreen, however, the isolation was infinitely preferable to the narrow-minded and unfriendly intimacy of society in a country town with its snobbery and cliques. To be mistress of her own home and to be able to look after and mother her dearly-loved brother was a pleasant change from her position as a cipher in the household of a crotchetty, unsympathetic, maiden aunt. And fortunately for her the charm of the silent forest around them, the romance of the mysterious jungle with its dangers and its wonders, appealed strongly to her, and she preferred them to all the pleasures that London could offer. And yet the delights of town were not unknown to her. Her father's first cousin, who had loved him but married a rich man, often invited the girl to stay with her in her house in Grosvenor Square. These visits gave her an insight into life in Mayfair with its attendant pleasures of dances in smart houses, dinners and suppers in expensive restaurants, the Opera and theatres, and afternoons at Ranelagh and Hurlingham. She enjoyed them all; she had enough money to dress well; and she was very popular. But London could not hold her. Her relative, who was childless, was anxious that Noreen should remain always with her, at least until she married - and the older woman determined that the girl should make an advantageous marriage. But the latter knew that her income was very welcome to her aunt and, with a spirit of self-sacrifice not usual in the young, gave up a gay, fashionable life for the dull existence of a paying drudge in the house of an ungrateful, embittered elderly spinster. Yet her heart rejoiced when she conscientiously felt that her brother needed her more and had a greater claim upon her; and gladly she went to keep house for him in India.

And she was happier than he in their new life. For in this land that is essentially a soldier's country, won by the sword, held by the sword, in spite of all that ignorant demagogues in England may say, Fred Daleham felt all the more keenly the disappointment of his inability to follow the career that he would have chosen. However, he was a healthy-minded young man, not given to brooding and vain regrets.

"Are you ready to start, dear?" he said to his sister now. "Shall I order the ponies?"

"I am ready. But have you finished your coffee?"

"Thanks, yes. We'll go off at once then, for I have a long morning's work, and we had better get our ride over while it's cool."

He shouted to his "boy" to order the *syces*, or grooms, to bring the ponies.

"Where are we going today, dear?" asked the girl, putting on her pith helmet.

"To the nursery first. I want to see if the young plants have suffered much from that hailstorm yesterday."

"Wasn't it awful? What would people in England say if they got hailstones like that on their heads?"

"Chunerbutty and I measured one that I picked up outside the withering shed," said the brother. "It was a solid lump of clear ice two inches long and one and a half broad."

"I couldn't have believed it if I hadn't seen them," observed the girl. "I wonder that everyone who is caught out in such a storm is not killed."

"Animals often are - and men, too, for that matter," replied Daleham.

Noreen tapped her smart little riding-boot with her whip.

"I'm glad we're going out to the nursery," she said. "It's my favourite ride."

"I know it is, but I don't like taking you there, Sis," replied her brother. "I always funk that short cut through the bit of jungle to it. I never feel sure that we won't meet a wild elephant in it."

"Oh; but I don't believe they are dangerous; and I do love the ride through that exquisite patch of forest. The trees look so lovely, now that the orchids on them are in flower."

"My dear girl, get that silly idea that elephants are not dangerous out of your head," said Daleham decidedly. "You ask any of the fellows."

"Mr. Parry says they're not."

"Old Parr's never seen any elephant but a tame one, unless it's a pink or speckled one with a brass tail climbing up the wall of his room when he's got D.T's. He never went out shooting in the jungle in his life. But you ask Payne or Reynolds or any of the chaps on the other gardens who know anything of the jungle."

The girl was unwilling to believe that her beloved forest could prove perilous to her, and she feared lest her excursions into it should be forbidden.

"Well, perhaps a rogue might be dangerous," she admitted grudgingly. "But I don't believe that even a rogue would attack you unprovoked."

"Wouldn't it? From all I've heard about them I'd be very sorry to give one of them the chance," said her brother. "I'd almost like you to meet one, just to teach you not to be such a cocksure young woman. Lord! wouldn't I laugh to see you trying to climb a tree - that is, if I were safe up one myself!"

The arrival of the ponies cut short the discussion. Daleham swung his sister up into the saddle of her smart little country-bred and mounted his own waler.

Out along the road through the estate they trotted in the cool northerly breeze that swept down from the mountains and tempered the sun's heat. The panorama of the Himalayas was glorious, although Kinchinjunga had now drawn up his covering of clouds over his face and the Snows had disappeared. The long orderly lines of tea-bushes were dotted here and there with splashes of colour from the bright-hued *puggris*, or turbans, of the men and the *saris* and petticoats of the female coolies, who were busy among the plants, pruning them or tending their wounds after the storm.

The brother and sister quickened their pace and, racing along the soft earthern road, soon reached the patch of forest that intervened between the garden and the nursery.

"I say, Noreen, I think we'd better go the long way round," said Daleham apprehensively, as he pulled up his waler.

"Oh, no, Fred. Don't funk it. Do come on," urged the girl. "If you don't, I'll go on by myself and meet you at the nursery."

The dispute was a daily occurrence and always ended in the man weakly giving in.

"That's a dear boy," said his sister consolingly, when she had gained her point.

"Yes, that's all very well," grumbled the brother. "You've got your own way, as usual. I hope you won't have cause to regret it one day."

"Don't be silly, dear. Come on!" she replied, touching her pony with the whip. The animal seemed to dislike entering the forest as much as the man did. "Oh, do go on, Kitty. Don't be tiresome."

The pony balked, but finally gave way under protest, and they rode on into the jungle. A bridle path wound through the undergrowth and between the trees, and this they followed.

It was easy to understand the girl's enthusiasm and desire to be in the forest. After the tameness of the tea-garden the wild beauty of the giant trees, their huge limbs clothed in the green leaves and drooping trails of blossoms of the orchids, the tangled pattern of the interlaced creepers, the flower-decked bushes and the high ferns, looked all the lovelier in their untrammelled profusion.

The nursery was visited and the damage done to the young plants inspected. Then they turned their ponies' heads towards home and went back through the strip of jungle. They rode over the whole estate, including the untidy ramshackle village of bamboo and palm-thatched huts of the garden coolies, where the little, naked, brown babies rushed out to salaam and smile at their friend Noreen.

As they came in sight of the ugly buildings of the engine and drying-houses with their corrugated iron roofs and rusty stove-pipe chimneys, Daleham said:

"Look here, old girl, while I go to the factory, you'd better hurry on and see to the drinks and things we've got to send to the club. I hope you haven't forgotten that it's our day to be 'at home' there."

"Of course I haven't, Fred. Is it likely?" exclaimed the justly-indignant housewife. "Long before you were awake I helped the cook to pack the cold meat and sweets and cakes, and they went off before we left the bungalow."

They were referring to a custom that obtains in the colonies of tea-planters who are scattered in ones, two, and threes on widely-separated estates. Their one chance of meeting others of their colour is at the weekly gathering in the so-called club of the district. This is very unlike the institutions known by that name to dwellers in civilised cities. No marble or granite palace is it, but a rough wooden shed with one or two rooms built out in the forest far from human habitations, but in a spot as central and equi-distant to all the planters of the district as possible. A few tennis courts are made beside it, or perhaps a stretch of jungle is cleared, the more obtrusive roots grubbed up, and the result is called a polo-ground, and on it the game is played fast and furiously.

A certain day in the week is selected as the one which the planters from the gardens for ten or twenty miles around will come together to it. Across rivers, through forest, jungle, and peril of wild beasts they journey on their ponies to meet their fellow men. Some of them may not have seen another white face since the last weekly gathering.

Each of them in turn acts as host. By lumbering bullock-cart or on the heads of coolies he sends in charge of his servants to the club-house miles away from his bungalow food and drink, crockery, cutlery, and glasses, for the entertainment of all who will foregather there.

And for a few crowded hours this lonely spot in the jungle is filled with the sound of human voices, with laughter, friendliness, and good fellowship. Men who have been isolated for a week rub off the cobwebs, lunch, play tennis, polo, and cards, and swap stories at the bar until the declining sun warns them of the necessity for departing before night falls on the forest. After hearty farewells they swing themselves up into the saddle again and dash off at breakneck speed to escape being trapped by the darkness.

Many and strange are the adventures that befall them on the rough roads or in the trackless wilds. Sometimes an elephant, a bear, or a tiger confronts them on their way. But the intrepid planter, and his not less courageous women-folk, if he has any to accompany him, gallops fearlessly by it or, perhaps, rides unarmed at the astonished beast and scares it by wild cries. Then on again to another week of lonely labour.

This day it had fallen to the lot of the Dalehams to be the hosts of their community. Noreen had superintended the preparation and despatch of the supplies for their guests and could ride home now with a clear conscience to wait for her brother to return for their second breakfast. The early morning repast, the *chota hazri* of an Anglo-Indian household, is a very light and frugal one, consisting of a cup of coffee or tea, a slice of toast, and one or two bananas.

As she pulled up her pony in front of the bungalow a man came down the steps of the verandah and helped her to dismount.

"Oh, thank you, Mr. Chunerbutty," she exclaimed, "and good morning."

"Good morning, Miss Daleham. Just back from your ride with Fred, I suppose?"

The newcomer was the engineer of the estate. The staff of the tea-garden of Malpura consisted of three persons, the manager, a hard-drinking old Welshman called Parry; the assistant manager, Daleham; and this man. As a rule the employees of these estates are Europeans. Chunerbutty was an exception. A Bengali Brahmin by birth, the son of a minor official in the service of a petty rajah of Eastern Bengal, he had chosen engineering instead of medicine or law, the two professions that appeal most to his compatriots. A certain amount of native money was invested in the company that owned the Malpura garden; and the directors apparently thought it good policy to employ an Indian on it.

Like many other young Hindus who have studied in England,

Chunerbutty professed to be completely Anglicised. In the presence of Europeans he sneered at the customs, beliefs, and religions of his fellow-countrymen and posed as an agnostic. It galled him that Englishmen in India thought none the more of him for foreswearing his native land, and he contrasted bitterly their manner to him with the reception that he had met with in the circles in which he moved in England. He had been regarded as a hero in London boarding-houses. His well-cut features and dark complexion had played havoc with the affections of shop-girls of a certain class and that debased type of young Englishwoman whose perverted and unnatural taste leads her to admire coloured men.

In one of these boarding-houses he had met Daleham, when the latter was a clerk in the city. It was at Chunerbutty's suggestion and with an introduction from him that Fred had sought for and obtained employment in the tea company, and as a result the young Englishman had ever since felt in the Bengali's debt. He inspired his sister with the same belief, and in consequence Noreen always endeavoured to show her gratitude to Chunerbutty by frank friendliness. They had all three sailed to India in the same ship, and on the voyage she had resented what seemed to her the illiberal prejudice of other English ladies on board to the Hindu. And all the more since she had an uncomfortable suspicion that deep down in her heart she shared their feeling. So she tried to seem the friendlier to Chunerbutty.

It said much for her own and her brother's popularity with the planters that their intimacy with him did not cause them to be disliked. These men as a class are not unjust to natives, but intimate acquaintance with the Bengali does not tend to make them love him. For the Dalehams' sake most of the men in the district received Chunerbutty with courtesy. But his manager, a rough Welshman of the bad old school, who openly declared that he "loathed all niggers," treated him with invariable rudeness.

As the Hindu engineer and Noreen ascended the steps of the

verandah together, the girl said:

"You are coming to the club this afternoon, are you not?"

"Yes, Miss Daleham, that is why I have been waiting at your bungalow to see you. I wanted to ask if we'd ride over together."

"Of course. We must start early, though. I want to see that the servants have everything ready."

"I don't think I'd be anxious to go if it were not *your*' At Home' day," said the Bengali, as they seated themselves in the drawing-room that Noreen had made as pretty as she could with her limited resources. "I don't like the club as a rule. The fellows are so stand-offish."

"You mustn't think so, Mr. Chunerbutty. They aren't really. You know Englishmen as a rule are not expansive. They often seem unfriendly when they don't mean to be."

"Oh, they mean it right enough here," replied the Hindu bitterly. "They all think they're better than I am, just because I am an Indian. It is that hateful prejudice of the English man and woman in this country. It is different in England. You know I was made a lot of in London. You saw how all the men in that boarding-house we stayed at before we sailed were my friends."

"Yes; that was so, Mr. Chunerbutty," replied Noreen, who was secretly tired of the subject, with which he regaled her every day.

"And as for the women - Of course I don't want to boast, but all the girls were keen to have me take them out and were proud to be seen with me. I know that if I liked I could have picked up lots of ladies, real ladies, I mean, not shop-girls. You should have seen the way they ogled me in the street. I can assure you that little red-haired girl from Manchester in the boarding-house, Lily -"

Noreen broke in quickly.

"Please don't tell me anything about her, Mr. Chunerbutty. You know that I don't like to hear you speak disrespectfully of ladies." Then, to change the disagreeable subject, she continued: "Fred will be back to breakfast soon. Will you stay for it? Then we can all ride together to the club."

"Thank you. I should like to," replied Chunerbutty. To show his freedom from caste prejudices he not only ate with Europeans, but even showed no objection to beef, much to the horror of all orthodox Hindus. That a Brahmin, of all men, should partake of the sacred flesh of the almost divine cow was an appalling sacrilege in their eyes.

Leaving him with a book she attended to the cares of her household, disorganised by the absence of cook and butler, who had gone on ahead to the club with the supplies.

When, after an eight miles' ride, the Dalehams and Chunerbutty reached the wooden shanty that was the rendezvous of the day, they found that they were not the first arrivals. Four or five young men swooped joyously down on Noreen and quarrelled over the right to help her from the saddle. While they were disputing vehemently and pushing each other away the laughing girl slipped unaided to the ground and ran up the wooden steps of the verandah. She was instantly pursued by the men, who followed her to the back verandah where she had gone to interview her servants. They clamoured to be allowed to help in any capacity, and she had to assume an indignation and a severity she was far from feeling to drive them away.

"Oh, do go away, please," she said. "You are only in the way. How can I look after *tiffin* if you interfere with me like this?

Now do be good boys and go off. There's Mrs. Rice arriving. Help her out of her trap."

They went reluctantly to the aid of the only other lady of their little community, who was apparently unable to climb down from her bamboo cart without help. Her husband and Daleham were already proferring their services, but they were seemingly insufficient.

Mrs. Rice belonged to the type of woman altogether unsuited to the life of a planter's wife. She was a shallow, empty-headed person devoid of mental resources and incapable of taking interest in her household or her husband's affairs. In her girlhood she had been pretty in a common style, and she refused to recognise that the days of her youth and good looks had gone by. On the garden she spent her time lounging in her bungalow in an untidy dressing-gown, skimming through light novels and the fashion papers and writing interminable letters to her family in Balham. Her elderly husband, a weak, easy-going man, tired of her constant reproaches for having dragged her away from the gay life of her London suburb to the isolation of a tea-garden, spent as much of his day as possible in the factory. In the bungalow he drank methodically and steadily until he was in a state of mellow contentment and indifferent to his wife's tongue.

On club days Mrs. Rice was a different woman. She arrayed herself in the latest fashions, or the nearest approach to them that could be reached by a native tailor working on her back verandah with the guidance of the fashion plates in ladies' journals. Her face thickly coated with most of the creams, powders, and complexion beautifiers on the market, she swathed her head in a thick veil thrown over her sun-hat. Then, prepared for conquest, she climbed into the strong, country-built bamboo cart in which her husband was graciously permitted to drive her to the club. Fortunately for her a passable road to it ran from her bungalow, for she could not ride.

Arrived at the weekly gathering-place she delighted to surround herself with all the men that she could cajole from the bar running down the side of the one room of the building. With the extraordinary power of self-deception of vain women she believed that most of them were secretly in love with her.

Noreen's arrival in the district the previous year and her instant popularity were galling to the older woman. But after a while, finding that her sneers and thinly-veiled bitter speeches against the girl had no effect on the men, she changed her tactics and pretended to make a bosom friend of her.

When all the company had assembled at the club, luncheon was served at a long, rough wooden table. Beside Noreen sat the man she liked best in the little colony, a grey-haired planter named Payne. Many of the younger men had striven hard to win her favour, and several had wished to marry her; but, liking them all, none had touched her heart. She felt most at ease with Payne, who was a quiet, elderly man and a confirmed bachelor. And he cordially reciprocated her liking.

During *tiffin* Fred Daleham called out from the far end of the table:

"I say, Payne, I wish you'd convince that young sister of mine that wild elephants can be dangerous beasts."

"They can indeed," replied Payne, turning to Noreen. "Take my advice and keep out of their way."

"Oh, but isn't it only rogues that one need be afraid of?" the girl asked. "And aren't they rare?"

"These jungles are full of them, Miss Daleham," said another planter. "We've had two men on our garden killed already this year."

"The Forest Officer told me that several guards and wood-cutters have been attacked lately," joined in another. "One brute has held up the jungles around Mendabari for months."

"Oh, don't tell us any more, Mr. Lane," cried Mrs. Rice with affected timidity. "I shall be afraid to leave the bungalow."

"I heard that the fellow commanding the Military Police detachment at Ranga Duar was nearly killed by a rogue lately," remarked an engineer named Goddard. "Our *mahout* had the story from one of the *mahouts* of the Fort. He had a cock-and-bull yarn about the sahib being saved by his tame elephant, a single-tusker, which drove off the rogue. But, as the latter was a double tusker, it's not a very likely tale."

"They've got a still more wonderful story about that fellow in Ranga Duar," remarked a planter named Lulworth. "They say he can do anything with wild elephants, goes about the jungle with a herd and they obey him like a pack of hounds."

The men near him laughed.

"Good old Lulworth!" said one. "That beats Goddard's yarn. Did you make it up on the spot or did it take you long to think it out?"

Lulworth smiled good humouredly.

"Oh, it's not an original lie," he replied. "I had it from a half-bred Gurkha living in the forest village near my garden."

"Who is commanding Ranga Duar?" asked Lane.

"A fellow called Dermot; a Major," replied Goddard.

"Dermot? I wonder if by any chance it's a man who used to be in these parts before - commanded Buxa Duar when there was a detachment of an Indian regiment there," said Payne.

"I believe it's the same," replied Goddard. "He knows these jungles well and did a lot of shooting in them. He bagged that *budmash* (rogue) elephant that killed so many people. You heard of it. He chased the brute for a fortnight."

"That's the man," said Payne. "I'm glad he's back. We used to be rather pals and stay with each other."

"Oh, do ask him again, Mr. Payne, and bring him to the club," chimed in Mrs. Rice. "It would be such a pleasant change to have some of the officers here. They are so nice, such men of the world."

A smile went round the table. All were so used to the lady's tactless remarks that they only amused. They had long lost the power to irritate.

"I'm afraid Dermot wouldn't suit you, Mrs. Rice," said Payne laughing. "He's not a lady's man."

"Indeed? Is he married?" she asked.

"No, he hasn't that reason to dislike your sex. At least, he wasn't married when I knew him. I wonder how he's escaped, for he's very well off for a man in the Indian Army and heir to an uncle who is a baronet. Good-looking chap, too. Clever beggar, well read and a good soldier, I believe. He has a wonderful way with animals. I had a pony that was a regular mad beast. It killed one *syce* and savaged another. It nearly did for me. I sent it to Dermot, and in a week he had it eating out of his hand."

"He seems an Admiral what-d'you-call-him - you know, that play they had in town about a wonderful butler," said Mrs. Rice.

"Admirable Crichton, wasn't it?"

"Yes, that was the name. Well, your Major seems a wonderful chap," she said. "Do ask him. Perhaps he'll bring some of his officers here."

"I hope he won't, Mrs. Rice," remarked Goddard. "If he does, it's evident that none of us will have a look in with you."
She smirked, well pleased, as she caught Noreen's eye and rose from the table.

Sets of tennis were arranged and the game was soon in full swing. Some of the men walked round to the back of the building to select a spot to be cleared to make a polo ground. Others gathered at the bar to chat.

Noreen had a small court round her, Chunerbutty clinging closely to her all the afternoon, to her secret annoyance. For whenever he accompanied her to the club he seemed to make a point of emphasising the friendly terms on which they were for the benefit of all beholders. As a matter of fact he did so purposely, because he knew that it annoyed all the other men of the community to see him apparently on intimate terms with the girl.

On the afternoon, when at her request he had gone out to the back verandah to tell her servants to prepare tea, he called to her across the club and addressed her by her Christian name. Noreen took it to be an accidental slip, but she fancied that it made Mrs. Rice smile unpleasantly and several of the men regard her curiously.

The day passed all too quickly for these exiled Britons, whose one bright spot of amusement and companionship it was in the week. The setting sun gave the signal for departure. After exchanging good-byes with their guests, the Malpura party mounted their ponies and cantered home.

One morning, a week later, Noreen over-slept herself, and, when she came out of her room for her *chota hazri*, she found that her brother had already started off to ride over the garden. Ordering her pony she followed him. She guessed that he had gone first to the nursery, and when she reached the short cut through the forest she rejoiced at being able to enter it without the usual battle. She urged the reluctant Kitty on, and rode into it carelessly.

Suddenly her pony balked and shied, flinging her to the ground. Then it turned and galloped madly home.

As Noreen, half stunned by the fall, picked herself up stiffly and stood dazed and shaken, she shrieked in terror. She was in the middle of a herd of wild elephants which surrounded her on every side; and, as she gazed panic-stricken at them, they advanced slowly upon her.

Gordon Casserly

CHAPTER IV

THE MADNESS OF BADSHAH

Badshah's rescue of Dermot from the rogue caused him to be more venerated than ever by the natives. The Mohammedan sepoys of the detachment, who should have had no sympathy with Hindu superstitions, began to regard him with awe, impressed by the firm belief in his supernatural nature held by their co-religionists among the *mahouts* and elephant coolies. Among the scattered dwellers in the jungle and the Bhuttias on the hills, his fame, already widespread, increased enormously; and these ignorant folk, partly devil-worshippers, looked on him as half-god, half-demon.

Dermot's feelings towards the gallant animal deepened into strong affection, and the perfect understanding between the two made the sympathy between the best-trained horse and its rider seem a very small thing. The elephant loved the man; and when the Major was on his neck, Badshah seemed to need neither touch of hand or foot nor spoken word to make him comprehend his master's wishes.

Such a state of affairs was very helpful to Dermot in the execution of his task of secret enquiry and exploration. He was thus able to dispense with any attendant for the elephant in his jungle wanderings, which sometimes lasted several days and nights without a return to the Fort. He wanted no witness to his actions at these times. Badshah needed no attention on these excursions. The jungle everywhere supplied him with food, and water was always to be found in gullies in the hills. It was unnecessary to shackle him at night when Dermot slept beside him in the forest. The elephant never strayed, but stayed by his man to watch over him through the dangerous hours of darkness. He either stood by the sleeper all night or else gently lay down near him with the same consummate carefulness that a cow-elephant uses when she lowers her huge body to the ground beside her young calf. When Badshah guarded Dermot no harm from beast of prey could come to him.

While the forest provided sustenance for the animal, the soldier, accustomed though he was to roughing it, found it advisable to supplement its resources for himself. But with some ship's biscuits and a few tins of preserved meat he was ready to face the jungle for days. Limes and bananas grew freely in the foothills. Besides his rifle he usually carried a shot gun, for jungle fowl abounded in the forest, and *kalej*, the black and white speckled pheasant, in the lower hills, and both were excellent eating.

Dermot carried out a thorough survey of the borderland between Bhutan and India, making accurate military sketches and noting the ranges of all positions suitable for defence, artillery, or observation. Mounted on Badshah's neck he ascended the steep hills - elephants are excellent climbers - and explored every known *duar* and defile.

At the same time he kept a keen look-out for messengers passing between disloyal elements inside the Indian frontier and possible enemies beyond it. His knowledge of the language spoken by the Bhuttia settlers within the border, mostly refugees from Bhutan who had fled thither to escape the tyranny and exactions of the officials, enabled him to question the hill-dwellers as to the presence and purpose of any strangers passing through. He gradually established a species of intelligence department among these colonists, whose dread and hatred of their former rulers have made them very pro-British. Through them he was able to keep a check on the comings and goings of trans-frontier Bhutanese, who are permitted to enter India freely, although an English subject is not allowed by his own Government to penetrate into Bhutan. Despite this prohibition - so Dermot discovered - many Bengalis had lately passed backwards and forwards across the frontier, a thing hitherto unheard of. That members of this timorous race should venture to enter such a lawless and savage country as Bhutan and that, having entered it, they lived to come back proved that there must be a strong understanding between many Bhutanese officials and a certain disloyal element in India.

Dermot was returning through the forest from one of his excursions in the hills, when an opportunity was afforded him of repaying the debt that he owed to Badshah for the saving of his life. They had halted at midday, and the man, seated on the ground with his back to a tree, was eating his lunch, while the elephant had strayed out of sight among the trees in search of food.

Beside Dermot lay his rifle and a double-barrelled shot gun, both loaded. Having eaten he lit a cheroot and was jotting down in his notebook the information that he had gathered that morning, when a shrill trumpet from the invisible Badshah made him grasp his rifle. Skilled in the knowledge of the various sounds that elephants make he knew by the brassy note of this that the animal was in deadly fear. He sprang up to go to his assistance, when Badshah burst through the trees and came towards him at his fastest pace, his drooping ears and tail and outstretched trunk showing that he was terrified.

Dermot, bringing his rifle to the ready, looked past him for the cause of his flight, but could see no pursuer. He wondered what could have so alarmed the usually courageous animal. Suddenly the knowledge came to him. As Badshah rushed towards him with every indication of terror the man saw that, moving over the ground with an almost incredible speed, a large serpent came in close pursuit. Even in the open across which Badshah was fleeing it was actually gaining on the elephant, as with an extraordinary rapidity it poured the sinuous curves of its body along the earth. It was evident that, if the chase were continued into the dense undergrowth which would hamper the animal more than the snake, the latter would prove the winner in the desperate race.

Dermot recognised the pursuer. From its size and the fact that it was attacking the elephant it could only be that most dreadful and almost legendary denizen of the forest, the hamadryad, or king-cobra. All other big snakes in India are pythons, which are not venomous. But this, the deadliest, most terrible of all Asiatic serpents, is very poisonous and will wantonly attack man as well as animals. Badshah had probably disturbed it by accident - it might have been a female guarding its eggs - and in its vicious rage it had made an onslaught on him.

The peril of the poisoned tooth is the sole one that a grown elephant need fear in the jungle, and Badshah seemed to know that only his man could save him. And so in his extremity he fled to Dermot.

The soldier hurriedly put down his rifle and picked up the fowling-piece. The elephant rushed past him, and then the snake seemed to sense the man - its feeble sight would not permit it to see him. It swerved out of its course and came towards him. When but a few feet away it suddenly checked and, swiftly writhing its body into a coil from which its head and about five feet of its length rose straight up and waved menacingly in the air, it gathered impetus to strike.

A deadly feeling of nausea and powerlessness possessed Dermot, as from the open mouth, in which the fatal fangs showed plainly while the protruding forked tongue darting in and out seemed to feel for him, came a fetid effluvia that had a paralysing effect on him. He was experiencing the extra-ordinary fascination that a snake exercises over its victims. His muscles seemed benumbed, as the huge head swayed from side to side and mesmerised him with its uncanny power. The gun almost dropped from his nerveless fingers. But with a fierce effort he regained the mastery of himself, brought the butt to his shoulder, and pressed both triggers.

At that short range the shot blew the snake's head off, and Dermot sprang back as the heavy body fell forward and lashed and heaved with convulsive writhing of the muscles, while the tail beat the ground heavily.

At the report of the gun Badshah stopped in his hurried retreat and turned. Then, still showing evidences of his alarm, he approached Dermot slowly.

"It's all right, old boy," said the Major to him. "The brute is done for."

The elephant understood and came to him. Dermot patted the quivering trunk outstretched to smell the dead snake and then went forward and grasped the hamadryad's tail with both hands, striving to hold it still. But it dragged him from side to side and the writhing coils of the headless body nearly enfolded him, so he let go and stepped back. As well as he could judge the king-cobra was more than seventeen feet long.

It took some time to reassure Badshah, for the elephant was badly frightened and, when Dermot mounted him, set off from the spot with a haste unlike his usual deliberate pace.

$$* \quad * \quad * \quad * \quad *$$

For a week after this occurrence the Major was busy in his bungalow in Ranga Duar drawing up reports for the Adjutant General and amplifying existing maps of the borderland, as well as completing his large-scale sketches of the passes. When his task was finished he filled his haversack with provisions one morning and, shouldering his rifle, descended the winding mountain road to the *peelkhana*. Long before this was visible through the trees of the foothills he was apprised by the trumpeting of the elephants and the loud shouts of men that there was trouble there. When he came out on the cleared stretch of ground in front of the stables he saw *mahouts* and coolies fleeing in terror in all directions, while the stoutly built *peelkhana* itself rocked violently as though shaken by an earthquake.

Then forth from it, to the accompaniment of terrified squealing and trumpeting from the female elephants, Badshah stalked, ears cocked and tail up and the light of battle in his eyes, broken iron shackles dangling from his legs.

"*Dewand hoyga* (he has gone mad)," cried the attendants, fleeing past the Major in such alarm that they almost failed to notice him. Last of all came Ramnath, who, recognising him, halted and salaamed.

"*Khubbadar* (take care), sahib!" he cried in warning. "The fit is on him again. The jungle calls him. He is mad."

Dermot paid no attention to him but hastened on to intercept the elephant which stalked on with ears thrust forward and tail raised, ready to give battle to any one that dared stop him.

The Major whistled. Badshah checked in his stride, then as a well-known voice fell on his ear he faltered and looked about him. Dermot spoke his name and the elephant turned and went straight to him, to the amazement of the *peelkhana* attendants watching from behind trees on the hillside. Yet they feared lest his intention was to attack the sahib, for when a tame tusker is seized with a fit of madness, it often kills even its *mahout*, to whom ordinarily it is much attached.

Dermot raised his hand. Badshah stopped and sank on his knees, while his master cast off the broken shackles and swung himself astride of his neck. Then the elephant rose again and of his own volition rolled swiftly forward into the jungle which closed around them and hid animal and man from the astounded watchers.

One by one the *mahouts* and coolies stole from the shelter of the trees and gathered together.

"*Wah! Wah!* the sahib has gone mad, too," exclaimed an old Mohammedan.

"He will never return alive," said another, shaking his head sorrowfully. "*Afsos hun* (I am sorry), for he was a good sahib. The *shaitan* (devil) has borne him away to *Eblis* (hell)."

Here Ramnath broke in indignantly:

"My elephant is no *shaitan*. He is *Gunesh*, the god *Gunesh* himself. He will let no harm come to the sahib, who is safe under his protection."

The other Hindus among the elephant attendants nodded agreement.

"*Such bath* (true words)," they said. "Who knows what the gods purpose? Which of you has ever before seen any man stop a *dhantwallah* (tusker) when the madness was upon him? Which of ye has known a white man to have a power that even we have not, we whose fathers, whose forefathers for generations, have tended elephants?"

"Ye speak true talk," said the first speaker. "The Prophet tells us there are no gods. But *afrits* there are, *djinns* - beings more than man. What know we of those with whom the sahib communes when he and Badshah go forth alone into the forest?"

"The sahib is not as other sahibs," broke in an old coolie. "I was with him before - in Buxa Duar. There is naught in the jungle that can puzzle him. He knows its ways, the speech of the men in it - ay, and of its animals, too. He was a great *shikari* (hunter) in those old days. Many beasts have fallen to his gun. Yet now he goes forth for days and brings back no heads. What does he?"

"For days, say you, Chotu?" queried another *mahout*. "Ay, for more than days. For nights. What man among us, what man even of these wild men around us, would willingly pass a night in the forest?"

"True talk," agreed the old Mohammedan. "Which of us would care to lie down alone beside his elephant in the jungle all night? Yet the sahib sleeps there - if he does sleep - without fear. And no harm comes to him."

Ramnath slowly shook his head.

"The sahib does not sleep. Nor is there aught in the forest that can do him harm. Or my elephant either. The *budmash* tried to kill the sahib, and Badshah protected him. When the big snake attacked Badshah, the sahib saved him.

"But what do they in the forest?" asked Chotu again. "Tell me that, Ramnath-*ji*."

Once more Ramnath shook his head.

"What know we? We are black men. What knowledge have we of what the sahibs do, of what they can do? They go under the sea in ships, beneath the land in carriages. So say the sepoys who have been to *Vilayet* (Europe). They fly in the air like birds. That have I seen with my own eyes at Delhi -"

"And I at Lahore," broke in the old Mohammedan.

"And I at Nucklao (Lucknow)," said a third.

"But never yet was there a man, black man or sahib, who could hold a *dhantwallah* when the mad fit was on him, as our sahib has done," continued Ramnath. "He is under the protection of the gods."

Even the Mohammedans among his audience nodded assent. Their *mullah* taught them that the gods of the Hindu were devils. But who knew? Mecca was far away, and the jungle with its demons was very near them. Among the various creeds in India there is a wide tolerance and a readiness to believe that there may be something of truth in all the faiths that men profess. A Hindu will hang a wreath of marigolds on the tomb of a Mohammedan *pir* - a Mussulman saint - and recite a *mantra*, if he knows one, before it as readily as he will before the shrine of Siva.

While the superstitious elephant attendants talked, Badshah was moving at a fast shambling pace along animal paths through the forest farther and farther away from the *peelkhana*. Wild beasts always follow a track through the jungle, even a man-made road, in preference to forcing a way through the undergrowth for themselves. As he was borne swiftly along, his rider felt that, although the elephant had allowed him to mount to his accustomed place, it would resent any attempts at restraint or guidance. But indeed Dermot had no wish to control it. He was filled with an immense desire to learn the mystery of Badshah's frequent disappearances. The Major was convinced that the animal had a definite objective in view, so purposeful was his manner. For he went rapidly on, never pausing to feed, unlike the usual habit of elephants which, when they can, eat all their waking time. But Badshah held straight on rapidly without stopping. He was proceeding in a direction that took him at an angle away from the line of the Himalayas, and the character of the forest altered as he went.

Near the foot of the hills the graceful plumes of the bamboo and the broad drooping leaves of the plantain, the wild banana, were interspersed with the vivid green leaves and fruit of the limes. Then came the big trees, from which the myriad creepers hung in graceful festoons. Here the undergrowth was scanty and the ground covered with tall bracken in the open glades, which gave the jungle the appearance of an English wood.

Farther on the trees were closer together and the track led through dense undergrowth. Then through a border of high elephant-grass with feathery tops it emerged on to a broad, dry river-bed of white sand strewn with rounded boulders rolled down from the hills. The sudden change from the pleasant green gloom of the forest to the harsh glare of the brilliant sunshine was startling. As they crossed the open Dermot looked up at the giant rampart of the mountains and saw against the dark background of their steep slopes the grey wall of Fort and bungalows in the little outpost of Ranga Duar high above the forest.

Then the jungle closed round them again, as Badshah plunged into the high grass bordering the far side of the river-bed, its feathery plumes sixteen feet from the ground. On through low thorny trees and scrub to the huge bulks and thick, leafy canopy of the giant *simal* and teak once more. The further they went from the hills the denser, more tropical became the undergrowth. The soil was damper and supported a richer, more luxuriant vegetation. Cane brakes through which even elephants and bison would find it hard to push a way, tree ferns of every kind, feathery bushes set thick with cruel hooked thorns, mingled with the great trees, between which the creepers rioted in wilder confusion than ever.

The heat was intense. The air grew moist and steamy, and the sweat trickled down Dermot's face. The earth underfoot was sodden and slushy. Little streams began to trickle, for the water from the mountains ten miles away that sinks into the soil at the foot of the hills and flows to the south underground, here rises to the surface and gives the whole forest its name - Terai, that is, "wet."

Slimy pools lurked in the undergrowth. In one the ugly snout of a small crocodile protruded from the muddy, noisome water, and the cold, unwinking eyes stared at elephant and man as they passed. The rank abundant foliage overhung the track and brushed or broke against Badshah's sides, as he shouldered his way through it.

Suddenly, without warning, Badshah came out on a stretch of

forest clear of undergrowth between the great tree-trunks, and to his amazement Dermot saw that it was filled with wild elephants. Everywhere, as far as the eye could range between the trees, they were massed, not in tens or scores, but in hundreds. On every side were vistas of multitudes of great heads with gleaming white tusks and restless-moving trunks, of huge bodies supported on ponderous legs. And with an unwonted fear clutching at his heart Dermot realised that all their eyes were turned in his direction.

Did they see him? Were they aware that Badshah carried a man? Dermot knew that beasts do not quickly realise a man's presence on the neck or back of a tame elephant. He had seen in a *kheddah*, when the *mahouts* and noosers had gone on their trained elephants in among the host of terrified or angry captured wild ones, that the latter seemed not to observe the humans.

So he hoped now that if he succeeded in turning his animal round and getting him away quickly, his presence would remain unnoticed. Grasping his rifle ready to fire if necessary, he tried with foot and hand to swing Badshah about. But his elephant absolutely ignored his efforts and for the first time in their acquaintance disobeyed him. Slowing down to a stately and deliberate pace the *Gunesh* advanced to meet the others.

Then, to Dermot's amazement, from the vast herd that now encompassed them on every side came the low purring that in an elephant denotes pleasure. Almost inaudible from one throat, it sounded from these many hundreds like the rumble of distant thunder. And in answer to it there came from Badshah's trunk a low sound, indicative of his pleasure. Then it dawned on Dermot that it was to meet this vast gathering of his kind that the animal had broken loose from captivity.

And the multitude of huge beasts was waiting for him. All the swaying trunks were lifted together and pointed towards him to sense him, with a unanimity of motion that made it seem as if they were receiving him with a salute. And, as Badshah moved on into the centre of the vast herd and stopped, again the murmured welcome rumbled from the great throats.

Dermot slung his rifle on his back. It would not be needed now. He resigned himself to anything that might happen and was filled with an immense curiosity. Was there really some truth in the stories about Badshah, some foundation for the natives' belief in his mysterious powers? This reception of him by the immense gathering of his kind was beyond credence Dermot knew that wild elephants do not welcome a strange male into a herd. He has to fight, and fight hard, for admission, which he can only gain by defeating the bull that is its leader and tyrant. But that several herds should come together - for that there were several was evident, since the greatest strength of a herd rarely exceeds a hundred individuals - to meet an escaped domesticated elephant, and apparently by appointment, was too fantastic to be credited by any one acquainted with the habits of these animals. Yet here it was happening before his eyes. The soldier gave up attempting to understand it and simply accepted the fact.

He looked around him. There were elephants of every type, of all ages. Some were very old, as he could tell from their lean, fleshless skulls, their sunken temples and hollow eyes, emaciated bodies and straight, thin legs. And the clearest proof of their age was their ears, which lapped over very much at the top and were torn and ragged at the lower edges.

There were bull-elephants in the prime of life, from twenty-five to thirty-five years old, with great heads, short, thick legs bowed out with masses of muscle, and bodies with straight backs sloping to the long, well-feathered tails. Most of them were tuskers - and the sight of one magnificent bull near Dermot made the sportsman's trigger-finger itch, so splendid were its tusks - shapely, spreading outward and upward in a graceful sweep, and each nearly six feet in length along the outside curve.

There was a large proportion of females and calves in the

Gordon Casserly

assemblage. The youngest ones were about four or five months old. A few had not shed their first woolly coat; and many of the male babies could not boast of even the tiniest tusks.

Badshah was now completely surrounded, for the elephants had closed in on him from every side. He raised his trunk. At once the nearest animals extended theirs towards him. These he touched, and they in their turn touched those of their neighbours beyond his reach. They did the same to others farther away, and so the action was repeated and carried on throughout the herd by all except the youngest calves.

Dermot was wondering whether this meant a greeting or a command from Badshah, when there was a sudden stir among the animals, and soon the whole mass was in motion. Then he saw that the elephants were moving into single file, the formation in which they always march. Badshah alone remained where he was.

Then the enormous gathering broke up and began to move. The oldest elephants led; and the line commenced to defile by Badshah, who stood as if passing them in review. As the first approached it lifted its trunk, and to Dermot's astonishment gently touched him on the leg with it. Then it passed on and the next animal took its place and in its turn touched the man. The succeeding ones did the same; and thus all the elephants defiled by their domesticated companion and touched or smelt Dermot as they went by.

Throughout the whole proceeding Badshah remained motionless, and his rider began to believe that he had ordered his wild kindred to make themselves acquainted with his human friend. It seemed a ridiculous idea, but the whole proceeding was so wildly improbable that the soldier felt that nothing could surprise him further.

As the elephants passed him he noticed on the legs of a few of them marks which were evidently old scars of chain or rope-galls. And the forehead of one or two showed traces of having been daubed with tar, while on the trunk of one very large tusker was an almost obliterated ornamental design in white paint, and his tusks were tipped with brass. So it was apparent that Badshah was not the only animal present that had escaped from captivity. The big tusker had probably belonged to the *peelkhana* of some rajah, judging by the pattern of the painted design.

Slowly the seemingly endless line of great animals went by. Hours elapsed before the last elephant had passed; and Dermot, cramped by sitting still on Badshah's neck, was worn out with heat and fatigue long before the slow procession ended.

When at last the almost interminable line had gone by, Badshah moved off at a rapid pace and passed the slow-plodding animals until he had overtaken the leaders. Dermot found that the herd was heading for the mountains and the oldest beasts were still in front. This surprised him, as it was altogether contrary to the custom of wild elephants. For usually on a march the cows with calves lead the way. This is logical and reasonable; because if an unencumbered tusker headed the line and set the pace, he would go too fast and too far for the little legs of the babies in the rear. They would fall behind; and, as their mothers would stay with them, the herd would soon be broken up.

But as Badshah reached the head of the file and, taking the lead, set a very slow pace, Dermot quickly understood why the old elephants were allowed to remain in front. For all of them were exceedingly feeble, and some seemed at death's door from age and disease. He would not have been surprised at any of them falling down at any moment and expiring on the spot.

Then he remembered the curious but well-known fact that no man, white or coloured, has ever yet found the body of a wild elephant that has died in the jungle from natural causes. Though few corners of Indian or Ceylon forests remain unexplored, no carcases or skeletons of these animals have ever been discovered. And yet, although in a wild state they reach the age of a hundred and fifty years, elephants must die at last.

Dermot was meditating on this curious fact of natural history when Badshah came out on the high bank of an empty river-bed and cautiously climbed down it. Ahead of them rose the long line of mountains clear and distinct in the rays of the setting sun. As he reached the far bank Dermot turned round to look back. Behind them stretched the procession of elephants in single file, each one stepping into the huge footprints of those in front of it. When Badshah plunged into the jungle again the tail of the procession had not yet come out on the white sand of the river-bed.

And when the sun went down they were still plodding on towards the hills.

CHAPTER V

THE DEATH-PLACE

An hour or two after night had fallen on the jungle Badshah stopped suddenly and sank down on his knees. Dermot took this as an invitation to dismount, and slid to the ground. When Badshah stopped, the long-stretching line behind him halted, too, and the elephants broke their formation and wandered about feeding. Soon the forest resounded with the noise of creepers being torn down, branches broken off, and small trees uprooted so that the hungry animals could reach the leafy crowns. Dermot realised that in the darkness he was in danger of being trodden underfoot among the hundreds of huge animals straying about. But Badshah knew it, too, and so he remained standing over his man, while the latter sat down on the ground, rested his aching back against a tree, and made a meal from the contents of his haversack. Badshah contented himself with the grass and leaves that he could reach without stirring from the spot, and then cautiously lowered himself to the ground and stretched his huge limbs out.

Dermot lay down beside him, as he had so often done before in the nights spent in the jungle. But, exhausted as he was, he could not sleep at first. The strangeness of the adventure kept him awake. To find his presence accepted by this vast gathering of wild elephants, animals which are usually extremely shy of human beings, was in itself extraordinary. Much as he knew of the jungle he had never dreamt of this. In Central Indian villages he had been told legends of lost

Gordon Casserly

children being adopted by wolves. But for elephants to admit a man into their herd was beyond belief. That it was due to Badshah's affection for him was little less remarkable than the fact itself. For it opened up the question of the animal's extraordinary power over his kind. And that was an unfathomable mystery.

Dermot found the riddle too difficult to solve. He ceased to puzzle over it. The noises in the forest gradually died down, and the intense silence that followed was broken only by the harsh call of the barking-deer or the wailing cry of the giant owl. Fatigue overcame him, and he slept.

It seemed to him that he had scarcely lost consciousness when he was awakened by a touch on his face. It was still dark; but, when he sprang up hastily, he could vaguely make out Badshah standing beside him. The elephant touched him with his trunk and then sank down on his knees. The invitation to mount was unmistakable; and Dermot slung his rifle on his back and climbed on to the elephant's neck. Badshah rose up and moved off, and apparently the other elephants followed him, for the noises that had filled the forest and showed them to be awake and feeding, ceased abruptly. Dermot could just faintly distinguish the soft footfall of the animal immediately behind him.

When Badshah reached the lowest hills and left the heavy forest behind the sky became visible, filled with the clear and vivid tropic starlight. An animal track led up between giant clumps of bamboos, by long-leaved plantain trees and through thick undergrowth of high, tangled bushes that clothed the foothills. Up this path, as a paling in the east betokened the dawn, the long line of elephants climbed in the same order of march as on the previous day. Badshah led; and behind him followed the oldest elephants, on which the steep ascent told heavily.

Two thousand feet above the forest the track led close to a Bhuttia village. As the rising sun streaked the sky with rose, the head of the long line neared the scattered bamboo huts perched on piles on the steep slopes. The track was not visible from the village, but a party of wood-cutters from the hamlet had just reached it on their way to descend to their day's work in the jungle below. They saw the winding file of ascending elephants some distance beneath them and in great alarm climbed up a big rubber tree growing close to the path. Hidden among its broad and glossy green leaves they watched the approaching elephants.

From their elevated perch they had a good view of the serpentining line. To their amazement they saw that a white man sat astride the neck of the first animal and was apparently conducting the enormous herd. One of the wood-cutters recognised Dermot, who had once visited this very village and interrogated this man among others. Petrified with fright, the Bhuttia and his companions watched the long line go by, and for fully an hour after the last elephant had disappeared they did not venture to descend from the tree.

When at last they did so there was no longer any thought of work. Instead, they fled hotfoot to the village to spread their strange news; and next day, when they went to their work below and explained to the enraged Gurkha overseer the reason of their absence on the previous day, they told him the full tale. No story is too incredible for the average native of India, and the overseer and various forest guards who also heard the narrative fully believed it and spread it through the jungle villages. It grew as it passed from tongue to tongue, until the story finally rivalled the most marvellous of the exploits of Krishna, that wonderful Hindu god.

Meanwhile Dermot and his mammoth companions were climbing steadily higher and ever higher into the mountains. A panther, disturbed by them in his sleep beside the bones of a goat, rose growling from the ground and slunk sullenly away. A pair of brilliantly-plumaged hornbills flew overhead with a loud and measured beat of wings. *Kalej* pheasants scuttled away among the bushes.

Gordon Casserly

But soon the jungle diminished to low scrub and finally fell away behind the ascending elephants, and they entered a region of rugged, barren mountains cloven by giant chasms and seamed by rocky *nullahs* down which brawling streams rushed or tumbled over falls. A herd of *gooral* - the little wild goat - rushed away before their coming and sprang in dizzy leaps down almost sheer precipices.

As the mountains closed in upon him in a narrow passage between beetling cliffs thousands of feet high, Dermot's interest quickened. For he knew that he was nearing the border-line between India and Bhutan; and this was apparently a pass from one country into the other, unknown and unmarked in the existing maps, one of which he carried in his haversack. He took it out and examined it. There was no doubt of it; he had made a fresh discovery.

He turned round on Badshah's neck and looked down on all India spread out beneath him. East and west along the foot of the mountains the sea of foliage of the Terai swept away out of sight. Here and there lighter patches of colour showed where tea-gardens dotted the darker forest. Thirty odd miles to the south of the foothills the jungle ended abruptly, and beyond its ragged fringe lay the flat and fertile fields of Eastern Bengal. A dark spot seen indistinctly through the hot-weather haze marked where the little city of Cooch Behar lay. Sixty miles and more away to the south-east the Garo Hills rose beyond the snaky line of the Brahmaputra River wandering through the plains of Assam.

A sharp turn in the narrow defile shut out the view of everything except the sheer walls of rock that seemed almost to meet high overhead and hide the sky. Even at noon the pass was dark and gloomy. But it came abruptly to an end, and as through a gateway the leading elephants emerged suddenly on a narrow jungle-like valley. The first line of mountains guarding Bhutan had been traversed. Beyond the valley lay another range, its southern face covered with trees.

Badshah halted, and the elephants behind him scattered as they came out of the defile. The aged animals among them, as soon as they had drunk from a little river running midway between the mountain chains and fed by streams from both, lay down to rest, too exhausted to eat. But the others spread out in the trees to graze.

Dermot, who had begun to fear that the supply of food in his haversack might run short, found a plantain tree and gathered a quantity of the fruit. After a frugal meal he wrote up his notes on the pass through which he had just come and made rough military sketches of it. Then he strolled among the elephants grazing near Badshah. They showed no fear or hostility as he passed, and some of the calves evinced a certain amount of curiosity in him. He even succeeded in making friends with one little animal about a year old, marked with whitish blotches on its forehead and trunk, which allowed him to touch it and, after due consideration, accepted the gift of a peeled banana. Its mother stood by during the proceeding and regarded the fraternising with her calf dubiously.

Not until dawn on the following day did the herd resume its onward movement. Dermot was awake even before Badshah's trunk touched his face to arouse him, and as soon as he was mounted the march began again. The route lay through the new mountain range; and all day, except for a couple of hours' halt at noon, the long line wound up a confusing jumble of ravines and passes. When night fell a plateau covered with tall deodar trees had been reached, and here the elephants rested.

Daybreak on the third morning found Badshah leading the line through a still more bewildering maze of narrow defiles and a forest with such dense foliage that, when the sun was high in the heavens, its rays scarcely lightened the gloom between the tree-trunks. Dermot wondered how Badshah found his way, for there was no sign of a track, but the elephant moved on steadily and with an air of assured purpose.

At one place he plunged into a deep narrow ravine filled with tangled undergrowth that constantly threatened to tear Dermot from his seat. Indeed, only the continual employment of the latter's *kukri*, with which he hacked at the throttling creepers and clutching thorny branches, saved him.

Darker and gloomier grew the way. The sides of the *nullah* closed in until there was scarcely room for the animals to pass, and then Dermot found Badshah had entered a natural tunnel in the mountain side. The interior was as black as midnight, and the soldier had to lie flat on the elephant's skull to save his own head.

Suddenly a blinding light made him close his eyes, as Badshah burst out of the darkness of the tunnel into the dazzling glare of the sunshine.

When his rider looked again he found that they were in an almost circular valley completely ringed in by precipitous walls of rock rising straight and sheer for a couple of thousand feet. Above these cliffs towered giant mountain peaks covered with snow and ice.

At the end of the valley farthest from them was a small lake. Near the mouth of the tunnel the earth was clothed with long grass and flowering bushes and dotted with low trees. But elsewhere the ground was dazzlingly white, as though the snow lay deep upon it. Badshah halted among the trees, and the old elephants passed him and went on in the direction of the lake. Dermot noticed that they seemed to have suddenly grown feebler and more decrepit.

He looked down at the white ground. To his surprise he found that from here to the lake the valley was floored with huge skulls, skeletons, scattered bones, and tusks. It was the elephants' Golgotha. He had penetrated to a spot which perhaps no other human being had ever seen - the death-place of the mammoths, the mysterious retreat to which the elephants of the Terai came to die.

He looked instinctively towards the aged animals, which alone had gone forward among the bones. And, as he gazed, one of them stumbled, recovered its footing, staggered on a few paces, then stopped and slowly sank to the ground. It laid its head down and stretched out its limbs. Tremors shook the huge body; then it lay still as though asleep. A second old elephant, and a third, stood for a moment, then slowly subsided. Another and another did the same; until finally all of them lay stretched out motionless - lifeless, dark spots on the white floor that was composed of bones of countless generations of their kind.

There was a strange impressiveness about the solemn passing of these great beasts. It affected the human spectator almost painfully. The hush of this fatal valley, the long line of elephants watching the death of their kindred, the pathos of the end of the stately animals which in obedience to some mysterious impulse, had struggled through many difficulties only to lie down here silently, uncomplainingly, and give up their lives, all stirred Dermot strangely. And when the thought of the incalculable wealth that lay in the vast quantity of ivory stored in this great charnel-house flashed through his mind, he felt that it would be a shameful desecration, inviting the wrath of the gods, to remove even one tusk of it.

He was not left long to gaze and wonder at the weird scene. To his relief Badshah suddenly turned and passed through the trees again towards the tunnelled entrance, and the hundreds of other elephants followed him in file. In a few minutes Dermot found himself plunged into darkness once more, and the Valley of Death had disappeared.

When they had passed through the tunnel, the elephants slipped and stumbled down the rock-encumbered ravines, for elephants are far less sure-footed in descent than when ascending. But they travelled at a much faster pace, being no longer hampered by the presence of the old and decrepit beasts. It seemed to take only a comparatively short time to reach the valley between the two mountain ranges. And here they stopped to feed and rest.

When morning came, Dermot found that the big assembly of elephants was breaking up into separate herds of which it was composed. The greater number of these moved off to the east and north, evidently purposing to remain for a time in Bhutan, where the young grass was springing up in the valleys as the lower snows melted. Only three herds intended to return to India with Badshah, of which the largest, consisting of about a hundred members, seemed to be the one to which he particularly belonged.

During the descent from the mountains into the Terai, Dermot wondered what would happen with Badshah when they reached the forest. Would the elephant persist in remaining with the herd or would it return with him to the *peelkhana?*

Night had fallen before they had got clear of the foothills, so that when they arrived in the jungle once more they halted to rest not far from the mountains. When Dermot awoke next morning he found that he and Badshah were alone, all the others having disappeared, and the animal was standing patiently awaiting orders. He seemed to recognise that his brief hour of authority had passed, and had become once more his usual docile and well-disciplined self. At the word of command he sank to his knees to allow his master to mount; and then, at the touch of his rider's foot, turned his head towards home and started off obediently.

As they approached the *peelkhana* a cry was raised, and the elephant attendants rushed from their huts to stare in awe-struck silence at animal and man. Ramnath approached with marked reverence, salaaming deeply at every step.

When Dermot dismounted it was hard for him to bid farewell to Badshah. He felt, too, that he could no longer make the elephant submit to the ignominy of fetters. So he bade Ramnath not shackle nor bind him again. Then he patted the huge beast affectionately and pointed to the empty stall in the *peelkhana*; and Badshah, seeming to understand and appreciate his being left unfettered, touched his white friend caressingly with his trunk and walked obediently to his brick standing in the stable. The watching *mahouts* and coolies nodded and whispered to each other at this, but Ramnath appeared to regard the relations between his elephant and the sahib as perfectly natural.

Dermot shouldered his rifle and started off on the long and weary climb to Ranga Duar. When he reached the parade ground he found the men of the detachment falling out after their morning drill. His subaltern, Parker, who was talking to the Indian officers of the Double Company, saw him and came to meet him.

"Hullo, Major; I'm glad to see you back again," he said, saluting. "I hardly expected to, after the extraordinary stories I've heard from the *mahouts*."

"Really? What were they?" asked his senior officer, leading the way to his bungalow.

"Well, the simplest was that Badshah had gone mad and bolted with you into the jungle," replied the subaltern. "Another tale was that he knelt down and worshipped you, and then asked you to go off with him on some mysterious mission."

Dermot had resolved to say as little as possible about his experiences. Europeans would not credit his story, and he had no desire to be regarded as a phenomenal liar. Natives would believe it, for nothing is too marvellous for them; but he had no wish that any one should know of the existence of the Death Place, lest ivory-hunters should seek to penetrate to it.

"Nonsense. Badshah wasn't mad," he replied. "It was just as I guessed when you first told me of these fits of his - merely the jungle calling him."

"Yes, sir. But the weirdest tale of all was that you were seen leading an army of elephants, just like a Hindu god, to invade Bhutan."

"Where did you hear that?" asked Dermot in surprise.

"Oh, the yarn came from the *mahouts*, who heard it from some of the forest guards, who said they'd been told it by Bhuttias from the hills. You know how natives spread stories. Wasn't it a silly tale?" And Parker laughed at the thought of it.

"Yes, rather absurd," agreed the Major, forcing a smile. "Yes, natives are really - Hello! who's done this?"

They had reached the garden of his bungalow. The little wooden gate-posts at the entrance were smeared with red paint and hung with withered wreaths of marigolds.

When a Hindu gets the idea into his head that a certain stone or tree or place is the abode of a god or godling or is otherwise holy, his first impulse is to procure marigolds and red paint and make a votive offering of them by making wreaths of the one and daubing everything in the vicinity with the other.

"By Jove, Major, I expect that some of the Hindus in the bazaar have heard these yarns about you and mean to do *poojah* (worship) to you," said Parker with a laugh. "I told you they regard Badshah as a very holy animal. I suppose some of his sacredness has overflowed on to you."

Dermot realised that there was probably some truth in the suggestion. He was annoyed, as he had no desire to be looked on by the natives as the possessor of supernatural powers.

"I must see that my boy has the posts cleaned," he said. "When you get to the Mess, Parker, please tell them I'll be up to breakfast as soon as I've had a tub and a shave."

Two hours later Dermot showed Parker the position of the

defile on the map and explained his notes and sketches of it; for it was important that his subordinate should know of it in the event of any mishap occurring to himself. But before he acquainted Army Headquarters in India with his discovery, he went to the pass again on Badshah to examine and survey it thoroughly. When this was done and he had despatched his sketches and report to Simla, he felt free to carry out a project that interested him. This was to seek out the herd of wild elephants with which Badshah seemed most closely associated and try to discover the secret of his connection with them.

Somewhat to his surprise he experienced no difficulty in finding them; as, when he set out from the *peelkhana* in search of them, Badshah seemed to know what he wanted and carried him straight to them. For each day the animal appeared to understand his man's inmost thoughts more and more, and to need no visible expression of them.

When they reached the herd, the elephants received Badshah without any demonstration of greeting, unlike the previous occasion. They showed no objection to Dermot's presence among them. The little animal with the blotched trunk recognised him at once and came to him, and the other calves soon followed its example and made friends with him. The big elephants betrayed no fear, and allowed him to stroll on foot among them freely.

This excursion was merely the first of many that Dermot made with the herd, with which he often roamed far and wide through the forest. And sometimes, without his knowing it, he was seen by some native passing through the jungle, who hurriedly climbed a tree or hid in the undergrowth to avoid meeting the elephants. From concealment the awed watcher gazed in astonishment at the white man in their midst, of whom such wonderful tales were told in the villages. And when he got back safely to his own hamlet that night the native added freely to the legends that were gathering around Dermot's name among the jungle and hill-dwellers.

On one occasion Dermot, seated on Badshah's neck, was following in rear of the herd when it was moving slowly through the forest a few miles from the foot of the hills. A sudden halt in the leisurely progress made him wonder at the cause. Then the elephants in front broke their formation and crowded forward in a body, and Dermot suddenly heard a human cry. Fearing that they had come unexpectantly on a native and might do him harm, he urged Badshah forward through the press of animals, which parted left and right to let him through. To his surprise he found the leading elephants ringed round a girl, an English girl, who, hatless and with her unpinned hair streaming on her shoulders, stood terrified in their midst.

CHAPTER VI

A DRAMATIC INTRODUCTION

When Noreen Daleham rose half-stunned from the ground where her pony had flung her and realised that she was surrounded by wild elephants she was terrified. The stories of their ferocity told her at the club flashed across her mind, and she felt that she was in danger of a horrible death. When the huge animals closed in and advanced on her from all sides she gave herself up for lost.

At that awful moment a voice fell on her ears and she heard the words:

"Don't be alarmed. You are in no danger."

In bewilderment she looked up and saw to her astonishment and relief a white man sitting on the neck of one of the great beasts.

"Oh, I am so glad!" she exclaimed. "I was terrified. I thought that these were wild elephants."

Dermot smiled.

"So they are," he said. "But they won't hurt you. Can I help you? What are you doing here? Have you lost your way in the jungle?"

　　　　　Gordon Casserly

By this time Noreen had recovered her presence of mind and began to realise the situation. It was natural that this man should be astonished to find an Englishwoman alone and in distress in the forest. Her appearance was calculated to cause him to wonder - and a feminine instinct made her hands go up to her untidy hair, as she suddenly thought of her dishevelled state. She picked up her hat and put it on.

"I've had a fall from my pony," she explained, trying to reduce her unruly tresses to order. "It shied at the elephants and threw me. Then I suppose it bolted."

She looked around but could see nothing except elephants, which were regarding her solemnly.

"But where have you come from? Are you far from your camp?" persisted Dermot. "Shall I take you to it?"

"Oh, we are not in camp," replied Noreen. "I live on a tea-garden. It is quite near. I can walk back, thank you, if you are sure that the elephants won't do me any harm."

But as she spoke she felt her knees give way under her from weakness, and she was obliged to sit down on the ground. The shock of the fall and the fright had affected her more than she realised.

Dermot laid his hand on Badshah's head, and the animal knelt down.

"I'm afraid you are not fit to walk far," said Dermot. "I must take you back."

As he spoke he slipped to the ground. From a pocket in the pad he extracted a flask of brandy, with which he filled a small silver cup.

"Drink this," he said, holding it to her lips. "It will do you good."

Noreen obeyed and drank a little of the spirit. Then, before she could protest, she was lifted in Dermot's arms and placed on the pad on Badshah's back. This cool disposal of her took her breath away, but to her surprise she felt that she rather liked it. There was something attractive in her new acquaintance's unconsciously authoritative manner.

Replacing the flask he said:

"Are you used to riding elephants?"

She shook her head.

"Then hold on to this rope across the pad, otherwise you may slip off when Badshah rises to his feet. You had better keep your hand on it as we go along, though there isn't much danger of your falling."

As he got astride the elephant's neck he continued: "Now, be ready. Hold on tightly. Uth, Badshah!"

Despite his warning Noreen nearly slipped off the pad at the sudden and jerky upheaval when the elephant rose.

"Now please show me the direction in which your garden lies, if you can," said Dermot.

"Oh, it is quite near," Noreen answered. "That is the road to it."

She let the rope go to point out the way, but instantly grasped it again. Dermot turned Badshah's head down the track.

"Oh, what about all these other elephants?" asked the girl apprehensively, looking at them where they were grouped together, gazing with curiosity at Badshah's passengers. "Will they come too?"

"No," said Dermot reassuringly, "you needn't be afraid. They won't follow. We'd create rather too much of a sensation if we arrived at your bungalow at the head of a hundred *hathis*."

"But are they really wild?" she asked. "They look so quiet and inoffensive now; though when I was on the ground they seemed very dreadful indeed. But I was told that wild elephants are dangerous."

"Some of them undoubtedly are," replied Dermot. "But a herd is fairly inoffensive, if you don't go too near it. Cow-elephants with young calves can be very vicious, if they suspect danger to their offspring."

A turn in the road through the jungle shut out the sight of the huge animals behind them, and Noreen breathed more freely. She began to wonder who her rescuer was and how he had come so opportunely to her relief. Their dramatic meeting invested him in her eyes with more interest than she would have found in any man whose acquaintance she had made in a more unromantic and conventional manner. And so she bestowed more attention on him and studied his appearance more closely than she would otherwise have done. He struck her at once as being exceedingly good looking in a strong and manly way. His profile showed clear-cut and regular features, with a mouth and chin bespeaking firmness and determination. His face in repose was grave, almost stern, but she had seen it melt in sudden tenderness as he sprang to her aid when she had felt faint. She noticed that his eyes were very attractive and unusually dark - due, although she did not know it, to the Spanish strain in him as in so many other Irish of the far west of Connaught - and with his darker hair, which had a little wave in it, and his small black moustache they gave him an almost foreign look. The girl had a sudden mental vision of him as a fierce rover of bygone days on the Spanish Main. But when, in a swift transition, little laughter-wrinkles creased around his eyes that softened in a merry smile, she wondered how she could have thought that he looked fierce or stern. Although, like many of her sex, she was a little prejudiced against handsome men, and he certainly was one, yet she was strongly attracted by his appearance. Probably the very contrast in colouring and type between him and her made him appeal to her. He was as dark as she was fair. And when he was standing on the ground she had seen that he was well above middle height with a lithe and graceful figure displayed to advantage by his careless costume of loose khaki shirt and Jodpur breeches. The breadth of his shoulders denoted strength, and his rolled-up sleeves showed muscular arms burned dark by the sun.

"How did you manage to come up just at the right moment to rescue me?" she asked. "I have not thanked you yet for saving me, but I do so now most heartily. I can't tell you how grateful I feel. I am sure, no matter what you say, that those elephants would have killed me if you hadn't come."

Dermot laughed.

"I'm afraid I cannot pose as a heroic rescuer. I daresay there might have been some danger to you, had I not been with them. For one can never tell what elephants will do. Out of sheer nervousness and fright they might have attacked you."

"You were with them?" she echoed in surprise. "But you said that these were wild ones."

"So they are. But this animal we are on is a tame one and was captured years ago in the jungle about here. I think he must have belonged to this particular herd, for they accept him as one of themselves."

"Yes; but you?"

"Oh, they have made me a sort of honorary member of the herd for his sake, I think. He and I are great pals," and Dermot laid his hand affectionately on Badshah's head. "He saved my life not long ago when I was attacked by a vicious rogue."

Noreen suddenly remembered the conversation at the club lunch.

"Oh, are you the officer from the Fort up at Ranga Duar?" she asked.

"One of them. I am commanding the detachment of Military Police there," he answered. "My name is Dermot."

"Then I've heard of you. I understand now. They said that you could do wonderful things with wild elephants, that you went about the forest with a herd of them."

"*They* said?" he exclaimed. "Who are 'they'?"

"The men at the club. We have a planters' club for the district, you know. At our last weekly meeting they spoke of you and said that you had nearly been killed by a rogue. Mr. Payne told us that he used to know you."

"What? Payne of Salchini? I knew him well. Awfully good chap."

"Yes, isn't he? I like him so much."

"I saw a lot of him when I was stationed at Buxa Duar with my Double Company. Hullo! here we are at a tea-garden."

They had suddenly come out of the forest on to the open stretch of furrowed land planted with the orderly rows of tidy bushes.

"Yes; it is ours. It's called Malpura," said Noreen. "My brother is the assistant manager. Our name is Daleham."

"Here comes somebody in a hurry," remarked Dermot, pointing to where, on the road ahead of them, a man on a pony was galloping towards them with a cloud of dust rising behind him.

"Yes, it's my brother. Oh, what's happening?" she exclaimed.

For as he approached his pony scented the elephant and stopped dead suddenly, nearly throwing its rider over its head.

"Fred! Fred! Here I am!" she cried.

But Daleham's animal was unused to elephants and positively refused to approach Badshah. In vain its rider strove to make it go on. It suddenly put an end to the dispute between them by swinging round and bolting back the way that it had come, despite its master's efforts to hold it.

Noreen looked after the pair anxiously.

"You needn't be alarmed, Miss Daleham," said Dermot consolingly. "Your brother is quite all right. Once he gets to a safe distance from Badshah the pony will pull up. Horses are always afraid of elephants until they get used to them. See, he is slowing up already."

When the girl was satisfied that her brother was in no danger she smiled at the dramatic abruptness of his departure.

"Poor Fred! He must have been awfully worried over me," she said. "He probably thought I was killed or at least had met with a bad accident. And now the poor boy can't get near me."

"I daresay he was alarmed if your pony went home riderless."

"Yes, it must have done so. Naughty Kitty. It must have bolted back to its stable and frightened my poor brother out of his wits."

"Well, he'll soon have you back safe and sound," said Dermot. "Hold on tightly now, and I'll make Badshah step out. *Mul!*"

The elephant increased his pace, and the motion sorely tried

Gordon Casserly

Noreen. As they passed through the estate the coolies bending over the tea-bushes stopped their work to stare at them. Noreen remarked that they appeared deeply interested at the sight of the elephant, and gathered together to talk volubly and point at it.

When they neared the bungalow they saw Daleham standing on the steps of the verandah, waiting for them. He had recognised the futility of struggling with his pony and had returned with it.

As they arrived he ran down the steps to meet them.

"Good gracious, Noreen, what has happened to you?" he cried, as Badshah stopped in front of the house. "I've been worried to death about you. When the servants came to the factory to say that Kitty had galloped home with broken reins and without you, I thought you had been killed."

"Oh, Fred, I've had such an adventure," she cried gaily. "You'll say it served me right. Wait until I get down. But how am I to do so, Major Dermot?"

"The elephant will kneel down. Hold on tightly," he replied. "*Buth*, Badshah." He unslung his rifle as he dismounted.

When her brother had lifted her off the pad, the girl kissed him and said:

"I'm so glad to get back to you, dear. I thought I never would. I know you'll crow over me and and say, 'I told you so.' But I must introduce you to Major Dermot. This is my brother, Major. Fred, if it had not been for Major Dermot, you wouldn't have a sister now. Just listen."

The men shook hands as she began her story. Her brother interrupted her to suggest their going on to the verandah to get out of the sun. When they were all seated he listened with the deepest interest.

At the end of her narrative he could not help saying:

"I warned you, young woman. What on earth would have happened to you if Major Dermot had not been there?" He turned to their visitor and continued: "I must thank you awfully, sir. There's no doubt that Noreen would have been killed without your help."

"Oh, perhaps not. But certainly you were right in advising her not to enter the forest alone."

"There, you see, Noreen?"

The girl pouted a little.

"Is it really so dangerous, Major Dermot?" she asked.

"Well, one ought never to go into it without a good rifle," he replied. "You might pass weeks, months, in it without any harm befalling you; but on the other hand you might be exposed to the greatest danger on your very first day in it. You've just had a sample."

"You were attacked yourself by a rogue, weren't you?" asked the girl. "You said that your elephant saved you? Was this the one? Do tell us about it."

Dermot briefly narrated his adventure with the rogue. Brother and sister punctuated the tale with exclamations of surprise and admiration, and at the conclusion of it, turned to look at Badshah, who had taken refuge from the sun's rays under a tree and was standing in the shade, shifting his weight from leg to leg, flapping his ears and driving away the flies by flicking his sides with a small branch which he held in his trunk. Dermot had taken off his pad.

"You dear thing!" cried the girl to him. "You are a hero. I'm very proud to think that I have been on your back."

"It was really wonderful," said Daleham. "How I should have liked to see the fight! I say, all our servants have come out to look at him. By Jove! any amount of coolies, too. One would think that they'd never seen an elephant before."

"I'm sure they've never seen such a splendid one," said his sister enthusiastically. "He is well worth looking at. But - oh, what is that man doing?"

One of the crowd of coolies that had collected had gone down on his knees before Badshah and touched the earth with his forehead. Then another and another imitated him, until twenty or thirty of them were prostrate in the dust, worshipping him.

"I must stop this," exclaimed Daleham. "If old Parr sees them he'll be furious. They ought to be at their work."

He ran down the steps of the verandah and ordered them away. His servants disappeared promptly, but the coolies went slowly and reluctantly.

"What were they doing, Major Dermot?" asked Noreen. "They looked as if they were praying to your elephant. Hadn't they ever seen one before?"

He explained the reason of the reverence paid to Badshah. Daleham, returning, renewed his thanks as his sister went into the bungalow to see about breakfast. When she returned to tell them that it was ready, Dermot hardly recognised in the dainty girl, clad in a cool muslin dress, the terrified and dishevelled damsel whom he had first seen standing in the midst of the elephants.

During the meal she questioned him eagerly about the jungle and the ways of the wild animals that inhabit it, and she and her brother listened with interest to his vivid descriptions. A chance remark of Daleham's on the difficulty of obtaining labour for the tea-gardens in the Terai interested Dermot and set him trying to extract information from his host.

"I suppose you know, sir, that as these districts are so sparsely populated and the Bhuttias on the hills won't take the work, we have to import the thousands of coolies needed from Chota Nagpur and other places hundreds of miles away," said Daleham. "Lately, however, we have begun to get men from Bengal."

"What? Bengalis?" asked Dermot.

"Yes. Very good men. Quite decent class. Some educated men among them. Why, I discovered by chance that one is a B.A. of Calcutta University."

"Do you mean for your clerical work, as *babus* and writers?"

"No. These chaps are content to do the regular coolie work. Of course we make them heads of gangs. I believe they're what are called Brahmins."

"Impossible! Brahmins as tea-garden coolies?" exclaimed Dermot in surprise.

"Yes. I'm told that they are Brahmins, though I don't know much about natives yet," replied his host.

Dermot was silent for a while. He could hardly believe that the boy was right. Brahmins who, being of the priestly caste, claim to be semi-divine rather than mere men, will take up professions or clerical work, but with all his experience of India he had never heard of any of them engaging in such manual labour.

"How do you get them?" he asked.

"Oh, they come here to ask for employment themselves," replied Daleham.

"Do they get them on many gardens in the district?" asked Dermot, in whose mind a vague suspicion was arising.

"There are one or two on most of them. The older planters are surprised."

"I don't wonder," commented Dermot grimly. "It's something very unusual."

"We have got most, though," added his host. "I daresay it's because our engineer is a Hindu. His name is Chunerbutty."

"Sounds as if he were a Bengali Brahmin himself," said Dermot.

"He is. His father holds an appointment in the service of the Rajah of Lalpuri, a native State in Eastern Bengal not far from here. The son is an old friend of ours. I met him first in London."

"In fact, it was through Mr. Chunerbutty that we came here," said Noreen. "He gave Fred an introduction to this company."

Dermot reflected. He felt that if these men were really Bengali Brahmins, their coming to the district to labour as coolies demanded investigation. Their race furnishes the extremist and disloyal element in India, and any of them residing on these gardens would be conveniently placed to act as channels of communication between enemies without and traitors within. He felt that it would be advisable for him to talk the matter over with some of the older planters.

"Who is your manager here?" he enquired.

"A Welshman named Parry."

"Are you far from Salchini?"

"You mean Payne's garden? Yes; a good way. He's a friend of

yours, isn't he?"

"Yes; I should like to see him again. I must pay him a visit."

"Oh, look here, Major," said Daleham eagerly. I've got an idea. Tomorrow is the day of our weekly meeting at the club. Will you let me put you up for the night, and we'll take you tomorrow to the club, where you will meet Payne?"

"Thank you; it's very kind of you; but -" began Dermot dubiously.

Noreen joined in.

"Oh, do stay, Major Dermot. We'd be delighted to have you."

Dermot needed but little pressing, for the plan suited him well.

"Excellent," said Daleham. "You'll meet Chunerbutty at dinner then. You'll find him quite a good fellow."

"I'd like to meet him," answered the soldier truthfully. He felt that the Bengali engineer might interest him more than his host imagined.

"I'll tell the boy to get your room ready," said Noreen. "Oh, what will you do with your elephant?"

"Badshah will be all right. I'll send him back to the herd."

"What, will he go by himself?" exclaimed Daleham. "How will you get him again?"

"I think he'll wait for me," replied Dermot.

They had finished breakfast by now and rose from the table. The Major went to Badshah, touched him and made him turn round to face in the direction whence they had come.

"Go now, and wait for me there," he said pointing to the forest.

The elephant seemed to understand, and, touching his master with his trunk, started off at once towards the jungle.

Daleham and his sister watched the animal's departure with surprise.

"Well, I'm blessed, Major. You certainly have him well trained," said Fred. "Now, will you excuse me, sir? I must go to the factory. Noreen will look after you."

He rose and took up his sun-hat.

"Oh, by the way, there is one of the fellows I told you of," he continued. "He is the B.A."

He pointed to a man passing some distance away from the bungalow. Dermot looked at him with curiosity. His head was bare, and his thick black hair shone with oil. He wore a European shirt and a *dhoti*, or cotton cloth draped round his waist like a divided skirt. His legs were bare except for gay-coloured socks and English boots. Gold-rimmed spectacles completed an appearance as unlike that of the ordinary tea-garden coolie as possible. He was the typical Indian student as seen around Gower Street or South Kensington, in the dress that he wears in his native land. There was no doubt of his being a Bengali Brahmin.

Daleham called him.

"Hi! I say! Come here!"

When the man reached the foot of the verandah steps the assistant manager said to him:

"I have told this sahib that you are a graduate of Calcutta University."

The Bengali salaamed carelessly and replied:

"Oah, yess, sir. I am B.A."

"Really? What is your name?" asked Dermot.

"Narain Dass, sir."

"I am sorry, Mr. Dass, that a man of your education cannot get better employment than this," remarked Dermot.

The Bengali smiled superciliously.

"Oah, yess, I can, of course. This -" He checked himself suddenly, and his manner became more cringing. "Yess, sir, I can with much facility procure employment of sedentary nature. But for reasons of health I am stringently advised by medical practitioner to engage in outdoor occupation. So I adopt policy of 'Back to the Land.'"

"I see, Mr. Dass. Very wise of you," remarked Dermot, restraining an inclination to smile. "You are a Brahmin, aren't you?"

"Yess, sir," replied the Bengali with pride.

"Well, Mr. Dass, I hope that your health will improve in this bracing air. Good-morning."

"Good-morning, sir," replied the Bengali, and continued on his way.

Dermot watched his departing figure meditatively. He felt that he had got hold of a thread, however slender, of the conspiracy against British rule.

"You seem very interested in that coolie, Major Dermot," remarked Noreen.

"Eh? Oh, I beg your pardon," he said, turning to her. "Yes. You see, it is very unusual to find such a man doing this sort of work."

He did not enter into any further explanation. The suspicion that he entertained must for the present be kept to himself.

When Daleham left them the girl felt curiously shy. Perfectly at her ease with men as a rule, she now, to her surprise, experienced a sensation of nervousness, a feeling almost akin to awe of her guest. Yet she liked him. He impressed her as being a man of strong personality. The fact that - unlike most men that she met - he made no special effort to please her interested her all the more in him. Gradually she grew more at her ease. She enjoyed his tales of the jungle, told with such graphic power of narrative that she could almost see the scenes and incidents that he depicted.

Dinner-time brought Chunerbutty, who did not conduce to harmony in the little party. Dermot regarded him with interest, for he wished to discover if the engineer played any part in the game of conspiracy and treason. Although the Hindu was ignorant of this, it was evident that he resented the soldier's presence, partly from racial motives, but chiefly from jealousy over Noreen. He was annoyed at her interest in Dermot and objected to her feeling grateful for her rescue. He tried to make light of the adventure and asserted that she had been in no danger. Gradually he became so offensive to the Major that Noreen was annoyed, and even her brother, who usually saw no fault in his friend, felt uncomfortable at Chunerbutty's incivility to their guest.

Dermot, however, appeared not to notice it. He behaved with perfect courtesy to the Hindu, and ignored his attempts at impertinence, much to Daleham's relief, winning Noreen's admiration by his self-control. He skilfully steered the conversation to the subject of the Bengalis employed on the estate. The engineer at first denied that there were Brahmins among them, but when told of Narain Dass's claim to be one, he pretended ignorance of the fact. This obvious falsehood confirmed Dermot's suspicion of him.

The Dalehams were not sorry when Chunerbutty rose to say good-night shortly after they had left the dining-room. He was starting at an early hour next morning on a long ride to Lalpuri to visit his father, of whose health he said he had received disquieting news.

When Noreen went to bed that night she lay awake for some time thinking of their new friend. In addition to her natural feeling of gratitude to him for saving her from deadly peril, there was the consciousness that he was eminently likable in himself. His strength of character, his manliness, the suggestion of mystery about him in his power over wild animals and the fearlessness with which he risked the dangers of the forest, all increased the attraction that he had for her. Still thinking of him she fell asleep.

And Dermot? Truth to tell, his thoughts dwelt longer on Chunerbutty and Narain Dass than on Miss Daleham. He liked the girl, admired her nature, her unaffected and frank manner, her kind and sunny disposition. He considered her decidedly pretty; but her good looks did not move him much, for he was neither impressionable nor susceptible, and had known too many beautiful women the world over to lose his heart readily. Possibly under other circumstances he might not have given the girl a second thought, for women had never bulked largely in his life. But the strange beginning of their acquaintance had given her, too, a special interest.

The Dalehams' arrival at the club the next day with their guest caused quite a sensation. At any time a stranger was a refreshing novelty to this isolated community. But in addition Dermot had the claim of old friendship with one of their members, and the other men knew him by repute. So he was welcomed with the open-hearted hospitality for which planters are deservedly renowned.

Mrs. Rice took complete possession of him as soon as he was introduced to her, insisted on his sitting beside her at lunch and monopolised him after it. Noreen, rather to her own surprise, felt a little indignant at the calm appropriation of her new friend by the older woman, and a faint resentment against Dermot for acquiescing in it. She was a little hurt, too, at his ignoring her.

But the soldier had not come there to talk to ladies. He soon managed to escape from Mrs. Rice's clutches in order to have a serious talk with his old friend Payne, which resulted in the latter adroitly gathering the older and more dependable men together outside the building on the pretext of inspecting the future polo ground. In reality it was to afford Dermot an opportunity of disclosing to them as much of the impending peril of invasion as he judged wise. The planters would be the first to suffer in such an event. He wanted to put them on their guard and enlist their help in the detection of a treacherous correspondence between external and internal foes. This they readily promised, and they undertook to watch the Bengalis among their coolies.

The Dalehams and their guest did not reach Malpura until after sundown, and Dermot was persuaded to remain another night under their roof.

On the following morning the brother and sister rode out with him to the scene of Noreen's adventure. He was on foot and was accompanied by two coolies carrying his elephant's pad. The girl was not surprised, although Fred Daleham was, at Badshah's appearance from the forest in response to a whistle from his master. And when, after a friendly farewell, man and animal disappeared in the jungle, Noreen was conscious of the fact that they had left a little ache in her heart.

CHAPTER VII

IN THE RAJAH'S PALACE

A rambling, many-storied building, a jumbled mass of no particular design or style of architecture, with blue-washed walls and close-latticed windows, an insanitary rabbit-warren of intricate passages, unexpected courtyards, hidden gardens, and crazy tenements kennelling a small army of servants, retainers, and indefinable hangers-on - such was the palace of the Rajah of Lalpuri. Here and there, by carved doors or iron-studded gates half off their hinges, lounged purposeless sentries, barefooted, clad in old and dirty red coatees, white cross-belts and ragged blue trousers. They leant on rusty, muzzle-loading muskets purchased from "John Company" in pre-Mutiny years, and their uniforms were modelled on those worn by the Company's native troops before the days of Chillianwallah.

The outer courtyard swarmed with a mob of beggars, panders, traders, servants, and idlers, through which occasionally a ramshackle carriage drawn by galled ponies, their broken harness tied with rope, and conveying some Palace official, made its way with difficulty. Sometimes the vehicle was closely shuttered or shrouded with white cotton sheets and contained some high-caste lady or brazen, jewel-decked wanton of the Court.

On one side were the tumble-down stables, near which a squealing white stallion with long, red-dyed tail was tied to a *peepul* tree. Its rider, a blue-coated *sowar*, or cavalryman, with bare feet thrust into heelless native slippers, sat on the ground near it smoking a hubble-bubble. A chorus of neighing answered his screaming horse from the filthy stalls, outside which stood foul-smelling manure-heaps, around which mangy pariah dogs nosed. In the blazing sun a couple of hooded hunting-cheetahs lay panting on the bullock-cart to which they were chained.

The Palace stood in the heart of the city of Lalpuri, a maze of narrow, malodorous streets off which ran still narrower and fouler lanes. The gaudily-painted houses, many stories high, with wooden balconies and projecting windows, were interspersed with ruinous palm-thatched bamboo huts and grotesquely decorated temples filled with fat priests and hideous, ochre-daubed gods, and noisy with the incessant blare of conch shells and the jangling of bells. Lalpuri was a byword throughout India and was known to its contemptuous neighbours as the City of Harlots and Thieves. Poverty, debauchery, and crime were rife. Justice was a mockery; corruption and abuses flourished everywhere. A just magistrate or an honourable official was as hard to find as an honest citizen or a virtuous woman.

Like people, like rulers. The State had been founded by a Mahratta free-booter in the days when the Pindaris swept across Hindustan from Poona almost to Calcutta. His successor at the time of the Mutiny was a clever rascal, who refused to commit himself openly against the British while secretly protesting his devotion to their enemies. He balanced himself adroitly on the fence until it was evident which side would prove victorious. When Delhi fell and the mutineers were scattered, he offered a refuge in his palace to certain rebel princes and leaders who were fleeing with their treasures and loot to Burmah. But the treacherous scoundrel seized the money and valuables and handed the owners over to the Government of India.

The present occupant of the *gadi* - which is the Hindustani equivalent of a throne - was far from being an improvement on his predecessors. He exceeded them in viciousness, though much their inferior in ability. As a rule the Indian reigning princes of today - and especially those educated at the splendid Rajkumar College, or Princes' School - are an honour to their high lineage and the races from which they spring. In peace they devote themselves to the welfare of their subjects, and in war many of them have fought gallantly for the Empire and all have given their treasures or their troops loyally and generously to their King-Emperor.

The Rajah of Lalpuri was an exception - and a bad one. Although not thirty years of age he had plumbed the lowest depths of vice and debauchery. Cruelty and treachery were his most marked characteristics, lust and liquor his ruling passions.

Of Mahratta descent he was of course a Hindu. While in drunken moments professing himself an atheist and blaspheming the gods, yet when suffering from illness caused by his excesses he was a prey to superstitious fears and as wax in the hands of his Brahmin priests. Although his territory was small and unimportant, yet the ownership of a Bengal coalfield and the judicious investment by his father of the treasure stolen from the rebel princes in profitable Western enterprises ensured him an income greater than that enjoyed by many far more important maharajahs. But his revenue was never sufficient for his needs, and he ground down his wretched subjects with oppressive taxes to furnish him with still more money to waste in his vices. All men marvelled that the Government of India allowed such a debauchee and wastrel to remain on the *gadi*. But it is a long-suffering Government and loth to interfere with the rulers of the native states. However, matters were fast reaching a crisis when the Viceroy and his advisers would be forced to consider whether they should allow this degenerate to continue to misgovern his State. This the Rajah realised, and it filled him with feelings of hostility and disloyalty to the Suzerain Power.

But the real ruler of Lalpuri State was the *Dewan* or Prime

Minister, a clever, ambitious, and unscrupulous Bengali Brahmin, endowed with all the talent for intrigue and chicanery of his race and caste as well as with their hatred of the British. He had persuaded himself that the English dominion in India was coming to an end and was ready to do all in his power to hasten the event. For he secretly nourished the design of deposing the Rajah and making himself the nominal as well as the virtual ruler of the State, and he knew that the British would not permit this. His was the brain that had conceived the project of uniting the disloyal elements of Bengal with the foreign foes of the Government of India, and he was the leader of the disaffected and the chief of the conspirators.

When Chunerbutty arrived in Lalpuri he rode with difficulty through the crowded, narrow streets. His sun-helmet and European dress earned him hostile glances and open insults, and more than one foul gibe was hurled at him as he went along by some who imagined him from his dark face and English clothes to be a half-caste. For the native, however humble, hates and despises the man of mixed breed.

When he reached the Palace he made his way through the throng of beggars, touts, and hangers-on in the outer courtyard, and, passing the sentries, all of whom recognised him, entered the building. Through the maze of passages and courts he penetrated to the room occupied by his father in virtue of his appointment in the Rajah's service.

He found the old man sitting cross-legged on a mat in the dirty, almost bare apartment. He was chewing betel-nut and spitting the red juice into a pot. He looked up as his son entered.

Among the other out-of-date customs and silly superstitions that the younger Chunerbutty boasted of having freed himself from, were the respect and regard due to parents - usually deep-rooted in all races of India, and indeed of the East generally. So without any salutation or greeting he sat down on the one ricketty chair that the room contained, and said ill-temperedly:

"Here I am, having ridden miles in the heat and endured discomfort for some absurd whim of thine. Why didst thou send for me? I told thee never to do so unless the matter were very important. I had to eat abuse from that drunken Welshman to get permission to come. I had to swear that thou wert on the point of death. Then he consented, but only because, as he said, I might catch thy illness and die too. May jackals dig him from his grave and devour his corpse!"

As the father and son sat confronting each other the contrast between them was significant of the old Bengal and the new. The silly, light-minded girls in England who had found the younger man's attractions irresistible and raved over his dark skin and the fascinating suggestion of the Orient in him, should have seen the pair now. The son, ultra-English in his costume, from his sun-hat to his riding-breeches and gaiters, and the old Bengali, ridiculously like him in features, despite his shaven crown with one oiled scalp-lock, his bulbous nose and flabby cheeks, and teeth stained red by betel-chewing. On his forehead were painted three white horizontal strokes, the mark of the worshippers of Siva the Destroyer. His only garment was a dirty old *dhoti* tied round his fat, naked paunch.

He grinned at his son's ill-temper and replied briefly:

"The Rajah wishes to see thee, son."

"Why? Is there anything new?"

"I do not know. Thou art angry at being torn from the side of the English girl. Art thou to marry her? Why not be satisfied to wed one of thine own countrywomen?"

The younger man spat contemptuously.

"I would not be content with a fat Hindu cow after having

known English girls. Thou shouldest see those of London, old man. How they love us of dark skin and believe our tales that we are Indian princes!"

The father leered unpleasantly.

"Thou hast often told me that these white women are shameless. Is it needful to pay the price of marriage to possess this one?"

"I want her, if only to anger the white men among whom I live," replied his son sullenly. "Like all the English out here they hate to see their women marry us black men."

"There is a white man in the Palace who is not like that."

"A white man in the Palace?" echoed his son. "Who is he? What does he here?"

"A Parliamentary-*wallah*, who is visiting India and will go back to tell the English monkeys in his country what we are not. He comes here with letters from the *Lat Sahib*."

"From the Viceroy?"

"Yes; thou knowest that any fool from their Parliament holds a whip over the back of the *Lat Sahib* and all the white men in this land. This one hath no love for his own country."

"How knowest thou that?"

"Because the *Dewan Sahib* loves him. Any foe of England is as welcome to the *Dewan* as the monsoon rain to the *ryot* whose crops are dying of drought. Thou wilt see this one, for he is ever with the *Dewan*, who has ordered that thou goest to him before seeing the Rajah.

"Ordered? I am sick of his orders," replied the son, petulantly. "Am I his dog that he should order me? I am not a Lalpuri now. I am a British subject."

"Thy father eats the Rajah's salt. Thou forgettest that the *Dewan* found the money to send thee across the Black Water to learn thy trade."

The younger man frowned discontentedly.

"Well, I see not the colour of his money now. Why should I obey him? I will not."

"Softly, softly, son. There be many knives in the bazaars of the city that will seek out any man's heart at the *Dewan's* bidding. Thou art a man of Lalpuri still."

His son rose discontentedly from his chair.

"*Kali* smite him with smallpox. I suppose it were better to see what he wants. I shall go."

Admitted to the presence of the *Dewan*, Chunerbutty's defiant manner dropped from him, for he had always held that official in awe. His swagger vanished; he bent low and his hand went up to his head in a salaam. The Premier of the State, a wrinkled old Brahmin, was seated on the ground propped up by white bolsters, with a small table, a foot high, crowded with papers in front of him. He was dressed simply and plainly in white cotton garments, a small coloured *puggri* covering his shaved head. Although reputed the possessor of finer jewels than the Rajah he wore no ornaments.

Sprawling in an easy chair opposite him was a fat European in a tight white linen suit buttoned up to the neck. He evidently felt the heat acutely, and with a large coloured handkerchief he incessantly wiped his red face, down which the sweat rolled in oily drops, and mopped his bald head.

When Chunerbutty entered the apartment the *Dewan*, without any greeting indicated him, saying:

Gordon Casserly

"This, Mr. Macgregor, is an example of what all we Indians shall be when relieved of the tyranny of British officials and allowed to govern ourselves."

His English was perfect.

The bearer of the historic Highland name, whose appearance suggested rather a Hebrew patronymic, removed from his mouth the cigar that he was smoking and asked in a guttural voice:

"Who is the young man?"

The *Dewan* briefly explained, then, turning to Chunerbutty, he said:

"This is Mr. Donald Macgregor, M.P., a member of the Labour Party and a true friend of India. You may speak freely before him. Sit down."

The engineer looked around in vain for another chair. The *Dewan* said sharply in Bengali, using the familiar, and in this case contemptuous, "thou":

"Sit on the floor, as thy fathers before thee have done, as thou didst thyself before thou began to think thyself an Englishman and despise thy country and its ways."

Chunerbutty collapsed and sat down hastily on a mat. Then in English the *Dewan* continued:

"Have you any news?"

"No; I have forwarded as they came all letters and messengers from Bhutan. The troops -" He stopped and looked at the Member of Parliament.

"Continue. There is no need of secrecy before Mr. Macgregor," said the *Dewan*. "I have said that he is a friend of India."

"It's all right, my boy," added the Hebrew Highlander encouragingly. "I am a Pacifist and a socialist. I don't hold with soldiers or with keeping coloured races enslaved. 'England for English and India for the Indians' is my motto."

"Well, I have already informed you that there is no truth in the reports that troops were to be sent again to Buxa Duar," said Chunerbutty, reassured. "On the frontier there are only the two hundred Military Police at Ranga Duar. They are Punjaubi Mohammedans. I made the acquaintance of the officer commanding them last night."

"Ah! What is he like?" enquired the *Dewan*, interested.

"Inquisitive, but a fool - like all these officers," replied the engineer contemptuously. "He noticed Narain Dass on our garden and saw that he was a Bengali. He learned that others of us were employed on our estate and was surprised that Brahmins should do coolie work. But he suspected nothing."

"You are sure?" asked the *Dewan*.

"Quite certain."

The *Dewan* shook his head doubtfully.

"These English officers are not always the fools they seem," he observed. "We must keep an eye on this inquisitive person. Now, how goes the work among the garden coolies? Are they ripe for revolt?"

"Not yet on all the estates. They are ignorant cattle, and to them the Motherland means nothing. But on our garden our greatest helper is the manager, a drunken bully. He ill-treats the coolies and nearly kicked one to death the other day."

"That's how the Englishman always treats the native, isn't it?"

asked the Hebrew representative of an English constituency.

"Always and everywhere," replied the engineer unhesitatingly, wondering if Macgregor were really fool enough to believe the libel, which one day's experience in India should have shown him to be false. But this foreign Jew turned Scotchman hated the country of his adoption, as only these gentry do, and was ready to believe any lie against it and eager to do all in his power to injure it.

The *Dewan* said:

"Mr. Macgregor has been sent to tell us that his party pledges itself to help us in Parliament."

"Yes, you need have no fear. We'll see that justice is done you," began the politician in his best tub-thumping manner. "We Socialists and Communists are determined to put an end to tyranny and oppression, whether of the downtrodden slaves of Capitalism at home or our coloured brothers abroad. The British working-man wants no colonies, no India. He is determined to change everything in England and do away with all above him - kings, lords, aristocrats, and the *bourgeoisie*. He demands Revolution, and we'll give it him."

"Pardon me, Mr. Macgregor," remarked the engineer. "I've lived among British working-men, when I was in the shops, but I never found that they wanted revolution."

The Member of Parliament looked at him steadily for a moment and grinned.

"You're no fool, Mr. Chunerbutty. You're a lad after my own heart. You know a thing or two. Perhaps you're right. But the British working-man lets us represent him, and we know what's good for him, if he don't. We Socialists run the Labour Party, and I promise you we'll back you up in Parliament if you rebel and drive the English out of India."

"We shalldo it, Mr. Macgregor," said the *Dewan*, confidently, "We are co-ordinating all the organisations in the Punjaub, Bombay, and Bengal, and we shall strike simultaneously. Afghan help has been promised, and the Pathan tribesmen will follow the Amir's regiments into India. As I told you, the Chinese and Bhutanese invasion is certain, and there are neither troops nor fortifications along this frontier to stop it."

"That's right. You'll do it," said Macgregor. "The General Election comes off in a few months, and our party is sure of victory. I am authorised to assure you that our first act will be to give India absolute independence. So you can do what you like. But don't kill the white women and children - at least, not openly. They might not like it in England, though personally I don't care if you massacre every damned Britisher in the country. From what I've seen of 'em it's only what they deserve. The insolence I've met with from those whipper-snapper officers! And the civil officials would be as bad, if they dared. Then their women - I wouldn't like to say what I think of *them*."

The *Dewan* turned to Chunerbutty.

"Go now; you have my leave. His Highness wishes to see you. I have sent him word that you are here."

The engineer rose and salaamed respectfully. Then, with a nod to Macgregor, he withdrew full of thought. He had not known before that the conspiracy to expel the British was so wide-spread and promising. He had not regarded it very seriously hitherto. But he had faith in the *Dewan*, and the pledge of the great political party in England was reassuring.

Admitted to the presence of the Rajah, Chunerbutty found him reclining languidly on a pile of soft cushions on the floor of a tawdrily-decorated room. The walls were crowded with highly-coloured chromos of Hindu gods and badly-painted indecent pictures. A cut-glass chandelier hung from the ceiling, and expensive but ill-assorted European furniture stood about the apartment. French mechanical toys under glass shades crowded the tables.

The Rajah was a fat and sensual-looking young man, with bloated face and bloodshot that eyes spoke eloquently of his excesses. On his forehead was painted a small semicircular line above the eyebrows with a round patch in the middle, which was the sect-mark of the *Saktas*. His white linen garments were creased and dirty, but round his neck he wore a rope of enormous pearls. His feet were bare. On a gold tray beside him were two liqueur bottles, one empty, the other only half full, and two or three glasses.

He looked up vacantly as Chunerbutty entered, then, recognising him, said petulantly:

"Where have you been? Why did you not come before?"

The engineer salaamed and seated himself on the carpet near him without invitation. He held the Rajah far less in awe than the Prime Minister, for he had been the former's boon-companion in his debauches too often to have much respect for him.

He answered the prince carelessly.

"The *Dewan* sent for me to see him before I came to you, *Maharaj Sahib*."

"Why? What for? That man thinks that he is the ruler of Lalpuri, not I," grumbled the Rajah. "I gave orders that you were to be sent to me as soon as you arrived. I want news of the girl. Is she still there?"

"Yes; she is still there."

"Listen to me," the Rajah leant forward and tapped him on the knee. "I must have that girl. Ever since I saw her at the *durbar* at Jalpaiguri I have wanted her."

"Your Highness knows that it is difficult to get hold of an Englishwoman in India."

"I know. But I do not care. I must have her. I *will* have her." He filled a tumbler with liqueur and sipped it. "I have sent for you to find a way. You are clever. You know the customs of these English. You have often told me how you did as you wished with the white women in England."

"That is very different. It is easy there," and Chunerbutty smiled at pleasant memories. "There the women are shameless, and they prefer us to their own colour. And the men are not jealous. They are proud that their daughters and sisters should know us."

He helped himself to the liqueur.

"Why do you not go to England?" he continued. "There every woman would throw herself at your feet. They make much of the Hindu students, the sons of fat *bunniahs* and shopkeepers in Calcutta, because they think them all Indian princes. For you who really are one they would do anything."

The Rajah sat up furious and dashed his glass down on the tray so violently that it shivered to atoms.

"Go to England? Have I not tried to?" he cried. "But every time I ask, the Viceroy refuses me permission. I, a rajah, the son of rajahs, must beg leave like a servant from a man whose grandfather was a nobody - and be refused. May his womenkind be dishonoured! May his grave be defiled!"

He filled another glass and emptied it before continuing.

"But, I tell you, I want this girl. I must have her. You must get her for me. Can you not carry her off and bring her here? You can have all the money you want to bribe any one. You said there are only two white men on the garden. I will send you a hundred soldiers."

Chunerbutty looked alarmed. He had no wish to be dragged into such a mad proceeding as to attempt to carry off an Englishwoman by force, and in a place where he was well known. For the girl in question was Noreen Daleham. The Rajah had seen her a few months before at a *durbar* or reception of native notables held by the Lieutenant Governor of Eastern Bengal, and been fired with an insane and unholy passion for her.

"Your Highness, it is impossible. Quite impossible. Do you not see that all the power of the *Sirkar* (the Government) would be put forth to punish us? You would be deposed, and I - I would be sent to the convict settlement in the Andaman Islands, if I were not hanged."

The Rajah abused the hated English, root and branch. But he was forced to admit that Chunerbutty was right. Open violence would ruin them.

He sank back on the cushions, exhausted by his fit of anger. Draining his glass he filled it up again. Then he clapped his hands. A servant entered noiselessly on bare feet, bringing two full bottles of liqueur and fresh tumblers. There was little difficulty in anticipating His Highness's requirements. The *khitmagar* removed the empty bottles and the broken glass and left the apartment.

The Rajah drank again. The strong liqueur seemed to have no effect on him. Then he said:

"Well, find a plan yourself. But I must get the girl."

Chunerbutty pretended to think. Then he began to expose tentatively, as if it were an idea just come to him, a plan that he had conceived weeks before.

"*Maharaj Sahib*, if I could make the girl my wife -"

The Rajah half rose up and spluttered out furiously:

"You dog, wouldst thou dare to rival me, to interfere between me and my desires?"

The engineer hastened to pacify the angry man.

"No, no, Your Highness. You misunderstand me. Surely you know that you can trust me. What I mean is that, if I married her, she would have to obey me, and -" he smiled insinuatingly and significantly - "I am a loyal subject of Your Highness."

The fat debauchee stared at him uncomprehendingly for a few moments. Then understanding dawned, and his bloated face creased into a lascivious smile.

"I see. I see. Then marry her," he said, sinking back on the cushions.

"Your Highness forgets that the salary they pay a tea-garden engineer is not enough to tempt a girl to marry him nor support them if she did."

"That is true," replied the Rajah thoughtfully. He was silent for a little, and then he said:

"I will give you an appointment here in the Palace with a salary of a *lakh* of rupees a year."

Chunerbutty's eyes glistened. A *lakh* is a hundred thousand, and at par fifteen rupees went to an English sovereign.

"Thank you, Your Highness," he said eagerly.

The Rajah held up a fat forefinger warningly.

"But not until you have married her," he said.

Chunerbutty smiled confidently. Much as he had seen of Noreen Daleham he yet knew her so little as to believe that the prospect of such an income, joined to the favour in which he believed she held him, would make it an easy matter to win her consent.

He imagined himself to be in love with the girl, but it was in the Oriental's way - that is, it was merely a matter of sensual desire. Although as jealous as Eastern men are in sex questions, the prospect of the money quite reconciled him to the idea of sharing his wife with another. His fancy flew ahead to the time, which he knew to be inevitable, when possession would have killed passion and the money would bring new, and so more welcome, women to his arms. The Rajah would only too readily permit, nay encourage him to go to Europe - alone. And he gloated over the thought of being again in London, but this time with much money at his command. What was any one woman compared with fifty, with a hundred, others ready to replace her?

So he calmly discussed with the Rajah the manner of carrying out their nefarious scheme; and His Highness, to show his appreciation, invited him to share his orgies that night. And in the smiles and embraces of a Kashmiri wanton, Chunerbutty forgot the English girl.

CHAPTER VIII

A BHUTTIA RAID

Dermot's friendship with the Dalehams made rapid progress, and in the ensuing weeks he saw them often. In order to verify his suspicions as to the Bengalis, he made a point of cultivating the acquaintance of the planters, paid several visits to Payne and other members of the community, and was a frequent guest at the weekly gatherings at the club.

On one of his visits to Malpura he found Fred recovering from a sharp bout of malarial fever, and Dermot was glad of an opportunity of requiting their hospitality by inviting both the Dalehams to Ranga Duar to enable Fred to recuperate in the mountain air.

The invitation was gladly accepted. Their host came to fetch them himself with two elephants; Badshah, carrying a *charjama*, conveying them, while the other animal bore their luggage and servants. With jealous rage in his heart Chunerbutty watched them go.

Noreen enjoyed the journey through the forest and up the mountains, with Dermot sitting beside her to act as her guide, for on this occasion Ramnath drove Badshah. As they climbed the steep, winding road among the hills and rose out of the damp heat of the Plains, Fred declared that he felt better at once in the cool refreshing breezes that swept down from the lofty peaks above. The forest fell away behind them. The great teak and *sal* trees gave place to the lighter growths of bamboo, plantain, and sago-palm. A troop of small brown monkeys, feasting on ripe bananas, sprang away startled on all fours and vanished in all directions. A slim-bodied, long-tailed mongoose, stealing across the road, stopped in the middle of it to rise up on his hind legs and stare with tiny pink eyes at the approaching elephants. Then, dropping to the ground again with puffed-out, defiant tail, he trotted on into the undergrowth angry and unafraid.

Arrived at Ranga Duar the brother and sister exclaimed in admiration at the beauty of the lonely outpost nestling in the bosom of the hills. They gazed with interest at the stalwart sepoys of the detachment in khaki or white undress whom they passed and who drew themselves up and saluted their commanding sahib smartly.

Dermot had given up his small bungalow to his guests and gone to occupy the one vacant quarter in the Mess. Noreen was to sleep in his bedroom, and, as the girl looked round the scantily-furnished apartment with its small camp-bed, one canvas chair, a table, and a barrack chest of drawers, she tried to realise that she was actually to live for a while in the very room of the man who was fast becoming her hero. For indeed her feeling for Dermot so far savoured more of hero-worship than of love. She looked with interest at his scanty possessions, his sword, the line of riding-boots against the wall, the belts and spurs hung on nails, the brass-buttoned greatcoat hanging behind the door. In his sitting-room she read the names of the books on a roughly-made stand to try to judge of his taste in literature. And with feminine curiosity she studied the photographs on the walls and tables and wondered who were the originals of the portraits of some beautiful women among them and what was their relation to Dermot.

While her brother, who picked up strength at once in the pure air, delighted in the military sights and sounds around him, the girl revelled in the loveliness of their surroundings, the beauty of the scenery, the splendour of the hills, and the glorious panorama of forest and plains spread before her eyes. To Parker, who had awaited their arrival at Dermot's gate and hurried forward to help down from Badshah's back the first Englishwoman who had ever visited their solitary station, she took an instant liking, which increased when she found that he openly admired his commanding officer as much as she did secretly.

In the days that followed it seemed quite natural that the task of entertaining Noreen should fall to the senior officer's lot, while the junior tactfully paired off with her brother and took him to shoot on the rifle range or join in games of hockey with the sepoys on the parade ground, which was the only level spot in the station.

Propinquity is the most frequent cause of love - for one who falls headlong into that passion fifty drift into it. In the isolation of that solitary spot on the face of the giant mountains, Kevin Dermot and Noreen Daleham drew nearer to each other in their few days together there than they ever would have done in as many months of London life. As they climbed the hills or sat side by side on the Mess verandah and looked down on the leagues of forest and plain spread out like a map at their feet, they were apt to forget that they were not alone in the world.

The more Dermot saw of Noreen, the more he was attracted by her naturalness and her unconscious charm of manner. He liked her bright and happy disposition, full of the joy of living. On her side Noreen at first hardly recognised the quiet-mannered, courteous man that she had first known in the smart, keen, and intelligent soldier such as she found Dermot to be in his own surroundings. Yet she was glad to have seen him in his little world and delighted to watch him with his Indian officers and sepoys, whose liking and respect for him were so evident.

When she was alone her thoughts were all of him. As she lay at night half-dreaming on his little camp-bed in his bare room she wondered what his life had been. And, to a woman, the inevitable question arose in her mind: Had he ever loved or was he now in love with someone? It seemed to her that any woman should be proud to win the love of such a man. Was there one? What sort of girl would he admire, she wondered. She had noticed that in their talks he had never mentioned any of her sex or given her a clue to his likes and dislikes. She knew little of men. Her brother was the only one of whose inner life and ideas she had any knowledge, and he was no help to her understanding of Dermot.

It never occurred to Noreen that there was anything unusual in her interest in this new friend, nor did she suspect that that interest was perilously akin to a deeper feeling. All she knew was that she liked him and was content to be near him. She had not reached the stage of being miserable out of his presence. The dawn of a woman's love is the happiest time in its story. There is no certain realisation of the truth to startle, perhaps affright, her, no doubts to depress her, no jealous fears to torture her heart - only a vague, delicious feeling of gladness, a pleasant rose-tinted glow to brighten life and warm her heart. The fierce, devouring flames come later.

The first love of a young girl is passionless, pure; a fanciful, poetic devotion to an ideal; the worship of a deified, glorious being who does not, never could, exist. Too often the realisation of the truth that the idol has feet of clay is enough to burst the iridescent glowing bubble. Too seldom the love deepens, develops into the true and lasting devotion of the woman, clear-sighted enough to see the real man through the mists of illusion, but fondly wise enough to cherish him in spite of his faults, aye, even because of them, as a mother loves her deformed child for its very infirmity.

So to Noreen love had come - as it should, as it must, to every daughter of Eve, for until it comes no one of them will ever be really content or feel that her life is complete, although when it does she will probably be unhappy. For it will surely bring to her more grief than joy. Life and Nature are harder to the woman than to the man. But in those golden days in the mountains, Noreen Daleham was happy, happier far than she had ever been; albeit she did not realise that love was the magician that made her so. She only felt that the world was a very delightful place and that the lonely outpost the most attractive spot in it.

Even when the day came to quit Ranga Duar she was not depressed. For was not her friend - so she named him now in her thoughts - to bring her on his wonderful elephant through the leagues of enchanted forest to her home? And had he not promised to come to it again very soon to visit - not her, of course, but her brother? So what cause was there for sadness?

Long as was the way - for forty miles of jungle paths lay between Malpura and Ranga Duar - the journey seemed all too short for Noreen. But it came to an end at last, and they arrived at the garden as the sun set and Kinchinjunga's fairy white towers and spires hung high in air for a space of time tantalisingly brief. Before they reached the bungalow the short-lived Indian twilight was dying, and the tiny oil-lamps began to twinkle in the palm-thatched huts of the toilers' village on the estate. And forth from it swarmed the coolies, men, women, children, not to welcome them, but to stare at the sacred elephant. Many heads bent low, many hands were lifted to foreheads in awed salutation. Some of the throng prostrated themselves to the dust, not in greeting to their own sahib but in reverence to the marvellous animal and the mysterious white man bestriding his neck who was becoming identified with him.

When Dermot rode away on Badshah the next morning the same scenes were repeated. The coolies left their work among the tea-bushes to flock to the side of the road as he passed. But he paid as little attention to them as Badshah did, and turned just before the Dalehams' bungalow was lost to sight to wave a last farewell to the girl still standing on the verandah steps. It was a vision that he took away with him in his heart.

But, as the elephant bore him away through the forest, Noreen faded from his mind, for he had graver, sterner thoughts to fill it. Love can never be a fair game between the sexes, for the man and the woman do not play with equal stakes. The latter risks everything, her soul, her mind, her whole being. The former wagers only a fragment of his heart, a part of his thoughts. Yet he is not to blame; it is Nature's ordinance. For the world's work would never go on if men, who chiefly carry it on, were possessed, obsessed, by love as women are.

So Dermot was only complying with that ordinance when he allowed the thoughts of his task, which indeed was ever present with him, to oust Noreen from his mind. He was on his way to Payne's bungalow to meet the managers of several gardens in that part of the district, who were to assemble there to report to him the result of their investigations.

His suspicions were more than confirmed. All had the same tale to tell - a story of strange restlessness, a turbulent spirit, a frequent display of insolence and insubordination among the coolies ordinarily so docile and respectful. But this was only in the gardens that numbered Brahmins in their population. The influence of these dangerous men was growing daily. This was not surprising to any one who knows the extraordinary power of this priestly caste among all Hindus.

There was evidence of constant communication between the Bengalis on the other estates and Malpura, which pointed to the latter as being the headquarters of the promoters of disaffection. But few of the planters were inclined to agree with Dermot in suspecting Chunerbutty as likely to prove the leader, for they were of opinion that his repudiation and disregard of all the beliefs and customs of the Brahmins would render him obnoxious to them.

From Payne's the Major went on to visit some other gardens. Everywhere he heard the same story. All the planters were convinced that the heart and the brain of the disaffection was to be found in Malpura. So Dermot determined to return there and expose the whole matter to Fred Daleham at last, charging him on his loyalty not to give the faintest inkling to Chunerbutty.

A delay in the advent of the rain, which falls earlier in the district of the Himalayan foothills than elsewhere in India, had rendered the jungle very dry. Consequently when Dermot on Badshah's neck emerged from it on to the garden of Malpura, he was not surprised to see at the far end of the estate a column of smoke which told of a forest fire. The wide, open stretch of the plantation was deserted, probably, so Dermot concluded, because all the coolies had been collected to beat out the flames. But, as he neared the Daleham's bungalow, he saw a crowd of them in front of it. Before the verandah steps a group surrounded something on the ground, while the servants were standing together talking to a man in European clothes, whom Dermot, when he drew nearer, recognised as Chunerbutty.

The group near the steps scattered as he approached, and Dermot saw that the object on the ground was a native lying on his back, covered with blood and apparently dead.

Chunerbutty rushed forward. He was evidently greatly agitated.

"Oh, Major Dermot! Major Dermot! Help! Help!" he cried excitedly. "A terrible thing has happened. Miss Daleham has been carried off by a party of Bhuttia raiders."

"Carried off? By Bhuttias?" exclaimed the soldier. "When?"

He made the elephant kneel and slipped off to the ground.

"Barely two hours ago," replied the engineer. "A fire broke out in the jungle at the south edge of the garden - probably started purposely to draw everyone away from the bungalows and factory. The manager, Daleham, and I went there to superintend the men fighting the flames. In our absence a party of ten or twenty Bhuttia swordsmen rushed the house. Miss Daleham had just returned from her ride. Poor girl!"

He broke down and began to cry.

"Pull yourself together man!" exclaimed Dermot in disgust. "Go on. What happened?"

"They seized and bound her," continued the Bengali, mastering his emotion. "These cowards" - with a wave of his hand he indicated the servants - "did nothing to protect her. Only the *syce* attempted to resist, and they killed him."

He pointed to the prostrate man.

"They tried to bear her off on her pony, but it took fright and bolted. Then they tied poles to a chair brought from the bungalow and carried her away in it."

"Didn't the servants give the alarm?" asked Dermot.

"No; they remained hiding in their quarters until we came. A coolie woman, who saw the raiders from a distance, ran to us and told us. Fred went mad, of course. He wanted to follow the Bhuttias, but I pointed out that it was hopeless."

"Hopeless? Why?"

"There were only three of us, and they were a large party," replied Chunerbutty.

"Yes; but you had rifles and should have been a match for fifty."

The Bengali shrugged his shoulders.

"We did not know in which way they had gone," he said. "We could not track them."

"I suppose not. Well?"

"Fred and Mr. Parry have ridden off in different directions to the neighbouring gardens to summon help. We sent two coolies with a telegram to you or any officer at Ranga Duar, to be sent from the telegraph office on the Barwahi estate. Then you came."

Dermot observed him narrowly. He was always suspicious of the Hindu; but, unless the engineer was a good actor, there was no doubt that he was greatly affected by the outrage. His distress seemed absolutely genuine. And certainly there seemed no reason for suspecting his complicity in the carrying off of Miss Daleham. So the Major turned to the servants and, taking them apart one by one, questioned them closely. Chunerbutty had given their story correctly. But Dermot elicited two new facts which they had not mentioned to the engineer. One raider at least was armed with a revolver, which was unusual for a Bhuttia, the difficulty of procuring firearms and ammunition in Bhutan being so great that even the soldiers of the Maharajah are armed only with swords and bows. The Dalehams' *khansamah*, or butler, stated that this man had threatened all the servants with this weapon, bidding them under pain of death remain in their houses without raising an alarm.

"Do you know Bhutanese?" asked Dermot.

"No, sahib. But he spoke Bengali," replied the servant.

"Spoke it well?"

"No, sahib, not well, but sufficiently for us to understand him."

Another servant, on being questioned, mentioned the curious fact that the man with the revolver conversed with another of the raiders in Bengali. This struck Dermot as being improbable, but others of the servants confirmed the fact. Having gathered all the information that they could give him he went over to look at the dead man.

The *syce*, or groom, was lying on his back in a pool of blood. He had been struck down by a blow from a sword which seemed to have split the skull. But, on placing his ear to the poor wretch's chest, Dermot thought that he could detect a faint fluttering of the heart. Holding his polished silver cigarette case to the man's mouth he found its brightness slightly clouded.

"Why, he is still living," exclaimed the soldier. "Quick! Bring water."

He hastily applied his flask to the man's lips. Although he grudged the time, Dermot felt that the wounded man's attempt to defend Noreen entitled him to have his wound attended to even before any effort was made to rescue her. So he had the *syce* carried to his hut, and then, taking out his surgical case, he cleansed and sewed up the gash. But his thoughts were busy with Noreen's peril. The occurrence astonished him. Bhuttias from the hills beyond the border occasionally raided villages and tea-gardens in British territory in search of loot, but were generally careful to avoid Europeans. Such an outrage as the carrying off of an Englishwoman had never been heard of on the North-East Frontier.

There was no time to be lost if the raiders were to be overtaken before they crossed the border. Indeed, with the start that they had, pursuit seemed almost hopeless. Nevertheless, Dermot resolved to attempt it, and single-handed. For he could not wait for the planters to gather, and summoning his men from Ranga Duar was out of the question. He did not consider the odds against him. Had Englishmen stopped to do so in India, the Empire would never have been founded. With his rifle and the prestige of the white race behind him he would not have hesitated to face a hundred such opponents. His blood boiled at the thought of the indignity offered to the girl; though he was not seriously concerned for her safety, judging that she had been carried off for ransom. But he pictured the distress and terror of a delicately nurtured Englishwoman at finding herself in the hands of a band of savage outlaws dragging her away to an unknown and awful fate. She was his friend, and he felt that it was his right as well as his duty to rescue her.

With a grim determination to follow her abductors even to Punaka, the capital of Bhutan, he swung his leg across Badshah's neck and set out, having bade Chunerbutty inform Daleham and the planters that he had started in pursuit.

The raiders had left the garden by a path leading to the north and headed for the mountains. When Dermot got well clear of the bungalow and reached the confines of the estate, he dismounted and examined the ground over which they had passed. In the dust he found the blurred prints of a number of barefooted men and in one place four sharply-defined marks which showed where they had set down the chair in which Noreen was being carried, probably to change the bearers. A mile or two further on the track crossed the dry bed of a small stream. In the sand Dermot noticed to his surprise the heel-mark of a boot among the footprints of the raiders, it being most unusual for Bhuttias to be shod.

As his rider knelt down to examine the tracks, Badshah stretched out his trunk and smelt them as though he under-stood the object of their mission. And, as soon as Dermot was again on his neck, he moved on at a rapid pace. It was neces-sary, however, to check constantly to search for the raiders' tracks. The Bhuttias had followed an animal path through the jungle, and Dermot seated on his elephant's neck with loaded rifle across his knees, scanned it carefully and watched the undergrowth on either side, noting here and there broken twigs or freshly-fallen leaves which marked the passage of the chair conveying Noreen. Such signs were generally to be found at sharp turnings of the path. Wherever the ground was soft enough or sufficient dust lay to show impressions he stopped to examine the spot carefully for footprints. Occasionally he detected the sharp marks of the chair-legs or of the boot.

The trial led towards the mountains, as was natural. But after several hours' progress Badshah turned suddenly to the left and endeavoured to continue on towards the west. Dermot was disappointed, for he had persuaded himself that the elephant quite understood the quest and was following the trail. He headed Badshah again towards the north, but with difficulty, for the animal obstinately persisted in trying to go his own way. When Dermot conquered finally they continued towards the mountains. But before long the soldier found that he had lost all traces of the raiding party. He cast around without success and wasted much time in endeavouring to pick up the trail again. At last to his annoyance he was forced to turn back and retrace his steps.

At the spot where the conflict of opinion between him and the elephant had taken place he cast about and found the track again. It led in the direction in which Badshah had tried to take him. The elephant had been wiser than he. Now, with an apologetic pat on the head, Dermot let him follow the new path, wondering at the change of route, for it was only natural to expect that the Bhuttias would have made for the hills by the shortest way to the nearest pass into Bhutan. As the elephant moved along his rider's eye was quick to recognise the traces of the passing of the raiders, where no sign would have been visible to one unskilled in tracking.

All at once Badshah slackened his pace and began to advance with the caution of a tusker stalking an enemy. Confident in the animal's extraordinary intelligence Dermot cocked his rifle. The elephant suddenly turned off the path and moved noiselessly through the undergrowth for a few minutes. Then he stopped on the edge of an open glade in the forest.

Scattered about in it, sitting or lying down half-asleep, were a number of short, sturdy, brown-faced men with close cropped bare heads. Each was clad in a single garment shaped like a Japanese *kimono* and kilted up to expose thick-calved, muscular bare legs by a girdle from which hung a *dah* - a short, straight sword. A little apart from them sat Noreen Daleham in a chair in which she was securely fastened and to which long carrying-poles were tied. She was dressed in riding costume and wore a sun-helmet.

The girl was pale, weary, and dejected, and looked so frail and unfitted to cope with so terrifying a situation that a feeling of immense tenderness and an instinctive desire to protect her filled Dermot as he watched her. Then passionate anger welled up in him as he turned his eyes again to her captors; and he longed to make them pay dearly for the suffering that she had endured.

But, despite his rage, he deliberated coolly enough on the best mode of attack, as he counted the number of the raiders. There were twenty-two. The soldier's quick eye instantly detected that one of them, although garbed similarly to the rest, was in features unlike a Bhuttia and had not the sturdy frame of a man of that race. He was wearing shoes and socks and was the only one of the party not carrying a *dah*.

Dermot's first idea was to open fire suddenly on the raiders and continue firing while moving about in cover from place to place on the edge of the glade, so as to give the impression of a numerous force. But he feared that harm might come to the girl in the fight if any of the Bhuttias carried fire-arms, for they would probably fire wildly, and a stray bullet might hit the girl. So he resolved on a bolder policy. While the raiders, who had put out no sentries, lay about in groups unconscious of the proximity of an enemy, Dermot touched Badshah with his hand, and the elephant broke noiselessly out of the undergrowth and suddenly appeared in their midst.

CHAPTER IX

THE RESCUE OF NOREEN

There was a moment's consternation among the Bhuttias. Then they sprang to their feet and began to draw their *dahs*. But suddenly one cried:

"The demon elephant! The devil man!"

Another and another took up the cry. Then all at once in terror they turned and plunged panic-stricken into the undergrowth. All but two - the wearer of shoes and a man with a scarred face beside him. While the rest fled they stood their ground and called vainly to their companions to come back. When they found themselves deserted the wearer of shoes pulled out a revolver and fired at Dermot, while his scarred comrade drew his sword and ran towards Noreen.

The soldier, ignoring his own danger but fearing for the girl's life, threw his rifle to his shoulder and sent a bullet crashing through her assailant's skull, then with his second barrel he shot the man with the pistol through the heart. The first raider collapsed instantly and fell in a heap, while the other, dropping his weapon, swayed for a moment, staggered forward a few feet, and fell dead.

Only then could Dermot look at Noreen. In the dramatic moment of his appearance the girl had uttered no sound, but sat rigid with her eyes fixed on him. When the swordsman rushed at her she seemed scarcely conscious of her peril but she started in terror and grew deadly pale when his companion fired at her rescuer. When both fell her tension relaxed. She sank back half-fainting in her chair and closed her eyes.

When she opened them again Badshah was kneeling a few yards away and Dermot stood beside her cutting the cords that bound her.

She looked up at him and said simply:

"I knew you would come."

With an affectation of light-heartedness that he was far from feeling he replied laughing:

"Of course you did. I am bound to turn up like the clown in the pantomime, saying, 'Here we are again.' Oh, I forgot. I am a bit late. I should have appeared on the scene when those beggars got to your bungalow."

He pretended to treat the whole affair lightly and made no further allusion to her adventure, asking no questions about it. He was afraid lest she should break down in the sudden relief from the strain and anxiety. But there was no cause to fear it. The girl was quietly brave and imitated his air of unconcern, behaving after the first moment as if they were meeting under the most ordinary circumstances. She smiled, though somewhat feebly, as she said:

"Oh, not a clown, Major Dermot. Rather the hero of a cinema drama, who always appears in time to rescue the persecuted maiden. I am beginning to feel quite like the unlucky heroine of a film play."

The cords fastening her had now been cut, so she tried to stand up but found no strength in her numbed limbs.

"Oh, I'm sorry. I'm - I'm rather stiff," she said, sinking back into the chair again. She felt angry at her weakness, but she was almost glad of it when she saw Dermot's instant look of concern.

"You are cramped from being tied up," he said. "Don't hurry."

The cords had chafed her wrists cruelly. He stooped to examine the abrasions, and the girl thrilled at his gentle touch. A feeling of shyness overcame her, and she turned her eyes away from his face. They fell on the bodies of the dead raiders, and she hastily averted her gaze.

"Hadn't we better hurry away from here?" she asked, apprehensively.

"No; I don't think there is any necessity. The men who ran away seemed too scared to think of returning. But still, we'll start as soon as you feel strong enough."

"What was it that they cried out?"

"Oh, merely an uncomplimentary remark about Badshah and me," he replied.

The girl made another attempt to rise and succeeded with his assistance. He lifted her on to Badshah's pad and went over to examine the dead men. After his first casual glance at the wearer of shoes he knelt down and looked closely into the face of the corpse. Then he pulled open the single garment. A thin cord consisting of three strings of spun cotton was round the body next the skin, passing over the left shoulder and under the right arm. This Dermot cut off. From inside the garment he took out some other articles, all of which he pocketed. He then searched the corpse of the scarred Bhuttia, taking a small packet tied up in cloth from the breast of the garment. Noreen watched him with curiosity and marvelled at his courage in handling the dead bodies.

He returned to the kneeling elephant and took his place on

the neck.

"Hold on now, Miss Daleham," he said. "Badshah's going to rise. *Uth*"

Noreen gripped the surcingle rope tightly as the elephant heaved up his big body and set off along a track through the jungle at a rapid pace.

"Now we are safe enough," said Dermot, turning towards his companion. "I have not asked you yet about your adventures. Tell me all that happened to you, if you don't mind talking about it."

"Oh, it was awful," she answered, shuddering at the remembrance. "And it was all so sudden. There was a fire in the jungle near the garden, and Fred went with the others to put it out. He wouldn't let me accompany him, but told me to go for my ride in the opposite direction. I didn't stay away long. I had just returned to the bungalow and dismounted and was giving my pony a piece of sugar, when several Bhuttias rushed at me from behind the house and seized me. Poor Lalla, my *syce*, tried to keep them off with his bare hands, but one brute struck him on the head with his sword. The poor boy fell, covered with blood. I'm afraid he was killed."

"No, he isn't dead," remarked Dermot. "I saw him, and I think that he'll live."

"Oh, I'm so glad to hear it," exclaimed the girl. "Ever since I saw it I've had before my eyes the dreadful sight of the poor lad lying on the ground covered with blood and apparently lifeless. Well, to go on. I called the other servants, but no one came. The Bhuttias tied my hands and tried to lift me on to my pony's back, but Kitty got frightened and bolted. Then they didn't seem to know what to do, and one went to a man who had remained at a distance from us and spoke to him. He apparently told them to fetch a chair from the bungalow and put me into it. I tried to struggle, but I was powerless in their grasp. I was fastened to the chair, poles were tied to it, and at a sign from the man who stood alone - he seemed to be the leader - I was lifted up and carried off."

"Did you notice anything about this man - the leader?" asked Dermot.

"Yes, he was not like the others in face. He didn't seem to me to be a Bhuttia at all. He was one of the two that you shot - the man with shoes. It seems absurd, but do you know, his face appeared rather familiar to me somehow. But of course I could never have seen him before."

"Are you sure that you hadn't? Think hard," said Dermot eagerly.

The girl shook her head.

"It's no use. I puzzled over the likeness most of the time that I was in their hands, but I couldn't place him."

Dermot looked disappointed.

The girl continued:

"We went through the forest for hours without stopping, except to change the bearers of my chair. I noticed that the leader spoke to one man only, the man with the scars on his face whom you shot, too, and he passed on the orders."

"Could you tell in what language these two spoke to each other?"

"No; they never talked in my hearing. In fact I noticed that the man with shoes always avoided coming near me. Well, we went on and on and never halted until we reached the place where you found us. It seemed to be a spot that they had aimed for. I saw the scarred man examining some marks on the trees in it and pointing them out to the leader, who then gave the order to stop."

"How did they behave to you?"

"No one took any notice of me. They simply carried me, lifted me up, and dumped me down as if I were a tea-chest," replied the girl. "Well, that is all my adventure. But now please tell me how you came so opportunely to my rescue. Was it by chance or did you follow us? Oh, I forgot. You said you saw Lalla, so you must have been at Malpura. Did Fred send you?"

Dermot briefly related all that had happened. When he told her of his dispute with Badshah about the route to be followed and how the elephant proved to be in the right she cried enthusiastically:

"Oh, the dear thing! He's just the most wonderful animal in the world. Forgive me for interrupting. Please go on."

When he had finished his tale there was silence between them for a little. Then Noreen said in a voice shaking with emotion:

"How can I thank you? Again you have saved me. And this time from a fate even more dreadful than the first. I'd sooner be killed outright by the elephants than endure to be carried off to some awful place by those wretches. Who were they? Were they brigands, like one reads of in Sicily? Was I to be killed or to be held to ransom?"

"Oh, the latter, I suppose," replied Dermot.

But there was a doubtful tone about his words. In fact, he was at a loss to understand the affair. It was probably not what he had thought it at first - an attempt on the part of enterprising Bhuttia raiders to carry off an Englishwoman for ransom. For when he overtook them they were on a path that led away from the mountains, so they were not making for Bhutan. And the identity of the leader perplexed him.

There could be no political motive for the outrage. The affair was a puzzle. But he put the matter aside for the time being and began to consider their position. The sun was declining, for the afternoon was well advanced. As far as he could judge they were a long way from Malpura, and it seemed to him that Badshah was not heading directly for the garden. But he had sufficient confidence in the animal's intelligence to refrain from interfering with him again. The pangs of hunger reminded him that he had had no food since the early morning cup of tea at the planter's bungalow where he had passed the night, for he had hoped to breakfast at Malpura. It occurred to him that his companion must be in the same plight.

"Are you hungry, Miss Daleham?" he asked.

"Hungry? I don't know. I haven't had time to think about food," she replied. "But I'm very thirsty."

"Would you like a cup of tea?"

"Oh, don't tantalise me, Major," she replied laughing. "I feel I'd give anything for one now. But unfortunately there aren't any tea-rooms in this wonderful jungle of yours."

Dermot smiled.

"Perhaps it could be managed," he said. "What I am concerned about is how to get something substantial to eat, for I foolishly came away from Granger's bungalow, where I stayed last night, without replenishing my stores, which had run low. I intended asking you for enough to carry me back to Ranga Duar. But when I heard what had happened - Hullo! with luck there's our dinner."

He broke off suddenly, for a jungle cock had crowed in the forest not far away.

"I wish I had a shot gun," he whispered. "But my rifle will have to do. *Mul*, Badshah."

He guided the elephant quietly and cautiously in the direction from whichthe sound had come. Presently they came to an open glade and heard the fowl crow again. Dermot halted Badshah in cover and waited. Presently there was a patter over the dry leaves lying on the ground, and a jungle cock, a bird similar to an English bantam, stalked across the glade twenty yards away. It stopped and began to peck. Dermot quietly raised his rifle and took careful aim at its head. He fired, and the body of the cock fell to the earth headless.

"What a good shot, Major!" exclaimed Noreen, who had been quite excited.

"It was an easy one, for this rifle's extremely accurate and the range was very short. I fired at the head, for if I had hit the body with such a big bullet there wouldn't have been much dinner left for us. Now I think that we shall have to halt for a little time. I know that you must be eager to get back home and relieve your brother's anxiety. But Badshah has been going for many hours on end and has not delayed to graze on the way, so it would be wise to give him a rest and a feed."

"Yes, indeed," said the girl. "He thoroughly deserves it."

She was not unwilling that the time spent in Dermot's company should be prolonged. It was a sweet and wonderful experience to be thus alone with him in the enchanted jungle. She had forgotten her fears; and the remembrance of her recent unpleasant adventure vanished in her present happiness. For she was subtly conscious of a new tenderness in his manner towards her.

The elephant sank down, and Dermot dismounted and lifted the girl off carefully. Noreen felt herself blushing as he held her in his arms, and she was thankful that he did not look at her, but when he had put her down, busied himself in taking off Badshah's pad and laying it on the ground. Unstrapping his blankets he spread one and rolled the other up as a pillow.

"Now please lie down on this, Miss Daleham," he said. "A rest will do you good, too. I am going to turn cook and show you how we fare in the jungle."

The girl took off her hat and was only too glad to stretch herself on the pad, which made a comfortable couch, for the emotions of the day had worn her out. She watched Dermot as he moved about absorbed in his task. From one pocket of the pad he took out a shallow aluminium dish and a small, round, convex iron plate. From another he drew a linen bag and a tin canister.

"You said that you would like tea, Miss Daleham," he remarked. "Well, you shall have some presently."

"Yes; but how can you make it?" she asked. "There's no water in the jungle."

"Plenty of it."

"Are we near a stream, then?"

"No; the water is all round us, waiting for me to draw it off."

The girl looked about her.

"What do you mean? I don't see any. Where is the water?"

"Hanging from the trees," he replied, laughing. "I'll admit you into one of the secrets of the jungle. But first I want a fire."

He gathered dried grass and sticks, cleared a space of earth and built three fires, two on the ground with a large lump of hard clay on either side of each, the third in a hole that he scraped out.

"To be consistent I ought to produce fire by rubbing two pieces of dried wood together, as they do in books of adventure," he said, turning to the interested girl. "It can be done. I have seen natives do it; but it is a lengthy process and I prefer a match."

He took out a box and lit the fires.

"Now," he said, "if you'll see to these for me, I'll go and get the kettle and crockery."

At the far end of the glade was a clump of bamboos. Dermot selected the biggest stem and hacked it down with his *kukri*. From the thicker end he cut off a length from immediately below a knot to about a foot above it, trimmed the edges and brought it to Noreen. It made a beautifully clean and polished pot, pale green outside, white within.

"There is your kettle and tea-pot," he said.

From a thinner part he cut off similarly two smaller vessels to serve as cups.

"Now then for the water to fill the kettle," he said, looking around among the creepers festooning the trees for the *pani bel*. When he found the plant he sought, he cut off a length and brought it to the girl, who had never heard of it. Asking her to hold the bamboo pot he filled it with water from the creeper, much to her astonishment.

"How wonderful!" she cried. "Is it really good to drink?"

"Perfectly."

"But how are you going to boil it?"

"In that bamboo pot."

"But surely that will burn?"

"No, the water will boil long before the green wood begins to be charred," replied Dermot, placing the pot over the first fire on the two lumps of clay, so that the flames could reach it.

Then he opened the linen bag, which Noreen found to contain *atta*, or native flour. Some of this he poured into the round aluminium dish and with water from the *pani bel* he mixed dough, rolled it into balls, and patted them into small flat cakes. Over the second fire he placed the iron plate, convex side up, and when it grew hot put the cakes on it.

"How clever of you! You are making *chupatis* like the natives do,"exclaimed Noreen. "I love them. I get the cook to give them to us for tea often."

She watched him with interest and amusement, as he turned the cakes over with a dexterous flip when one side browned; then, when they were done, he took them off and piled them on a large leaf.

"Who would ever imagine that you could cook?" Noreen said, laughing. "Do let me help. I feel so lazy."

"Very well. Look after the *chupatis* while I get the fowl ready," he replied.

He cleaned the jungle cock, wrapped it up in a coating of wet clay and laid it in the hot ashes of the third fire, covering it over with the red embers.

Just as he had finished the girl cried: "The water is actually boiling? Who would have believed it possible?"

"Now we are going to have billy tea as they make it in the bush in Australia," said Dermot, opening the canister and dropping tea from it into the boiling water.

Noreen gathered up a pile of well-toasted *chupatis* and turned a smiling, dimpled face to him.

"This is the jolliest picnic I've ever had," she cried. "It was worth being carried off by those wretches to have all these delightful surprises. Now, tea is ready, sir. Please may I pour it out?"

He wrapped his handkerchief round the pot before handing it to her.

"I suppose you haven't a dairy in your wonderful jungle?" she asked, laughing.

"No; I'm sorry to say that you must put up with condensed milk," he replied, producing a tin from a pocket of the pad and opening it with his knife.

"What a pity! That spoils the illusion," declared the girl. "I ought to refuse it; but I'll pass it for this occasion, as I don't like my tea unsugared and milkless. No, I refuse to have a spoon." For he took out a couple and some aluminium plates from the inexhaustible pad. "I'll stir my tea with a splinter of bamboo and eat my *chupatis* off leaves. It is more in keeping with the situation."

Like a couple of light-hearted children they sat side by side on the pad, drank their tea from the rude bamboo cups and devoured the hot *chupatis* with enjoyment; while, invisible in the dense undergrowth, Badshah twenty yards away betrayed his presence by tearing down creepers and breaking off branches. In due time Dermot took from the hot ashes a hardened clay ball, broke it open and served up the jungle fowl, from which the feathers had been stripped off by the process of cooking. Noreen expressed herself disappointed when her companion produced knives and forks from the magic pockets of the pad.

"We ought to be consistent and use our fingers," she said.

When they had finished their meal, which the girl declared was the most enjoyable one that she had ever had, Dermot made her rest again on the pad while he cleaned and replaced his plates, cutlery, and cooking vessels. Then, leaning his back against a tree, he filled and lit his pipe, while Noreen watched him stealthily and admiringly. In the perfect peace and silence of the forest encompassing them she felt reluctant to leave the enchanted spot.

But suddenly the charm was rudely dispelled. A shot rang out close by, and Dermot's hat was knocked from his head as a bullet passed through it and pierced the bark of the tree half an inch above his hair. As though the shot were a signal, fire was opened on the glade from every side, and for a moment the air seemed full of whistling bullets. The soldier sprang to Noreen, picked her up like a child in his arms, and ran with her to an enormously thick *simal* tree, behind which he placed her. Then he gathered up the pad and piled it on her exposed side as some slight protection. At least it hid her from sight.

As he did so the firing redoubled in intensity and bullets whistled and droned through the glade. One grazed his cheek, searing the flesh as with a red-hot iron. Another wounded him slightly in the neck, while a third cut the skin of his thigh. He seemed to bear a charmed life; and the girl watching him felt her heart stop, as the blood showed on his face and neck. The flying lead sent leaves fluttering to the ground, cut off twigs, and struck the tree-trunks with a thud. Flinging himself at full length on the ground Dermot reached his rifle, then crawled to shelter behind another tree.

He looked eagerly around for his assailants. At first he could see no one. Suddenly through the undergrowth about thirty yards away the muzzle of an old musket was pushed out, and then a dark face peered cautiously behind it. The eyes in it met Dermot's, but that glance was their last. The soldier's rifle spoke, and the face disappeared as its owner's body pitched forward among the bushes and lay still. At the sharp report of the white man's weapon the firing all around ceased suddenly. But the intense silence that followed was broken by a strange sound like the shrill blast of a steam whistle mingled with the crackling of sheets of tin rapidly shaken and doubled. Noreen, crouching submissively in the shelter where Dermot had placed her, thrilled and wondered at the uncanny sound.

The soldier knew well what it was. It was Badshah's appeal for help, and he wondered why the animal had given it then, so late. But far away a wild elephant trumpeted in reply. There was a crashing in the undergrowth as Badshah dashed away and burst through the cordon of enemies encircling them. Dermot's heart sank; for, although he rejoiced that his elephant was out of danger, his sole hope of getting Noreen and himself away had lain in running the gauntlet on the animal's back through their invisible foes.

As he gripped his rifle, keenly alert for a mark to aim at, his thoughts were busy. He was amazed at this unexpected attack and utterly unable to guess who their assailants could be. They were not the Bhuttias again, for those had no guns. And the man that he had just shot was not a mountaineer. Although it was evident that the firearms used were mostly old smooth-bore muskets, and the smoke from the powder rose in clouds over the undergrowth and drifted to the tree-tops, he had detected the sharp crack of a modern rifle occasionally among the duller reports of the more ancient weapons. The mysterious attackers were apparently numerous and completely surrounded them. Dermot cursed himself for his folly in halting for food instead of pushing on to safety without a stop. But he had calculated on the superstitious fears of the Bhuttias who had been scared away by the sight of him and Badshah; and indeed to all appearance he was right in so doing. He could not reckon on new enemies springing up around them. Who could they be? It was almost inconceivable that in this quiet corner of the Indian Empire two English people could be thus assailed. The only theory that he could form was that the attackers were a band of Bengali political *dacoits*.

The firing started again. Dermot appeared to be so well hidden that none of their enemies had discovered him, except the one unlucky wretch whose courage had proved his ruin. The shots were being fired at random and all went high. But there seemed no hope of escape; for it was evident from the sounds and the smoke that the girl and he were completely surrounded. For one wild moment he thought of rising suddenly to his feet and making a dash through the cordon, hoping to draw all their enemies after him and give his companion a chance of escape. But the plan was futile; for she would never find her way alone through the jungle and would fall at once into the hands of her foes.

Suddenly a heavy bullet struck the tree a foot above his head, evidently fired from behind him. He instantly rolled over on his back and lay motionless with his eyes half-closed, looking in the direction from which the shot must have come. The bushes not ten yards away were parted quietly; and a head was thrust out. With a swift motion Dermot swung his rifle round until the muzzle pointed over his toes and, holding the weapon in one hand like a pistol, fired point-blank at the assailant who had crept up quietly behind him. Shot through the head the man pitched forward on his face, almost touching the soldier's feet. Dermot saw that the corpse was that of a low-caste Hindu, clad only in a dirty cotton *koorta* and *dhoti*. A Tower musket lay beside him.

The wild firing died down again. The sun was setting; and the soldier judged that the attackers were probably waiting for darkness to rush him. Why they did not do so at once, since they were so numerous, surprised him; but he surmised that it was lack of courage. It was maddening to be obliged to await their pleasure. He was far more concerned about the girl than for himself. A feeling of dread pity filled his heart when he thought of what her fate would be when he was no longer alive to protect her. Should he kill her, he asked himself, and give her a swift and merciful death instead of the horrors of outrage and torture that would probably be her lot if she fell alive into the hands of these murderous scoundrels? In those moments of tension and terrible strain he realised that she was very dear to him, that she evoked in his heart a feeling that no other woman had ever aroused in him.

The sun was going down; and with it Dermot felt that his life was passing. He grudged losing it in an obscure and causeless scuffle, instead of on an honourable field of battle as a soldier should. He wished that he had a handful of his splendid sepoys with him. They would have made short work of a hundred of such ruffians as now threatened him. But it was useless to long for them. He drew his *kukri* and laid it on the ground beside him, ready for the last grim struggle. He had resolved to crawl to the girl when darkness settled on the forest, and, before the rush came, give her the chance of a swift and honourable death, shoot her if she chose it - as he was confident that she would - then close with his foes until death came.

The light grew fainter. Dermot nerved himself for the terrible task before him and was about to move, when with a light and unfaltering step Noreen came to him.

CHAPTER X

A STRANGE HOME-COMING

Dermot dragged the girl down to the ground beside him as a shot rang out.

"I suppose they will kill us, Major Dermot," she said calmly. "But couldn't you manage to get away in the darkness? You know the jungle so well. Please don't hesitate to leave me, for I should only hamper you. Won't you go?"

Emotion choked the soldier for a moment. He gripped her arm and was about to speak when suddenly the forest on every side of them resounded to a pandemonium of noise: a chorus of wild shrieks, shots, the crashing of trampled undergrowth, the death-yells of men amid the savage screams and fierce trumpetings of a herd of elephants.

"Oh, what's that? What terrible thing is happening?" cried the girl.

Dermot seized her and dragged her close against the trunk of the tree. In the gloom they saw men flying madly past them pursued by elephants. One wretch not ten yards from them was overtaken by a great tusker, which struck him to the ground, trampled on him, kicked and knelt upon his lifeless body until it was crushed to a pulp, then placing one forefoot on the man's chest, wound his trunk round the legs and seized them in his mouth, tore them from the body, and threw them twenty yards away. All around similar tragedies were being enacted; for the herd of wild elephants had charged in among the attackers.

Dermot gathered the terrified girl in his arms and held her face against his breast, so that she should be spared the horror of the sights about them; but he could not shut out the terrible sounds, the agonised shrieks, the despairing yells of the wretches who were meeting with an awful fate. He remained motionless against the tree, hoping to escape the notice of the fierce animals, whom he could see plunging through the jungle in pursuit of their prey, for they were hunting the men down. Suddenly one elephant came straight towards them with trunk uplifted. Dermot put the girl behind him and raised his rifle; but with a low murmur from its throat the animal lowered its trunk, and he recognised it.

"Thank God! we are saved," he said. "It's Badshah. He has brought his herd to our rescue."

The girl clung to him convulsively and scarcely heard him; for the tumult in the jungle still continued, though the terrible pursuit seemed to be passing farther away. The giant avengers were still crashing through the jungle after their prey; and an occasional heartrending shriek told of another luckless wretch who had met his doom.

Dermot gently disengaged the clinging hands and repeated his words. The girl, still shuddering, made an effort and rose to her knees.

Dermot went forward and laid his hand on the elephant's trunk.

"Thank you, Badshah," he said. "I am in your debt again."

The tip of the trunk touched his face in a gentle caress. Then he stepped back and said: "Now we'll go at once, Miss Daleham. We won't stop this time until we reach your bungalow."

The girl had already recovered her courage and stood beside him.

"But you are wounded. There's blood on your face and on your neck. Are you badly hurt?"

Dermot laughed reassuringly.

"To tell you the truth I had forgotten all about it. They are only scratches. The skin is cut, that's all. Come, we mustn't delay any longer."

At a word from him Badshah knelt. He hurriedly threw the pad on the elephant's back and made him rise so that the surcingle rope could be fixed. Then he brought the animal to his knees again and lifted Noreen on to the pad. But before he took his own seat he searched the undergrowth around the glade and found many corpses of men almost unrecognisable as human bodies, so crushed and battered were they. From the number that he came upon it was evident that most of their assailants had been slain. But all the elephants except his had disappeared; and the sounds of the massacre were dying away.

Slinging his rifle he climbed on to the pad; and Badshah rose and went swiftly along a track that seemed to Dermot to lead towards Malpura. He did not attempt to guide the elephant, but placed himself so that his body would shield the girl from the danger of being struck by overhanging boughs. He held her firmly as they were borne through the darkness that now filled the forest; for the swift-coming Indian night had fallen.

"Keep well down, Miss Daleham," he said. "You must be on your guard against being swept off the pad by the low branches."

"Oh, Major Dermot," cried the girl with a shudder, "have all these terrible things really happened in the last few hours or has it all been a hideous nightmare?"

"Please try not to think of them," he answered. "You are safe now."

"Yes; but you? You have to face these dangers again, since you are so much in the jungle. Oh, my forest that I thought a fairyland! That such terrible things can happen in it!"

"I can assure you that they are very unusual," he replied with a cheery laugh. "You have been very fortunate; for you have crammed more excitement and adventure into one day than I have seen previously in all my time in the jungle."

"It all seems so incredible," she said. "Did you really mean that Badshah brought his herd to our rescue? But I know he did. I heard him call them. When he ran off I thought that he was frightened and had abandoned us. But I did him a great injustice."

Her companion was silent for a moment. Then he said:

"Look here, Miss Daleham, we had better not tell that tale of Badshah quite in that way. It would seem impossible, and no European would credit it. Natives would, of course, for as it is they seem to look upon him as a god already."

"Yes; but you think as I do, don't you?" she exclaimed in surprise. "Surely you believe that he did bring the other elephants to save us."

"Yes, I do. I know that he did, for I - well, between ourselves I have seen him do even more wonderful things. But others wouldn't believe us, and I don't want to emphasise the marvellous part of the story. I'd rather people thought that the *dacoits*, or whoever those men were who attacked us, accidentally fell foul of a herd of wild elephants."

"Perhaps you are right. But *we* know. It will be just our own secret and Badshah's," she said dreamily.

Then she relapsed into silence. In spite of the terrible experiences through which she had just passed she felt happy at the pressure of Dermot's arm about her and the sensation of being utterly alone with him in a world of their own, as they were borne on through the darkness. Fatigue made her drowsy, and the swaying motion of the elephant's pace lulled her to sleep.

She woke suddenly and for an instant wondered where she was. Then remembrance came and she felt the warm blood mantle her face as she realised that she was nestling in Dermot's arms. But, drowsy and content, she did not move. Looking up she saw the stars overhead. They were out of the forest.

"I must have been asleep," she said. "Where are we?"

"At Malpura. There are the lights of your bungalow," replied Dermot. He said it almost with regret, for he had found the long miles through the forest almost short, while the girl nestled confidingly, though unconsciously, in his arms and he held her against his heart.

As the elephant neared the house Dermot gave a loud shout.

Instantly the verandah filled with men who rushed out of the lighted rooms and tried to pierce the darkness. A little distance from the bungalow a large number of coolies, seated on the ground, rose up and pressed forward to the road. From behind the house several white-clad servants ran out.

Dermot shouted again and called out Daleham's name.

There was a frantic rush down the verandah steps.

"Hurrah! it's the Major," cried a planter.

"And - and - yes, Miss Daleham's with him. Hooray!" yelled another.

"Good old Dermot!" came in Payne's voice.

Through the throng of shouting, excited men the girl's brother broke.

"Noreen! Noreen! My God, are you there? Are you safe?" he cried frantically.

Almost before Badshah sank to the ground, the girl, with a little sob, sprang into her brother's arms and clung to him, while Dermot was dragged off the pad by the eager hands of a dozen men who thumped him on the back, pulled him from one to another, and nearly shook his arm off. The servants had brought out lamps to light up the scene.

From the verandah steps Chunerbutty looked jealously on. He had been relieved at knowing that the girl had returned, but in his heart he cursed the man who had saved her. He was roughly thrust aside by Parry, who dashed up the steps, ran into the house, and emerged a minute later holding a large tumbler in his hand.

"Where is he, where is he? Look you, I know what he wants. Here's what will do you good, Major," he shouted.

Dermot laughed and, taking the tumbler, drank its contents gratefully, though their strength made him cough, for the bibulous Celt had mixed it to his own taste.

"Major, Major, how can we thank you?" said Fred Daleham, coming to him with his sister clinging to his arm.

But she had to release him and shake hands over and over again with all the planters and receive their congratulations and expressions of delight at seeing her safe and sound. Meanwhile her brother was endeavouring in the hubbub to thank her rescuer. But Dermot refused to listen.

"Oh, there's nothing to make a fuss about I assure you, Daleham," he said. "It was just that I had the luck to be the first to follow the raiders. Any one else would have done the same."

"Oh, nonsense, old man," broke in Payne, clapping him on the back. "Of course we'd all have liked to do it, but none of us could have tracked the scoundrels like you could. How did you do it?"

"Yes; tell us what happened, Major."

"How did you find her, Dermot?"

"What occurred, Miss Daleham?"

"Did they put up a fight, sir?"

The eager mob of men poured a torrent of questions on the girl and her rescuer.

"Easy on, you fellows," said Dermot, laughing. "Give us time. We can't answer you all at once."

"Yes, give them a chance, boys. Don't crowd," cried one planter.

"Here! We can't see them. Let's have some light," shouted another.

"Where are those servants? Bring out all the lamps!"

"Lamps be hanged! Let's have a decent blaze. We'll have a bonfire."

Several of the younger planters ran to the stable and outhouses and brought piles of straw, old boxes, anything that would burn. Others despatched coolies to the factory near by to fetch wood, broken chests, and other fuel. Several bonfires were made and the flames lit up the scene with a blaze of light.

"Why, you're wounded, Dermot!" exclaimed Payne.

"Oh, no. Just a scratch."

"Yes, he is wounded, but he pretends it's nothing," said Noreen. "Do see if it's anything serious, Mr. Payne."

"I assure you it's nothing," protested the soldier, resisting eager and well-meant attempts to drag him into the house and tend his hurts by force. But attention was diverted when a planter cried:

"Good Heavens! what's this? The elephant's tusk is covered with blood."

"Tusk! Why, he's blood to the eyes," exclaimed another.

For the leaping flames revealed the fact that Badshah's tusk, trunk, and legs were covered with freshly-dried blood.

"Good Heavens! he's been wading in it."

"What's that on his tusk? Why, it's fragments of flesh. Oh, the deuce!"

There were exclamations of surprise and horror from the white men. But the mass of coolies, who had been pressing forward to stare, drew back into the darkness and muttered to each other.

"The god! The god! Who can withstand the god?" they whispered.

"*Arhe, bhai!* (Aye, brother!) But which is the god? The

elephant or his rider? Tell me that!" exclaimed a grey-haired coolie.

Among the Europeans the questions showered on Dermot redoubled.

"Look here, you fellows. I can't answer you all at once," he expostulated. "It's a long story. But please remember that Miss Daleham has had a tiring day and must be worn out."

"Oh, no, I'm not," exclaimed the girl. "Not now. I was fatigued, but I'm too excited to rest yet."

"Come into the bungalow everyone and we'll have the whole story there," said her brother. "The servants will get supper ready for us. We must celebrate tonight."

"Indeed, yes. Look you, it shall be very wet tonight in Malpura, whateffer," cried Parry, who was already half drunk. "Here, boy! Boy! Where is that damned black beastie of mine? Boy!"

His *khitmagar* disengaged himself from the group of servants and approached apprehensively, keeping out of reach of his master's fist.

"Go to the house," said Parry to him in Bengali. "Bring liquor here. All the liquor I have. Hurry, you dog!"

He aimed a blow at him, which the *khitmagar* dodged with the ease of long practice and ran to execute his master's bidding.

Daleham gave directions to his butler and cook to prepare supper, and led the way into the house with his arm round his sister, who, woman-like, escaped to change her dress and make herself presentable, as she put it. She had already forgotten the fatigues of the day in the hearty welcome and the joy of her safe home-coming.

But before Dermot entered the bungalow he had water brought and washed from Badshah's head and legs the evidences of the terrible vengeance that he had taken upon their assailants. And from the verandah the planters looked at animal and master and commented in low tones on the strange tales told of both, for the reputation of mysterious power that they enjoyed with natives had reached every white man of the district.

The crowd of coolies drifted away to their village on the tea-garden, and there throughout the hot night hours the groups sat on the ground outside the thatched bamboo huts and talked of the animal and the man.

"It is not well to cross this sahib who is not as other sahibs," said a coolie, shaking his head solemnly.

"Sahib, say you? Is he only a sahib?" asked an old man. "Is he truly of the *gora logue* (white folk)?"

"Why, what else is he? Is not his skin white?" said a youth, presumptuously thrusting himself into the conclave of the elders.

"Peace! Since when was it meet for children to prattle in the presence of their grandsires?" demanded a grey-haired coolie contemptuously. "Know, boy, that Shri Krishn's skin was of the same colour when he moved among us on earth."

Krishna, the Second Person of the Hindu Trinity, the best-loved god of all their mythological heaven, is represented in the cheap coloured oleographs sold in the bazaars in India as being of fair complexion.

"Is he Krishna himself?" asked a female coolie eagerly, the glass bangles on her arm rattling as she raised her hand to draw her *sari* over her face when she thus addressed men. "Is he Krishna, think you? He is handsome enough to be the Holy One."

Gordon Casserly

"Who knows, daughter? It may be. Shri Krishn has many incarnations," said the old man solemnly.

"Nay, I do not think that he is Krishna," remarked an elderly coolie. "It may be that he is another of the Holy Ones."

"Perhaps he is *Gunesh*," ventured a younger man.

"No; he bestrides *Gunesh*. I think he must be Krishna," chimed in another. "What lesser god would dare to use Gunesh as his steed?"

"He is *Gunesh* himself," asserted a grey-beard. "Does he not range the jungle and the mountains at the head of all the elephants of the Terai? Can he not call them to his aid as Hanuman did the monkeys?"

"He is certainly a Holy One or else a very powerful demon," declared the old man. "It is an evil and a dangerous thing to molest those whom he protects. The Bhuttias, ignorant pagans that they are, carried off the missie *baba* he favours. What, think ye, has been their fate? With your own eyes ye have all seen the blood and the flesh of men upon the tusk and legs of his sacred elephant."

And so through the night the shuttle of superstitious talk went backward and forward and wove a still more marvellous garment of fancy to drape the reputation of elephant and man. The godship that the common belief had long endowed Badshah with was being transferred to his master; and a mere Indian Army Major was transformed into a mysterious Hindu deity.

Meanwhile in the well-lighted bungalow in which all the sahibs were gathered together the servants were hurriedly preparing a supper such as lonely Malpura had never known. And Noreen's pretty drawing-room was crowded with men in riding costume or in uniform - for most of the planters belonged to a Volunteer Light Horse Corps, and some of them, expecting a fight, had put on khaki when they got Daleham's summons. Their rifles, revolvers, and cartridge belts were piled on the verandah. Chunerbutty, feeling that his presence among them would not be welcomed by the white men that night, had gone off to his own bungalow in jealous rage. And nobody missed him. Dermot, despite his protests, had been dragged off to have his hurts attended to, and it was then seen that he had been touched by three bullets.

When all were assembled in the room the planters demanded the tale of Noreen's adventures; and the girl, looking dainty and fresh in a white muslin dress, unlike the heroine of her recent tragic experience, smilingly complied and told the story up to the point of Dermot's unexpected and dramatic intervention.

"Now you must go on, Major," she said, turning to him.

"Yes, yes, Dermot. Carry on the tale," was the universal cry.

Everyone turned an expectant face towards where the soldier sat, looking unusually embarrassed.

"Oh, there's nothing much to tell," he said. "The raiders - they were Bhuttias - had left a trail easy enough to see, though I confess that I would have lost it once but for my elephant. When I came up to them, as Miss Daleham has just told you, they all ran away except two."

"What did these two do?" asked Granger, his host of the previous night.

"Not much. They tried to stand their ground, but didn't really give much trouble. So I took Miss Daleham up on my elephant and we started back. But like a fool I stopped on the way to have grub, and somebody began shooting at us from the jungle, until wild elephants turned up and cleared them off. Then we came on here. That's all."

These was a moment's silence. Then Granger, in disgusted tones, exclaimed:

"Well, Major, of all the poor story-tellers I've ever heard, you're the very worst. One would think you'd only been for a stroll in a quiet English lane. 'Then we came on here. That's all.'"

"Oh, yes, you can't ask us to believe it was as tame as that, Major," said another planter. "We expected to hear something a little more exciting."

"You go out after thirty or forty raiders -"

"No, only twenty-two all told," corrected Dermot.

"All right, only twenty-two, come back with three hits on you and your elephant up to his eyes in blood and - and - well, hang it all, Major, let's have some more details."

"Come, Miss Daleham," Payne broke in, "you tell us what happened. I know Dermot, and we won't get any more out of him."

"Yes; let's hear all about it, Noreen," said her brother. "I'm sure it wasn't as tame as the Major says."

"Tame?" echoed the girl, smiling. "I've had enough excitement to last me all my life, dear. I think that Major Dermot has put it rather mildly. I'm sure even I could tell the story better."

She narrated their adventures, giving her rescuer, despite his protests, full credit for his courage and resource, only omitting the details of their picnic meal and slurring over their relief by the wild elephants. The planters listened eagerly to her tale, breaking into applause at times. When she had finished Parry laid a heavy hand on Dermot's shoulder and said solemnly, though thickly:

"Look you, you are a bad liar, Major Dermot. Your story would not deceive a child, whatetfer. But I am proud of you. You should have been a Welshman."

The rest overwhelmed the soldier with compliments and congratulations, much to his embarrassment, and when Noreen left the room to supervise the arrangement of the supper-table they plied him with questions without extracting much more information from him. But when a servant came to announce that the meal was ready and the planters rose to troop to the dining-room, Dermot reached the door first and held up his hand to stop them.

"Gentlemen, one moment, please," he said. Then he looked out to satisfy himself that the domestic was out of hearing and continued: "I'd be obliged if during supper you'd make no allusion before the servants to what has happened today. Afterwards I shall have something to say to you in confidence that will explain this request of mine."

The others looked at him in surprise but readily agreed. Before they left the room Daleham noticed the Hindu engineer's absence for the first time.

"By Jove, I'd forgotten Chunerbutty," he exclaimed. "I wonder where he is? Perhaps he doesn't know we're going to have supper. I'd better send the boy to tell him."

"Indeed no, he is fery well where he is," hiccoughed Parry, who, seated by a table on which drinks had been placed, had not been idle. "This is not a night for black men, look you."

"Yes, Daleham, Parry's right," said Granger. "Let us keep to our own colour tonight. Things might be said that wouldn't be pleasant for an Indian to hear."

"Forgive my putting a word in, Daleham," added Dermot. "But I have a very particular reason, which I'll explain afterwards, for asking you to leave Chunerbutty out."

"Yes, we don't want a damned Bengali among us tonight, Fred," said a young planter bluntly.

"Oh, very well; if you fellows would rather I didn't ask him I won't," replied their host. "But I'm afraid his feelings will be hurt at being left out when we're celebrating my sister's safe return. He's such an old friend."

"Oh, hang his feelings! Think of ours," cried another of the party.

"All right. Have it your own way. Let's go in to supper," said the host.

The hastily improvised meal was a merry feast, and the loud voices and the roars of laughter rang out into the silent night and reached the ears of Chunerbutty sitting in his bungalow eating his heart out in bitterness and jealousy. Noreen, presiding at one end of the long table, was the queen of the festival and certainly had never enjoyed any supper in London as much as this impromptu meal. General favourite as she always was with every man in the district, this night there was added universal gladness at her escape and the feeling of satisfaction that the outrage on her had been so promptly avenged. While the girl was pleased with the warmth and sincerity of the congratulations showered upon her, she was secretly delighted to see the high esteem in which all the other men held Dermot. He was seated beside her and shared with her the good wishes of the company. His health was drunk with all the honours after hers, and the planters did not spare his blushes in their loudly-expressed praises of his achievements. Cordiality and good humour prevailed, and, although the fun was fast and furious, Parry was the only one who drank too much. Before he became objectionable, for he was usually quarrelsome in his cups, he was dexterously cajoled out of the room and safely shepherded to his bungalow.

CHAPTER XI

THE MAKING OF A GOD

Parry's departure served as a hint to Noreen that it was time for her to say good-night to her guests and withdraw. As soon as she left the room there was an instant hush of expectancy, and all eyes were turned to Dermot. The servants had long since gone, but, after asking his host's permission, he rose from his place and strolled with apparent carelessness to each doorway in turn and satisfied himself that there were no eavesdroppers. Then he shut the doors and asked members of the party to station themselves on guard at each of them. The planters watched these precautions with surprise.

Having thus made sure that he would not be overheard Dermot said:

"Gentlemen, a few of you already know something of what I am going to tell you. I want you to understand that I am now speaking officially and in strict confidence."

He turned to his host.

"I must ask you, Mr. Daleham (Fred looked up in surprise at the formality of the mode of address) to promise to divulge nothing of what I say to your friend, Mr. Chunerbutty."

"Not tell Chunerbutty, sir?" repeated the young planter in astonishment.

"No; the matter is one which must not be mentioned to any but Europeans."

"Oh, but I assure you, Major, Chunerbutty's thoroughly loyal and reliable," said Daleham warmly.

"I repeat that you are not to give him the least inkling of what I am going to say," replied Dermot in a quiet but stern voice. "As I have already told you, I am speaking officially."

The boy was impressed and a little awed by his manner.

"Oh, certainly, sir. I give you my word that I shan't mention it to him."

"Very well. The fact is, gentlemen, that we are on the track of a vast conspiracy against British rule in India, and have reason to believe that the activity of the disloyalists in Bengal has spread to this district. We suspect that the Brahmins who, very much to the surprise of any one acquainted with the ways of their caste, are working as coolies on your gardens, are really emissaries of the seditionists."

"By George, is that really so, Major?" asked a young planter in a doubting tone. "We have a couple of these Bengalis on our place, and they seem such quiet, harmless chaps."

"The Major is quite right. I know it," said one of the oldest men present. "I confess that it didn't occur to me as strange that Brahmins should take such low-caste work until he told me. But I have found since, as others of us have, that these men are the secret cause of all the trouble and unrest that we have had lately among our coolies, to whom they preach sedition and revolution."

Several other estate managers corroborated his statement.

"But surely, sir, you don't suspect Chunerbutty of being mixed up in this?" asked Daleham. "He's been a friend of mine for a long time. I lived with him in London, and I'm certain he is quite loyal and pro-British."

"I know nothing of him, Daleham," replied the soldier. "But he is a Bengali Brahmin, one of the race and caste that are responsible for most of the sedition in India, and we must take precautions."

"I'd stake my life on him," exclaimed the boy hotly. "He's been a good friend to me, and I'll answer for him."

Dermot did not trouble to argue the matter further with him, but said to the company generally:

"This outrageous attempt to carry off Miss Daleham -"

"Oh, but you said yourself, sir, that the ruffians were Bhuttias," broke in the boy, still nourishing a grievance at the mistrust of his friend.

Dermot turned to him again.

"Do Bhuttias talk to each other in Bengali? The leader gave his orders in that language to one man - who, by the way, was the only one he spoke to - and that man passed them on to the others in Bhutanese."

This statement caused a sensation in the company.

"By Jove, is that a fact, Dermot?" cried Payne.

"Yes. These two were the men I shot. Do Bhuttias, unless they have just looted a garden successfully - and we know these fellows had not - carry sums like this?" And Dermot threw on the supper-table a cloth in which coins were wrapped. "Open that, Payne, and count the money, please."

All bent forward and watched as the planter opened the knot fastening the cloth and poured out a stream of bright rupees, the silver coin of India roughly equivalent to a florin. There was silence while he counted them.

"A hundred," he said.

Dermot laid on the table a new automatic pistol and several clips of cartridges.

"Bhuttias from across the border do not possess weapons like these, as you know. Nor do they carry English-made pocket-books with contents like those this one has."

He handed a leather case to Granger who opened it and took out a packet of bank notes and counted them. "Eight hundred and fifty rupees," he said.

The men around him looked at the notes and at each other. A young engineer whistled and said: "Whew! It pays to be a brigand. I'll turn robber myself, I think. Poor but honest man that I am I have never gazed on so much wealth before. Hullo! What's that bit of string?"

Dermot had taken from his pocket the cord that he had cut from the corpse of the second raider and laid it on the table.

"Perhaps some of you may not be sufficiently well acquainted with Indian customs to know what this is."

"I'm blessed if I am, Major," said the engineer. "What is it?"

"It's the *janeo*, or sacred cord worn by the three highest of the original Hindu castes as a symbol of their second or spiritual birth and to mark the distinction between their noble twice-born selves and the lower caste once-born Sudras. You see it is made up of three strings of spun cotton to symbolise the Hindu *Trimurti* (Trinity), Brahma, Vishnu, and Siva, and also Earth, Air, and Heaven, the three worlds pervaded by their essence."

"Oh, I see. But where did you get it?" asked the engineer.

"Off the body of the second man that I shot, together with the pistol and pocket-book. Now, Bhuttias do not wear the *janeo*, not being Hindus. But high-caste Hindus do - and a Brahmin would never be without it."

"Oh, no. So you mean that the man wasn't a Bhuttia?"

"This is the last exhibit, as they say in the Law Courts," said Dermot, producing a pair of gold-rimmed spectacles. "You don't find Bhuttias wearing these."

"By Jove, no," said Granger, taking them up and trying them. "Damned good glasses, these, and cost a bit, too."

Dermot turned towards Daleham.

"Do you remember showing me on this garden one day a coolie whom you said was a B.A. of Calcutta University?"

"Yes; he was called Narain Dass," replied Fred. "We spoke to him, you recollect, Major? He talked excellent English of the *babu* sort."

"What has happened to him?"

"I don't know. He disappeared a short time ago. Deserted, I suppose, though I don't see why he should. He was getting on well here."

Dermot smiled grimly and touched the cord and spectacles.

"The man who wore these, who led the Bhuttias in the raid, was Narain Dass."

These was a moment's amazed silence in the room. Then a hubbub arose, and there was a chorus of exclamations and questions.

"Good Heavens, is it possible, Major? He appeared to be such a decent, civil chap," exclaimed Daleham.

"His face seemed familiar to me, as he lay dead on the ground," replied Dermot. "I couldn't place him, though, until I found the spectacles. I put them on his nose, and then I knew him. His hair was cropped close, he was wearing Bhuttia clothes, but it was Narain Dass, the University graduate who was working as a coolie for a few *annas* a day."

"And he had eight hundred and fifty rupees on him," added the young engineer.

"Yes; and if all the Bhuttias had as much as the one shot that meant over two thousand."

"Where did they get it?"

"Who is behind all this?"

"The seditionists, of course," said an elderly planter.

"Yes; but today it isn't a question of an isolated outrage on one Englishwoman, nor of a few Bengali lawyers in Calcutta and their dupes among hot-headed students and ignorant peasants," said Dermot. "It's the biggest thing we've ever had to face yet in India. What we want to get at is the head and brains of the conspiracy."

"What do you make of this attempt on Miss Daleham?" asked Granger. "What was the object of it?"

"Probably just terrorism. They wanted to show that no one is secure under our rule. It may be that Narain Dass, who had worked on this garden and seen Miss Daleham, suggested it. They may have thought that the carrying off of an English-woman would make more impression than the mere bombing of a police officer or a magistrate - we are too used to that."

"But why employ Bhuttias?" asked Payne.

"To throw the pursuers off the track and prevent their being run down. The search would stop if we thought they'd gone across the frontier, so they could get away easily. When they had got Miss Daleham safely hidden away in the labyrinths of a native bazaar, perhaps in Calcutta, they'd have let everyone know who had carried her off."

"Who was the other fellow with Narain Dass - the chap who talked Bengali?"

"Probably a Bhuttia who knew the language was given the Brahmin as an interpreter."

"But I say, Major," cried a planter, "who the devil were the lot that attacked you?"

"I'm hanged if I know," Dermot answered. "I have been inclined to believe them to be a gang of political *dacoits*, probably coming to meet the Bhuttias and take Miss Daleham from them, but in that case they would have been young Brahmins and better armed. This lot were low-caste men and their weapons were mostly old muzzle-loading muskets."

"Perhaps they were just ordinary *dacoits*," hazarded a planter.

"Possibly; but they must have been new to the business," replied the Major. "For there wouldn't be much of an opening for robbers in the middle of the forest."

"It's a puzzle. I can't make it out," said Granger, shaking his head.

The others discussed the subject for some time, but no one could elucidate the mystery. At length Dermot said to Daleham:

"No answer has come to that telegram you sent to Ranga

Duar, I suppose?"

"No, Major; though there's been plenty of time for a reply."

"It's strange. Parker would have answered at once if he'd got the wire, I know," said Dermot. "But did he? Most of the telegraph clerks in this Province are Brahmins - I don't trust them. Anyhow, if Parker did receive the wire, he'd start a party off at once. It's a long forty miles, and marching through the jungle is slow work. They couldn't get here before dawn. And the men would be pretty done up."

"I bet they would if they had to go through the forest in the dark," said a planter.

"Well, I want to start at daybreak to search the scene of the attack on us and the place where I came on the Bhuttias. Will some of you fellows come with me?"

"Rather. We'll all go," was the shout from all at the table.

"Thanks. We may round up some of the survivors."

"I say, Major, would you tell us a thing that's puzzled me, and I daresay more than me?" ventured a young assistant manager, voicing the thoughts of others present. "How the deuce did those wild elephants happen to turn up just in the nick of time for you?"

"They were probably close by and the firing disturbed them," was the careless answer.

"H'm; very curious, wasn't it, Major?" said Granger. "You know the habits of the *jungli hathi* better than most other people. Wouldn't they be far more likely to run away from the firing than right into it?"

"As a rule. But when wild elephants stampede in a panic they'll go through anything."

The assistant manager was persistent.

"But how did your elephant chance to join up with them?" he asked. "Judging by the look of him he took a very prominent part in clearing your enemies off."

"Oh, Badshah is a fighter. I daresay if there was a scrap anywhere near him he'd like to be in it," replied Dermot lightly, and tried to change the conversation.

But the others insisted on keeping to the subject. They had all been curious as to the truth of the stories about Dermot's supposed miraculous power over wild elephants, but no one had ever ventured to question him on the subject before.

"I suppose you know, Major, that the natives have some wonderful tales about Badshah?" said a planter.

"Yes; and of you, too, sir," said the young assistant manager. "They think you both some special brand of gods."

"I'm not surprised," said the Major with assumed carelessness. "They're ready to deify anything. They will see a god in a stone or a tree. You know they looked on the famous John Nicholson during the Mutiny as a god, and made a cult of him. There are still men who worship him."

"They're prepared to do that to you, Major," said Granger frankly. "Barrett is quite right. They call you the Elephant God."

Dermot laughed and stood up.

"Oh, natives will believe anything," he said. "If you'll excuse me now, Daleham, I'll turn in - or rather, turn out. I'd like to get some sleep, for we've an early start before us."

"Yes, we'd better all do the same," said Granger, rising too. "How are you going to bed us all down, Daleham? Bit of a job, isn't it?"

"We'll manage all right," replied the young host. "I told the servants to spread all the mattresses and charpoys that they could raise anywhere out on the verandah and in the spare rooms. I'm short of mosquito curtains, though. Some of you will get badly bitten tonight."

"I'll go to old Parr's bungalow and steal his," said Granger. "He's too drunk to feel any 'skeeter biting him."

"I pity the mosquito that does," joined in a young planter laughing. "The poor insect would die of alcoholic poisoning."

"I've given you my room, Major," said Daleham. "I know the other fellows won't mind."

No persuasion, however, could make Dermot accept the offer. While the others slept in the bungalow, he lay under the stars beside his elephant. The house was wrapped in darkness. In the huts in the compound the servants still gossiped about the extraordinary events of the day, but gradually they too lay down and pulled their blankets over their heads, and all was silence. But a few hundred yards away a lamp still burned in Chunerbutty's bungalow where the Hindu sat staring at the wall of his room, wondering what had happened that day and what had been said in the Dalehams' dining-room that night. For he had prowled about their house in the darkness and seen the company gathered around the supper-table. And he had watched Dermot shut the door between the room and the verandah, and guessed that things were to be said that Indians were not meant to hear. So through the night he sat motionless in his chair with mind and heart full of bitterness, cursing the soldier by all he held unholy.

Long before dawn Noreen, refreshed by sleep and quite recovered from the fatigues and alarms of the previous day, was up to superintend the early meal that her servants prepared for the departing company. No one but her brother was returning to Malpura, the others were to scatter to their own gardens when Dermot had finished with them.

As the girl said good-bye to the planters she warmly thanked each one for his chivalrous readiness to come to her aid. But to the soldier she found it hard, impossible, to say all that was in her heart, and to an onlooker her farewell to him would have seemed abrupt, almost cold. But he understood her, and long after he had vanished from sight she seemed to feel the friendly pressure of his hand on hers. When she went to her rooms the tears filled her eyes, as she kissed the fingers that his had held.

Out in the forest the Major led the way on Badshah, the ponies of his followers keeping at a respectful distance from the elephant. When nearing the scene of the fight the tracks of the avenging herd were plain to see, and soon the party came upon ghastly evidences of the tragedy. The buzzing of innumerable flies guided the searchers to spots in the undergrowth where the scattered corpses lay. As each was reached a black cloud of blood-drunk winged insects rose in the air from the loathsome mass of red, crushed pulp, but trains of big ants came and went undisturbed. The dense foliage had hidden the battered, shapeless bodies from the eyes of the soaring vultures high up in the blue sky, otherwise nothing but scattered bones would have remained. Now the task of scavenging was left to the insects.

Over twenty corpses were found. When an angry elephant has wreaked his rage on a man the result is something that is difficult to recognise as the remains of a human being. So out of the twenty, the attackers shot by Dermot were the only ones whose bodies were in a fit state to be examined. But they afforded no clue to the identity of the mysterious assailants. The men appeared to have been low-caste Hindus of the coolie class. They carried nothing on their persons except a little food - a few broken *chupatis*, a handful of coarse grain, an onion or two, and a few *cardamoms* tied up in a bit of cloth. Each had a powder-flask and a small bag with some spherical bullets in it hung on a string passed over one shoulder. The weapons found were mostly old Tower muskets, the marks on which showed that at one time they had belonged to various native regiments in the service of the East India Company. But there were two or three fairly modern rifles of French or German make.

These latter Dermot tied on his elephant, and, as there was nothing further to be learned here, he led the way to the other spot which he wished to visit. But when, after a canter along the narrow, winding track through the dense undergrowth, jumping fallen trees and dodging overhanging branches, the party drew near the open glade in which Dermot had overtaken the raiders, a chorus of loud and angry squawks, the rushing sound of heavy wings and the rustling of feathered bodies prepared them for disappointment. When they entered it there was nothing to be seen but two struggling groups of vultures jostling and fighting over what had been human bodies. For the glade was open to the sky and the keen eyes of the foul scavengers had detected the corpses, of which nothing was left now but torn clothing, mangled flesh, and scattered bones. So there was no possibility of Daleham's deciding if Dermot had been right in believing that one of the two raiders that he had killed was the Calcutta Bachelor of Arts. On the whole the search had proved fruitless, for no further clue to the identity of either body of miscreants was found.

So the riders turned back. At various points of the homeward journey members of the party went off down tracks leading in the direction of their respective gardens, and there was but a small remnant left when Dermot said good-bye, after hearty thanks from Daleham and cheery farewells from the others.

He did not reach the Fort until the following day. There he learned that Parker had never received the telegram asking for help. Subsequent enquiries from the telegraph authorities only elicited the statement that the line had been broken between Barwahi and Ranga Duar. As where it passed through the forest accidents to it from trees knocked down by elephants or brought down by natural causes were frequent, it was impossible to discover the truth, but the fact that nearly all the telegraph officials were Bengali Brahmins made Dermot doubtful. But he was able to report the happenings to Simla by cipher messages over the line.

Parker was furious because the information had failed to reach him. He had missed the opportunity of marching a party of his men down to the rescue of Miss Daleham and his commanding officer, and he was not consoled by the latter pointing out to him that it would have been impossible for him to have arrived in time for the fight.

Two days after Dermot's return to the Fort he was informed that three Bhuttias wanted to see him. On going out on to the verandah of his bungalow he found an old man whom he recognised as the headman of a mountain village just inside the British border, ten miles from Ranga Duar. Beside him stood two sturdy young Bhuttias with a hang-dog expression on their Mongol-like faces.

The headman, who was one of those in Dermot's pay, saluted and, dragging forward his two companions, bade them say what they had come there to say. Each of the young men pulled out of the breast of his jacket a little cloth-wrapped parcel, and, opening it, poured a stream of bright silver rupees at the feet of the astonished Major. Then they threw themselves on their knees before him, touched the ground with their foreheads, and implored his pardon, saying that they had sinned against him in ignorance and offered in atonement the price of their crime.

Dermot turned enquiringly to the headman, who explained that the two had taken part in the carrying off of the white *mem*, and being now convinced that they had in so doing offended a very powerful being - god or devil - had come to implore his pardon.

Their story was soon told. They said that they had been approached by a certain Bhuttia who, formerly residing in British territory, had been forced to flee to Bhutan by reason of his many crimes. Nevertheless, he made frequent secret visits across the border. For fifty rupees - a princely sum to them - he induced them to agree to join with others in carrying off Miss Daleham. They found subsequently that the real leader of the enterprise was a Hindu masquerading as a Bhuttia.

When they had succeeded in their object they were directed to go to a certain spot in the jungle where they were to be met by another party to which they were to hand over the Englishwoman. Having reached the place first they were waiting for the others when Dermot appeared. So terrible were the tales told in their villages about this dread white man and his mysterious elephant that, believing that he had come to punish them for their crime, all but the two leaders fled in panic. Several of the fugitives ran into the party of armed Hindus which they were to meet, a member of which spoke a certain amount of Bhutanese. Having learned what had happened he ordered them to guide the newcomers' pursuit.

When the attack began the Bhuttias, having no fire-arms, took refuge in trees. So when the herd swept down upon the assailants all the hillmen escaped. But they were witnesses of the terrible vengeance of the powerful devil-man and devil-elephant. When at last they had ventured to descend from the trees that had proved their salvation and returned to their villages these two confided the story to their headman. At his orders they had come to surrender the price of their crime and plead for pardon.

Their story only deepened the mystery, for, when Dermot eagerly questioned them as to the identity of the Hindus, he was again brought up against a blank wall, for they knew nothing of them. He deemed it politic to promise to forgive them and allow them to keep the money that they had received, after he had thoroughly impressed upon them the enormity of their guilt in daring to lay hands upon a white woman. He ordered them as a penance to visit all the Bhuttia villages on each side of the border and tell everyone how terrible was the punishment for such a crime. They were first to seek out their companions in the raid and lay the same task on them. He found afterwards that these latter had hardly waited to be told, for they had already spread broadcast the tale, which grew as it travelled. Before long every mountain and jungle village had heard how the Demon-Man had overtaken the raiders on his marvellous winged elephant, slain some by breathing fire on them and called up from the Lower Hell a troop of devils, half dragons, half elephants, who had torn the other criminals limb from limb or eaten them alive. So, not the fear of the Government, as Dermot intended, but the terror of him and his attendant devil Badshah, lay heavy on the border-side.

Chunerbutty, kept at the soldier's request in utter ignorance of more than the fact that Noreen had been rescued by him from the raiders, had concluded at first that the crime was what it appeared on the surface - a descent of trans-frontier Bhuttias to carry off a white woman for ransom. But when these stories reached the tea-garden villages and eventually came to his ears he was very puzzled. For he knew that, in spite of their extravagance, there was probably a grain of truth somewhere in them. They made him suspect that some other agency had been at work and another reason than hope of money had inspired the outrage.

In the Palace at Lalpuri a tempest raged. The Rajah, mad with fury and disappointed desire, stormed through his apartments, beating his servants and threatening all his satellites with torture and death. For no news had come to him for days as to the success or failure of a project that he had conceived in his diseased brain. Distrusting Chunerbutty, as he did everyone about him, he had sent for Narain Dass, whom he knew as one of the *Dewan's* agents, and given him the task of executing his original design of carrying off Miss Daleham. To the Bengali's subtle mind had occurred the idea of making the outrage seem the work of Bhuttia raiders. But for Dermot's prompt pursuit his plan would have been crowned with success. The girl, handed over as arranged to a party of the Rajah's soldiers in disguise, would have been taken to the Palace at Lalpuri, while everyone believed her a captive in Bhutan.

At length a few poor wretches, who had escaped their comrades' terrible doom under the feet of the wild elephants and, mad with terror, had wandered in the jungle for days, crept back starved and almost mad to the capital of the State. Only one was rash enough to return to the Palace, while the others, fearing to face their lord when they had only failure to report, hid in the slums of the bazaar. This one was summoned to the Rajah's presence. His tale was heard with unbelief and rage, and he was ordered to be trampled to death by the ruler's trained elephants. Search was made through the bazaar for the other men who had returned, and when they were caught their punishment was more terrible still. Inconceivable tortures were inflicted on them and they were flung half-dead into a pit full of live scorpions and cobras. Even in these enlightened days there are dark corners in India, and in some Native States strange and terrible things still happen. And the tale of them rarely reaches the ear of the representatives of the Suzerain Power or the columns of the daily press.

CHAPTER XII

THE LURE OF THE HILLS

A dark pall enveloped the mountains, and over Ranga Duar raged one of the terrifying tropical thunderstorms that signalise the rains of India. Unlike more temperate climes this land has but three Seasons. To her the division of the year into Spring, Summer, Autumn, and Winter means nothing. She knows only the Hot Weather, the Monsoon or Rains, and the Cold Weather. From November to the end of February is the pleasant time of dry, bright, and cool days, with nights that register from three to sixteen degrees of frost in the plains of Central and Northern India. In the Himalayas the snow lies feet deep. The popular idea that Hindustan is always a land of blazing sun and burning heat is entirely wrong. But from March to the end of June it certainly turns itself into a hell of torment for the luckless mortals that cannot fly from the parched plains to the cool mountains. Then from the last days of June, when the Monsoon winds bring up the moisture-laden clouds from the oceans on the south-west of the peninsula, to the beginning or middle of October, India is the Kingdom of Rain. From the grey sky it falls drearily day and night. Outside, the thirsty soil drinks it up gladly. Green things venture timidly out of the parched earth, then shoot up as rapidly as the beanstalk of the fairy tale. But inside houses dampness reigns. Green fungus adorns boots and all things of leather, tobacco reeks with moisture, and the white man scratches himself and curses the plague of prickly heat.

But while tens of thousands of Europeans and hundreds of millions of natives suffer greatly in the tortures of Heat and Wet for eight weary months of the year in the Plains of India, up in the magic realm of the Hills, in the pleasure colonies like Simla, Mussourie, Naini Tal, Darjeeling, and Ootacamund, existence during those same months is one long spell of gaiety and comfort for the favoured few. These hill-stations make life in India worth living for the lucky English women and men who can take refuge in them. And incidentally they are responsible for more domestic unhappiness in Anglo-Indian households than any other cause. It is said that while in the lower levels of the land many roads lead to the Divorce Court, in the Hills *all* do.

For wives must needs go alone to the hill-stations, as a rule. India is not a country for idlers. Every white man in it has work to do, otherwise he would not be in that land at all. Husbands therefore cannot always accompany their spouses to the mountains, and, when they do, can rarely contrive to remain there for six months or longer of the Season. Consequently the wives are often very lonely in the big hotels that abound on the hill-tops, and sometimes drift into dependence on bachelors on leave for daily companionship, for escort to the many social functions, for regular dancing partners. And so trouble is bred.

Major Dermot was no lover of these mountain Capuas of Hindustan, and had gladly escaped from Simla, chiefest of them all. Yet now he sat in his little stone bungalow in Ranga Duar, while the terrific thunder crashed and roared among the hills, and read with a pleased smile an official letter ordering him to proceed forthwith to Darjeeling - as gay a pleasure colony as any - to meet the General Commanding the Division, who was visiting the place on inspection duty. For the same post had brought him a letter from Noreen Daleham which told him that she was then, and had been for some time, in that hill-station.

The climate of the Terai, unpleasantly but not unbearably hot in the summer months, is pestilential and deadly during the rains, when malaria and the more dreaded black-water fever take toll of the strongest. Noreen had suffered in health in the hot weather, and her brother was seriously concerned at the thought of her being obliged to remain in Malpura throughout the Monsoon. He could not take her to the Hills; it was impossible for him to absent himself even for a few days from the garden, for the care and management of it was devolving more and more every day on him, owing to the intemperate habits of Parry.

Fred Daleham's relief was great when his sister unexpectedly received a letter from a former school-friend who two years before had married a man in the Indian Civil Service. Noreen, who was a good deal her junior, had corresponded regularly with her, and she now wrote to say that she was going to Darjeeling for the Season and suggested that Noreen should join her there. Much as the prospect of seeing a friend whom she had idolised, appealed to the girl (to say nothing of the gaieties of a hill-station and the pleasure of seeing shops, real shops, again), she was nevertheless unwilling to leave her brother. But Fred insisted on her going.

From Darjeeling she told Dermot in a long and chatty epistle all her sensations and experiences in this new world. It was her first real letter to him, although she had written him a few short notes from Malpura. It was interesting and clever, without any attempt to be so, and Dermot was surprised at the accuracy of her judgment of men and things and the vividness of her descriptions. He noticed, moreover, that the social gaieties of Darjeeling did not engross her. She enjoyed dancing, but the many balls, At Homes, and other social functions did not attract her so much as the riding and tennis, the sight-seeing, the glimpses of the strange and varied races that fill the Darjeeling bazaar, and, above all, the glories of the superb scenery where the ice-crowned monarch of all mountains, Kinchinjunga, forty miles away - though not seeming five - and twenty-nine thousand feet high, towers up above the white line of the Eternal Snows.

Dermot was critically pleased with the letter. Few men - and he least of all - care for an empty-headed doll whose only thoughts are of dress and fashionable entertainments. He liked the girl for her love of sport and action, for her intelligence, and the interest she took in the varied native life around her. He was almost tempted to think that her letter betrayed some desire for his companionship in Darjeeling, for in it she constantly wondered what he would think of this, what he would say of that.

But he put the idea from him, though he smiled as he re-read his orders and thought of her surprise when she saw him in Darjeeling. Would she really be pleased to meet her friend of the jungle in the gay atmosphere of a pleasure colony? Like most men who are not woman-hunters he set a very modest value on himself and did not rate highly his power of attraction for the opposite sex. Therefore, he thought it not unlikely that the girl might consider him as a desirable enough acquaintance for the forest but a bore in a ballroom. In this he was unjust to her.

He was surprised to discover that he looked forward with pleasure to seeing her again, for women as a rule did not interest him. Noreen was the first whom he had met that gave him the feeling of companionship, of comradeship, that he experienced with most men. She was not more clever, more talented, or better educated than most English girls are, but she had the capacity of taking interest in many things outside the ordinary range of topics. Above all, she inspired him with the pleasant sense of "chum-ship," than which there is no happier, more durable bond of union between a man and a woman.

The Season brought the work in which Dermot was engaged to a standstill, and, keen lover of sport as he was, he was not tempted to risk the fevers of the jungle. Life in the small station of Ranga Duar was dull indeed. Day and night the rain rattled incessantly on the iron roofs of the bungalows - six or eight inches in twenty-four hours being not unusual.

Thunderstorms roared and echoed among the hills for twenty or thirty hours at a stretch. All outdoor work or exercise was impossible. The outpost was nearly always shrouded in dense mist. Insect pests abounded. Scorpions and snakes invaded the buildings. Outside, from every blade of grass, every leaf and twig, a thin and hungry leech waved its worm-like, yellow-striped body in the air, seeming to scent any approaching man or beast on which it could fasten and gorge itself fat with blood. Certainly a small station on the face of the Himalayas is not a desirable place of residence during the rains, and to persons of melancholy temperament would be conducive to suicide or murder. Fortunately for themselves the two white men in Ranga Duar took life cheerily and were excellent friends.

* * * * *

By this time Noreen considered herself quite an old resident of Darjeeling. But she had felt the greatest reluctance to go when her brother had helped her into the dogcart for the long drive to the railway. Fred was unable to take her even as far as the train, for his manager had one of his periodic attacks of what was euphemistically termed his "illness." But Chunerbutty volunteered to escort Noreen to the hills, as he had been summoned again to his sick father's side, the said parent being supposed to be in attendance on his Rajah who had taken a house in Darjeeling for the season. As a matter of fact his worthy progenitor had never left Lalpuri. However, Daleham knew nothing of that, and, being empowered to do so when Parry was incapacitated, gladly gave him permission to go and gratefully accepted his offer to look after the girl on the journey.

Noreen would much have preferred going alone, but her brother refused to entertain the idea. Although she knew nothing of the suspicions of her Bengali friend entertained by Dermot, she sensed a certain disapproval on his part of Fred's and her intimacy with Chunerbutty, and it affected her far more than did the open objection of the other planters to the

Hindu. Besides, she was gradually realising the existence of the "colour bar," illiberal as she considered it to be. But it will always exist, dormant perhaps but none the less alive in the bosoms of the white peoples. It is Nature herself who has planted it there, in order to preserve the separation of the races that she has ordained. So Noreen, though she hated herself for it, felt that she would rather go all the way alone than travel with the Hindu.

The thirty miles' drive to the station of the narrow-gauge branch railway which would convey them to the main line did not seem long. For several planters who resided near her road had laid a *dak* for her, that is, had arranged relays of ponies at various points of the way to enable the journey to be performed quickly. Noreen's heavy luggage had gone on ahead by bullock cart two days before, so the pair travelled light.

After her long absence from civilisation the diminutive engine and carriages of the narrow-gauge railway looked quite imposing, and it seemed to the girl strange to be out of the jungle when the toy train slid from the forest into open country, through the rice-fields and by the trim palm-thatched villages nestling among giant clumps of bamboo.

In the evening the train reached the junction where Noreen and Chunerbutty had to transfer to the Calcutta express, which brought them early next morning to Siliguri, the terminus of the main line at the foot of the hills, whence the little mountain-railway starts out on its seven thousand feet climb up the Himalayas.

Out of the big carriages of the express the passengers tumbled reluctantly and hurried half asleep to secure their seats in the quaint open compartments of the tiny train. White-clad servants strapped up their employers' bedding - for in India the railway traveller must bring his own with him - and collected the luggage, while the masters and mistresses crowded into the refreshment room for *chota hazri*, or early breakfast. Noreen was unpleasantly aware of the curious and semi-hostile looks cast at her and her companion by the other Europeans, particularly the ladies, for the sight of an English girl travelling with a native is not regarded with friendly eyes by English folk in India.

But she forgot this when the toy train started. As they climbed higher the vegetation grew smaller and sparser, until it ceased altogether and the line wound up bare slopes. And as they rose they left the damp heat behind them, and the air grew fresher and cooler.

The train twisted among the mountains and crawled up their steep sides on a line that wound about in bewildering fashion, in one place looping the loop completely in such a way that the engine was crossing a bridge from under which the last carriage was just emerging. Noreen delighted in the journey. She chatted gaily with her companion, asking him questions about anything that was new to her, and striving to ignore the looks of curiosity, pity, or disgust cast at her by the other European passengers, among whom speculation was rife as to the relationship between the pair.

The leisurely train took plenty of time to recover its breath when it stopped at the little wayside stations, and many of its occupants got out to stretch their legs. Two of them, Englishmen, strolled to the end of the platform at a halt. One, a tall, fair man, named Charlesworth, a captain in a Rifle battalion quartered in Lebong, the military suburb of Darjeeling, remarked to his companion:

"I wonder who is the pretty, golden-haired girl travelling with that native. How the deuce does she come to be with him? She can't be his wife."

"You never know," replied the other, an artillery subaltern named Turner. "Many of these Bengali students in London marry their landladies' daughters or girls they've picked up in the street, persuading the wretched women by their lies that they are Indian princes. Then they bring them out here to herd with a black family in a little house in the native quarter."

"Yes; but that girl is a lady," answered Charlesworth impatiently. "I heard her speak on the platform at Siliguri."

"She certainly looks all right," admitted his friend. "Smart and well-turned out, too. But one can never tell nowadays."

"Let's stroll by her carriage and get a nearer view of her," said Charlesworth.

As they passed the compartment in which Noreen was seated, the girl's attention was attracted by two gaily-dressed Sikkimese men with striped petticoats and peacocks' feathers stuck in their flowerpot-shaped hats, who came on to the platform.

"Oh, Mr. Chunerbutty, look at those men!" she said eagerly. "What are they?"

The Hindu had got out and was standing at the door of the compartment.

"Did you notice that?" said Charlesworth, when he and Turner had got beyond earshot. "She called him Mr. Something-or-other."

"Yes; deuced glad to hear it, too," replied the gunner. "I'd hate to see a white woman, especially an English lady, married to a native. I wonder how that girl comes to be travelling with the beggar at all."

"I'd like to meet her," said Charlesworth, who was returning from ten days' leave in Calcutta. "If I ever do, I'll advise her not to go travelling about with a black man. I suppose she's just out from England and knows no better."

"She'd probably tell you to mind your own business," observed his friend.

"Hullo! it looks as if the engine-driver is actually going to get a move on this old hearse. Let's go aboard."

More spiteful comments were made on Noreen by the Englishwomen on the train, and the girl could not help remarking their contemptuous glances at her and her escort.

When the train ran into the station at Darjeeling she saw her friend, Ida Smith, waiting on the platform for her. As the two embraced and kissed each other effusively Charlesworth muttered to Turner:

"It's all right, old chap. I'll be introduced to that girl before this time tomorrow, you bet. I know her friend. She's from the Bombay side - wife of one of the Heaven Born."

By this lofty title are designated the members of the Indian Civil Service by lesser mortals, such as army officers - who in return are contemptuously termed "brainless military popinjays" by the exalted caste.

Their greeting over, Noreen introduced Chunerbutty to Ida, who nodded frigidly and then turned her back on him.

"Now, dear, point out your luggage to my servant and he'll look after it and get it up to the hotel. Oh, how do you do, Captain Charlesworth?"

The Rifleman, determined to lose no time in making Noreen's acquaintance, had come up to them.

"I had quite a shock, Mrs. Smith, when I saw you on the platform, for I was afraid that you were leaving us and had come to take the down train."

"Oh, no; I am only here to meet a friend," she replied. "Have you just arrived by this train? Have you been away?"

Charlesworth laughed and replied:

"What an unkind question, Mrs. Smith! It shows that I haven't been missed. Yes, I've been on ten days' leave to Calcutta."

"How brave of you at this time of year! It must have been something very important that took you there. Have you been to see your tailor?" Then, without giving him time to reply, she turned to Noreen. "Let me introduce Captain Charlesworth, my dear. Captain Charlesworth, this is Miss Daleham, an old school-friend, who has come up to keep me company. We poor hill-widows are so lonely."

The Rifleman held out his hand eagerly to the girl.

"How d'you do, Miss Daleham? I hope you've come up for the Season."

"Yes, I think so," she replied. "It's a very delightful change from down below. This is my first visit to a hill-station."

"Then you'll be sure to enjoy it. Are you going to the Lieutenant-Governor's ball on Thursday?"

"I don't suppose so. I don't know anything about it," she replied. "You see, I've only just arrived."

"You are, dear," said Ida. "I told Captain Craigie, one of the A.D.C.'s, that you were coming up, and he sent me your invitation with mine."

"Oh, how jolly!" exclaimed the girl. "I do hope I'll get some partners."

"Please accept me as one," said Charlesworth. Then he tactfully added to Ida, "I hope you'll spare me a couple of dances, Mrs. Smith."

"With pleasure, Captain Charlesworth," she replied. "But do come and see us before then."

"I shall be delighted to. By the way, are you going to the gymkhana on the polo-ground tomorrow?"

"Yes, we are."

Charlesworth turned to Noreen.

"In that case, Miss Daleham, perhaps you'll be good enough to nominate me for some of the events. As you have only just got here you won't have been snapped up yet by other fellows. I know it's hopeless to expect Mrs. Smith not to be."

Ida smiled, well pleased at the flattery, although, as a matter of fact, no one had yet asked her to nominate him.

"I'm afraid I wouldn't know what to do," answered Noreen. "I've never been to a gymkhana in India. I haven't seen or ridden in any, except at Hurlingham and Ranelagh."

Charlesworth made a mental note of this. If the girl had taken part in gymkhanas at the London Clubs she must be socially all right, he thought.

"They're just the same," he said. "In England they've only copied India in these things. Have you brought your habit with you?"

"Yes; Mrs. Smith told me in her letters that I could get riding up here."

"Good. I've got a ripping pony for a lady. I'll raise a saddle for you somewhere, and we'll enter for some of the affinity events."

The girl's eyes sparkled.

"Oh, how delightful. Could I do it, Ida?"

"Yes, certainly, dear."

"I should love to. It's very kind of you, Captain Charlesworth. Thank you ever so much. It will be splendid. I hope I shan't disgrace you."

"I'm sure you won't. I'll call for you and bring you both down to Lebong if I may, Mrs. Smith."

"Will you lunch with us then?" asked Ida. "You know where I am staying - the Woodbrook Hotel. Noreen is coming there too."

"Thank you, I'll be delighted," replied the Rifleman.

"Very well. One o'clock sharp. Now we'll say good-bye for the present."

Charlesworth shook hands with both ladies and strode off in triumph to where Turner was awaiting him impatiently.

"Now, dear, we'll go," said Ida. "I have a couple of *dandies* waiting for us."

"*Dandies?*" echoed the girl in surprise. "What do you mean?"

The older woman laughed.

"Oh, not dandies like Captain Charlesworth. These are chairs in which coolies carry you. In Darjeeling you can't drive. You must go in *dandies*, or rickshas, unless you ride. Here, Miguel! Have you got the missie *baba's* luggage?" This to her Goanese servant.

"Yes, *mem sahib*. All got," replied the "boy," a native Christian with the high sounding name of Miguel Gonsalves Da Costa from the Portugese Colony of Goa on the West Coast of India below Bombay. In his tweed cap and suit of white ducks he did not look as imposing as the Hindu or Mohammedan butlers of other Europeans on the platform with their long-skirted white coats, coloured *kamarbands*, and big *puggris*, or turbans, with their employers' crests on silver brooches pinned in the front. But Goanese servants are excellent and much in demand in Bombay.

"All right. You bring to hotel *jeldi* (quickly). Come along, Noreen," said Mrs. Smith, walking off and utterly ignoring the Hindu engineer who had stood by unnoticed all this time with rage in his heart.

Noreen, however, turned to him and said:

"What are you going to do, Mr. Chunerbutty? Where are you staying?"

"I am going to my father at His Highness's house," he replied. "I should not be very welcome at your hotel or to your friends, Miss Daleham."

"Oh, of course you would," replied the girl, feeling sorry for him but uncertain what to say. "Will you come and see me tomorrow?"

"You forget. You are going to the gymkhana with that insolent English officer."

"Now don't be unjust. I'm sure Captain Charlesworth wasn't at all insolent. But I forgot the gymkhana. You could come in the morning. Yet, perhaps, I may have to go out calling with Mrs. Smith," she said doubtfully. "And how selfish of me! You have your own affairs to see to. I do hope that you'll find your father much better."

"Thank you. I hope so."

"Do let me know how he is. Send me a *chit* (letter) if you have time. I am anxious to hear. Now I must thank you ever so much for your kindness in looking after me on the journey. I don't know what I'd have done without you."

"It was nothing. But you had better go. Your haughty friend is looking back for you, angry that you should stop here talking to a native," he said bitterly.

Ida was beckoning to her; even at that distance they could see that she was impatient. So Noreen could only reiterate her thanks to the Hindu and hurry after her friend, who said petulantly when she came up:

"I do wish you hadn't travelled up with that Indian, Noreen. It isn't nice for an English girl to be seen with one, and it will make people talk. The women here are such cats."

Noreen judged it best to make no reply, but followed her irate friend in silence. Their *dandies* were waiting outside the station, and as the girl got into hers and was lifted up and carried off by the sturdy coolies on whose shoulders the poles rested, she thought with a thrill of the last occasion on which she had been borne in a chair.

CHAPTER XIII

THE PLEASURE COLONY

A town on the hill-tops; a town of clubs, churches, and hotels, of luxury shops, of pretty villas set in lovely gardens bright with English flowers and shaded by great orchid-clad trees; of broad, well-kept roads - such is Darjeeling, seven thousand feet above the sea.

At first sight there is nothing Oriental about it except the Gurkha policemen on point duty or the laughing groups of fair-skinned, rosy-cheeked Lepcha women that go chattering by him. But on one side the steep hills are crowded with the confused jumble of houses in the native bazaar, built higgledy-piggledy one on top of the other and lining the narrow streets and lanes that are thronged all day by a bright-garbed medley of Eastern races - Sikkimese, Bhuttias, Hindus, Tibetans, Lepchas. Set in a beautiful glen are the lovely Botanical Gardens, which look down past slopes trimly planted with rows of tea-bushes into the deep valleys far below.

As Noreen was borne along in her *dandy* she thought that she had never seen a more delightful spot. Everything and everyone attracted her attention - the scenery, the buildings, the varied folk that passed her on the road, from well set-up British soldiers in red coats and white helmets, smartly-dressed ladies in rickshas, Englishmen in breeches and gaiters riding sleek-coated ponies, to yellow-gowned lamas and Lepcha girls with massive silver necklaces and turquoise ornaments. She

Gordon Casserly

longed to turn her chair-coolies down the hill and begin at once the exploration of the attractive-looking native bazaar - until she reached the English shops with the newest fashions of female wear from London and Paris, set out behind their plate-glass windows. Here she forgot the bazaar and would willingly have lingered to look, but Ida's *dandy* kept steadily alongside hers and its occupant chattered incessantly of the many forth-coming social gaieties, until they turned into the courtyard of their hotel and stepped out of their chairs.

When Ida had shown her friend into the room reserved for her she said:

"Take off your hat, dear, and let me see how you look after all these years. Why, you've grown into quite a pretty girl. What a nice colour your hair is! Do you use anything for it? I don't remember its being as golden as all that at school."

The girl laughed and shook the sunlit waves of it down, for it had got untidy under her sun-hat.

"No, Ida darling, of course I don't use anything. The colour is quite natural, I assure you. Have you forgotten you used sometimes to call me Goldylocks at school?"

"Did I? I don't remember. I say, Noreen, you're a lucky girl to have made such a hit straight away with Captain Charlesworth. He's quite the rage with the women here."

"Is he? Why?" asked the girl carelessly, pinning up her hair.

"Why? My dear, he's the smartest man in a very smart regiment. Very well off; has lots of money and a beautiful place at home, I believe. Comes from an excellent family. And then he's so handsome. Don't you think so?"

"Yes; he's rather good-looking. But he struck me as being somewhat foppish."

"Oh, he's always beautifully dressed, if that's what you mean. You saw that, even when he had just come off a train journey. He's a beautiful dancer. I'm so glad he asked me for a couple of dances at the L.G.'s ball. I'll see he doesn't forget them. I'll keep him up to his word, though Bertie won't like it. He's fearfully jealous of me, but I don't care."

"Bertie? Who is - ? I thought that your husband's name was William?" said Noreen wonderingly.

Ida burst into a peal of laughter.

"Good gracious, child! I'm not talking of my husband. Bill's hundreds of miles away, thank goodness! I wouldn't mind if he were thousands. No; I'm speaking of Captain Bain, a great friend of mine from the Bombay side. He's stationed in Poona, which is quite a jolly place in the Season, though of course not a patch on this. But he got leave and came here because I did."

"Oh, yes, I see," replied Noreen vaguely, puzzled by Ida's remark about her husband. She had seen the Civil Servant at the wedding and remembered him as a stolid, middle-aged, and apparently uninteresting individual. But the girl was still ignorant enough of life not to understand why a woman after two years of marriage should be thankful that her husband was far away from her and wish him farther.

"But I'm not going to let Bertie monopolise me up here," continued Mrs. Smith, taking off her hat and pulling and patting her hair before the mirror. "I like a change. I've come here to have a good time. I think I'll go in and cut you out with Captain Charlesworth. He's awfully attractive."

"You are quite welcome to him, dear," said the girl.

"Oh, wait until you see the fuss the other women make of him. He's a great catch; and all the mothers here with marriageable daughters and the spins themselves are ready to scratch each other's eyes out over him."

"Don't be uncharitable, Ida dearest."

"It's a fact, darling. But I warn you that he's not a marrying man. He has the reputation of being a terrible flirt. I don't think you'll hold him long. He's afraid of girls - afraid they'll try to catch him. He prefers married women. He knows we're safe."

Noreen said nothing, but began to open and unpack her trunks. In India, the land of servants, where a bachelor officer has seven or more, a lady has usually to do without a maid, for the *ayah*, or native female domestic, is generally a failure in that capacity. In the hotels Indian "boys" replace the chambermaids of Europe.

Ida rattled on.

"Of course, Bertie's awfully useful. A tame cat - and he's a well-trained one - is a handy thing to have about you, especially up here. You need someone to take you to races and gymkhanas and to fill up blanks on your programme at dances, as well as getting your ricksha or *dandy* for you when they're over."

Noreen laughed, amused at the frankness of the statement.

"And where is the redoubtable Captain Bain, dear?"

"You'll see him soon. I let him off today until it's time for him to call to take us to the Amusement Club. He was anxious to see you. He wanted to come with me to the station, but I said he'd only be in the way. I knew Miguel would be much more useful in getting your luggage. Bertie's so slow. Still, he's rather a dear. Remember, he's my property. You mustn't poach."

Noreen laughed again and said:

"If he admires you, dear, I'm sure no one could take him from you."

"My dear girl, you never can trust any man," said her friend seriously. Then, glancing at herself in the mirror, she continued modestly:

"I know I'm not bad-looking, and lots of men do admire me. Bertie says I'm a ripper."

She certainly was decidedly pretty, though of a type of beauty that would fade early. Vain and empty-headed, she was, nevertheless, popular with the class of men who are content with a shallow, silly woman with whom it is easy to flirt. They described her as "good fun and not a bit strait-laced." Noreen knew nothing of this side of her friend, for she had not seen her since her marriage, and honestly thought her beautiful and fascinating.

Ida picked up her hat and parasol and said:

"Now I'll leave you to get straight, darling child, and come back to you later on."

She looked into the glass again and went on:

"It's so nice to have you here. A woman alone is rather out of it, especially if she comes from the other side of India and doesn't know Calcutta people. Now it'll be all right when there are two of us. The cats can't say horrid things about me and Bertie - though it's only the old frumps that can't get a man who do. I *am* glad you've come. We'll have such fun."

* * * * *

Captain Bain, a dapper little man, designed by Nature to be the "tame cat" of some married woman, was punctual when the time came to take the two ladies to the Amusement Club. Noreen had very dubiously donned her smartest frock which, having just been taken out of a trunk after a long journey, seemed very crushed, creased, and dowdy compared with the freshness and daintiness of Ida's *toilette.* Men as a rule understand nothing of the agonies endured by a woman who must face the unfriendly stares of other women in a gown that she feels will invite pitiless criticism.

But for the moment the girl forgot her worries as they turned out of the hotel gate and reached the Chaurasta, the meeting of the "four-ways," nearly as busy a cross-roads as (and infinitely more beautiful than) Carfax at Oxford or the Quattro Canti in Palermo. To the east the hill of Jalapahar towered a thousand feet above Darjeeling, crowned with bungalows and barracks. To the north the ground fell as sharply; and a thousand feet below Darjeeling lay Lebong, set out on a flattened hilltop. On three sides of this military suburb the hill sloped steeply to the valleys below. But beyond them, tumbled mass upon mass, rose the great mountains barring the way to Sikkim and Tibet, towering to the clouds that hid the white summits of the Eternal Snows.

Bain walked his pony beside Noreen's chair and named the various points of the scenery around them. Then, when Noreen had inscribed her name in the Visitors' Book at Government House, they entered the Amusement Club.

Noreen was overcome with shyness at finding herself, after her months of isolation, among scores of white folk, all strangers to her. Ida unconcernedly led the way into the large hall which was used as a roller-skating rink, along one side of which were set out dozens of little tables around which sat ladies in smart frocks that made the girl more painfully conscious of what she considered to be the deficiencies of her own costume. She saw one or two of the women that had travelled up in the train that day stare at her and then lean forward and make some remark about her to their companions at the table. She was profoundly thankful when the ordeal was over and, in Ida's wake, she had got out of the rink. Conscious only of the critical glances of her own sex, she was not aware of the admiring looks cast at her by many men in the groups around the tables.

But later on in the evening she found herself seated at one of those same tables that an hour before had seemed to her a bench of stern judges. She formed one of a laughing, chattering group of Ida's acquaintances. More at ease now, the girl watched the people around her with interest. For a year she had seen no larger gathering of her own race than the weekly meetings at the planters' little club in the jungle, with the one exception of a *durbar* at Jalpaiguri.

Yet despite Ida's company she was feeling lonely and a little depressed, a stranger in a crowd, when she saw Captain Charlesworth enter the rink, accompanied by another man. Recent as had been their meeting, he seemed quite an old friend among all these unknown people about her, and she almost hoped that he would come and speak to her. He sauntered through the hall, bowing casually to many ladies, some of whom, the girl noticed, made rather obvious efforts to detain him. But he ignored them and looked around, as if in search of some particular person. Suddenly his eyes met Noreen's, and he promptly came straight to her table. He shook hands with Mrs. Smith and bowed to the other ladies in the group, introduced his companion, a new arrival to his battalion, and, securing a chair beside Noreen, plunged into a light and animated conversation with her. The girl could not help feeling a little pleased when she saw the looks of surprise and annoyance on the faces of some of the women at the other tables. But Charlesworth was not allowed to have it all his own way with her. Bain and an Indian Army officer named Melville also claimed her attention. The knowledge that we are appreciated tends to make most of us appear at our best, and Noreen soon forgot her shyness and loneliness and became her usual natural, bright self. Ida looked on indulgently and smiled at her patronisingly, as though Noreen's little personal triumph were due to her.

Noreen slept soundly that night, and although she had meant to get up early and see Kinchinjunga and the snows when the sun rose, it was late when her hostess came to her room. After breakfast Ida took her out shopping. Only a woman can realise what a delight it was to the girl, after being divorced for a whole year from the sight of shops and the possibility of replenishing her wardrobe, or purchasing the thousand little necessities of the female toilet, to enter milliners' and dressmakers' shops where the latest, or very nearly the latest, *modes* of the day in hats and gowns were to be seen.

Charlesworth came to lunch in a smart riding-kit, looking particularly well-groomed and handsome. The girl was quite excited about the gymkhana, and plied him with innumerable questions as to what she would have to do. She learned that they were to enter for two affinity events. In one of these the lady was to tilt with a billiard-cue at three suspended rings, while the man, carrying a spear and a sword, took a tent-peg with the former, threw the lance away, cut off a Turk's head in wood with the sword, and then took another peg with the same weapon. The other competition was named the Gretna Green Stakes, and in it the pair were to ride hand in hand over three hurdles, dismount and sign their names in a book, then mount again and return hand in hand over the jumps to the winning-post.

The polo-ground at Lebong that afternoon presented an animated scene, filled with colour by the bright-hued garments of the thousands of native spectators surrounding it, the uniforms of the British soldiers in the crowd, and the frocks of the English ladies in the reserved enclosure, where in large white marquees the officers of Charlesworth's regiment acted as hosts to the European visitors. Down the precipitous road to it from Darjeeling came swarms of mixed Eastern races in picturesque garb, Gurkha soldiers in uniform, and British gunners from Jalapahar; and through the throngs Englishmen on ponies, and *dandies* and rickshas carrying ladies in smart summer frocks, could scarcely make their way.

When Mrs. Smith's party reached the enclosure and shook hands with the wife of the Colonel of the Rifles, who was the senior hostess, Noreen was not troubled by the feeling of shyness that had assailed her at the Club on the previous evening. She had the comforting knowledge that her habit and boots from the best West End makers were beyond cavil. But she was too excited at the thought of the approaching contests to think much of her appearance. Charlesworth took her to see the pony that she was to ride, and, as she passed through the enclosure, she did not hear the admiring remarks of many of the men and, indeed, of some of the women. For in India even an ordinarily pretty girl will be thought beautiful, and Noreen was more than ordinarily pretty. Her mount she found to be a well-shaped, fourteen-two grey Arab, with the perfect manners of his race; and she instantly lost her heart to him as he rubbed his velvety muzzle against her cheek.

The gymkhana opened with men's competitions, the first event in which ladies were to take part, the Tilting and Tent-pegging, not occurring until nearly half-way down the programme. Noreen was awaiting it too anxiously to enjoy, as she otherwise would, the novel scene, the gaiety, the band in the enclosure, the well-dressed throngs of English folk, the gaudy colours of the crowds squatting round the polo-ground and wondering at the strange diversions of the sahib-*logue*. Charlesworth did well in the men's event, securing two first prizes and a third, and Noreen could not help admiring him in the saddle. He was a graceful as well as a good rider. Indeed, he was No. 2 in the regimental polo team, which was one of the best in India at the time.

When the moment for their competition came at last and he swung her up into her saddle, Noreen's heart beat violently and her bridle-hand shook. But when, after other couples had ridden the course, their names were called and a billiard-cue given her, the girl's nerves steadied at once and she was perfectly cool as she reined back her impatient pony at the starting-line. The signal was given, and she and her partner dashed down the course at a gallop. They did well, Charlesworth securing the two pegs and cutting the Turk's head, while his affinity carried off two rings and touched the third. No others had been as fortunate, and cheers from the soldiers and plaudits from the enclosure greeted their success. Noreen was encouraged, and a becoming colour flushed her

Gordon Casserly

face at the applause. The last couple to ride tied with them, the lady taking all the rings, her partner getting the Turk's head and one peg and touching the second. The tie was run off at once. Noreen, to her delight, found the three rings on her cue when she pulled up at the end of the course, although she hardly remembered taking them, while Charlesworth had made no mistake. Daunted by this result, their rivals lost their heads and missed everything in their second run.

Noreen, on her return to the enclosure, was again loudly cheered by the men, the applause of the ladies being noticeably fainter, possibly because they resented a new arrival's success. But the girl was too pleasantly surprised at her good luck to observe this, and responded gratefully to the congratulations showered on her. She was no longer too excited to notice her surroundings, and now was able to enjoy the scenery, the music, the gay crowds, the frocks, as well as her tea when Charlesworth escorted her to the Mess Tent.

In the Gretna Green Stakes she and her partner were not so fortunate. Over the second hurdle in the run home Charlesworth's pony blundered badly and he was forced to release his hold on the girl's hand. When the event came for which he had originally requested her to nominate him, she suggested that he should ask Mrs. Smith to do so instead. He was skilled enough in the ways of women not to demur, and he did as he was wanted so tactfully that Ida believed it to be his own idea. So, when the gymkhana ended and Noreen and her chaperone said good-bye, he felt that he had advanced a good deal in the girl's favour.

During the afternoon Noreen caught sight of Chunerbutty talking to a fat and sensual-looking native in white linen garments with a string of roughly-cut but very large diamonds round his neck and several obsequious satellites standing behind him. They were covertly watching her, but when, catching the engineer's eye, she bowed to him, the fat man leant forward and stared boldly at her. She guessed him to be the Rajah of Lalpuri, who had been pointed out to her once at the Lieutenant-Governor's *durbar* at Jalpaiguri.

That evening a note from Chunerbutty, telling her that his father was better though still in a precarious state, was left at her hotel. But the engineer did not call on her.

The ball on the Thursday night at Government House was all that Noreen anticipated it would be. Among the hundreds of guests there were a few Indian men of rank and a number of Parsis of both sexes - the women adding bright colours to the scene by the beautiful hues of their *saris*, as the silk shawls worn over their heads are called. During the evening Noreen saw Chunerbutty standing at the door of the ballroom with the fat man, who was now adorned with jewels and wearing a magnificent diamond *aigrette* in his *puggri*, and gloating with a lustful gaze over the bared necks and bosoms of the English ladies. The native of India, where the females of all races veil their faces, looks on white women, who lavishly display their charms to the eyes of all beholders, as immodest and immoral. And he judges harshly the freedom - the sometimes extreme freedom - of intercourse between English wives and men who are not their husbands.

Later in the evening, when Noreen was sitting in the central lounge with Captain Bain during an interval, Chunerbutty approached her with the fat man. Coming up to her alone the engineer said:

"Miss Daleham, may I present His Highness the Rajah of Lalpuri to you?"

Noreen felt Captain Bain stiffen, but she replied courteously:

"Certainly, Mr. Chunerbutty."

The Rajah stepped forward, and on being introduced held out a fat and flabby hand to her, speaking in stiff and stilted English, for he did not use it with ease. He spoke only a few conventional sentences, but all the while Noreen felt an inward shiver of disgust. For his bloodshot eyes seemed to burn her bared flesh, as he devoured her naked shoulders and breast with a hot and lascivious stare. After replying politely but briefly to him she turned to the engineer and enquired after his father's health. The music beginning in the ball-room for the next dance gave her a welcome excuse for cutting the interview short, as Bain sprang up quickly and offered her his arm. Bowing she moved away with relief.

"I suppose that fellow in evening dress was the man from your garden, Miss Daleham?" asked Bain, as they entered the ballroom.

"Yes; that was Mr. Chunerbutty, who escorted me to Darjeeling," she answered.

"Well, if he's a friend of your brother, he ought to know better than to introduce that fat brute of a rajah to you."

"Oh, he is staying at the Rajah's house here, as his father, who is ill, is in His Highness's service."

"I don't care. That beast Lalpuri is a disreputable scoundrel. There are awful tales of his behaviour up here. It's a wonder that the L.G. doesn't order him out of the place."

"Really?"

"Yes; he's a disgraceful blackguard. None of the other Rajahs of the Presidency will have anything to do with him, I believe; and the two or three of them up here now who are really splendid fellows, refuse to acknowledge him. Everybody wonders why the Government of India allows him to remain on the *gadi*."

The Rajah had watched Noreen with a hungry stare as she walked towards the ballroom. When she was lost to sight in the crowd of dancers he turned to Chunerbutty and seized his arm with a grip that made the engineer wince.

"She is more beautiful than I thought," he muttered. "O you fools! You fools, who have failed me! But I shall get her yet."

He licked his dry lips and went on:

"Let us go! Let us go from here! I am parched. I want liquor. I want women."

And they returned to a night of revolting debauchery in the house that was honoured by being the temporary residence of His Highness the Rajah of Lalpuri, wearer of an order bestowed upon him by the Viceroy and ruler of the fate of millions of people by the grace and under the benign auspices of the Government of India.

CHAPTER XIV

THE TANGLED SKEIN OF LOVE

The Lieutenant-Governor's ball was for Noreen but the beginning of a long series of social entertainments, of afternoon and evening dances, receptions, dinner and supper parties, concerts, and amateur theatrical performances that filled every date on the calendar of the Darjeeling Season. Only in winter sport resorts like St. Moritz and Muerren had she ever seen its like. But in Switzerland the visitors come from many lands and are generally strangers to each other, whereas in the Hills in India the summer residents of the villas and the guests at the big hotels are of the same race and class, come from the same stations in the Plains or know of each other by repute. For, with the exception of the comparatively few lawyers, planters, merchants, or railway folk, the names of all are set forth in the two Golden Books of the land, the Army List and the Civil Service List; and hostesses fly with relief to the blessed "Table of Precedence" contained in them, which tells whether the wife of Colonel This should go in to dinner before or after the spouse of Mr. That. The great god Snob is the supreme deity of Anglo-India.

Many hill-stations are the Hot Weather headquarters of some important Government official, such as the Governor of the Presidency or the Lieutenant-Governor or Chief Commissioner of the Province. These are great personages indeed in India. They have military guards before their doors. The Union Jack waves by command above their august heads. They have Indian Cavalry soldiers to trot before their wives' carriages when these good ladies drive down to bargain in the native bazaar. But to the hill visitors their chief reason for existing is that their position demands the giving of official entertainments to which all of the proper class (who duly inscribe their names in the red-bound, gold-lettered book in the hall of Government House) have a prescriptive right to be invited.

Noreen revelled in the gaieties. Her frank-hearted enjoyment was like a child's, and made every man who knew her anxious to add to it. She could not possibly ride all the ponies offered to her nor accept half the invitations that she got. Even among the women she was popular, for none but a match-making mother or a jealous spinster could resist her.

Proposals of marriage were not showered on her, as persons ignorant of Anglo-Indian life fondly believe to be the lot of every English girl there. While a dowerless maiden still has a much better chance of securing a husband in a land where maidens are few and bachelors are many, yet the day has long gone by when every spinster who had drawn a blank in England could be shipped off to India with the certainty of finding a spouse there. Frequent leave and fast steamers have altered that. When a man can go home in a fortnight every year or second year he is not as anxious to snatch at the first maiden who appears in his station as his predecessor who lived in India in the days when a voyage to England took six months. And men in the East are as a rule not anxious to marry. A wife out there is a handicap at every turn. She adds enormously to his expenses, and her society too often lends more brightness to the existence of his fellows than his own. Children are ruinous luxuries. Bachelor life in Mess or club is too pleasant, sport that a single man can enjoy more readily than a married one too attractive, rupees too few for what Kipling terms "the wild ass of the desert" to be willing to put his head into the halter readily.

Yet men do marry in India - one wonders why! - and a girl

there has so many opportunities of meeting the opposite sex every day, and so little rivalry, that her chances in the matrimonial market are infinitely better than at home. In stations in the Plains there are usually four or five men to every woman in its limited society, and the proportion of bachelors to spinsters is far greater. Sometimes in a military cantonment with five or six batteries and regiments in it, which, with departmental officers, may furnish a total of eighty to a hundred unmarried men from subalterns to colonels, there may be only one or two unwedded girls. The lower ranks are worse off for English spinster society; for the private soldier there is none.

Noreen's two most constant attendants were Charlesworth and Melville. The Indian Army officer's devotion and earnestness were patent to the world, but the Rifleman's intentions were a problem and a source of dispute among the women, who in Indian stations not less than other places watch the progress of every love-affair with the eyes of hawks. It was doubtful if Charlesworth himself knew what he wanted. He was a man who loved his liberty and his right to make love to each and every woman who caught his fancy. Noreen's casual liking for him but her frank indifference to him in any other capacity than that of a pleasant companion with whom to ride, dance, or play tennis, piqued him, but not sufficiently to make him risk losing his cherished freedom.

Chunerbutty left Darjeeling after a week's stay. Parry, having become sufficiently sober to enquire after him and learn of his absence, demanded his instant return in a telegram so profanely worded that it shocked even the Barwahi post-office *babu*. The engineer called on Noreen to say good-bye, and offered to be the bearer of a message to her brother. He kept up to the end the fable of his sick father.

He could not tell her the real reason of his coming to Darjeeling. The truth was that he had learned that the Rajah had inspired the attempt by the Bhuttias to carry off Noreen and wanted to see and upbraid him for his deceit and treachery to their agreement. There had been a furious quarrel when the two accomplices met. The Rajah taunted the other with his lack of success with Noreen and the failure of his plan to persuade her to marry him. Chunerbutty retorted that he had not been allowed sufficient time to win the favour of an English girl, who, unlike Indian maidens, was free to choose her own husband. And he threatened to inform the Government if any further attempt against her were made without his knowledge and approval. But the quarrel did not last long. Each scoundrel needed the help of the other. Still, Chunerbutty judged it safer to remove himself from the Rajah's house and find a lodging elsewhere, lest any deplorable accident might occur to him under his patron's roof.

After the engineer's departure Noreen seldom saw the Rajah, and then only at official entertainments, to which his position gained him invitations. He spoke to her once or twice at these receptions, but as a rule she contrived to elude him.

So far she had got on very well with Mrs. Smith. Their wills had never clashed, for the girl unselfishly gave in to her friend whenever the latter demanded it, which was often enough. Ida's ways were certainly not Noreen's, and the latter sometimes felt tempted to disapprove of her excessive familiarity with Captain Bain and one or two others. But the next moment she took herself severely to task for being censorious of the elder woman, who must surely know better how to behave towards men than a young unmarried girl who had been buried so long in the jungle. And Ida did not guess why sometimes her repentant little friend's caresses were so fervent and her desire to please her so manifest, and ascribed it all to her own sweetness of nature.

The coming of the Rains did not check the gaiety of the dwellers on the mountain-tops, though torrential downpours had to be faced on black nights in shrouded rickshas and dripping *dandies*, though incessant lightning lit up the road to the club or theatre, and the thunder made it difficult to hear the music of the band in the ballroom. Noreen missed nothing of the revels. But in all the whirl of gaiety and pleasure in which her days were passed her thoughts turned more and more to the great forest lying thousands of feet below her, and the man who passed his lonely days therein.

Little news of him came to her. He never wrote, and her brother seldom mentioned him in his letters; for during Parker's absence on two months' privilege leave from Ranga Duar Dermot did not quit it often and very rarely visited the planters' club or the bungalows of any of its members. And Noreen wanted news of him. Much as she saw of other men now - many of them attractive and some of whom she frankly liked - none had effaced Dermot's image or displaced him from the shrine that she had built for him in her inmost heart. Mingled with her love was hero-worship. She dared not hope that he could ever be interested in or care for any one as shallow-minded as she. She could not picture him descending from the pedestal on which she had placed him to raise so ordinary a girl to his heart. She could not fancy him in the light, frothy life of Darjeeling. She judged him too serious to care for frivolities, and it inspired her with a little awe of him and a fear that he would despise her as a feather-brained, silly woman if he saw how she enjoyed the amusements of the hill-station. But she felt that she would gladly exchange the gaieties and cool climate of Darjeeling for the torments of the Terai again, if only it would bring him to her side. For sometimes the longing to see him grew almost unbearable.

As the days went by the power of the gay life of the Hills to satisfy her grew less, while the ache in her heart for her absent friend increased. If only she could hear from him she thought she could bear the separation better. From her brother she learned by chance that he was alone in Ranga Duar, the only news that she had had of him for a long time. The Rains had burst, and she pictured the loneliness of the one European in the solitary outpost, cut off from his kind, with no one of his race to speak to, deprived of the most ordinary requirements, necessities, of civilisation, without a doctor within hundreds of miles.

At that thought her heart seemed to stop beating. Without a doctor! He might be ill, dying, for all she knew, with no one of his colour to tend him, no loving hand to hold a cup to his fevered lips. Even in the short time that she had been in India she had heard of many tragedies of isolation, of sick and lonely Englishmen with none but ignorant, careless native servants to look after them in their illness, no doctor to alleviate their sufferings, until pain and delirium drove them to look for relief and oblivion down the barrel of a too-ready pistol.

Thus the girl tortured herself, as a loving woman will do, by imagining all the most terrible things happening to the man of her heart. She feared no longer the perils of the forest for him. She felt that he was master of man or beast in it. But fever lays low the strongest. It might be that while she was dancing he was lying ill, dying, perhaps dead. And she would not know. The dreadful idea occurred to her after her return from a ball at which she had been universally admired and much sought after. But, as she sat wrapped in her blue silk dressing-gown, her feet thrust into satin slippers of the same colour, her pretty hair about her shoulders, instead of recalling the triumphs of the evening, the compliments of her partners, and the unspoken envy of other girls, her thoughts flew to one solitary man in a little bungalow, cloud-enfolded and comfortless, in a lonely outpost. The sudden dread of his being ill chilled her blood and so terrified her that, if the hour had not made it impossible, she would have gone out at once and telegraphed to him to ask if all were well.

Yet the next instant her face grew scarlet at the thought. She sat for a long time motionless, thinking hard. Then the idea occurred to her of writing to him, writing a chatty, almost impersonal letter, such as one friend could send to another without fear of her motives being misunderstood. She had too high an opinion of Dermot to think that he would deem her forward, yet it cost her much to be the first to write. But her anxiety conquered pride. And she wrote the letter that Dermot read in his bungalow in Ranga Duar while the storm shook the hills.

The girl counted the days, the hours, until she could hope for an answer. Would he reply at once, she wondered. She knew that, even shut up in his little station, he had much work to occupy him. He could not spare time, perhaps, for a letter to a silly girl. And the thought of all that she had put in hers to him made her face burn, for it seemed so vapid and frivolous that he was sure to despise her.

On the fourth day after she had written to Dermot she was engaged to ride in the afternoon with Captain Charlesworth. But in the morning a note came to her from him regretting his inability to keep the appointment, as the Divisional General had arrived in Darjeeling and intended to inspect the Rifles after lunch. Noreen was not sorry, for she was going to a dance that evening and did not wish to tire herself before it.

Distracted and little in the mood for gaiety as she felt that night, yet when she entered the large ballroom of the Amusement Club she could not help laughing at the quaint and original decorations for the occasion. For the entertainment was one of the great features of the Season, the Bachelors' Ball, and the walls were blazoned with the insignia of the Tribe of the Wild Ass. Everywhere was painted its coat-of-arms - a bottle, slippers, and a pipe crossed with a latch-key, all in proper heraldic guise. Captain Melville, who was a leading member of the ball committee and who was her particular host that night, spirited her away from the crowd of partner-seeking men at the doorway and took her on a tour of the room to see and admire the scheme of decoration. She was laughing at one original ornamentation when a well-known voice behind her said:

"May I hope for a dance tonight, Miss Daleham?"

The girl started and turned round incredulously, feeling that her ears had deceived her. To her astonishment Dermot stood before her. For a few seconds she could not trust herself to reply. She felt that she had grown pale. At last she said, and her voice sounded strange in her own ears:

"Major Dermot! Is it possible? I - I thought you -"

She could not finish the sentence. But neither man observed her emotion, for Melville had suddenly seized Dermot's hand and was shaking it warmly. They had been on service together once and had not met since. The next moment, a committee man being urgently wanted, Melville was called away and left Dermot and the girl together.

"I suppose you thought me shut up in my mountain home," the man said, "and probably wondered why I had not answered your very interesting letter. It was so kind of you in all your gaiety here to think of me in my loneliness."

Noreen had quite recovered from her surprise and smiled brightly at him.

"Yes, I believed you to be in Ranga Duar," she said. "How is it you are here?"

"An unexpected summons reached me at the same time as your letter. Four days ago I had no idea that I should be coming here."

"How could you bear to leave your beloved jungle and that dear Badshah? I know you dislike hill-stations," said the girl, laughing and tremulously happy. The world seemed a much brighter place than it did five minutes before.

"My beloved jungle has no charm for me at this season," he said. "But Badshah - ah, that was another matter. I have seldom felt parting with a human friend as much as I did leaving him. The dear old fellow seemed to know that I was going away from him. But I was very pleased to come here to see how you were enjoying yourself in this gay spot. I was glad to know that you were out of the Terai during the Rains."

So he had wanted to see her again. Noreen blushed, but

Dermot did not observe her heightened colour, for he had taken her programme out of her hand in his usual quiet, masterful manner and was scrutinising it.

"You haven't said yet if I may have a dance," he continued. "But I know that on an occasion like this I must lose no time if I want one."

"Oh, do you dance?" she asked in surprise. Somehow she had never associated him with ballrooms and social frivolities.

Dermot laughed.

"You forget that I was on the Staff in Simla. I shouldn't have been kept there a day if I hadn't been able to dance. What may I have?"

Noreen felt tempted to bid him take all her programme.

"Well, I'm engaged for several. They are all written down. Take any of the others you like," she said demurely, but her heart was beating fast at the thought of dancing with him.

"H'm; I see that all the first ones are booked. May I - oh, I see you have the supper dances free. May I take you in to supper?"

"Yes, do, please. We haven't met for so long, and I have heaps to tell you," the girl said. "We can talk ever so much better at the supper-table than in an interval."

"Thank you. I'll take the supper dances then."

"Wouldn't you care for any others?" she asked timidly. What would he think of her? Yet she didn't care. He was with her again, and she wanted to see all she could of him.

"I should indeed. May I have this - and this?"

"With pleasure. Is that enough?"

"I'll be greedy. After all, the men up here have had dances from you all the Season, and I have never danced with you yet. I'll take these, too, if you can spare them."

She looked at him earnestly.

"I owe you more than a few dances can pay," she said simply.

"Thank you, little friend," he said, and a happy feeling thrilled her at his words. He had not forgotten her, then. He used to call her that sometimes in Ranga Duar. She was still his little friend. What a delightful place the world was after all!

As he pencilled his initials on her programme a horde of dance-hungry men swooped down on Noreen and almost pushed him aside. He bowed and strolled away to watch the dancing. He had no desire to obtain other partners and was content to watch his little friend of the forest, who seemed to have suddenly become a very lovely woman. She seemed very gay and happy, he thought. He noticed that she danced oftenest with Melville and a tall, fair man whom he did not know.

Never had the early part of a ball seemed to Noreen to drag so much as this one did. She felt that her partners must find her very stupid indeed, for she paid no attention to what they said and answered at random.

At last almost in a trance of happiness she found herself gliding round the room with Dermot's arm about her. The band was playing a dreamy waltz, and her partner danced perfectly. Neither of them spoke. Noreen could not; she felt that all she wanted was to float, on air it seemed, held close to Dermot's breast. She gave a sigh when the dance ended. In the interval she did not want to talk; it was enough to look at his face, to hear his voice. She hated her next partner when he came to claim her.

But she had two more dances with Dermot before the band

struck up "The Roast Beef of Old England," and the ballroom emptied. At supper he contrived to secure a small table at which they were alone; so they were able to talk without constraint. She began to wonder how she had ever thought him grave and stern or felt in awe of him. For in the gay atmosphere his Irish nature was uppermost; he was as light-hearted as a boy, and his conversation was almost frivolous.

During supper Noreen saw Ida watching her across the room, and later on, when the dancing began again, her friend cornered her.

"I say, darling, who is the new man you've been dancing with such a lot tonight? You had supper with him, too. I've never seen him before. He's awfully good-looking."

"Oh, that is - I suppose you mean Major Dermot," replied the girl, feeling suddenly shy.

"Major Dermot? Who's he? What is - Oh, is it the wonderful hero from the Terai, the man you told me so much about when you came up?"

"Yes; he is the same."

"Really? How interesting! He's so distinguished-looking. When did he come up? Why didn't you tell me he was coming?"

"I didn't know it myself."

"I should love to meet him. Introduce him to me. Now, at once."

With a hurried apology to her own partner and Noreen's she dragged the girl off in search of the fresh man who had taken her fancy, and did not give up the chase until, with Melville's aid, Dermot was run to earth in the cardroom and introduced to her. Ida did not wait for him to ask her to dance but calmly ran her pencil through three names on the programme and bestowed the vacancies thus created on him in such a way that he could not refuse them. Dermot, however, did not grumble. She was Noreen's friend; if not the rose, she was near the rose.

Ida was not the only one who noticed how frequently the girl had danced with him. Charlesworth, disappointed at finding vacancies on her programme, for which he had hoped, already filled, commented on it and asked who the stranger was in a supercilious tone that made her furious and gained for him a well-merited snubbing.

Indifferent to criticism, kind or otherwise, Noreen gave herself up for the evening to the happiness of Dermot's presence, trying to trick herself into the belief that he was still only a dear friend to whom she owed an immense debt of gratitude for saving her life and her honour. Never had a ball seemed so enjoyable - not even her first. Never had she had a partner who suited her so well. Certainly he danced to perfection, but she knew that if he had been the worst dancer in the room she still would have preferred him to all others. And never had she hated the ending of an entertainment so much. But Dermot walked beside her *dandy* to the gate of her hotel, calmly displacing Charlesworth, much to the fury of the Rifleman, who had begun to consider this his prerogative.

Ida and she sat up for hours in her room discussing the ball and all its happenings, but the older woman's most constant topic was Dermot. It was a subject of which Noreen felt that she could never weary; and she drew her friend on to talk of him, if the conversation threatened to stray to anything less interesting. The girl was used to Ida's sudden fancies for men, for the married woman was both susceptible and fickle, and Noreen judged that this sudden predilection for Dermot would die as quickly as a hundred others before it. But this time she was wrong.

The Major was not to remain many days in Darjeeling, but Noreen hoped that he would give her much of his spare time while there. She was disappointed, however, to find that although he was frequently in her and Ida's company at the Amusement Club or elsewhere, he made no effort to compete with Charlesworth or Melville or any other man who sought to monopolise her, but drew back and allowed him to have a clear field while he himself seemed content to talk to Mrs. Smith. At first she was hurt. He was her friend, not Ida's. But he never sought to be alone with her, never asked her to ride with him, or do anything that would take her away from the others.

Then she grew piqued. If he did not value her society he should see that others did, and she suddenly grew more gracious to Charlesworth, who seemed to sense in Dermot a more dangerous rival than was Melville or any of the others and began to be more openly devoted and to put more meaning into his intentions.

One hateful night when she had been with Charlesworth to a private dance to which Ida had refused to go, dining instead with Dermot, who had no invitation to the affair, the blow fell. After her return to the hotel her treacherous friend had crept into her room, weeping and imploring her sympathy. Too late, she sobbed on Noreen's shoulder, she had found her soul-mate, the man destined for her through the past aeons, the one man who could make her happy and whose existence she alone could complete. Why had she met Dermot too late? Why was she tied to a clod, mated to a clown? Why were two lives to be wrecked?

As Noreen listened amazed an icy hand seemed to clutch her shrinking heart. Was this true? Did Dermot really care for Ida? Could the man whom she had revered as a white-souled knight be base enough to make love to another man's wife?

Then the demon of jealousy poisoned her soul. She got the weeping Ida back to her bed, and sat in her own dark room until the dawn came, her brain in a whirl, her heart filled with a fierce hatred of Dermot. And when next day, his business finished, he had to leave Darjeeling, she made a point of absenting herself with Charlesworth from the hotel at the time when Dermot had arranged to come to say good-bye.

But long before the train in which he travelled down to the Plains was half-way to Siliguri, the girl lay on her bed, her face buried in her pillow, her body shaken with silent but convulsive sobs.

And Dermot stared out into the thick mist that shrouded the mountains and enfolded his downward-slipping train and wondered if his one-time little friend of the forest would be happy in the new life that, according to her bosom-friend and confidant, Mrs. Smith, would open to her as Charlesworth's wife as soon as she spoke the word that was trembling on her lips.

And he sighed unconsciously. Then he frowned as the distasteful memory recurred to him of the previous night, when a wanton woman, misled by vanity and his courteous manner, had shamelessly offered him what she termed her love and forced him to play the Joseph to a modern Mrs. Potiphar.

CHAPTER XV

THE FEAST OF THE GODDESS KALI

The Rains were nearing their end, and with them the Darjeeling Season was drawing to a close. To Noreen Daleham it had lost its savour since Dermot's departure. Her feelings towards Ida had undergone a radical change; her admiration of and affection for her old schoolfellow had vanished. Her eyes were opened, and she now saw plainly the true character of the woman whom once she was proud to call her friend. The girl wondered that she could have ever been deceived, for she now understood the many innuendoes that had been made in her hearing against Mrs. Smith, as well as many things in that lady's own behaviour that had perplexed her at the time.

But towards the man her feelings were frankly anger and contempt. He had rudely awakened her from a beautiful dream; for that she could never forgive him. Her idol was shattered, never again to be made whole, so she vowed in the bitterness of her desolate soul. It was not friendship that she had felt for him - she realised that now. It was love. She had given him her whole heart in a girl's first, pure, ideal love. And he had despised the gift and trampled it in the mire of unholy passion. She knew that it was the love of her life. Never could any man be to her what he had been.

But what did it matter to Dermot? she thought bitterly. She had passed out of his life. She had never been anything in it. He had been amused for an idle moment by her simplicity, tool that she was. What he had done, had risked for her, he would have done and risked for any other woman. Why did he not write to her after his departure as he might have done? She almost hoped that he would, so that she could answer him and pour out on him, if only on paper, the scorn and disgust that filled her. But no; she would not do that. The more dignified course would be to ignore his letter altogether. If only she could hurt him she felt that she would accept any other man's offer of marriage. But even then he wouldn't care. He had always stood aside in Darjeeling and let others strive for her favour. And she was put to the test, for first Charlesworth and then Melville had proposed to her.

Though Noreen's heart was frozen towards her quondam friend, Ida never perceived the fact. For the elder woman was so thoroughly satisfied with herself that it never occurred to her that any one whom she honoured with her liking could do aught but be devoted to her in return. And against the granite of her self-sufficiency the iron of the girl's proud anger broke until at length, baffled by the other's conceit, Noreen drifted back into the semblance of her former friendliness. And Ida never remarked any difference.

A hundred miles away Dermot roamed the hills and forest again. The interdict of the Rains was lifted, and the game was afoot once more.

The portents of the coming storm were intensified. Much that the Divisional Commander, General Heyland, had revealed to him in their confidential interviews at Darjeeling was being corroborated by happenings in other parts of the Peninsula, in Afghanistan, in China, and elsewhere. Signs were not wanting on the border that Dermot had to guard. Messengers crossing and re-crossing the Bhutan frontier were increasing in numbers and frequency; and he had at length succeeded in tracking some of them to a destination that first gave him a clue to the seat and identity of the organisers of the conspiracy in Bengal.

For one or two Bhutanese had been traced to the capital of the

Native State of Lalpuri, and others, having got into Indian territory, had been met by Hindus who were subsequently followed to the same ill-famed town. But once inside the maze of its bazaars their trail was hopelessly lost. It was useless to appeal to the authorities of the State. Their reputation and the character of their ruler were so bad that it was highly probable that the Rajah and all his counsellors were implicated in the plot. But how to bring it home to them Dermot did not know. By his secret instructions several of the messengers to and from Bhutan were the victims of apparent highway robbery in the hills. But no search of them revealed anything compromising, no treasonable correspondence between enemies within and without. The men would not speak, and he could not sanction the proposals made to him by which they should be induced so to do.

The planters began to report to him a marked increase in the mutinous spirit exhibited by their coolies; arms were found in the possession of these men, and there was reason to fear a combined rising of the labourers on all the estates of the Duars. Dermot advised Rice to send his wife to England, but the lady showed no desire to return to her loudly-regretted London suburb.

Every time that the Major met Daleham he expected to be told of Noreen's engagement, perhaps even her wedding. But he heard nothing. When he found that Fred was beginning to arrange for her return to Malpura and that - instigated by Chunerbutty - he refused to consider the advisability of her remaining away until conditions were better in the Terai, Dermot persuaded him to replace his untrustworthy Bengali house-servants by reliable Mussulman domestics, warlike Punjaubis, whom the soldier procured. They were men not unused to firearms, and capable of defending the bungalow if necessary.

He and Badshah, who was happy to have his man with him again, kept indefatigable watch and ward along the frontier. Sometimes Dermot assembled the herd, which had learned to obey him almost like a pack of hounds, and, concealed among them, penetrated across the border into Bhutan and explored hidden spots where hostile troops might be concentrated. Only rarely a wandering Bhuttia chanced to see him, and then the terrified man would veil his eyes, fearing to behold the doings of the terrible Elephant God.

The constant work and preoccupation kept Dermot from dwelling much on Noreen. Nevertheless, he thought often of the girl and hoped that she would be happy when she married the man she was said to have chosen. He felt no jealousy of Charlesworth; on the contrary, he admired him as a good sportsman and a manly fellow, as well as he could judge from the little that he had seen of him. The very fact that the girl who was his friend had chosen the Rifleman as her husband, according to Mrs. Smith, made him ready to like the man. He was not in love with the girl and had no desire to marry, for he was wedded to his profession and had always held that a soldier married was a soldier marred.

Thus while Dermot thought far seldomer of Noreen, whom he acknowledged to himself he liked more than any other woman he had ever met, she, who assured herself every day that she hated and despised him, could not keep him out of her mind. And all the more so as she began to have doubts of the truth of Ida's story. For the girl, who could not resist watching her friend's post every day, much as she despised herself for doing it, observed that no letter ever came to Mrs. Smith in Dermot's handwriting. And, although Ida had talked much and sentimentally of him for days after his departure, she appeared to forget him soon, and before long was engrossed in a good-looking young civilian from Calcutta. Bain had long since left Darjeeling.

Could it all have been a figment of the woman's imagination and vanity? - for Noreen now realised how colossally vain she was. Had she misunderstood or, worse still, misrepresented him? But that thought was almost more painful to the girl than the certainty of his guilt. For if it were true, how cruelly, how vilely unjust she had been to the man who had saved her at the peril of his life, the man who had called her his friend, who had trusted in her loyalty! No, no; better that he were proved worthless, dishonourable. That thought were easier to bear.

Sometimes the girl almost wished that she could see him again so that she might ask him the truth. She could learn nothing now from Ida, who calmly ignored all attempts to extract information from her. Yet how could she question him, Noreen asked herself. She could not even hint to him that she had any knowledge of the affair, for her friend had divulged it to her in confidence. If only she were back at Malpura! He might come to her again there and perhaps of his own free will tell her what to believe of him. But when in a letter she broached the subject of her return to her brother, Fred bade her wait, for he hoped that he might be able to join her in Darjeeling for a few days during the Puja holidays.

During the great festival of Durga-Puja, or the Dussera, as it is variously called, no Hindu works if he can help it, especially in Bengal. As all Government and private offices in Calcutta are closed for it, every European there, who can, escapes to Darjeeling, twenty-four hours away by rail, and the Season in that hill-station dies in a final blaze of splendour and gaiety in the mad rush of revelry of the Puja holidays. And Fred hoped that he might he there to see its ending, if Parry would keep sober long enough to let his assistant get away for a few days. When he returned, Daleham wrote, he would bring Noreen back with him.

Dermot's activities on the frontier were not passing unmarked by the chief conspirators in Lalpuri. His measures against their messengers focussed attention on him. The *Dewan*, a far better judge of men and things than Chunerbutty, did not make the mistake of despising him merely because he was a soldier. The old man realised that it was not wise to count British officers fools. He knew too well how efficient the Indian Military Intelligence Department had proved itself. So he began to collect information about this white man who might seriously inconvenience them or derange their plans. And he came to the conclusion that the inquisitive soldier must be put out of the way.

Assassination can be raised to a fine art in a Native State - where a man's life is worth far less than a cow's if the State be a Hindu one - provided that the prying eyes of British Political Officers are not turned that way. True, Dermot was in British territory, but in such an uncivilised part of it that his removal ought not to be difficult considering his habit of wandering alone about the hills and jungle.

So thought the *Dewan*. But the old man found to his surprise that it was very difficult to put his hand on any one willing to attempt Dermot's life. No sum however large could tempt any Bhuttia on either side of the border-line, or any Hindu in the Duars. Even the Brahmin extremists acting as missionaries on the tea-gardens fought shy of him. Superstition was his sure shield.

Then the *Dewan* fell back on the bazaar of Lalpuri City. But in that den of criminals there was not one cut-throat that did not know of the terrible Elephant God-Man and the appalling vengeance that he had wreaked on the Rajah's soldiers in the forest. The *Dewan* might cajole or threaten, but there was not one ruffian in the bazaar who did not prefer to risk his anger to the certainty of the hideous fate awaiting the rash mortal that crossed the path of this dread being who fed his magic elephants on the living flesh of his foes.

The *Dewan* was not baffled. If the local villains failed him an assassin must be imported from elsewhere. So the extremist leaders in Calcutta, being appealed to, sent more than one fanatical young Brahmin from that city to Lalpuri, where they were put in the way to remove Dermot. But when in bazaar or Palace his reputation reached their ears they drew back. One was sent direct from Calcutta to the Terai, so that he would not be scared by the foolish tales of the men of Lalpuri. But his first enquiries among the countryfolk as to where to find

Dermot brought him such illuminating information that, not daring to return unsuccessful to those who had sent him, he turned against his own breast the weapon that he had meant for the British officer.

Then the *Dewan* sent for Chunerbutty and took counsel with him, as being more conversant with European ways. And the result was a cunning and elaborate plot, such as from its very tortuousness and complexity would appeal to the heart of an Oriental.

The Rajah of Lalpuri, being of Mahratta descent, tried to copy in many things the great Mahratta chiefs in other parts of India, such as the Gaekwar of Baroda and the Maharajah Holkar of Indore. He had long been anxious to imitate Holkar's method of celebrating the Dussera or Durga Festival, particularly that part of it where a bull is sacrificed in public by the Maharajah on the fourth day of the feast. The *Dewan* had always opposed it, but now he suddenly veered round and suggested that it should be done. In Indore all the Europeans of the cantonment and many of the ladies and officers from the neighbouring military station of Mhow were always invited to be present on the fourth day. The old plotter proposed that, similarly, some of the English community of the Duars, the Civil Servants and planters, should receive invitations to Lalpuri. It would seem only natural to include the Officer Commanding Ranga Duar. And to tempt Dermot into the trap Chunerbutty suggested Noreen as a bait, undertaking to persuade her brother to bring her.

The Rajah was delighted at the thought of her presence in the Palace. The *Dewan* smiled and quoted two Hindu proverbs:

"Where the honey is spread there will the flies gather," said he. "Any lure is good that brings the bird to the net."

The consequence of the plotting was that Noreen Daleham, fretting in Darjeeling at having to wait for her brother to come there for the Puja holidays, received a letter from him saying that he had changed his mind and had accepted an invitation from the Rajah of Lalpuri for her and himself to be present at the celebrations of the great Hindu festival at the Palace. She was to pack up and leave at once by rail to Jalpaiguri, where he would meet her with a motor-car lent him for the purpose by the Lalpuri Durbar, or State Council. If Mrs. Smith cared to accompany her an invitation for her would be at once forthcoming. Fred added that he was making up a party from their district which included Payne, Granger, and the Rices. From Lalpuri Noreen would return with him to Malpura.

The girl was delighted at the thought of leaving Darjeeling sooner than she had expected. To her surprise Ida announced her intention of accompanying her to Lalpuri. But the fact that her Calcutta friend was returning to the city on the Hoogly and that by going with Noreen she could travel with him as far as Jalpaiguri explained it.

Chunerbutty, deputed by the Rajah to act as host to his European guests, met Daleham's party when they arrived at the gates of Lalpuri and conducted them to the Palace. They passed through the teeming city with its thronged bazaar, its narrow, winding streets hemmed in by the overhanging houses with their painted walls and closely-latticed windows through which thousands of female eyes peered inquisitively at the white women, the brightly dressed crowds flattening themselves against the walls to get out of the way of the two cavalry soldiers of the Rajah's Bodyguard who galloped recklessly ahead of the car. Soon they reached the *Nila Mahal*, or Blue Palace, as His Highness's residence was called, with its iron-studded gates, carved doors, and countless wooden balconies. A swarm of retainers in magnificent, if soiled, gold-laced liveries filled the courtyards, and bare-footed sepoys in red coats, generally burst at the seams and lacking buttons, and old shakoes with white cotton flaps hanging down behind, guarded the entrance.

A wing of the Palace had been cleared out and hastily furnished in an attempt to suit European tastes. The guests were accommodated in rooms floored with marble, generally badly stained or broken. Two large chambers tiled and wainscoted with wonderfully carved blackwood panels were apportioned as dining-hall and sitting-room for the English visitors. All the windows of the wing, many of them closely screened, looked on an inner courtyard which was bounded on two sides by other buildings of the Palace. The fourth side was divided off from another courtyard by a high blank wall pierced by a large gateway, the leaves of the gate hanging broken and useless from the posts.

Ida and Noreen were given rooms beside each other and were amused at the heterogeneous collection of odd pieces of furniture in them. The old four-posted beds with funereal canopies and moth-eaten curtains had probably been brought from England a hundred years before. In small chambers off their rooms, with marble walls and floors, and windows filled with thin slabs of alabaster carved in the most exquisite tracery as delicate as lace, galvanised iron tubs to be used as baths looked sadly out of place.

When they had freshened themselves up after their long motor drive they went down to the dining-hall, where lunch was to be served. And when she entered the room the first person that Noreen saw was Dermot, seated at a small table with Payne and Granger.

On his return from a secret excursion across the Bhutan border the Major had found awaiting him at Ranga Duar the official invitation of the Lalpuri Durbar. He was very much surprised at it; for he knew that the State had never encouraged visits from Europeans, and had, when possible, invariably refused admission to all except important British officials, who could not be denied. Such a thing as actually entertaining Englishmen of its own accord was unknown in its annals. So he stared at the large card printed in gold and embossed with the coat-of-arms of Lalpuri in colours, and wondered what motive lay behind the invitation. That it betokened a fresh move in the conspiracy he was certain; but be the motive what it might he was glad of the unexpected opportunity of visiting Lalpuri and meeting those whom he believed to be playing a leading part in the plot. So he promptly wrote an acceptance.

He reached the Palace only half an hour before Daleham's party arrived from another direction, and had just met his two planter friends when Noreen entered the room. He had not known that she was to be at Lalpuri. The three men rose and bowed to her, and Dermot looked to see if Charlesworth were with her. But only the two women and Daleham followed Chunerbutty as he led the way to a table at the far end of the room.

There were about twenty English guests altogether, eight or nine of whom were from the district in which Malpura was situated, the Rices among them. The rest were planters from other parts of the Duars, a few members of the Indian Civil Service or Public Works Departments, and a young Deputy Superintendent of Police from Jalpaiguri.

At Chunerbutty's table the party consisted of the Rices, one of the Civil Servants, the Dalehams, and Noreen's friend. The planter's wife neglected the man beside her to stare at Mrs. Smith, taking in every detail of her dress, while Ida chattered gaily to Fred, whose good looks had attracted her the moment that she first saw him on the platform of Jalpaiguri station. She was already apparently quite consoled for the loss of her Calcutta admirer.

Noreen sat pale and abstracted beside Chunerbutty, answering his remarks in monosyllables, eating nothing, and alleging a headache as an explanation of her mood. The unexpected sight of Dermot had shaken her, and she dreaded the moment when she must greet him. Yet she was anxious to witness his meeting with Ida, hoping that she might glean from it some idea of how matters really stood between them.

After *tiffin* a move was made into the long chamber arranged as the guests' lounge. Here introductions between those who had not previously known each other and meetings between old acquaintances took place; and with an inward shrinking Noreen saw Dermot approaching. She was astonished to observe that Ida's careless and indifferent greeting was responded to by him in a coldly courteous manner almost indicative of strong dislike. The girl wondered if they were both consummate actors. Dermot turned to her. He spoke in his usual pleasant and friendly manner; but she seemed to detect a trace of reserve that he had never showed before. She was almost too confused to reply to him and turned with relief to shake hands with Payne and Granger, who had come up with him.

Chunerbutty played the host well, introduced those who were strangers to each other, and saw that the Palace servants, who were unused to European habits, brought the coffee, liqueurs, and smokes to all the guests, where they gathered under the long punkah that swung lazily from the painted ceiling and barely stirred the heated air.

As soon as it was cool enough to drive out in the State carriages and motor-cars that waited in the outer courtyard, the afternoon was devoted to sight-seeing. Chunerbutty, in the leading car with Noreen and the District Superintendent of Police, acted as guide and showed them about the city. Dermot noted the lowering looks of many of the natives in the narrow streets, and overhead more than one muttered insult to the English race from men huddling against the houses to escape the carriages.

The visitors were invited by Chunerbutty to enter an ornate temple of Kali, in which a number of Hindu women squatted on the ground before a gigantic idol representing the goddess in whose honour the Puja festival is held. The image was that of a fierce-looking woman with ten arms, each hand holding a weapon, her right leg resting on a lion, her left on a buffalo-demon.

"I say, Chunerbutty, who's the lady?" asked Granger. "I can't say I like her looks."

"No, she certainly isn't a beauty," said the Brahmin with a contemptuous laugh. "Yet these superstitious fools believe in her, ignorant people that they are."

He indicated the female worshippers, who had been staring with malevolent curiosity at the English ladies, the first that most of them had ever seen. So these were the *mem-logue*, they whispered to each other, these shameless white women who went about openly with men and met all the world brazenly with unveiled countenances. And the whisperers modestly drew their *saris* before their own faces.

"She is the goddess Kali or Durga, the wife of Shiva, one of the Hindu Trinity. She is supposed to be the patron of smallpox and lots of other unpleasant things, so no wonder she is ugly," continued Chunerbutty.

"Oh, you have goddesses then in the Hindu religion," observed Ida carelessly.

"Yes, Mrs. Smith; but these are the sort we have in India," he answered with an unpleasant leer. "The English people are more fortunate, for they have you ladies."

The remark was one that would have gained him smiles and approbation from his female acquaintances in the Bayswater boarding-house, but Ida glared haughtily at him and most of the men longed to kick him.

Dreading a cutting and sarcastic speech from her friend, Noreen hurriedly interposed.

"Isn't the Puja festival in her honour, Mr. Chunerbutty?"

"Yes, Miss Daleham, it is. It is another of these silly superstitions of the Hindus that make one really ashamed of being an Indian. The festival is meant to commemorate the old lady's victory over a buffalo-headed demon. Hence the weird-looking beast under her left leg."

"And do these people really believe in that sort of rot?" asked Mrs. Rice.

"Oh, yes, lots of the ignorant, uneducated lower class do," replied the atheistical Brahmin. "Durga is the favourite deity. Her husband and Krishna and old Brahma are back numbers. The fact is that the common people are afraid of Kali. They think she can do them such a lot of harm."

"What does the festival consist of, old chap?" asked Daleham. "What do the Hindus do?"

"Well, the image is worshipped for nine days and then chucked into the water," replied the engineer. "Tomorrow, the fourth day, is the one on which the sacrifices are made - sheep, buck goats, and buffaloes are used. Their heads are cut off before this idol and their heads and blood are offered to it. Tomorrow you'll see the Rajah kill the bull that is to be the sacrifice. At least, he'll start the killing of it. Now, we'll go along back to the Palace."

The visitors' dinner that night was quite a magnificent affair. The catering for the time of their stay had been confided to an Italian firm in Calcutta. The cooking was excellent, but the waiting by the awkward Palace retainers was very bad. The food was eaten off the Rajah's State silver service, made in London for his father for the entertainment of a Viceroy. The wine was very good. So the guests enjoyed their meal, and most of them were quite prepared to think the Rajah a most excellent fellow when, at the conclusion of the meal, he entered the dining-room and came to the long table to propose and drink the health of the King-Emperor. He left the room immediately afterwards. This is the usual procedure on the part of Hindu rulers in India, since they are precluded by their religion and caste-customs from eating with Europeans.

After dinner the guests went to the lounge, where coffee was served. They broke up into groups or pairs and sat or stood about the room chatting. Mrs. Rice, who had been much impressed by Ida's appearance and expensive gowns, secured a chair beside her and endeavoured to monopolise her, despite many obvious snubs. At last Ida calmly turned her back on her and called Daleham to talk to her. Then the planter's wife espied Dermot sitting alone and pounced on him. He had tried to speak to Noreen after dinner, but it was so apparent that she wished to avoid him that he gave up the attempt. He endured Mrs. Rice's company with admirable resignation, but was thankful when the time for "good-night" came at last.

The men stayed up an hour or two later, and then after a final "peg" went off to bed. Dermot walked upstairs with Barclay, the young police officer, who was his nearest neighbour, although the Major's room was at the end of the building and separated from his by a long, narrow passage and several empty chambers.

CHAPTER XVI

THE PALACE OF DEATH

When they reached the door of the police officer's apartment Dermot wished him good-night and proceeded down the passage, which was lit only by a feeble lamp placed in a niche high up in the wall. He had to grope his way through the outer chambers by the aid of matches, and when he reached his room, was surprised to find it in darkness, for he had left a light burning in it. He struck more matches, and was annoyed to discover that his lamp had been taken away. Being very tired he felt inclined to undress and go to bed in the dark, but, suddenly remembering the small light in the passage, determined to fetch it. Making his way back to the passage he tried to take the little lamp down. But it was too high up, and the noise that he made in his efforts to reach it brought Barclay to his door.

When he heard of Dermot's difficulty he said:

"I'm not sleepy yet, Major, so I'll bring my lamp along to your room and smoke a cheroot while you undress. Then I'll go off with it as soon as you've turned in."

Dermot thanked him, and the young policeman went with him, carrying the lamp, which had a double wick and gave a good light. Putting it down on the dressing-table he lit a cheroot and proceeded to seat himself in a chair beside the bed. Like the room itself and the rest of the furniture, it was covered with dust.

"By George, what dirty quarters they've given you, sir," he exclaimed. "Just look at the floor. I'll bet it's never been swept since the Palace was built. The dust is an inch deep near the bed." He polished the seat of the chair carefully before he sat down.

The heat in the room was stifling, and the police officer, even in his white mess uniform, felt it acutely.

"By Jove, it's steamy tonight," he remarked, wiping his face.

"Yes, I hate October," replied Dermot. "It's the worst month in the year, I think. Its damp heat, when the rain is drying up out of the ground, is more trying than the worst scorching we get in May and June."

"Well, you don't seem to find it too hot, Major," said the other laughing. "It looks as if you'd got a hot-water bottle in the foot of your bed."

"Hot-water bottle? What do you mean?" asked Dermot in surprise, throwing the collar that he had just taken off on to the dressing-table and turning round.

"Why, don't you see? Under the clothes at the foot," said his companion, pointing with the Major's cane to a bulge in the thin blanket and sheet covering the bed. He got up and strode across to it. "What on earth have you got there? It does look - Oh, good heavens, keep back!" he cried suddenly.

Dermot was already bending over the bed, but the police officer pushed him forcibly back and snatched up the cane which he had laid down. Then, cautiously seizing the top of the blanket and sheet near the pillow, he whisked them off with a sudden vigorous jerk. At the spot where the bulge had betrayed it a black cobra, one of the deadliest snakes in India, lifted its head and a foot of its length from its shining coils.

The forked tongue darted and quivered incessantly, and the unwinking eyes glistened as with a loud hiss it raised itself higher and poised its head to strike.

Barclay struck it sharply with the cane, and it fell writhing on the bed, its spine broken. The coils wound and unwound vigorously, the tail convulsively lashing the sheet. He raised the stick to strike it again, but, paused with arm uplifted, for the snake could not move away or raise its head.

Seeing that it was powerless the young Superintendent swung round to Dermot.

"Have you a pistol, Major?" he whispered.

Without a word the soldier unlocked his despatch-box and took out a small automatic.

"Loaded?"

The soldier nodded.

"Give it to me."

Taking the weapon he tiptoed to the door, listened awhile, then opened it sharply. But there was no one there.

"Bring the lamp," he whispered.

Dermot complied, and together they searched the ante-rooms and passages. They were empty. Then they looked into the small room in which the zinc bath-tub stood. There was no one there.

The Deputy Superintendent closed the door again, and, as it had neither lock nor bolt, placed a heavy chair against it. Taking the lamp in his hand he bent down and carefully examined the dusty floor under and around the bed. Then he put down the lamp and drew Dermot into the centre of the room.

"Has your servant any reason to dislike you?" he asked in a low voice.

Dermot answered him in the same tone:

"I have not brought one with me."

The D.S.P. whistled faintly, then looked apprehensively round the room and whispered:

"Have you any enemies in the Palace or in Lalpuri?"

Dermot smiled.

"Very probably," he replied. Then in a low voice he continued: "Look here, Barclay, do you know anything of the state of affairs in this province? I mean, politically."

The police officer nodded.

"I do. I'm here in Lalpuri to try to find out things. The root of the trouble in Bengal is here."

"Then I can tell you that I have been sent on a special mission to the border and have come to this city to try to follow up a clue."

The D.S.P. drew a deep breath.

"That accounts for it. Look here, Major, I've seen this trick with the snake before. Not long ago I tried to hang the servant of a rich *bunniah* for murdering his master by means of it, but the Sessions Judge wouldn't convict him. If you look you'll see that that brute" - he pointed to the cobra writhing in agony on the bed and sinking its fangs into its own flesh - "never got up there by itself. It was put there. Otherwise it would have left a clear trail in the thick dust on the floor, but there isn't a sign."

Gordon Casserly

"Yes, I spotted that," said Dermot, lighting a cigarette over the lamp chimney. "I see the game. My lamp - which was here, for I dressed for dinner by its light - was taken away, so that I'd have to go to bed in the dark; and, by Jove, I very nearly did! Then I'd have kicked against the cobra as I got in, and been bitten. The lamp would have been put back in the morning before I was 'found.' Look here, Barclay, I owe you a lot. Without you I'd be dead in two hours."

"Or less. Sometimes the bite is fatal in forty minutes. Yes, there's no doubt of it, you'd have been done for. Lucky thing I hadn't gone to bed and heard you. Now, what'll we do with the brute?"

He looked at the writhing snake.

"Wait a minute. Where are the matches?"

He picked up a box from the dressing-table, moved the chair from the door and left the room. In a minute or two he returned, carrying an old porcelain vase, and shut the door.

"I found this stuck away with a lot of rubbish in the outer room," he said. "I don't suppose any one will miss it."

Dermot watched him with curiosity as he placed the vase on the floor near the bed and picked up the cane. Putting its point under the cobra he lifted the wriggling body on the stick and with some difficulty dropped the snake into the vase, where they heard its head striking the sides with furious blows.

"I hope it won't break the damned thing just when I'm carrying it," he said, regarding the vase anxiously.

"What are you doing that for?" asked Dermot.

The police officer lowered his voice.

"Well, Major, we don't want these would-be murderers to

know how their trick failed. That's the reason I didn't pound the brute to a jelly on the bed, for it would have made such a mess on the sheet. Now there isn't a speck on it. I'll take the vase with me into my room and finish the cobra off. In the morning I'll get rid of its body somehow. When these devils find tomorrow that you're not dead, they'll be very puzzled. Now, the question is, what are you going to do?"

"Going to bed," answered Dermot, continuing to undress. "There's nothing else to be done at this hour, is there?"

The police officer looked at him with admiration.

"By George, sir, you've got pluck. If it were I, I'd want to sit up all night with a pistol."

"Not you. Otherwise you wouldn't be in the place at all. Besides you are qualifying for delicate little attentions like this." And Dermot flicked the ash of his cigarette into the vase in which the cobra still writhed and twisted.

"Oh, well, they haven't tumbled to me yet," said the young police officer, making light of his own courage. "I suppose you won't make any fuss about this?"

"Of course not. We've got no proof against any one."

"But do you think it wise for you to stay on here, sir? They'll only try again."

Dermot lit a fresh cigarette.

"Well, it can't be helped. It's all in the day's work. I'm due to stay here two days more, and I'm damned if I'm going to move before then. As you know, it doesn't do to show these people the white feather. Besides, I'm rather interested to see what they'll try next."

"You're a cool hand, Major. Well, since you look at it that

way, there's nothing more to be said. I see you're ready for bed, so I'll take my lamp and bit of pottery, and trek."

"Oh, just one moment, Barclay." Dermot sank his voice. "Did you notice the Rajah's catch-'em-alive-ohs on sentry?"

"You mean his soldiers? No, I can't say I did."

"Well, just have a look at them tomorrow. I want to have a talk with you about them."

"I'd like to strip these bed-clothes off. I don't fancy them after the snake. Luckily it's so hot that one doesn't want even a sheet tonight. Let me see if there's another cobra under the pillow. It's said that they generally go about in pairs." He turned over the pillow. "No; that's all right."

"Hold on a minute," whispered Barclay, raising the lamp above his head with his left hand. "Let's see if there's any concealed entrance to the room. I daresay these old palaces are full of secret passages and masked doors."

He sounded the walls and floors and examined them carefully.

"Seems all right. I'll be off now. Good-night, Major. I hope you'll not be disturbed. If there's any trouble fire a shot and I'll be here in two shakes. I've got a pistol, and by Jingo I'll have it handy tonight. Keep yours ready, too."

"I shall. Now a thousand thanks for your help, Barclay," said the soldier, shaking his friend's hand.

Then he closed the door behind the police officer and by the light of a match piled chairs against it. Then he lay down on the bed, put the pistol under the edge of the mattress and ready to his hand, and fell asleep at once.

Early in the morning he was aroused by a vigorous knocking and heard Barclay's voice outside the door.

"Are you all right, Major?" it said.

"Yes, thanks. Good-morning," replied the soldier. "Come in. No, wait a minute."

He jumped out of bed and removed the barricade. Barclay entered in his pyjamas. Lowering his voice he said:

"Anything happen during the night?"

"I don't think so. I slept soundly and heard nothing. You're up early," replied the soldier, picking up the blankets and sheets from the floor and spreading them carelessly on the bed to make it look as if he had used them.

"Yes; those infernal birds make such a confounded row. It's like being in an aviary," said Barclay.

Dermot threw open the wooden shutters. Outside the window was a small balcony. On the roofs and verandahs of the Palace scores of grey-hooded crows were perched, filling the air with discordant sounds. Up in the pale blue sky the wheeling hawks whistled shrilly. Down in the courtyard below yellow-beaked *mynas* chattered volubly.

"Don't they make a beastly row? How is a fellow to sleep?" grumbled Barclay. "Look at that cheeky beggar."

A hooded crow perched on the railing of the balcony and, apparently resenting his remarks, cawed defiantly at him. The Deputy Superintendent picked up one of Dermot's slippers and was about to hurl it at the bird, when a voice from the doorway startled him.

"*Char, Huzoor!* (Tea, Your Excellency!)"

He looked round. One of the Palace servants stood at the door holding a tray containing tea and buttered toast.

Dermot directed the man to put the tray on the dressing-table, and when the servant had salaamed and left the room, he walked over to it and looked at the food.

"Now, is it safe to eat that?" he said. "I've no fear of the grub they serve in the dining-hall, for they wouldn't dare to poison us all. But somehow I have my doubts about any nice little meal prepared exclusively for me."

"I think you're right there, Major," said Barclay, who was sitting on the edge of the bed.

"We'll see. There isn't the usually handy pi-dog to try it on. But we'll make use of our noisy friend here. He won't be much loss to the world if it poisons him," and Dermot broke off a piece of the toast and threw it on the floor of the balcony. The crow stopped his cawing, cocked his head on one side, and eyed the tempting morsel. Buttered toast did not often come his way. He dropped down on to the balcony floor, hopped over to the toast, pecked at it, picked it up in his strong beak, and flew with it to the roof of the building opposite. In silence the two men watched him devour it.

"That seems all right, Major," said the police officer. "You've made him your friend for life. He's coming back for more."

The crow perched on the rail again and cawed loudly.

"Oh, shut up, you greedy bird. Here's another bit for you. That's all you'll have. I want the rest myself," said Dermot, laughing. He broke off another piece and threw it out on to the balcony.

The crow looked at it, ruffled its feathers, shook itself - and then fell heavily to the floor of the balcony and lay still.

"Good heavens! What an escape!" ejaculated Barclay, suddenly pale.

The two men stared at each other and the dead bird in silence. Then Dermot murmured:

"This is getting monotonous. Hang it! They *are* in a hurry. Why, they couldn't even know whether I was alive or not. If the snake trick had come off, I'd be a corpse now and this nice little meal would have been wasted. Really, they are rather crowding things on me."

"They're taking no chances, the devils," said the younger man, who was more upset by the occurrence than his companion.

"Well, I'll have to do without my *chota hazri*; and I do like a cup of tea in the morning," said the soldier; and he began to shave. Glancing out of the window he continued: "They've got a fine day for the show anyway."

Barclay sprang up from the chair on which he had suddenly sat down. His nerve was shaken by the two attempts on his companion's life.

"Damn them and their shows, the infernal murderers," he muttered savagely, and rushed out of the room.

"Amen!" said Dermot, as he lathered his face. Death had been near him too often before for him to be disturbed now. So he went on shaving.

Before he left the room he poured tea into the cup on the tray and got rid of the rest of the toast, to make it appear that he had freely partaken of the meal. He wrapped up the dead crow in paper and locked it in his despatch-case, until he could dispose of it that evening after dark.

Noreen had slept little during the night. All through the weary hours of darkness she had tossed restlessly on her bed, tortured by thoughts that revolved in monotonous circles around Dermot. What was she to believe of him? What were the relations between him and her friend? He had seemed very cold to Ida when they met and had avoided her all day. And she did not appear to mind. What had happened between them? Had they quarrelled? It did not disturb Ida's rest, for the girl could hear her regular breathing all night long, the door between their rooms being open. Was it possible that she and Dermot were acting indifference to deceive the people around them?

Only towards morning did Noreen fall into a troubled, broken sleep, and she dreamt that the man she loved was in great danger. She woke up in a fright, then dozed again. She was hollow-eyed and unrefreshed when a bare-footed native "boy" knocked at her door and left a tray with her *chota hazri* at it. She could not eat, but she drank the tea thirstily.

Pleading fatigue she remained in her room all the morning and refused to go down to *tiffin*. When the other guests were at lunch in the dining-hall a message was brought her that Chunerbutty begged to see her urgently. She went down to the lounge, where he was waiting. Struck by her want of colour, he enquired somewhat tenderly what ailed her. She replied impatiently that she was only fatigued by the previous day's journey, and asked rather crossly why he wanted to see her.

"I have something nice for you," he said smiling. "Something I was to give you."

Glancing around to make sure that they were unobserved, he opened a sandalwood box that he held in his hand and took out a large, oval leather case, which he offered to her.

"What is this?" she asked in surprise.

"Open it and see," he replied.

The girl did so unsuspectingly. It was lined with blue velvet, and resting in it was a necklace of diamonds in quaint and massive gold setting, evidently the work of a native jeweller. The stones, though badly cut, were very large and flashed and sparkled with coloured fires. The ornament was evidently extremely valuable. Noreen stared at it and then at Chunerbutty in surprise.

"What does this mean?" she demanded, an ominous ring in her voice.

"Just a little present to you from a friend," replied the Hindu, evidently thinking that the girl was pleased with the magnificent gift.

"For me? Are these stones real?" she asked quietly.

"Rather. Why, that necklace must be worth thousands of pounds. The fact is that it's a little present from the Rajah, who admires you awfully. He -"

Noreen's eyes blazed, and she was on the point of bursting into angry words; but, controlling herself with an effort, she thrust the case back into his hands and said coldly:

"You know little of English women, Mr. Chunerbutty, if you think that they accept presents like that from strangers. This may be the Rajah's ignorance, but it looks more like insolence."

She turned to go; but, stopping her, he said:

"Oh, but you don't understand. He's a great friend of mine and he knows that I'm awfully fond of you, little girl. So he's ready to do anything for us and give me a -"

She walked past him, her eyes blazing with anger, with so resolute an air that he drew back and watched her go. She went straight to her room and remained there until Ida came to tell her that it was time to dress for the celebration of the Puja festival.

* * * * *

In the outer courtyard of the Palace six of the Rajah's State elephants, their tusks gilded and foreheads gaudily painted, caparisoned with rich velvet housings covered with heavy gold embroidery trailing almost to the ground, bearing on their backs gold or silver howdahs fashioned in the shape of temples, awaited the European guests. Chunerbutty, when allotting positions as Master of Ceremonies, took advantage of his position to contrive that Noreen should accompany him on the elephant on which he was to lead the line. The girl discovered too late that they were to be alone on it, except for the *mahout* on its neck. Dermot and Barclay managed to be together on another animal.

When all were in position in the howdahs, to which they climbed by ladders, the gates were thrown open, and through a mob of salaaming retainers the elephants emerged with stately tread on the great square in front of the Palace and proceeded through the city. The houses were gaily decorated. Flags and strips of coloured cloth fluttered from every building; gaudy carpets and embroideries hung from the innumerable balconies and windows. The elephants could scarcely force a passage through the narrow streets, so crowded were they with swarms of men, women, and children in holiday attire, all going in one direction. Their destination was the park of the *Moti Mahal* or Pearl Palace, the Rajah's summer residence outside the walls of the city.

There the enormous crowd was kept back by red-robed retainers armed with *tulwars* - native curved swords - leaving clear a wide stretch of open ground, in the centre of which on a gigantic altar was the image of the Goddess Kali. Before it a magnificent bull was firmly secured by chains and ropes to stout posts sunk deep in the earth. The animal's head drooped and it could hardly stand up, for it had been heavily drugged for the day's ceremony and was scarcely conscious.

The Rajah's army was drawn up in line fronting the altar, but some distance away from it. Two old muzzle-loading nine-pounder guns, their teams of powerful bullocks lying contentedly behind on the grass, formed the right of the line. Then came the cavalry, consisting of twenty *sowars* on squealing white stallions with long tails dyed red. Left of them was the infantry, two hundred sepoys in shakoes, red coatees, white trousers, and bare feet, leaning on long percussion-capped muskets with triangular bayonets.

Shortly after the Europeans had arrived and their elephants taken up their position on one side of the ground, cheering announced the coming of the Rajah. The cannons were discharged by slow matches and the infantrymen, raising their muskets, fired a ragged volley into the air. Then towards the altar of Kali the Rajah was seen approaching in a long gilded car shaded by a canopy of cloth-of-gold and drawn by an enormous elephant, richly caparisoned. Two gold-laced, scarlet-clad servants were perched on the back of the car, waving large peacock-feather fans over their monarch. A line of carriages followed, conveying the *Dewan*, the Durbar officials, the Ministers of the State and the leading nobles of Lalpuri. After the first volley, which scattered the horses of the cavalry, the artillery and infantry loaded and fired independently as fast as their antiquated weapons permitted, until the air was filled with smoke and the acrid smell of gunpowder.

The Rajah, hemmed in by spearmen with levelled points and followed by all his suite with drawn swords, timidly approached the bull, *tulwar* in hand. The animal was too dazed to lift its head. The Rajah raised his gleaming blade and struck at the nape of its neck, and at the same moment two swordsmen hamstrung it. Immediately the *Dewan*, Ministers, and nobles crowded in and hacked at the wretched beast as it lurched and fell heavily to the ground. The warm blood spurted out in jets and covered the officials and nobles as they cut savagely at the feebly struggling carcase, and the red liquid splashed the Rajah as he stood gloating over the gaping wounds and the sufferings of the poor sacrifice, his heavy face lit up by a ghastly grin of delight.

The horrible spectacle shocked and disgusted the European

spectators. Ida nearly fainted, and Mrs. Rice turned green. Noreen shuddered at Chunerbutty's fiendish and bestial expression, as he leaned forward in the howdah, his face working convulsively, his eyes straining to lose no detail of the repulsive sight. He was enjoying it, like the excited, enthralled mobs of Indians of all ages around, who pressed forward, gradually pushing back the line of retainers struggling to keep the ground.

Suddenly the swarming thousands broke loose. They surged madly forward, engulfing and sweeping the soldiers along with them, and rushed on the dying bull. They fought savagely to reach it. Those who succeeded threw themselves on the quivering carcase and with knives or bare hands tore pieces of still living flesh from it and thrust them into their mouths. Then, blooded to the eyes, they raised their reddened arms aloft, while from thousands of throats rang out the fanatical cry:

"*Kali Ma ki jai!* (Victory to Mother Kali!)"

They surged around the altar. The Rajah was knocked down and nearly trampled on by the maddened, hysterical crowd. *Dewan*, Ministers, officials, guards were hustled and swept aside. The cavalry commander saw his ruler's danger and collecting a dozen of his *sowars* charged the religious-mad mob and rescued the Rajah from his dangerous position, riding down and sabring men, women, and children, the fierce stallions savaging everyone within reach with their bared teeth.

Chunerbutty, in whom old racial instincts were rekindled, had scarcely been able to restrain himself from climbing down and joining in the frenzied rush on the bull. But the turn of events sobered him and induced him to listen at last to Noreen's entreaties and angry demands from the Englishmen who bade him order the *mahouts* to take the visitors away from the horrible spectacle. As they left they saw the Rajah's golden chariot and the carriages of the officials being driven helter-skelter across the grass with their blood-stained and terrified occupants. And the madly fanatical crowds surged wildly around the altar, while their cries to Kali rent the air.

The elephants lumbered swiftly in file through the deserted city, for it was now emptied of its inhabitants. Merchants, traders, shopkeepers, workers, harlots, and criminals, all had flocked to the *Moti Mahal* to witness the sacrifice.

As they entered the Palace gates the *mahout* of the animal carrying Barclay, Dermot, and two planters called to a native standing idly in the courtyard:

"Why wert thou not out with thy elephant, Ebrahim?"

The man addressed, a grey-bearded Mussulman, replied:

"Shiva-*ji* is bad today. I fear him greatly."

"Is it the madness of the *dhantwallah*?"

"It is the madness."

And the speaker cracked his finger-joints to avert evil luck.

Dinner was not a very jovial meal among the English guests that night. Much to their relief the Rajah did not come in to them. The ladies retired early to their rooms, and the men were not long in following their example.

Barclay and Dermot, who were the only occupants of the floor on which their rooms were situated - it was the top one of the wing - went upstairs together. At the Deputy Superintendent's door a man squatted and, as they approached, rose, and saluted them in military fashion. It was Barclay's police orderly.

"Hast got it?" asked his master in the vernacular.

"I have got it, Sahib. It is here," and the man placed a small covered basket in his hands.

"*Bahut atcha. Ruksat hai*" (very good. You have leave to go), said his officer, using the ordinary Indian formula for dismissing a subordinate.

"Salaam, Sahib."

The orderly saluted and went away down the passage.

"Wait a moment, Major; I'm going with you to your room," said the Deputy Superintendent, opening his door. "Do you mind bringing my light along, as yours may be gone again. My hands are full with this basket."

When they reached Dermot's apartment they found a lamp burning feebly in it, smoking, and giving little light.

"Looks as if there's a fresh game on tonight," said Dermot in a low voice. "This is not the lamp I had before dinner. That was a large and brilliant one. I'm glad we brought yours along."

"Barricade the door, Major," whispered Barclay. "Are the shutters closed? Yes; that's all right."

"What have you got in that mysterious basket?" his companion asked.

"You'll see presently."

He set it down on the floor and raised the lid. A small, sharp-muzzled head with fierce pink eyes popped up and looked about suspiciously. Then its owner climbed cautiously out on to the floor. It was a slim, long-bodied little animal like a ferret, with a long, furry tail.

"Hullo! A mongoose? You think they'll try the same trick again?" asked Dermot.

He glanced at the bed and picked up his cane.

"Just stand still, Major, and watch. If there's anything in the snake line about our young friend here will attend to it."

The mongoose trotted forward for a few steps, then sat down and scratched itself. It rose, yawned, stretched its legs, and looked up at the two men, betraying no fear of them. Then it lifted its sharp nose into the air, sniffed, and pattered about the room, stopping to smell the legs of the dressing-table and a cap of Dermot's lying on the floor. It investigated several rat-holes at the bottom of the walls and approached the bed. Under it a pair of the soldier's slippers were lying. The mongoose, passing by them, turned to smell them. Suddenly it sprang back, leaping a couple of feet into the air. When it touched the floor it crouched with bared teeth, the hair on its back bristling and its tail fluffed out until it was bigger than the body of the fierce little animal.

"By Jove, it has found something!" exclaimed Barclay.

The two men leant forward and watched intently. The mongoose approached the slippers again in a series of bounds, jumped around them, crouched, and then sprang into the air again.

Suddenly there was a rush and a scurry. The mongoose had pounced on one slipper and was shaking it savagely, beating it on the floor, rolling over and over and leaping into the air with it. Its movements were so rapid that for a few moments the watchers could distinguish nothing in the miniature cyclone of slipper and ball of fluffy hair inextricably mingled. Then there was a pause. The mongoose stood still, then backed away with stiffened legs, its sharp teeth fixed in the neck of a small snake about ten inches long, which it was trying to drag out of the slipper.

"Good heavens! This is worse than last night," cried Barclay. "It's a *karait.*"

This reptile is almost more poisonous than a cobra, and, as it is thin and rarely exceeds twelve inches in length, it can hide anywhere and is an even deadlier menace in a house.

The mongoose backed across the room, dragging the snake and with it the slipper.

"Why the deuce doesn't it pull the *karait* out?" said Dermot, bending down to look more closely, as the mongoose paused. "By George! Look at this, Barclay. The snake's fastened to the inside of the slipper by a loop and a bit of thin wire."

"What a devilish trick!" cried Barclay.

"Well, I hope that concludes the entertainment for tonight," said Dermot. "Enough is as good as a feast."

When next morning the servant brought in his tray, Dermot was smoking a cigarette in an easy chair, and he fancied that there was a scared expression in the man's eyes, as the fellow looked covertly at the slippers on the Major's feet.

CHAPTER XVII

A TRAP

In the forenoon of the fifth day of the Durga-Puja Festival the *Dewan* and Chunerbutty sat on the thick carpet of the Rajah's apartment, which was in that part of the Palace facing the wing given up to the visitors. It formed one of the sides of the square surrounding the paved courtyard below, which was rarely entered. Only one door led into it from the buildings which lined it on three sides, a door under the Rajah's suite of apartments.

That potentate was sprawling on a pile of soft cushions, glaring malevolently at his Chief Minister, whom he hated and feared.

"Curses on thee, *Dewan-ji!*" he muttered, turning uneasily and groaning with the pain of movement. For he was badly bruised, sore, and shaken, from his treatment by the crowd on the previous day.

"Why on me, O Maharaj?" asked the *Dewan*, looking at him steadily and with hardly-veiled contempt.

"Because thine was the idea of this foolish celebration yesterday. Mother Durga was angry with me for introducing this foreign way of worship," answered the superstitious atheist, conveniently forgetting that the idea was his own. "It will cost me large sums to these greedy priests, if she is not to punish me further."

"Not for that reason, but for another, is the Holy Mother enraged, O Maharaj," replied his Minister. "For the lack of a sweeter sacrifice than we offered her yesterday."

"What is that?" demanded the Rajah suspiciously. He distrusted his *Dewan* more than any one else in his service.

"Canst thou ask? Thou who bearest on thy forehead the badge of the Saktas?"

"Thou meanest a human sacrifice?"

"I do."

"I have given Durga many," grumbled the Rajah. "But if she be greedy, let her have more. There are girls in my *zenana* that I would gladly be rid of."

"The Holy Mother demands a worthier offering than some wanton that thou hast wearied of."

Chunerbutty spoke for the first time.

"She wants the blood of one of the accursed race; of a *Feringhi*; of this soldier and spy."

The Rajah shifted uneasily on his cushions. He hated but he feared the white men, and he had not implicit faith in the *Dewan's* talk of their speedy overthrow.

"Mother Durga has rejected him," he said. "Have ye not all tried to slay him and failed?"

The *Dewan* nodded his head slowly and stared at the carpet.

"There is some strange and evil influence that sets my plans at naught."

"The gods, if there be gods as you Brahmins say, protect him. I think evil will come to us if we harm him. And can we? Did he not lie down with the hooded death itself, a cobra, young, active, full of venom, and rise unhurt?"

"True. But perhaps the snake had escaped from the bed before the *Feringhi* entered it," said the *Dewan* meditatively.

"To guard against that, did they not fasten the *karait* in his shoe?"

"He may have discovered it in time," said the engineer. "Englishmen fear snakes greatly and always look out for them."

"Ha! and did he not eat and drink the poisoned meal prepared for him by our skilfullest physician?"

There was no answer to this. The mystery of Dermot's escape from death was beyond their understanding.

"There is certainly something strange about him," said Chunerbutty. "At least, so it is reported in our district, though to me he seems a fool. But there all races and castes fear him. Curious tales are told of him. Some say that *Gunesh*, the Elephant-headed One, protects him. Others hold that he is *Gunesh* himself. Can it be so?"

The *Dewan* smiled.

"Since when hast thou believed in the gods again?" he asked.

"Well, it is hard to know what is true or false. If there be no gods, perhaps there are devils. My Christian friends are more impressed by the latter."

The Rajah shook his head doubtfully.

"Perhaps he is a devil. Who knows? They told me that he summoned a host of devils in the form of elephants to slay my soldiers. Pah! it is all nonsense. There are no such things."

With startling distinctness the shrill trumpeting of an elephant rang through the room.

"Mother Kali preserve me!" shrieked the superstitious Rajah, flinging himself in terror on his face. "That was no mortal elephant. Was it *Gunesh* that spoke?" He lifted his head timidly. "It is a warning. Spare the *Feringhi*. Let him go."

"Spare him? Knowest thou, O Maharaj, that the girl thou dost desire loves him? But an hour ago I heard her tell him that she wished to speak with him alone," said Chunerbutty.

"Alone with him? The shameless one! Curses on him! Let him die," cried the jealous Rajah, his fright forgotten.

The *Dewan* smiled.

"There was no need to fear the cry of that elephant," he said. "It was your favourite, Shiva-*ji*. He is seized with the male-madness. They have penned him in the stone-walled enclosure yonder. He killed his *mahout* this morning."

"Killed Ebrahim? Curse him! If he had not cost me twenty thousand rupees I would have him shot," growled the Rajah savagely. "Killed Ebrahim, my best *mahout*? Why could he not have slain this accursed *Feringhi* if he had the blood-lust on him?"

"In the name of Siva the Great One!" exclaimed the *Dewan* piously. "It is a good thought. Listen to me, Maharaj! Listen, thou renegade" (this to Chunerbutty, who dared not resent the old man's insults).

The three heads came together.

* * * * *

After lunch that day Dermot sat smoking in his room. Although it had no punkah and the heat was great, he had escaped to it from the crowded lounge to be able to think quietly. But his thoughts were not of the attempts on his life and the probability that they would be repeated. His mind was filled with Noreen to the temporary exclusion of all other subjects. She puzzled him. He had supposed her engaged, or practically engaged, to Charlesworth. Yet she had come away from Darjeeling at its gayest time and here seemed to be engrossed with Chunerbutty. She was always with him or he with her. He never left her side. She sat by him at every meal. She had gone alone with him in his howdah to the *Moti Mahal*, when every other elephant had carried more than two persons. He knew that she had always regarded the Hindu as a friend, but he had not thought that she was so attracted to him. Certainly now she did not appear content away from him. What would Charlesworth, who hated natives, think of it?

As for himself, their former friendship seemed dead. He had naturally been hurt when she had not waited in the hotel at Darjeeling, though she knew that he was coming to say good-bye to her. But perhaps Charlesworth had kept her out, so he could not blame her. But why had she deliberately avoided him here in the Palace? What was the reason of her unfriendliness? Yet that morning in the lounge after breakfast he had chanced to pass her where she stood beside Chunerbutty, who was speaking to a servant. She had detained him for a moment to tell him that she wished to see him alone some time, for she wanted his advice. She seemed rather mysterious about it, and he remembered that she had spoken in a low tone, as if she did not desire any one else to hear what she was saying.

What did it all mean? Well, if he could help her with advice or anything else he would. He had not realised how fond he was of her until this estrangement between them had arisen.

As he sat puzzling over the problem the servant who waited on him entered the room and salaamed.

Gordon Casserly

"*Ghurrib Parwar!* (Protector of the Poor.) I bring a message for Your Honour. The English missie *baba* sends salaams and wishes to speak with you."

Dermot sprang up hastily.

"Where is she, Rama? In the lounge?"

"No, *Huzoor.* The missie *baba* is in the Red Garden."

"Where is that?"

"It is the Rajah's own private garden, through there." The servant pointed down to the gateway in the high wall of the courtyard below. He had opened the shutter of the window by which they were standing. "I will guide Your Honour. We must go through that door over there under His Highness's apartments."

"*Bahut atcha*, Rama. I will come with you. Give me my *topi*," cried Dermot, feeling light-hearted all at once. Perhaps the misunderstanding between Noreen and him would be cleared up now. He took his sun-hat from the man and followed him out of the room.

* * * * *

Noreen was greatly perplexed about the insult, as she considered it, of the Rajah's offer of the necklace. She feared to tell her brother, who might be angry with her for suspecting his friend of condoning an impertinence to her. Equally she felt that she could not confide in Ida or any one else, lest she should be misjudged and thought to have encouraged the engineer and his patron. To whom could she turn, sure of not being misunderstood? If only Dermot had remained her friend!

She was torn with longings to know the truth about his relations with Ida. The uncertainty was unbearable. That morning in her room she had boldly attacked Ida and asked her frankly. The other woman made light of the whole affair, pretended that Noreen had misunderstood her on that night in Darjeeling, and laughed at the idea of any one imagining that she had ever been in love with Dermot.

The girl was more puzzled than ever. Her heart ached for an hour or two alone with her one-time friend of the forest. O to be out with him on Badshah in the silent jungle, no matter what dangers encircled them! Perhaps there the cloud between them would vanish. But could she not speak to him here in the Palace? He seemed to be no longer fascinated with Ida, if indeed he ever had been. She could tell him of the Rajah's insult. He would advise her what to do, for she was sure that he would not misjudge her. And perhaps - who knew? - her confiding in him might break down the wall that separated them. She forgot that it had been built by her own resentment and anger, and that she had eluded his attempts to approach her. Even now she felt that she could not speak to him before others.

Growing desperate, she had that morning snatched at the opportunity to ask him for an interview. Chunerbutty, who seemed always to cling to her now with the persistence of a leech, had as usual been with her, but his attention had been distracted from her for a moment. She hoped that the Hindu had not overheard her. Yet what did it matter if he had? Dermot had understood and nodded, as he passed on with the old, friendly look in his eyes. Perhaps all would come right.

She had seen him leave the lounge after lunch, but she remained there confident that he would return. She felt she could not talk to the others so she withdrew to a table near one of the shuttered windows and pretended to read the newspapers on it.

Payne was there, deep in the perusal of an article in an English journal on the disturbed state of India. Mrs. Rice, impervious to snubs, was trying to impress the openly bored Ida with accounts of the gay and fashionable life of Balham. The men

Gordon Casserly

were scattered about the room in groups, some discussing in low tones the occurrences of the day before at the *Moti Mahal*, others talking of the illuminations and fireworks which were to wind up their entertainment in Lalpuri on this the last night of their stay. For all were leaving on the morrow.

Suddenly there was a wild outcry outside. Loud cries, the shouts of men, the terrifying trumpeting of an elephant, resounded through the courtyard below and echoed weirdly from the walls of the buildings. A piercing shriek of agony rang high above the tumult of sound and chilled the blood of the listeners in the lounge.

Payne tore fiercely at the stiff wooden shutters of the window near him, which led out to the long balcony. Suddenly they burst open and he sprang out.

"Good God!" he cried in horror. "Look! Look! Dermot's done for!"

*　*　*　*　*

The soldier had followed Rama, who led him through an unfamiliar part of the Palace along low passages, down narrow winding staircases, through painted rooms, in some of which female garments flung carelessly on the cushions seemed to indicate that they were passing through a portion of the *zenana*. Finally they reached a marble-paved hall on the ground-floor, where two attendants, the first persons whom they had seen on their way, lounged near a small door. They were evidently the porters and appeared to expect them, for they opened the door at Rama's approach. Through it Dermot followed his guide out into the courtyard on which he had often looked from the balcony of his room. He looked up at the lounge, two stories above his head, its long casements shuttered against the heat. Then he noticed that in none of the buildings surrounding the court were there any windows lower than the second story, and the only entrance into it from the Palace was the small door through which he had just passed.

Almost at the moment he stepped into the courtyard a familiar sound greeted his ears. It was the trumpeting of an elephant. But there was a strange note of rage and excitement in it, and he thought of the remarks of the *mahouts* the previous day on the return from the *Moti Mahal*. Probably the *must* elephant of which they spoke was chained somewhere close by.

As he crossed the courtyard he chanced to glance up at the shuttered windows of the apartments which he had been told were occupied by the Rajah. At that moment one of them was opened and a white cloth waved from it by an unseen hand. He wondered was it a signal. He stooped to fasten a bootlace, and Rama, who was making for the gateway in the high wall forming the fourth side of the courtyard, called impatiently to him to hasten. The servant's tone was impertinent, and Dermot looked up in surprise.

Then suddenly Hell broke loose. From the direction in which they were proceeding came fierce shouts of men, yells of terror, and the angry trumpeting of an elephant mingled with the groaning of iron dragged over stone and the crashing of splintered wood. Rama, who was a few yards ahead, turned and ran past the white man, his face livid. Dermot looked after him in surprise. The man had dashed back to the little door and was beating on it madly with his fists. It was opened to admit him and then hastily closed. The soldier heard the rusty bolts grinding home in their sockets.

Scenting danger and fearing a trap he stood still in the middle of the courtyard.

The uproar continued and drew nearer. Suddenly it was dominated by a blood-curdling shriek of agony. Through the wide gateway he saw five or six men fleeing across the farther courtyard, which was surrounded by a high wall. Behind them rushed a huge tusker elephant, ears and tail cocked, eyes aflame with rage. He overtook one man, struck him down with his trunk, trod him to pulp, and then pursued the others. Some of them, crazed with terror, tried to climb the walls. The savage

Gordon Casserly

brute struck them down one after another, gored them or trampled them to death.

Three terrified wretches fled through the gateway into the courtyard in which Dermot was standing. One stumbled and the elephant caught him up. The demented man turned on it and tried to beat it off with his bare hands. With a scream of fury the maddened beast drove his blood-stained tusk into the wretch's body, pitched him aloft, then hurled him to the ground and gored him again and again. The dying shriek that burst from the labouring lungs turned Dermot's blood cold. The body was kicked, trampled on, and then torn limb from limb.

The two other men had dashed wildly across the courtyard. One reached the small door and was beating madly on it with bleeding knuckles, but it remained implacably closed. The other, driven mad by fear, was running round and round the courtyard like a caged animal, stopping occasionally to raise imploring hands and eyes to the windows of the Palace, which were now filled with spectators. Even the roofs were crowded with natives looking down on the tragedy being enacted below.

Dermot realised that he had been trapped. There was no escape. He looked up at the Rajah's windows. One had been pushed open, and he thought that he could see the *Dewan* and his master watching him. He determined that he would not afford them the gratification of seeing him run round and round the walls of the courtyard like a rat in a trap until death overtook him. So, when the elephant at last drew off from its victim and stood irresolute for a moment, he turned to face it.

It seemed to him that he heard his voice called, faintly and from far away, but all his faculties were intent on watching the death that approached him in such hideous guise. Dermot's thoughts flew to Badshah for a moment, but swung back to centre on the coming annihilation. With flaming eyes, trunk curled, and head thrown up, the elephant charged.

For one brief instant the man felt an insane desire to flee but, mastering it, he faced the on-rushing brute. A minute more, and all would be over. The soldier was unconscious of the shouts that rent the air, of the spectators crowding the balconies and windows. He felt perfectly cool now and had but one regret - that he had not been able to see Noreen again, as she had wished, before he died.

He drew a deep breath, his last perhaps before Death reached him, and took a step forward to meet his doom.

But at his movement a miracle happened. Not five yards from him the charging elephant suddenly tried to check its rush, flung all its weight back and, unable to halt, slid forward with stiffened fore-legs over the paving-stones. When at last it stopped one tusk was actually touching the man. Tail, ears, and trunk drooped, and it backed with every evidence of terror. Some instinct had warned it at the last moment that this man was sacred to the mammoth tribe.

Like a flash enlightenment came to Dermot. Once again a mysterious power had saved him. The elephant knew and feared him. Yet he seemed as one in a dream. He looked up at the native portion of the Palace and became aware of the spectators on the roofs, the staring faces at the windows, the eyes of the women peering at him through the latticed casements of the *zenana*. The Rajah and the *Dewan*, all caution forgotten in their excitement, had thrown open the shutters from behind which they had hoped to witness his death, and were leaning out in full view.

Dermot laughed grimly, and the thought came to him to impress these treacherous foes more forcibly. He walked towards the shrinking elephant, raised his hand, and commanded it to kneel. The animal obeyed submissively. The soldier swung himself on to its neck, and the animal rose to its feet again.

He guided it across the courtyard until it stood under the window from which the Rajah and the *Dewan* stared down at him in amazement and superstitious dread. Then he said to the animal:

"*Salaam kuro!* (Salute!)"

It raised its trunk and trumpeted in the royal salutation. With a mocking smile, Dermot lifted his hat to the shrinking pair of murderers and turned the elephant away.

Then for the first time he became aware that the balcony of the lounge was crowded with his fellow-countrymen. Ida and Mrs. Rice were sobbing hysterically on each other's shoulders. Noreen, clinging to her brother, whose arm was about her, was staring down at him with a set, white face. And as he looked up and saw them the men went mad. They burst into a roar of cheering, of greeting, and applause that drove the Rajah and his Minister into hiding again, for the shouts had something of menace in them.

Dermot took off his hat in acknowledgment of the cheers and, seeing the Hindu engineer shrinking behind the others with an expression of amazed terror on his face, called to him:

"Would you kindly send one of your friends to open the door, Mr. Chunerbutty? It seems to have got shut by some unfortunate accident."

He brought the elephant to its knees and dismounted. Then as it rose he pointed to the gateway and said in the *mahout's* tongue:

"Return to your stall."

The animal walked away submissively. The two surviving natives shrank against the buildings in deadly fear, but the animal disappeared quietly.

Dermot went to the door and waited. Soon he heard the key turned in the lock and the rusty bolts drawn back. The door was then flung open by one of the porters, while the others huddled against the wall, for Barclay stood in front of them with a pistol raised. He sprang forward and seized Dermot's hand.

"Heaven and earth! How are you alive?" he cried. "I thought the devils had got you this time. I was tempted to shoot these swine here for being so long in opening the door."

There was a clatter of boots on the marble floor, as Payne and Granger, followed by the rest of the Englishmen, ran up the hall, cheering. They crowded round Dermot, nearly shook his arm off, thumped him on the back, and overwhelmed him with congratulations.

As Dermot thanked them he said:

"I didn't know that you fellows were looking on, otherwise I wouldn't have done that little bit of gallery-play. But I had a reason for it." "Yes; we know," said Payne significantly. "Barclay told us."

Then they dragged him protesting upstairs to the lounge, that the women might congratulate him too; which they did each in her own fashion. Ida was effusive and sentimental, Mrs. Rice fatuous, and Noreen timid and almost stiff. The girl, who had endured an agony worse than many deaths, could not voice her feelings, and her congratulations seemed curt and cold to others besides Dermot.

She had no opportunity of speaking to him apart, even for a minute, for the men surrounded him and insisted on toasting him and questioning him until it was time to dress for dinner. And even then they formed a guard of honour and escorted him to his room.

Noreen, utterly worn out by her sleepless nights and the storm of emotions that had shaken her, was unable to come down to dinner, and at her brother's wish went to bed instead. And so she did not learn that Dermot was leaving the Palace at the early hour of four o'clock in the morning.

That night as Dermot and Barclay went upstairs together the police officer said:

"I wonder if they'll dare to try anything against you tonight, Major. I should say they'd give you a miss in baulk, for they must believe you invulnerable. Still, I'm going with you to your room to see."

When they reached it and threw open the door a figure half rose from the floor. Barclay's hand went out to it with levelled pistol, but the words arrested him.

"*Khodawund!* (Lord of the World!) Forgive me! I did not know. I did not know."

It was the treacherous Rama who had tried to lead Dermot to his death. He lay face to the ground.

"Damned liar!" growled Barclay in English.

"Did not know that thou wert leading me under the feet of the *must* elephant?" demanded Dermot incredulously.

"Aye, that I knew of course, *Huzoor.* How can I deceive thee? But thee I knew not; though the elephant Shiva-*ji* did, even in his madness. It is not my fault. I am not of this country. I am a man of the Punjaub. I know naught of the gods of Bengal."

Barclay had heard from the planters the belief in Dermot's divinity which was universal in their district, and perceived that the legend had reached this man. He was quick to see the advantages that they could reap from his superstitious fears. He signed to Dermot to be silent and said in solemn tones:

"Rama, thou hast grievously offended the gods. Thou knowest the truth at last?"

"I do, Sahib. The talk through the Palace, aye, throughout the city, is all of the God of the Elephants, of the Terrible One who feeds his herd of demons on the flesh of men. The temple of *Gunesh* will be full indeed tonight. But alas! I am an ignorant man. I knew not that the holy one took form among the *gora-logue* (white folk)."

"The gods know no country. The truth, Rama, the truth," said Barclay impressively. "Else thou art lost. Shiva-*ji*, mayhap, is hungry and needs his meal of flesh."

"Ai! sahib, say not so," wailed the terror-stricken man. "He has feasted well today. With my own eyes I saw him feed on Man Singh the Rajput."

Natives believe that an elephant, when it seizes in its mouth the limbs of a man that it has killed and is about to tear in pieces, eats his flesh. In dread of a like doom, of the terrible vengeance of this mysterious Being, god, man, or demon, perhaps all three, from whom death shrank aside, whom neither poison of food nor venom of snake could harm, who used mad, man-slaying elephants as steeds, Rama unburdened his soul. He told how the *Dewan's* confidential man had bade him carry out the attempts on Dermot's life. He showed them that the Major's suspicions when he saw the Rajah's soldiery were correct, and that from Lalpuri came the inspiration of the carrying-off of Noreen. He told them of a party of these same soldiers that had gone on a secret mission into the Great Jungle, from which but a few came back after awful sufferings, and the strange tales whispered in the bazaar as to the fate of their comrades.

He disclosed more. He spoke of mysterious travellers from many lands that came to the Palace to confer with the *Dewan* - Chinese, Afghans, Bhutanese, Indians of many castes and races, white men not of the sahib-*logue*. He said enough to convince his hearers that many threads of the world-wide conspiracy against the British Raj led to Lalpuri. There was not proof enough yet for the Government of India to take action against its rulers, perhaps, but sufficient to show where the arch-conspirators of Bengal were to be sought for.

Rama left the room, not pardoned indeed, but with the promise of punishment suspended as long as he was true to the oath he had sworn by the Blessed Water of the Ganges, to be true slave and bearer of news when Dermot needed him.

Long after he left, the two sat and talked of the strange happenings of the last few days, and disclosed to each other what they knew of the treason that stalked the land, for each was servant of the Crown and his knowledge might help the other. And when the hoot of Payne's motor-horn in the outer courtyard told them that it was time for Dermot to go, they said good-bye in the outwardly careless fashion of the Briton who has looked into another's eyes and found him true man and friend.

Then through the darkness into the dawn Dermot sped away with his companions from the City of Shame and the Palace of Death.

And Noreen woke later to learn that the man she loved had left her again without farewell, that the fog of misunderstanding between them was not yet lifted.

CHAPTER XVIII

THE CAT AND THE TIGER

Several weeks had passed since the Durga Puja Festival. Over the Indian Empire the dark clouds were gathering fast. The Pathan tribes along the North-west Frontier were straining at the leash; Afridis, Yusufzais, Mohmands, all the *Pukhtana*, were restless and excited. The *mullahs* were preaching a holy war; and the *maliks*, or tribal elders, could not restrain their young men. Raids into British Indian territory were frequent.

There was worse menace behind. The Afghan troops, organised, trained, and equipped as they had never been before in their history, were massing near the Khyber Pass. Some of the Penlops, the great feudal chieftains of little-known Bhutan, were rumoured to have broken out into rebellion against the Maharajah because, loyal to his treaties with the Government of India, he had refused a Chinese army free passage through the country. All the masterless Bhuttia rogues on both sides of the border were sharpening their *dahs* and looking down greedily on the fertile plains below.

All India itself seemed trembling on the verge of revolt. The Punjaub was honeycombed with sedition. Men said that the warlike castes and races that had helped Britain to hold the land in the Black Year of the Mutiny would be the first to tear it from her now. In the Bengals outrages and open disloyalty were the order of the day. The curs that had fattened under England's protection were the first to snap at her heels. The

Day of Doom seemed very near. Only the great feudatories of the King-Emperor, the noble Princes of India, faithful to their oaths, were loyal.

Through the borderland of Bhutan Dermot and Badshah still ranged, watching the many gates through the walls of mountains better than battalions of spies. The man rarely slept in a bed. His nights were passed beside his faithful friend high up in the Himalayan passes, where the snow was already falling, or down in the jungles still reeking of fever and sweltering in tropic heat. By his instructions Parker and his two hundred sepoys toiled to improve the defences of Ranga Duar; and the subaltern was happy in the possession of several machine guns wrung from the Ordnance Department with difficulty.

Often, as Dermot sat high perched on the mountain side, searching the narrow valleys and deep ravines of Bhutan with powerful glasses, his thoughts flew to Noreen safe beyond the giant hills at his back. It cheered him to know that he was watching over her safety as well as guarding the peace of hundreds of millions in the same land. He had seldom seen her since their return from Lalpuri, and on the rare occasions of their meeting she seemed to avoid him more than ever. Chunerbutty was always by her side. Could there be truth, then, in this fresh story that Ida Smith had told him on their last night at the Palace, when she said that she had discovered that she was mistaken in believing in Noreen's approaching betrothal to Charlesworth, of which she had assured him in Darjeeling? For at Lalpuri she said she had extracted from the girl the confession that she had refused the Rifleman and others for love of someone in the Plains below. And Ida, judging from Chunerbutty's constant attendance on, and proprietorial manner with Noreen, confided to Dermot her firm belief that the Bengali was the man.

The thought was unbearable to the soldier. As he sat in his lonely eyrie he knew now that he loved the girl, that it would be unbearable for him to see her another's wife. Those few days at Lalpuri, when first he felt the estrangement between them, had revealed the truth to him. When in the courtyard of the Palace he saw Death rushing on him he had given her what he believed would be his last thought.

He recalled her charm, her delightful comradeship, her brightness, and her beauty. It was hateful to think that she would dower this renegade Hindu with them all. Dermot had no unjust prejudice against the natives of the land in which so much of his life was passed. Like every officer in the Indian Army he loved his sepoys and regarded them as his children. Their troubles, their welfare, were his. He respected the men of those gallant warrior races that once had faced the British valiantly in battle and fought as loyally beside them since. But for the effeminate and cowardly peoples of India, that ever crawled to kiss the feet of each conqueror of the peninsula in turn and then stabbed him in the back if they could, he had the contempt that every member of the martial races of the land, every Sikh, Rajput, Gurkha, Punjaubi had.

The girl would scarcely have refused so good a match as Charlesworth or come away heart-whole from Darjeeling, where so many had striven for her favour, if she had gone there without a prior attachment. That she cared for no man in England he was sure, for she had often told him that she had no desire to return to that country. He had seen her among the planters of the district and was certain that she loved none of them. Only Chunerbutty was left; it must indeed be he.

He shut up his binoculars and climbed down the rocky pinnacle on which he had been perched, and went to eat a cheerless meal where Badshah grazed a thousand feet below.

In Malpura Noreen was suffering bitterly for her foolish pride and jealous readiness to believe evil of the man she loved. She knew that she was entirely to blame for her estrangement from him. He never came to their garden now; and to her dismay her brother ignored all hints to invite him. For the boy was divided between loyalty to Chunerbutty (whom he had to thank for his chance in life) and the man who had twice saved his sister. Chunerbutty had reproached him with forgetting what he, the now despised Hindu, had done for him in the past, and complained sadly that Miss Daleham looked down on him for the colour of his skin. So Fred felt that he must choose between two friends and that honour demanded his clinging to the older one. Therefore he begged Noreen for his sake not to hurt the engineer's feelings and to treat him kindly. She could not refuse, and Chunerbutty took every advantage of her sisterly obedience. Whenever they went to the club he tried to monopolise her, and delighted in exhibiting the terms of friendship on which they appeared to be. The girl felt that even her old friends were beginning at last to look askance at her; consequently she tried to avoid going to the weekly gatherings.

It happened that on the occasion when Dermot, having arrived at Salchini on a visit to Payne, again made his appearance at the club, Daleham had insisted on his sister accompanying him there, much against her will. Chunerbutty was unable to go with them, being confined to his bungalow with a slight touch of fever.

That afternoon Noreen was more than ever conscious of a strained feeling and an unmistakable coldness to her on the part of the men whom she knew best. And worse, it seemed to her that some young fellows who had only recently come to the district and with whom she was little acquainted, were inclined to treat her with less respect than usual. She had seen Dermot arrive with his host; but, although Payne came to sit down beside her and chat, his guest merely greeted her courteously and passed on at once.

All that afternoon it seemed to the girl that something in the atmosphere was miserably wrong, but what it was she could not tell. She was bitterly disappointed that Dermot kept away from her. It was not the smart of a hurt pride, but the bewildered pain of a child that finds that the one it values most does not need it. Indeed her best friends, all except Payne, seemed to have agreed to ignore her.

Mrs. Rice, however, was even sweeter in her manner than usual when she spoke to the girl.

"Where is Mr. Chunerbutty today, dear?" she asked after lunch from where she sat on the verandah beside Dermot. Noreen was standing further along it with Payne, watching the play on the tennis-court in front of the club house.

"He isn't very well," replied the girl. "He's suffering from fever."

"Oh, really? I am so sorry to hear that," exclaimed the older woman. "So sad for you, dear. However did you force yourself to leave him?"

Noreen looked at her in surprise.

"Why not? We could do nothing for him," she said. "We sent him soup and jelly made by our cook, and Fred went to see him before we started. But he didn't want to be disturbed."

Mrs. Rice's manner grew even more sweetly sympathetic.

"I *am* so sorry," she said. "How worried you must be!"

The girl stared at her in astonishment. She had never expected to find Mrs. Rice seriously concerned about any one, and least of all the Hindu, who was no favourite of hers.

"Oh, there's really nothing to worry about," she exclaimed impatiently. "Fred said he hadn't much of a temperature."

"Yes, I daresay. But you can't help being anxious, I know. I wonder that you were able to bring yourself to come here at all, dear," said the older woman in honeyed tones.

"But why shouldn't I?"

Noreen's eyebrows were raised in bewilderment. She felt instinctively that there was some hidden unfriendliness at the back of Mrs. Rice's sympathetic words. She felt that Dermot was watching her.

"Oh, forgive me, dear. I am afraid I'm being indiscreet. I forgot," said the other woman. She rose from her chair and turned to the man beside her.

"Major, do take me out to see how the coolies are getting on with the polo ground. I hope when it's finished you'll come here to play regularly. These boys want someone to show them the game. You military men are the only ones who know how it should be played."

She put up her green-lined white sun-umbrella and led the way down the verandah steps. With a puckered brow Noreen watched her and her companion until they were out of sight round the corner of the little wooden building.

"What does Mrs. Rice mean?" she demanded. "I'm sure there's something behind her words. She never pretended to like Mr. Chunerbutty. Why should she be concerned about him now? Why does she seem to expect me to stay behind to nurse him? Of course I would, if he were dangerously ill. But he's not."

Payne glanced around. Some of the men, who were sitting near, had heard the conversation with Mrs. Rice, and Noreen felt that there was something hostile in the way in which they looked at her.

Payne answered in a careless tone:

"Let's sit down. There are a couple of chairs. We'll bag them."

He pointed to two at the far end of the verandah and led the way to them.

When they were seated he said:

"Haven't you any idea of what she means, Miss Daleham?"

The girl stared at him anxiously.

"Then she does mean something, and you know it. Mr. Payne, you have always been good to me. Won't you help me? Everyone seems to have grown suddenly very unfriendly."

The grey-haired man looked pityingly at her.

"Will you be honest with me, child?" he asked. "Are you engaged to Chunerbutty?"

"Engaged? What - to marry him? Good gracious, no!" exclaimed the astonished girl, half rising from her chair.

"Will you tell me frankly - have you any intention of marrying him?" he persisted.

Noreen stared at him, her cheeks flaming.

"Marry Mr. Chunerbutty? Of course not. How could you think so! Why, he's not even a white man."

"Thank God!" Payne exclaimed fervently. "I'm delighted to hear it. I couldn't believe it - yet one never knows."

"But what on earth put such a preposterous idea into your head, Mr. Payne?" asked Noreen. "And what has this got to do with Mrs. Rice?"

"Because Mrs. Rice said that you were engaged to Chunerbutty."

For a moment Noreen could find no words. Then she leaned forward, her eyes flashing.

"Oh, how could she - how could she think so?"

"Perhaps she didn't. But she wanted us to. She said that you had told her you were engaged to him, but wanted it kept secret for the present. So naturally she told everyone."

"Told everyone that I was going to marry a native? Oh, how cruel of her! How could she be so wicked!" exclaimed the girl, much distressed. Then she added: "Did *you* believe it?"

Payne shook his head.

"Candidly, child, I didn't know what to think. I hoped it wasn't true. But of late that damned Bengali seemed so intimate with you. He apparently wanted everyone to see on what very friendly terms you and he were."

"Did Major Dermot believe it too?"

"I don't know," said Payne doubtfully. "Dermot's not the fellow to talk about women. He's never mentioned you."

"But how do you know that Mrs. Rice said such a thing? Did she tell you?"

"No; she knows that I am your friend, and I daresay she was afraid to tell me such a lie. But she told others."

He turned in his chair and called to a young fellow standing near the bar of the club.

"I say, Travers, do you mind coming here a moment? Pull up a chair and sit down."

Travers was a straight, clean-minded boy, one of those of their community whom Noreen liked best, and she had felt hurt at his marked avoidance of her all the afternoon.

"Look here, youngster," said Payne in a low voice, "did Mrs. Rice tell you that Miss Daleham was engaged to Chunerbutty?"

Travers looked at him in surprise.

"Yes. I told you so the other day. She said that Miss Daleham had confided to her that they were engaged, but wanted it kept secret for a time until he could get another job."

"Then, my boy, you'll be pleased to hear it's a damned lie," said Payne impressively. "Miss Daleham would never marry a black man."

The boy's face lit up.

"I am glad!" he cried impulsively. "I'm very, very sorry, Miss Daleham, for helping to spread the lie. But I only told Payne. I knew he was a friend of yours, and I hoped he'd be able to contradict the yarn. For I felt very sick about it."

"Thank you, Mr. Travers," the girl said gratefully. "But I'm glad that you did tell him. Otherwise I might not have heard it, at least not from a friend."

Just then the four men on the tennis-court finished their game and came in to the bar. Fred Daleham and another took their places and began a single. Mrs. Rice, with Dermot and several other men, came up the steps of the verandah, and, sitting down, ordered tea for the party.

Noreen looked at her with angry eyes, and, rising, walked along the verandah to where she was sitting surrounded by the group of men.

Her enemy looked up as she approached.

"Are you coming to have tea, dear?" she said sweetly. "I haven't ordered any for you, but I daresay they'll find you a cup."

Dermot rose to offer the girl his chair; but, ignoring him, she confronted the other woman. "Mrs. Rice, will you please tell me if it is true that you said I was engaged to Mr.

Chunerbutty?" she demanded in a firm tone.

It was as if a bomb had exploded in the club. Noreen's voice carried clearly through the building, so that everyone inside it heard her words distinctly. The only two members of their little community who missed them were her brother and his opponent on the tennis-court.

Mrs. Rice gasped and stared at the indignant girl, while the men about her sat up suddenly in their chairs.

"I said so? What an idea!" ejaculated the planter's wife. Then in an insinuating voice she added: "You know I never betray secrets."

"There is no secret. Please answer me. Did you say to any one that I had told you I was engaged to him?" persisted the girl.

The older woman tried to crush her by a haughty assumption of superiority.

"You absurd child, you must be careful what accusations you bring. You shouldn't say such things."

"Kindly answer my question," demanded the angry girl.

Mrs. Rice lay back in her chair with affected carelessness.

"Well, aren't you engaged to him? Won't even he - ?" she broke off and sniggered impertinently.

"I am not. Most certainly not," said Noreen hotly. "I insist on your answering me. Did you say that I had told you we were and asked you to keep it a secret?"

"No, I did not. Who did I tell?" snapped the other woman.

"Me for one," broke in a voice; and Dermot took a step forward. "You told me very clearly and precisely, Mrs. Rice, that Miss Daleham had confided to you under the pledge of secrecy - which, by the way, you were breaking - that she was engaged to this man."

There was an uncomfortable pause. Noreen glanced gratefully at her champion. The other men shifted uneasily, and Mrs. Rice's husband, who was standing at the bar, hastily hid his face in a whiskey and soda.

Noreen turned again to her traducer.

"Will you kindly contradict your false statement?" she asked.

The other woman looked down sullenly and made no reply.

"Then I shall," continued the girl. She faced the group of men before her, Payne and Travers by her side.

"I ask you to believe, gentlemen, that there never was nor could be any question of an engagement between Mr. Chunerbutty and me," she said firmly. "And I give you my word of honour that I never said such a thing to Mrs. Rice."

She waited for a moment, then turned and walked away down the verandah, followed by Payne and Travers, leaving a pained silence behind her. Mrs. Rice tried to regain her self-confidence.

"The idea of that chit talking to me like that!" she exclaimed. "It was only meant for a joke, if I did say it. Who'd have ever thought she'd have taken it that way?"

"Any decent man - or woman, Mrs. Rice," said Dermot severely. Then, after looking at Rice to see if he wished to take up the cudgels on his wife's behalf, and failing to catch that gentleman's carefully-averted eye, the soldier turned and walked deliberately to where Noreen was sitting, now suffering from the reaction from her anger and frightened at the memory of her boldness.

Gordon Casserly

The other men got up one by one and went to the bar, from which the hen pecked Rice was peremptorily called by his angry wife and ordered to drive her home.

After the Dalehams had returned to their bungalow the girl told her brother of what had happened at the club. He was exceedingly angry and agreed that it would be wiser for her to keep Chunerbutty at a distance in future. And later on he had no objection to her inviting Dermot to pay them a flying visit when he was again in their neighbourhood. For the incident at the club had brought about a resumption of the old friendly relations between Noreen and Dermot, who occasionally invited her to accompany him on Badshah for a short excursion into the forest, much to her delight. She confided to him the offer of the necklace and learned in return his belief that the Rajah was the instigator of the attempt to carry her off. When her brother heard of this and of Chunerbutty's action in the matter of the jewels he was so enraged that he quarrelled for the first time with his Hindu friend.

*　　*　　*　　*　　*

Dermot was kept informed of whatever happened in Lalpuri by the repentant Rama through the medium of Barclay. For the Deputy Superintendent had been appointed to a special and important post in the Secret Police and told off to watch the conspiracy in Bengal. This he owed to a strong recommendation from Dermot to the Head of the Department in Simla. Rama proved invaluable. Through him they learned of the despatch of an important Brahmin messenger and intermediary from the Palace to Bhutan, by way of Malpura, where he was to visit some of his caste-fellows on Parry's garden. The information reached Dermot too late to enable him to seize the man on the tea-estate. So he hurried to the border to intercept the messenger before he crossed it. But here, too, he was unsuccessful. Certain that the Brahmin had not slipped through the meshes of the net formed by his secret service of subsidised Bhuttias, Dermot returned to the jungle to make search for him along the way. But all to no avail, much to his chagrin; for he had reason to hope that he would find on the emissary proof enough of the treason of the rulers of Lalpuri to hang them. He went back to Malpura to prosecute enquiries.

To console himself for his disappointment Dermot determined to have a day's shooting in the jungle, a treat he rarely had leisure for now. He invited the Dalehams to accompany him. Noreen accepted eagerly, but her brother was obliged to decline, much to his regret. For Parry was now always in a state bordering on lunacy, and his brutal treatment of the coolies, when his assistant was not there to restrain him, several times nearly drove them into open revolt. So Dermot and his companion set off alone.

As they went along they chanced to pass near a little village buried in the heart of the jungle. A man working on the small patch of cleared soil in which he and his fellows grew their scanty crops saw them, recognised Badshah and his male rider, and ran away shouting to the hamlet. Then out of it swarmed men, women, and children, the last naked, while only miserable rags clothed the skinny frames of their elders. All prostrated themselves in the dust in Badshah's path. The elephant stopped. Then a wizened old man with scanty white beard raised his hands imploringly to Dermot.

"Lord! Holy One! Have mercy on us!"

The rest chorused: "Have mercy!"

"Spare thy slaves, O Lord!" went on the old man. "Spare us ere all perish. We worship at thy shrine. We grudge not thy elephants our miserable crops. Are they not thy servants? But let not the Striped Death slay all of us."

Dermot questioned him and then explained to Noreen that a man-eating tiger had taken up its residence near the village and was rapidly killing off its inhabitants.

"Oh, do help them," she said. "Can't you shoot it?"

He reflected for a few moments.

"Yes, I think I know how to get it. Will you wait for me in the village?"

"What? Mayn't I go with you to see you kill it? Please let me. I promise I'll not scream or be stupid."

He looked at her admiringly.

"Bravo!" he said. "I'm sure you'll be all right. Very well. I promise you you shall see a sight that not many other women have seen."

He borrowed a *puggri* - a strip of cotton cloth several yards long - from a villager, and bade them show him where the tiger lay up during the heat of the day. When they had done so from a safe distance, he turned Badshah, and, to Noreen's surprise, sped off swiftly in the opposite direction.

Suddenly the girl touched his arm quietly.

"Look! I see a wild elephant. There's another! And another!" she whispered.

"Yes; I've come in search of them," he replied in his ordinary tone. "It's Badshah's herd."

"Is it really? How wonderful! How did you know where to find them?" she cried, thrilled by the sight of the great beasts all round them and exclaiming with delight at the solemn little woolly babies, many newly born. For this was the calving season.

Dermot uttered a peculiar cry that sent the cow-elephants huddling together, their young hiding under their bodies, while from every quarter the great tuskers broke out through the undergrowth and came to him in a mass. Then, as Badshah turned and set off at a rapid pace, the bull-elephants followed.

When he arrived near the spot in which the man-eater was said to have his lair, Dermot stopped them all. Despite her protests he tied Noreen firmly with the *puggri* to the rope crossing Badshah's pad. Then he drove his animal into the herd of tuskers, which had crowded together, and divided them into two bodies. The tiger was reported to lie up in a narrow *nullah* filled and fringed with low bushes. From the near bank to where Badshah stood the forest was free from undergrowth, which came to within a score of yards of the far bank.

Badshah smelled the ground, and the other elephants followed his example and, when they scented the tiger's trail, began to be restless and excited. A sharp cry from Dermot and the two bodies of tuskers separated and moved away, branching off half right and left, and disappeared in the undergrowth.

Dermot cocked his double-barrelled rifle. There was a long pause. A strange feeling of awe crept over Noreen at the realisation of her companion's strange power over these great animals. No wonder the superstitious natives believed him to be a god.

Presently there was a loud crashing in the undergrowth beyond the *nullah*, and Noreen saw the saplings in it agitated, as if by the passage of the elephants. The tiger gave no sign of life. The girl's heart beat fast, and her breath came quickly. But her companion never moved.

Suddenly Noreen gasped, for through the screen of thin bushes that fringed the edge of the *nullah* a hideous painted mask was thrust out. It was a tiger's face, the ears flattened to the skull, the eyes flaming, the lips drawn back to bare the teeth in a ghastly snarl. The brute saw Badshah and drew quietly back. A pause. Then it sprang into full view and poised for a single instant on the far bank. But at that very moment the line of tuskers burst out of the tangled undergrowth and the tiger jumped down into the *nullah* again.

Then like a flash it leaped into sight over the near bank, bounding in a furious charge straight at Badshah. Noreen held her breath as it crouched to spring. Dermot's rifle was at his shoulder, and he pressed the trigger. There was a click - the cartridge had missed fire. And the tiger sprang full at the man.

But as it did so Badshah swung swiftly round - well for Noreen that she was securely fastened - for he had been standing a little sideways. And with an upward sweep of his head he caught the leaping tiger in mid-air on the point of his tusk, hurling it back a dozen yards.

As the baffled brute struck the ground with a heavy thud it lay still for a second and then sprang up, but at that moment Dermot's second barrel rang out, and, shot through the brain, the tiger collapsed, its head resting on its paws. A tremor shook the powerful frame, the tail twitched feebly, then all was still.

The long line of elephants halted on the far bank of the *nullah*, swung into file, and moved swiftly out of sight. Their work was done.

Dermot reloaded and urged Badshah forward, covering the tiger with his rifle. There was no need. It was dead.

Noreen leant forward and looked down at the striped body.

"What a splendid beast!" she exclaimed.

Dermot turned to her.

"You kept your word well, Miss Daleham," he said. "I congratulate you on your pluck. The highest compliment I can pay you is to say that I forgot you were there. Not many men would have sat as quiet as you did when the cartridge missed fire and the brute sprang."

The girl's eyes sparkled and she blushed. His praise was very dear to her.

In a lighter tone he continued:

"As a reward and a souvenir you shall have the skin. I'll get the villagers to take it off. Now stay on Badshah, please, while I slip down and have a look at the tiger's little nest."

With rifle at the ready, lest the dead animal should have had a mate, he climbed down into the *nullah*. He had not gone ten yards before his foot struck against something hard. In the pressed-down weeds was the half-gnawed skull of a man. The skin and flesh of the face were fairly intact. He took the head up in his hands. On the forehead were painted three white horizontal strokes. The tiger's last prey had been a Brahmin. A thought flashed across Dermot's mind. He searched about. A few bones, parts of the hands and feet, some rags of clothing - and a long flat narrow leather case. He tore this open and hastily took out the papers it contained; and as he skimmed through them his eyes glistened with delight.

He sprang up out of the *nullah* and ran towards Badshah. When the elephant's trunk had swung him up on to the massive head he said:

"We must go back at once. I'll tell the villagers as we pass to flay the tiger. I must borrow your brother's pony and ride as fast as I can to Salchini to get Payne's motor to take me to the railway."

"The railway?" exclaimed the girl. "Why, what is the matter? Where are you going?"

"To Simla. I've found the lost messenger. Aye, and perhaps information that may save India and proofs that will hang our friends in the Palace of Lalpuri. *Mul*, Badshah!"

CHAPTER XIX

TEMPEST

The storm had burst on India. In the Khyber Pass there was fiercer fighting than even that blood-stained defile had ever seen. The flames kindled by fanaticism and lust of plunder blazed up along the North-west Frontier and burned fiercest around Peshawar, where the Pathan tribes gathered thickest. No news came from the interior of Bhutan.

So far, however, the interior of the land was comparatively tranquil. Sporadic outbreaks in the Bombay Presidency and the Punjaub had been crushed promptly. The great plan of a wide-spread concerted rising throughout the peninsula had come to naught, thanks to the papers that Dermot had found in the man-eater's den. He had carried them straight to Simla himself, for closer examination had confirmed his first impression and shown him that they were far too important to be confided to any one else.

The information in them proved to be of the utmost value, for they disclosed the complete plans of the conspirators and told the very dates arranged for the advance of the Afghan army and the attacks of the Pathans, which were to take place simultaneously with the general rising in India. This latter the military authorities were enabled to deal with so effectively that it came to nothing.

Incidentally the papers conclusively proved the treason of the

Rajah and the *Dewan* of Lalpuri, and that the Palace was one of the most important centres of the conspiracy. To Dermot's amazement no action was taken against the two arch-plotters, owing to the incredible timidity of the chief civil authorities in India and their susceptibility to political influences in England. For Lalpuri and its rulers had been taken under the very particular protection of the Socialist Party; and the Government of India feared to touch the traitors. The excuse given for this leniency was that any attempt to punish them might be the signal for the long delayed rising in Lalpuri and Eastern Bengal generally.

A few days after Dermot's return from Simla orders came to him from the Adjutant General to hand over the command of the detachment to Parker, as he himself had been appointed extra departmental Political Officer of the Bhutan Border, with headquarters at Ranga Duar. This released him from the responsibilities of his military duties and left him free to devote himself to watching the frontier. He was able to keep in communication with Parker by means of signal stations established on high peaks near the Fort, visible from many points in the mountains and the forest; for he carried a signalling outfit always with him.

Thanks to this precaution the garrison of the outpost was not taken by surprise when one morning the hills around Ranga Duar were seen to be covered with masses of armed men, and long lines of troops wound down the mountain paths. For from the peaks above the pass through which he had once gone to the Death Place of the elephants, Dermot had looked down upon an invading force of Chinese regulars supported by levies of Bhutanese from the interior and a wild mob of masterless Bhuttias from both sides of the border. He had flashed a warning to Parker in ample time, returned to the *peelkhana* and bidden Ramnath hide with Badshah in a concealed spot in the foothills where he could easily find them, sent the other *mahouts* and elephants out of reach of the invaders, and climbed up to the Fort to watch with his late subaltern the arrival of the enemy.

Gordon Casserly

"Well, Major, it's come our way at last," said Parker as they greeted each other. "Thanks to your warning we're ready for them. But we are not the only people who've been expecting them. The wires are cut, the road blocked, and we are isolated."

"Yes, I know. Many messengers have got through from the enemy; for my cordon of faithful Bhuttias has disappeared. The members of it have joined the invaders in the hope of loot." Parker looked up at the hills, black with descending forms.

"There's a mighty lot of the beggars," he said simply. "Do you remember our discussing this very happening once and your saying that we weren't equal to stopping a whole army? What's your advice now?"

"See it out. We're bound to go under in the end, but we'll be able, I hope, to keep them off for a few days. And every hour we hold them up will be worth a lot to those below. We shan't be relieved, for there aren't any men to spare in India. But we'll have done our part."

"I say, Major, wasn't it lucky we got those machine guns in time? I've plenty of ammunition, so we ought to be able to put up a good fight. What'll they do first?"

"Try to rush the defences at once. They have a lot of irregulars whom the Chinese General won't be able to keep in hand. He won't mind their being wiped out either. I see you've made a good job of clearing the foreground. You haven't left them much cover. So you blew up our poor old Mess and the bungalows?"

"Yes. The rubble came in handy for filling in that *nullah*. Hullo!" Parker's glasses went to his eyes. "You're right, by Jingo! They're gathering for an assault. Gad! what a beautiful mark for shrapnel. I wish we'd a gun or two."

A storm of shells from the mountain batteries, the only artillery that the enemy had been able to bring with them through the Himalayas, fell on the Fort and its defences. Then masses of men rushed down the hills to the attack. Not a shot was fired at them. Encouraged by the garrison's silence and carried away by the prospect of an easy victory, they lost all formation and crowded together in dense swarms.

The two British officers watched them from the central redoubt. Parker held his binoculars to his eyes with his right hand, while his left forefinger rested on a polished button in a little machine on the table beside him. The assailants, favoured by the fall of the ground, soon reached the limits of the cantonments, bare now of buildings and trees. There were trained Chinese troops, some tall, light-complexioned Northerners of Manchu blood, others stocky, yellow men from Canton and the Southern Provinces. Mobs of Bhutanese with heads, chests, legs, and feet bare, fierce but undisciplined fighters, armed with varied weapons, led the van. Uttering weird yells and brandishing their *dahs*, spears, muskets, and rifles, they rushed towards the fort, from which no shot was fired. Accustomed to the lofty *jongs*, or castles, of their own land they deemed the breastworks and trenches unworthy of notice. And the stone barracks and walls in the Fort were rapidly melting away under the rain of shells.

Flushed with victory the swarming masses came on. But suddenly the world upheaved behind the leaders. Rocks, earth, and rubble went up in clouds into the air, and with them scores of the Chinese regular troops, under whose very feet mines of the new explosive had been fired by Parker. And the howling mobs in front were held up by barbed wire, while from the despised trenches and breastworks a storm of lead swept the crowded masses of the attackers away. At that close range every bullet from the machine guns and rifles of the defenders drove through two or three assailants, every bomb and grenade slew a group. Only in one spot by sheer weight of numbers did they break through.

But like a thunderbolt fell the counter-attack. Stalwart Punjaubi Mohammedans, led by Dermot, swept down upon them, and with bomb and bayonet drove them out. The survivors turned and staggered up the hills again, withering away under the steady fire of the sepoys, who adjusted their sights with the utmost coolness as the range increased.

Again and again the assaults were repeated and repulsed, until the undisciplined and demoralised Bhutanese refused to advance, and the Chinese regulars attacked alone. But fresh mines exploded under them; the deadly fire of the defenders' machine guns blasted them; and the Pekin general looked anxious as his best troops melted away. He would not go far into India if every small body of its soldiers took equally heavy toll of his force. So he ordered a cessation of the assaults.

But there was no respite for the little garrison. Day and night the pitiless bombardment by the mountain batteries and long-range fire of rifles and machine guns never ceased. And death was busy among the defenders.

On the third night of the siege Dermot and the subaltern knelt side by side in what was now the last line of the defence.

"I ought not to ask you to go, Major," whispered Parker. "It's not possible to get through, I'm afraid. I can't forget the awful sight of the fiendish tortures they inflicted on poor Hikmat Khan and Shaikh Ismail today in full view of us all. They tried to slip through last night with their naked bodies covered with oil. It's a terrible death for you if they catch you. It would be much easier to die fighting. Yet someone ought to go."

"Yes, they must be told at Headquarters," replied his companion in an equally low tone. "We can't hold them two days longer."

"Not that, if they try to rush us again. Our ammunition is giving out," said Parker. "I'd go myself if I weren't commanding here. But I'd have no chance of getting through. You are our only hope. Oh, I don't mean of relief. There's no possibility of that."

"No; if I do manage to get into touch with Headquarters, it would be too late, even if they could spare any troops."

"Yes, it's all over now, bar the shouting. Well, we've had some jolly times together, sir, you and I, in this little place, haven't we? Do you remember when the Dalehams were up here? What a nice girl she was. I hope she's safe."

"I hope to Heaven she is," muttered Dermot. "Well, Parker, I must say good-bye. We've been good friends, you and I; and I'm sorry it's the end."

In the darkness their hands met in a firm grip.

"One word, sir," whispered the subaltern. "If you do pull through, you've got my mother's address. You'll let her know? She thinks a lot of me, poor old lady."

Dermot answered him only by a pressure of the hand. The next moment he was gone. Parker, straining eyes and ears, saw nothing, heard nothing.

Half an hour later a picquet of slant-eyed men lying on the steep slopes of the hill below the Fort saw above them a man's figure dark against the paling stars. They challenged and sprang towards it with levelled bayonets. The next instant they were hurled apart, dashed to the ground, trampled to death. One as he expired had a shadowy vision of some awful bulk towering black against the coming dawn.

The sun was low in the heavens when Dermot awoke in a bracken-carpeted glade of the forest thirty miles away from Ranga Duar. Over him Badshah stood watchfully. The man yawned, rubbed his eyes and sat up. He looked at his watch.

"Good Heavens! I've slept for hours!" he cried.

Overcome by fatigue, for he had not even lain down once since the siege began, and finding that he was in danger of falling off the elephant, he had dismounted for a few minutes' rest. But exhausted Nature had conquered him, and he had fallen into a deep sleep. Haggard, hollow-eyed, and worn out, despite the rest, he staggered to his feet and was swung up to Badshah's neck by the crooked trunk and started again.

He was hastening towards Salchini, where he hoped to secure Payne's car, if the owner had not fled, and try to get into touch with Army Headquarters. But what to do if his friend had gone he hardly knew. The heavy firing at Ranga Duar, echoed by the mountains, must have been heard in the district; and all the planters had probably taken the warning and gone away. He was racked with anxiety as to Noreen's fate and could only hope that at the first alarm her brother had hurried her off. But there was no military station nearer than Calcutta or Darjeeling, and by this time it was probable that the whole of Eastern Bengal was in revolt. God help the Englishwoman that fell into its people's hands! The temptation to turn aside to Malpura was great. But Dermot overcame it. His duty came first.

Darkness had fallen on the jungle now. Except to lessen his speed it made little difference to the elephant; but for the man it was harder to find his way. On the twisting jungle tracks his luminous compass was of little use. He was forced to trust mainly to the animal.

But soon a suspicion arose in his mind that Badshah had swerved away from the direction in which Salchini lay and was heading for Malpura. It became certainty when they reached a deep *nullah* in the forest which Dermot knew was on the route to that garden. He tried to turn the elephant. Badshah paid no heed to him and held on his way with an invincible determination that made the man suspect there was a grave reason for his obstinacy. He knew too well the animal's strange and mysterious intelligence. He gave up contending uselessly and was borne along through the dark forest unresisting. Over the tree-tops floated the long, wailing cry of a Giant Owl circling against the stars. Close to their path the warning bark of a *khakur* deer was answered by the harsh braying roar of a tiger. Far away the metallic trumpeting of a wild elephant rang out into the night.

Presently Dermot saw a red glow through the trees ahead. Badshah never checked his pace but swept on until the glow became a ruddy glare staining the tree-trunks. Suddenly the stars shone overhead. They were clear of the jungle; and as they emerged on the open clearing of the tea-garden a column of fire blazed up ahead of them.

A chill fear smote Dermot. He would have urged Badshah on, but the elephant did not need it. Rapidly they sped along the soft road towards the leaping flames, which the soldier soon realised rose from the burning factory and withering sheds. And black against the light danced hundreds of figures, while yells and wild cries rent the air. And, well to one side, a fresh burst of flame and sparks leapt up into the night. It was one of the bungalows afire. Round it more figures moved fantastically. A groan came from the man's lips. Was it Daleham's bungalow that burned?

All at once Badshah stopped of his own accord and sank down on his knees. Mechanically his rider slipped to the ground and stood staring at the strange scene. He hardly noticed that the elephant rose, touched him caressingly with its trunk, swung round and sped away towards the forest. Half-dazed and heedless of danger Dermot hurried forward. Again the flames shot up, and by their light he saw to his relief that the Dalehams' bungalow was still standing. Parry's house was burning furiously. Pistol in hand he ran forward, scarcely cognizant of the crowds of shifting figures around the blazing buildings, deaf to their triumphant yells. Groups of natives crossed his path, shouting and leaping into the air excitedly, but they paid no attention to him. But, as he ran, he hit up against one man who turned and, seeing his white face, yelled and sprang away.

As Dermot neared the Dalehams' bungalow he saw that it was surrounded by a cordon of coolies armed with rifles and strung out many yards apart. He raced swiftly for a gap between two of them; but a man rose from the ground and snatched at him. The soldier struck savagely at him with the hand in which the pistol was firmly clenched, putting all his weight into the blow. The native crumpled and fell in a heap.

Dashing on Dermot shouted Daleham's name. From behind a barricade of boxes on the verandah a stern voice which he recognised as belonging to one of the Punjaubi servants whom· he had provided, called out:

"*Kohn hai? Kohn atha?* (Who is there? Who comes?)"

"Sher Afzul! It is I. Dermot Sahib," he replied, as he sprang up the verandah steps.

The muzzle of a rifle was pointed at him over the barricade, and a bearded face peered at him.

"It is the Major Sahib!" said the Mohammedan. "In the name of Allah, Sahib, have you brought your sepoys?"

"No; I am alone. Where are the Sahib and the missie *baba?*"

"In the bungalow. Enter, Sahib."

Dermot climbed over the barricade and pushed open the door of the dining-room, which was in darkness. But the heavy curtain dividing it from the drawing-room was dragged aside and Daleham appeared in the doorway, outlined against the faint light of a turned-down lamp. Behind him Noreen was rising from a chair.

"Who's there?" cried the boy, raising a revolver.

"It's all right, Daleham. It's I, Dermot. I'm alone, I'm sorry to say."

A stifled cry burst from the girl.

"Oh, you are safe, thank God!" she cried, her hand at her heart.

"What has happened here?" asked Dermot, entering the room.

Fred let fall the curtain as he answered:

"Hell's broke loose on the garden, sir. The coolies have mutinied. Parry's dead, murdered; and we're alive only by the kind mercies of that brute Chunerbutty, damn him! You were right about him, Major; and I was a fool.... Is it true you've been attacked up in Ranga Duar?" he continued.

"Are you wounded, Major Dermot?" broke in the girl anxiously.

"No, Miss Daleham. I'm quite safe and sound."

Then he told them briefly what had happened. When he had finished he asked them when the trouble began at Malpura.

"Three days ago," replied Fred. "The wind was blowing from the north, and we heard firing up in the mountains. I thought you were having an extra go of musketry there. But the coolies suddenly stopped work and gathered outside their village, where those infernal Brahmins harangued them. I went to order them back to their jobs -".

"Where was Parry?"

"Lying dead drunk in his bungalow. Well, some of the coolies attacked me with *lathis*, others tried to protect me. The Brahmins told me that the end of the British *Raj* (dominion) had come and that you were being attacked in Ranga Duar by a big army from China and would be wiped out. Then I was hustled back to the bungalow where those Mohammedan servants that you got for us - lucky you did! - turned out with rifles, which they said afterwards you'd given them, and wanted to fire on the mob. But I stopped them."

"Where was Chunerbutty?"

"Oh, he hadn't thrown off the mask yet. He came to me and said he was a prisoner and would not be allowed to leave the estate. But he advised me to ride over to Granger or some of the other fellows and get their help. But I wouldn't leave Noreen; and Sher Afzul told me that it was as bad on the other gardens. But only today the real trouble began."

"What happened?"

"Some news apparently reached the coolies that drove them mad with delight. They murdered the Parsi storekeeper, looted his place, and got drunk on his *daru*. Then they started killing the few Mohammedans we had on the estate. Some of the women and children got to us and we took them in. But the rest, even the little babies, were murdered by the brutes.

"I went over to Parry, but he was still too drunk to understand me. I was trying to rouse him when I heard shouts and ran out on the verandah. All the coolies, men, women, and children, were streaming towards the bungalows, mad with excitement, screaming and yelling. The men and even most of the boys carried weapons. The Brahmins were leading them. They made for Chunerbutty's house first. I was going to run to his assistance, when he came out and they cheered him like anything. He was in native dress and had marks painted on his forehead like the other Brahmins."

"Yes; go on. What happened then?"

"The engineer seemed as excited and mad as the rest. He ran down his steps, put himself at the head of the mob, shouted out something, and pointed to Parry's bungalow. They all rushed over to it, yelling like mad. Poor old Parr heard them and, dazed and drunk, staggered out on the verandah in his pyjamas and bare feet. Chunerbutty and the Brahmins came up the steps, driving back the crowd, which tried to follow them, howling like demons."

Fred passed his hand across his eyes. Dermot bent forward and stared eagerly at him, while Noreen looked only at the soldier.

"I called out to the engineer and asked him what it all meant," went on the boy, "but he took no notice of me. Parry tottered towards him, abusing him. Chunerbutty let him come to within a yard or two, then pulled out a pistol and fired three shots straight at the old man's heart. Poor old Parr fell dead."

Daleham paused for a moment.

"Poor old chap! He had his faults; but he had his good points, too. Well, I rushed towards him, but the Bengalis fell on me, knocked me down, and overpowered me. The mob outside yelled for my blood; but Chunerbutty shut them up. I was allowed to get on my feet again; and Chunerbutty held a pistol to my head, and cursed me and ordered me to go back to my bungalow and wait. He said that somebody would come here tomorrow to settle what was to be my fate and to take Noreen."

The girl sprang up.

"You never told me that," she cried.

"No; it wasn't any use distressing you," replied her brother. "But I had to tell the Major."

She turned impetuously to Dermot and stretched out her arms to him.

"You won't let them take me, will you? Oh, say you won't!" she said with a little sob.

He took both her hands in his.

"No, little girl, I won't. Not while I live."

"You'll kill me first? Promise me."

"On my honour."

She gave a sigh of relief and, strangely content, sank back into her chair. But she still held one of his hands clasped tightly in both of hers.

"Well, that's pretty well all there is to tell, Major," her brother went on. "I came back here, and the servants and I tried to put the house into a state of defence. No one's come near us so far."

"So Chunerbutty was at the head of affairs here. I thought so, I suppose the someone is that scoundrelly Rajah. He'll make his conditions known and, if you don't surrender, they'll attack us. Now, let's see what we've got as garrison. We two and the servants - seven. How are you off for weapons? I left my rifle behind."

"The servants have got their rifles and plenty of ammunition. I have a double-barrelled .400 cordite rifle and a shot-gun. If it comes to a scrap I'll take that and leave you the rifle. You're a much better shot; and I can't miss at close quarters with a scatter-gun."

"Do you think there's any hope for us?" asked the girl quietly.

"Frankly, I don't. I'd not put it so bluntly, only I've seen you in a tight corner before, Miss Daleham, and you weren't afraid."

"I am not now," she replied calmly.

"I believe we'd hold off these coolies, aye, and the Rajah's soldiers too, if they came. But we may have the Chinese troops on us at any minute; and that's a different matter."

"But why should you stay with us, Major Dermot?" said the girl anxiously. "As you got in through these men, surely you could escape the same way."

"I'll be candid with you, Miss Daleham, and tell you that if I could I would. For it's my duty to go on and report. But I'm stranded without my elephant, and even if I had him it wouldn't be much good unless I had Payne's car. And what has happened here must have happened on the other gardens. Without the motor I'd be too late with my news. So I'll stay here and take my chance."

Then he laughed and added:

"But cheer up; we're not dead yet. If only I'd Badshah I'd take you both up on him and we'd break through the whole Chinese Army."

The girl shook her head.

"We couldn't go. We couldn't leave those poor women and children and the servants."

"I forgot them. No; you're right. Well, I haven't lost all hope. I have great faith in old Badshah. I shouldn't be surprised if he got us out of this scrape, as he did before."

"Oh, I forgot him. I believe he'll help us still," cried the girl. "Where did you leave him?"

"He left me. He's quite able to take care of himself," replied Dermot grimly. "Now, Daleham, please take me round the house and show me the defences; and we'll arrange about the roster of sentry-duty with the servants. Please excuse me, Miss Daleham."

Through the weary night the two men, when not taking their turn on guard, sat and talked with Noreen in the drawing-room. For the girl refused to go to bed and, only to content them, lay back on a settee.

When she and Dermot were left alone she sighed and said:

"Ah, my beautiful forest! I must say good-bye to it. How I have enjoyed the happy days in it."

"Some of them were too exciting to be pleasant," he replied smiling.

"But the others made up for them. I like to think of you in the forest best," she said dreamily. "We were real friends there."

"And elsewhere, I hope."

"No. In Darjeeling you didn't like me."

"I did. Tonight I can be frank and tell you that I was glad to go to it because you were there."

She looked at him wonderingly.

"But you wouldn't take any notice of me there," she said.

"No. I was told that you were engaged, or practically engaged, to Charlesworth, and disliked any one else taking up your time."

She sat up indignantly.

"To Captain Charlesworth? How absurd! I suppose I've Ida to thank for that. I wouldn't have married him for anything."

"Is that so? What a game of cross-purposes life is! But that's why I didn't try to speak to you much."

"Did you want to? I thought you disliked me. And it hurt me so much. Do you know, I used to cry about it sometimes. I wanted you to be my friend."

He walked over to her settee.

"Noreen, dear, I wanted to be your friend and you to be mine," he said, looking down at her. "I liked you so much. At least, I thought I liked you."

"And - and don't you?" she asked, looking up at him.

He knelt beside her.

"No, little friend, I don't like you. Because I -" He paused.

"What?" she whispered faintly.

"I love you, dear. Do you think it absurd?"

She was silent for a moment. Then she looked slowly up at him; and in her eyes he read her answer.

"Sweetheart! Little sweetheart!" he whispered, and held out his arms to her.

With a little cry she crept into them; and he pressed her to his heart. At that moment enemies, danger, death, were forgotten. For Noreen her whole world lay within the circle of his arms.

"Do you really, really love me?" she asked wonderingly.

He held her very close to his heart and looked fondly, tenderly down into the lovely upturned face.

"Love you, my dearest? I love you with all my heart, my soul, my being," he whispered. "How could I help loving you?"

And bending down he kissed her fondly.

"It's all so wonderful," she murmured. "I didn't think that you cared for me, that you could ever care. You seemed so far away, too occupied with important things to spare a thought for me.

Gordon Casserly

So serious a person, and sometimes so stern, that I was afraid of you."

He laughed amusedly.

"The wonder is that you ever came to care for me. You do care, don't you, beloved?"

She looked up at him earnestly.

"Dear, do I seem forward, bold? But our time together is too short for pretence. Yes, I do care. I love you? I seem to have always loved you. Or at least to have waited always to love you. I don't think I knew what love was until now. Until now. Now I do know."

She paused and stared across the room, seeing the vision of her childhood, her girlhood. From outside came intermittent shouts and an occasional random shot. But she did not hear them.

"As a child, as a schoolgirl, even afterwards, I used to day-dream. I used to wonder if any one would ever love me, ever teach me what love is. I dreamt of a Fairy Prince who would come to me one day, of a strong, brave, tender man who would care for me, who would want me to care for him. I often laughed at myself for it afterwards. For in London men all seemed so very unlike my dream-hero."

She turned her face to him and looked tenderly at him.

"But when I met you," she continued, "I think I knew that you were He. But I never dared hope that you would learn to care for me."

"Dearest heart," he replied, "I think I must have fallen in love with you the first moment I saw you. I can see you now as you stood surrounded by the elephants, a delightful but most unexpected vision in the jungle."

"Did you - oh, did you really like me that very first day?" she asked eagerly. At the moment the answer seemed to her the most important thing in the world.

As a lover will do Dermot deceived himself and imagined that his love had been born at the first sight of her. He told her so; and the girl forgot the imminent, deadly peril about them in the glow of happiness that warms the heart of a loving woman who hears that she has been beloved from the beginning.

"But I looked so absurd," she said dreamily; "so untidy, when you first saw me. Why, my hair was all down."

He laughed again; but the laughter died from his lips as the remembrance of their situation returned to him. Death was ordinarily little to him; though now life could be so sweet since she loved him. It seemed a terrible thing that this young girl must die so soon - and probably by his own hand to save her from a worse fate.

She guessed his thoughts.

"Is this really the end, dear?" she asked, unwilling but unafraid to meet death. "Is there no hope for us?"

"I fear not, beloved."

"I - I don't want to die so soon. Before you came tonight I wouldn't have minded very much; for I was not happy. But now it's a little hard, just as this wonderful thing has happened to me."

She sighed. He held out his arms again, and she crept into them and nestled into his embrace.

"Well, if it must be so, I'll try to be worthy of my soldier and not disgrace you, dear," she said fondly, bravely. "Let's try to forget it for a while and not let it spoil our last hours together. Let's 'make-believe,' as the children say. Let's pretend that this is all a hideous nightmare, that our lives and our love are before us."

So through the long, dread night with the hideous menace never out of their minds they talked bravely of what they would like to do, to be - if only they were not to die so soon. Several times Noreen left him and went to comfort, to console the poor Mohammedan women and children to whom she had given shelter. Her brother refused to allow Dermot to relieve him on watch, saying that he could not sleep or rest, and begging him instead to remain with the girl to cheer her, to hearten her in the awful hours of waiting for the end.

So Dermot was with her when a sudden uproar outside caused him to dash out on to the verandah. From behind the barricade on the front verandah Daleham was watching.

"What is it? Are they attacking?" cried the soldier.

"No. It's not an attack. They're cheering somebody, I think, and firing into the air."

Dermot stared out. Men ran forward to the smouldering ruins of the factory and threw on them tins of kerosene oil, looted from the murdered Parsi's shop, until the flames blazed up again and lit up the scene. The hundreds of coolies were cheering and crowding round a body of men in red coats.

"I believe it's the Rajah's infantry," said Dermot. "Are they going to attack? Sher Afzul, wake up the others and tell them to be on their guard. Give me that rifle, Daleham."

So Noreen did not see her lover again until the sun rose on a scene of desolation and ruin. Smoke and sparks still came from the blackened heaps of the destroyed buildings. The cordon of sentries had apparently been withdrawn; but when Daleham climbed up on the barricade to get a better view a shot was fired from somewhere and a bullet tore up the ground before the bungalow.

A couple of hours dragged slowly by; and then a servant doing sentry on the front verandah reported a cloud of dust on the road from the forest leading to the village. Dermot went out on the front verandah which looked towards the coolie lines and put up the glasses.

"Some men on horses. Yes, and a motor-car coming slowly behind them," he said to Daleham and his sister, who had followed him out. "It's the Rajah and his escort, I suppose. Things will begin to move now."

When the newcomers reached the village a storm of shouting arose. Volley after volley of shots were fired, conch-shells blown, tom-toms beaten.

"Yes, there's no doubt of it. It must be that fat brute," said Daleham.

Half an hour went by. The sun was high in the heavens. The landscape was bare of life. Not a man was visible. But presently from the village came a little figure, a naked little coolie boy. He moved slowly towards the bungalow, stopping every few minutes to look back to the huts, then advancing again with evident reluctance.

Dermot watched him through the glass. The whole garrison was on the verandah.

"He's a messenger. I see a letter in his hand," said the soldier. "Poor little devil, he's in an awful funk. None of the cowards dared do it themselves, so they beat this child and made him come."

At last the frightened infant reached the bungalow, and Sher Afzul met him and took the letter from him. Fred tore it open. It was written by Chunerbutty and couched in the most offensive terms. If within half an hour Miss Daleham came willingly to the Rajah, her brother's life would be spared and he would be given a safe conduct to Calcutta. But everyone else in the bungalow would be put to death, including the white man reported to have entered it during the night. If the girl did not surrender, her brother would be killed with the rest and she herself taken by force.

Dermot acquainted the Mohammedan servants with the contents, to show them that there was no hope for them, so that they would fight to the death. The little boy was told that there was no answer, and Daleham gave him a few copper coins; but the scared child dropped them as though they were red hot and scampered back to the village as fast as his little legs would carry him.

CHAPTER XX

THE GOD OF THE ELEPHANTS

At the end of the half hour a tempest of noise arose from the village; tom-toms were beaten, conch-shells blown and vigorous cheering was heard. Then from the huts long lines of coolies carrying weapons of every sort, rifles, old muskets, spears, and swords streamed out and encircled the bungalow at a distance. A little later the Rajah's twenty horsemen rode out of the village on their raw-boned stallions, followed by a hundred infantry soldiers who, Dermot observed, were now armed with rifles in place of their former muskets.

The dismounted troops formed up before the bungalow but half a mile away, in two lines in open order. But the cavalry kept together in a body; and the officer, turning in his saddle to speak to his men, pointed to the house with his sword.

"I believe they're going to charge us," said Dermot.

He had divided up the garrison to the four sides of the bungalow; but now, leaving one man with the shot gun to keep a watch on the back, he collected the rest on the front verandah. Noreen was inside, feeding the hungry children and consoling the mothers.

"Now, Daleham, don't fire until they are close, and then aim at the horses," said the Major, repeating the instruction to the servants in Urdu.

The Punjaubis grinned and patted their rifles.

The cavalry advanced. The *sowars* ambled forward, brandishing their curved sabres and uttering fierce yells. Dermot, knowing Sher Afzul and another man to be good shots, ordered them to open fire when the horsemen were about four hundred yards away. He himself took a steady aim at the commander and pressed the trigger. The officer, shot through the body, threw up his arms and fell forward on his horse's head. The startled animal shied and bolted across the furrows; and the corpse, dropping from the saddle, was dragged along the ground, one foot being caught in a stirrup. The cavalry checked for an instant; and Dermot fired again. A *sowar* fell. The rest cantered forward, yelling and waving their *tulwars*. Sher Afzul and the other servants opened fire. A second horseman dropped from his saddle, a stallion stumbled and fell, throwing its rider heavily. The firing grew faster. Two or three more horses were wounded and galloped wildly off. The rest of the cavalry came on, but, losing their nerve, checked their pace instead of charging home.

Dermot, loading and firing rapidly, bringing a *sowar* down with each shot, suddenly found Noreen crouching beside him behind the barricade. She was holding a revolver.

"For Heaven's sake, get into the house, darling!" he cried.

"No; I have Fred's pistol and know how to use it," she answered, calmly. "I have often practised with it."

He could not stop to argue with her, for the troopers still came on. But they bunched together, knee to knee, in a frontal attack, instead of assaulting from all four sides at once. They made a splendid target and suffered heavily. But some brought their horses' heads almost against the verandah railing. All the garrison rose from behind the barricade and fired point-blank at them. The girl, steadying her hand on a box, shot one *sowar* through the body. The few survivors turned and galloped madly away, leaving most of their number on the ground. To cover their retreat a ragged volley broke from the infantry; and a storm of bullets flew over and around the bungalow, ricocheted from the ground or struck the walls. But one young Mohammedan servant, who had incautiously exposed himself, dropped back shot through the lungs.

Then from every side fire was opened, the coolies blazing wildly; but as none of them had ever had a rifle in his hands before, the firing was for the most part innocuous. Yet it served to encourage them, and they drew nearer. The garrison, with only one or two defenders to each side of the house, could not keep them at a distance. The infantry began to crawl forward. The circle of foes closed in on the bungalow and its doomed inhabitants. Shrieks and cries rose from the women and children inside.

But although every bullet from the garrison found its billet, the issue was only a matter of time. Ill-directed as was the assailants' fire, the showers of bullets were too thick not to have some effect. Another servant was killed, a third wounded. Daleham was struck on the shoulder by a ricochet but only scratched. A rifle bullet, piercing the barricade, passed through Noreen's hair, as she crouched beside her lover, whom she resolutely refused to leave. The ring of enemies constricted.

Suddenly a bugle sounded from the village; and after a little the firing from the attackers ceased. Dermot, who with Noreen and Sher Afzul, was defending the front verandah, looked cautiously over the barricade. A white flag appeared in the village. The Major shouted to the others in the house to hold their fire but be on their guard.

After a pause the flag advanced, borne by a coolie. It was followed by a group of men; and Dermot through the glasses recognised the Rajah and Chunerbutty accompanied by several Brahmins. They advanced timidly towards the bungalow and stopped a hundred yards away. After some urging Chunerbutty stepped to the front and called for Daleham to appear.

Fred came through the house from the back verandah, where his place was taken by Sher Afzul. He looked over the barricade. Chunerbutty came nearer and shouted:

"Daleham, the Rajah gives you one more chance to surrender. You see your case is hopeless. You can have a quarter of an hour to think things over. If at the end of that time you and your sister don't come out, we'll rush the bungalow and finish you all."

Standing under the white flag he drew out his watch.

"Thank you," said Daleham; "and our reply is that if in a quarter of an hour you're still there, you'll get a bullet through you, white flag or no white flag."

He turned to Dermot whose arm was around Noreen as she crouched beside him.

"Well, Major, it's fifteen more minutes of life, that's all."

"Yes, it's nearly the end now. I've only two cartridges left."

"We're all in the same box. Getting near time we said good-bye. It was jolly good of you to stick by us, when you might have got away last night."

Dermot gripped the outstretched hand.

"If I go under first, you'll not let Noreen fall alive into the hands of those brutes, will you, sir?"

The girl raised her revolver.

"I'll keep the last cartridge for myself, dear," she said.

She looked lovingly at Dermot whose arm was still about her. Her brother betrayed no surprise.

"I'm not afraid to die, dear one," she whispered to her lover. "I couldn't live without you now. And I'm happy at this moment, happier than I've ever been, I think. But I wish you had saved yourself."

He mastered his emotion with difficulty.

"Darling, life without you wouldn't be possible for me either."

He could not take his eyes from her; and the minutes were flying all too swiftly. At last he looked at his watch and held out his hand to the boy.

"Good-bye, Daleham, you've got your wish. You're dying like a soldier for England," he said. "We've done our share for her. Now, we've three minutes more. If the Rajah and Chunerbutty come into view again I'll have them with my last two shots."

He turned to the girl and took her in his arms for a last embrace.

"Good-bye, sweetheart. Dear love of my heart. Pray that we may be together in the next world."

He paused and listened.

"Are they coming?"

But he did not put her from him. One second now was worth an eternity.

Then suddenly a distant murmur swelled through the strange silence. Daleham looked out over the barricade.

"They're - No. What is it? What are they doing?"

All round the circle of besiegers there was an eerie hush. No voice was heard. All - the Rajah, the flag-bearer, Brahmins, soldiers, coolies - had turned their faces away from the

Gordon Casserly

bungalow and were staring into the distance. And as the few survivors of the garrison looked up over the barricade an incredible sight met their eyes.

From the far-off forest, bursting out at every point of the long-stretching wall of dark undergrowth that hemmed in the wide estate, wild elephants appeared. Over the furrowed acres they streamed in endless lines, trampling down the ordered stretch of green bushes. In scores, in hundreds, they came, silently, slowly; the great heads nodding to the rhythm of their gait, the trunks swinging, the ragged ears flapping, as they advanced. Converging as they came, they drew together in a solid mass that blotted out the ground, a mass sombre-hued, dark, relieved only by flashes of gleaming white. For on either side of every massive skull jutted out the sharp-pointed, curving ivory. Of all save one.

For the mammoth that led them, the splendid beast that captained the oncoming array of Titans under the ponderous strokes of whose feet the ground trembled, had one tusk, one only. And as though the white flag were a magnet to him, he moved unerringly towards it, the immense, earth-shaking phalanx following him.

The awestruck crowds of armed men, so lately flushed with fanatical lust of slaughter, stood as though turned to stone, their faces set towards the terrifying onset. Their pain unheeded, their groans silenced, the wounded staggered to their feet to look. Even the dying strove to raise themselves on their arms from the reddened soil to gaze, and, gazing, fell back dead. Slowly, mechanically, silently, the living gave way, the weapons dropping from their nerveless grip. Step by step they drew back as if compelled by some strange mesmeric power.

And on the verandah the few survivors of the little band stood together, silent, amazed, scarce believing their eyes as they stared at the incredible vision. All but Dermot. His gaze was fixed on the leader of that terrible army; and he smiled, tenderly yet proudly. His arm drew the girl beside him still closer to him, as he murmured:

"He comes to save us for each other, beloved!"

Nothing was heard, save the dull thunder of the giant feet. Then from the village the high-pitched shriek of a woman pierced the air and shattered the eerie silence of the terror-stricken crowds. Murmurs, groans, swelled into shouts, wild yells, the appalling uproar of panic; and strong and weak, hale men and those from whose wounds the life-blood dripped, turned and fled. Fled past their dead brothers, past the little group of leaders whose power to sway them had vanished before this awful menace.

Petrified, rooted to the ground as though their quaking limbs were incapable of movement, the Rajah and his satellites stood motionless before the oncoming elephants. But when the leader almost towered above him, Chunerbutty was galvanised to life again. In mad panic he raised a pistol in his trembling hand and fired at the great beast. The next instant the huge tusk caught him. He was struck to the earth, gored, and lifted high in air. An appalling shriek burst from his bloodless lips. He was hurled to the ground with terrific force and trodden under foot. The Rajah screamed shrilly and turned to flee. Too late! The earth shook as the great phalanx moved on faster and passed without checking over the white-clad group, blotting them out of all semblance to humanity.

The dying yell of the renegade Hindu, arresting in its note of agony, caused the fleeing crowds to pause and turn to look. And as they witnessed the annihilation of their leaders they saw a yet more wondrous sight. For the dark array of monsters halted as the leader reached the house; and with the sea of twisted trunks upraised to salute him and a terrifying peal of trumpeting, they welcomed the white man who walked out from the shot-torn building towards the leader of the vast herd. Then in a solemn hush he was raised high in air and held aloft for all to see, beasts and men. And in the silence a single voice in the awestruck crowds cried shrilly:

"*Hathi ka Deo ki jai!* (Victory to the God of the Elephants!)"

In wonder, in dread, in superstitious reverence, hundreds of voices took up the refrain: *"Hathi ka Deo! Hathi ka Deo ki jai!"*

And leaving his thousand companions behind, the sacred elephant that all recognised now advanced towards the shrinking crowds, bearing the dread white god upon its neck. Had he not come invisibly among them again? Had they not witnessed the fate of those that opposed him? Had he not summoned from all Hindustan his man-devouring monsters to punish, to annihilate his enemies. Forgetful of their hate, their bloodthirst, their lust of battle, conscious only of their guilt, the terror-stricken crowds surged forward and flung themselves down in supplication on the earth. They wept, they wailed, they bared their heads and poured dust upon them, in all the extravagant demonstration of Oriental sorrow. Out from the village streamed the women and children to add their shrill cries to the lamentations.

With uplifted hand, Dermot silenced them. An awful hush succeeded the tumult. He swept his eyes slowly over them all, and every head went down to the dust again. Then he spoke, solemnly, clearly; and his voice reached everyone in the prostrate mob.

"My wrath is upon you and upon your children. Flee where you will, it shall overtake you. You have sinned and must atone. On those most guilty punishment has already fallen. Where are they that misled you? Go look for them under the feet of my elephants. Yet from you, ye poor deluded fools, for the moment I withhold my hand. But touch a single hair of those in your midst whom I protect, and you perish."

Not a sound was heard.

Then he said:

"Men of Lalpuri, who have come among these fools in thirst for blood. You have heard of me. You have seen my power. You see me. Go back to your city. Tell them there that I, who fed my elephants on the flesh of your comrades in the forest, shall come to them riding on my steed sacred to *Gunesh*. If they spare the evil counselors among them, then them I will not spare. Of their city no stone shall remain. Go back to them and bear this message to all within and without the walls, 'The British *Raj* shall endure. It is my will.' Tell them to engrave it on their hearts, on their children's hearts."

He paused. Then he spoke again:

"Rise, all ye people. Ye have my leave to go."

Noiselessly they obeyed. He watched them move away in terrified silence. Not a whisper was heard.

Then he smiled as he said to himself:

"That should keep them quiet."

He turned Badshah towards the bungalow.

Forty miles away, when darkness fell on the mountains that night, the army of the invaders slept soundly in their bivouacs around the doomed post of Ranga Duar. On the morrow the last feeble resistance of its garrison must cease, and happy those of the defenders who died. Luckless they that lived. For the worst tortures that even China knew would be theirs.

But when the morrow came there was no longer an investing army. Panic-stricken, the scattered remnants of the once formidable host staggered blindly up the inhospitable mountains only to perish in the snows of the passes. For in the dark hours annihilation had come upon the rest. Countless monsters, worse, far worse, than the legendary dragons of their native land, had come from the skies, sprung from the earth. And under their huge feet the army had perished.

When the sun rose Dermot knelt beside the mattress on which Parker lay among the heaps of rubble that had once been the Fort. An Indian officer, the only one left, and a few haggard sepoys stood by. The rest of the few survivors of the gallant band had thrown themselves down to sleep haphazard among the ruins that covered the bodies of their comrades.

"Is it all true, Major? Are they really gone?" whispered the subaltern feebly.

"Yes, Parker, it's quite true. They've gone. You've helped to save India. You held them off - God knows how you did it. Your wound's a nasty one; but you'll get over it."

He rose and held out his hands to the others. *"Shabash!* (Well done!) *Subhedar Sahib*, Mohammed Khan, Gulab Khan, Shaikh Bakar, well done."

And the men of the alien race pressed round him and clasped his hands gratefully.

The defeat of the invaders in this little-known corner of the Indian Empire was but the forerunner of the disasters that befell the other enemies of the British dominion, though many months passed before peace settled on the land again. But Lalpuri had not so long to wait for Dermot to redeem his promise to visit it. When he did he rode on Badshah at the head of a British force. The gates were flung open wide; and he passed through submissive crowds to see the blackened ruins of the Palace that, stormed, looted, and burnt by its rebel soldiery, hid the ashes of the *Dewan*.

A year had gone by. In the villages perched on the steep sides of the mountains the Bhuttia women rejoiced to know that the peace of the Borderland would never be broken again while the dread hand of a god lay on it. And in their bamboo huts they tried to hush their little children with the mention of his name. But the sturdy, naked babies had no fear of him. For they all knew him; and he was kind and far less terrible than the gods and demons that the old lama showed them in the painted Wheel of Life sent him from Tibet. Moreover, the white god's wife was kinder even than he. But that was because she was not a goddess. Only a girl.

On the high hills, up above the villages, a couple stood. No god and goddess: just a man and a woman. And the woman looked down past the huts, down to the great Terai Forest lying like a vast billowy sea of foliage far below them. Then, as her husband's arm stole round her, she turned her eyes from it and gazed into his and whispered:

"I love it more than even you do. For it gave you to me."

A crashing in the clump of hill bamboos at their feet attracted their attention; and with a smile he pointed down to the great elephant with the single tusk who was dragging down the feathery plumes with his curving trunk.

But Noreen looked up at Dermot again and said:

"I love you more than even Badshah does."

And their lips met.

Choose from Thousands of 1stWorldLibrary Classics By

A. M. Barnard
Ada Leverson
Adolphus William Ward
Aesop
Agatha Christie
Alexander Aaronsohn
Alexander Kielland
Alexandre Dumas
Alfred Gatty
Alfred Ollivant
Alice Duer Miller
Alice Turner Curtis
Alice Dunbar
Ambrose Bierce
Amelia E. Barr
Amory H. Bradford
Andrew Lang
Andrew McFarland Davis
Andy Adams
Anna Sewell
Annie Besant
Annie Hamilton Donnell
Annie Payson Call
Annonaymous
Anton Chekhov
Arnold Bennett
Arthur Conan Doyle
Arthur M. Winfield
Arthur Ransome
Atticus
B.H. Baden-Powell
B. M. Bower
Baroness Emmuska Orczy
Baroness Orczy
Basil King
Bayard Taylor
Ben Macomber
Bertha Muzzy Bower
Bjornstjerne Bjornson
Booth Tarkington
Boyd Cable
Bram Stoker
C. Collodi
C. E. Orr
C. M. Ingleby
Carolyn Wells
Catherine Parr Traill
Charles A. Eastman
Charles Dickens

Charles Dudley Warner
Charles Farrar Browne
Charles Ives
Charles Kingsley
Charles Klein
Charles Amory Beach
Charles Hanson Towne
Charles Lathrop Pack
Charles Whibley
Charles Willing Beale
Charlotte M. Braeme
Charlotte M. Yonge
Charlotte Perkins Stetson
Clair W. Hayes
Clarence Day Jr.
Clarence E. Mulford
Clemence Housman
Confucius
Cornelis DeWitt Wilcox
Cyril Burleigh
D. H. Lawrence
Daniel Defoe
David Garnett
Dinah Craik
Don Carlos Janes
Donald Keyhoe
Dorothy Kilner
Dougan Clark
Douglas Fairbanks
E. Nesbit
E.P.Roe
E. Phillips Oppenheim
Earl Barnes
Edgar Rice Burroughs
Edith Van Dyne
Edith Wharton
Edward J. O'Biren
Edward S. Ellis
Edwin L. Arnold
Eleanor Atkins
Eliot Gregory
Elizabeth Gaskell
Elizabeth McCracken
Elizabeth Von Arnim
Ellem Key
Emerson Hough
Emilie F. Carlen
Emily Dickinson
Enid Bagnold

Enilor Macartney Lane
Erasmus W. Jones
Ernie Howard Pie
Ethel Turner
Ethel Watts Mumford
Eugenie Foa
Eugene Wood
Eustace Hale Ball
Evelyn Everett-green
Everard Cotes
F. H. Cheley
F. J. Cross
Federick Austin Ogg
Ferdinand Ossendowski
Francis Bacon
Francis Darwin
Frances Hodgson Burnett
Frances Parkinson Keyes
Frank Gee Patchin
Frank Harris
Frank Jewett Mather
Frank L. Packard
Frank V. Webster
Frederic Stewart Isham
Frederick Trevor Hill
Frederick Winslow Taylor
Friedrich Kerst
Friedrich Nietzsche
Fyodor Dostoyevsky
G.A. Henty
G.K. Chesterton
Gabrielle E. Jackson
Garrett P. Serviss
Gaston Leroux
George A. Warren
George Ade
Geroge Bernard Shaw
George Durston
George Ebers
George Eliot
George Gissing
George MacDonald
George Meredith
George Orwell
George Sylvester Viereck
George Tucker
George W. Cable
George Wharton James
Gertrude Atherton

Grace E. King
Grace Gallatin
Grant Allen
Guillermo A. Sherwell
Gulielma Zollinger
Gustav Flaubert
H. A. Cody
H. B. Irving
H.C. Bailey
H. G. Wells
H. H. Munro
H. Irving Hancock
H. Rider Haggard
H. W. C. Davis
Hamilton Wright Mabie
Hans Christian Andersen
Harold Avery
Harold McGrath
Harriet Beecher Stowe
Harry Houidini
Helent Hunt Jackson
Helen Nicolay
Hendrik Conscience
Hendy David Thoreau
Henri Barbusse
Henrik Ibsen
Henry Adams
Henry Ford
Henry Frost
Henry James
Henry Jones Ford
Henry Seton Merriman
Henry W Longfellow
Herbert A. Giles
Herbert N. Casson
Herman Hesse
Homer
Honore De Balzac
Horace Walpole
Horatio Alger Jr.
Howard Pyle
Howard R. Garis
Hugh Lofting
Hugh Walpole
Humphry Ward
Ian Maclaren
Inez Haynes Gillmore
Irving Bacheller
Israel Abrahams
Ivan Turgenev
J.G.Austin

J. Henri Fabre
J. M. Barrie
J. Macdonald Oxley
J. S. Fletcher
J. S. Knowles
J. Storer Clouston
Jack London
Jacob Abbott
James Allen
James Andrews
James Baldwin
James DeMille
James Joyce
James Lane Allen
James Lane Allen
James Oliver Curwood
James Oppenheim
James Otis
James R. Driscoll
Jane Austen
Janet Aldridge
Jens Peter Jacobsen
Jerome K. Jerome
John Burroughs
John Cournos
John F. Kennedy
John Gay
John Glasworthy
John Habberton
John Joy Bell
John Kendrick Bangs
John Milton
John Philip Sousa
Jonas Lauritz Idemil Lie
Jonathan Swift
Joseph A. Altsheler
Joseph Carey
Joseph Conrad
Joseph E. Badger Jr
Joseph Hergesheimer
Joseph Jacobs
Jules Vernes
Julian Hawthrone
Julie A Lippmann
Justin Huntly McCarthy
Kakuzo Okakura
Kenneth Grahame
Kenneth McGaffey
Kate Langley Bosher
Kate Langley Bosher
Katherine Cecil Thurston

Katherine Stokes
L. A. Abbot
L. T. Meade
L. Frank Baum
Latta Griswold
Laura Lee Hope
Laurence Housman
Lawrence Beasley
Leo Tolstoy
Leonid Andreyev
Lewis Carroll
Lewis Sperry Chafer
Lilian Bell
Lloyd Osbourne
Louis Hughes
Louis Tracy
Louisa May Alcott
Lucy Fitch Perkins
Lucy Maud Montgomery
Lydia Miller Middleton
Lyndon Orr
M. Corvus
M. H. Adams
Margaret E. Sangster
Margaret Vandercook
Margret Penrose
Maria Edgeworth
Maria Thompson Daviess
Mariano Azuela
Marion Polk Angellotti
Mark Overton
Mark Twain
Mary Austin
Mary Catherine Crowley
Mary Cole
Mary Hastings Bradley
Mary Roberts Rinehart
Mary Rowlandson
M. Wollstonecraft Shelley
Maud Lindsay
Max Beerbohm
Myra Kelly
Nathaniel Hawthrone
Nicolo Machiavelli
O. F. Walton
Oscar Wilde
Owen Johnson
P.G. Wodehouse
Paul and Mabel Thorne
Paul G. Tomlinson
Paul Severing

Percy Brebner
Peter B. Kyne
Plato
R. Derby Holmes
R. L. Stevenson
R. S. Ball
Rabindranath Tagore
Rahul Alvares
Ralph Bonehill
Ralph Henry Barbour
Ralph Victor
Ralph Waldo Emmerson
Rene Descartes
Rex Beach
Rex E. Beach
Richard Harding Davis
Richard Jefferies
Richard Le Gallienne
Robert Barr
Robert Frost
Robert Gordon Anderson
Robert L. Drake
Robert Lansing
Robert Lynd
Robert Michael Ballantyne
Robert W. Chambers
Rosa Nouchette Carey
Rudyard Kipling
Samuel B. Allison

Samuel Hopkins Adams
Sarah Bernhardt
Sarah C. Hallowell
Selma Lagerlof
Sherwood Anderson
Sigmund Freud
Standish O'Grady
Stanley Weyman
Stella Benson
Stephen Crane
Stewart Edward White
Stijn Streuvels
Swami Abhedananda
Swami Parmananda
T. S. Ackland
T. S. Arthur
The Princess Der Ling
Thomas A. Janvier
Thomas A Kempis
Thomas Anderton
Thomas Bailey Aldrich
Thomas Bulfinch
Thomas De Quincey
Thomas H. Huxley
Thomas Hardy
Thomas More
Thornton W. Burgess
U. S. Grant
Valentine Williams

Various Authors
Vaughan Kester
Victor Appleton
Virginia Woolf
Walter Camp
Walter Scott
Washington Irving
Wilbur Lawton
Wilkie Collins
Willa Cather
Willard F. Baker
William Dean Howells
William le Queux
W. Makepeace Thackeray
William W. Walter
Winston Churchill
Yei Theodora Ozaki
Yogi Ramacharaka
Young E. Allison
Zane Grey

www.ingramcontent.com/pod-product-compliance
Lightning Source LLC
Chambersburg PA
CBHW020436270626
47155CB00022B/440